The Riverbend Romances

A Collection of Christian Romance Novellas

Valerie Comer

ISBN-13: 978-1988068077

This is a work of fiction set in a redrawn British Columbia, Canada. Any resemblance to real events or to actual persons, living or dead, is coincidental.

Published by GreenWords Media

Printed in the United States of America

Welcome to Riverbend!

Riverbend, BC, is the quaint Canadian town you wish you were from, where everyone knows everyone, seasons are celebrated, and love is in the air.

Riverbend and Castlebrook are fictional communities.

Canadian Tire, Tim Hortons, Shoppers Drug Mart, Chapters, and Save-On-More Foods are real Canadian businesses, but I've made up others for the stories.

In Canada, a stocking cap or beanie is called a tuque (rhymes with fluke). Distance is measured in meters and kilometers, and temperatures are in Celsius. And in British Columbia, yes, beginning drivers are required to have a magnetic L (for learners, first level) or N (for novice, second level) on the back of the vehicle.

Secretly Yours

Chef Lindsey Solberg agrees to cater the church's Valentine's Day fundraising banquet as a favor to her teen sister, but she's shocked to discover the bad boy from her high school days is now Riverbend's youth pastor. Seriously? How could he have changed that much?

Nick Harrison has prayed for years for an opportunity to make amends. Now Lindsey's back in Riverbend and won't give him the time of day. What's a guy to do except leave a trail of gifts from a secret admirer?

Lindsey's heart takes a beating when she realizes the boy who was never good enough is now a far better man than she deserves.

Pinky Promise

Kelly Bryant's young daughter wants a daddy and sets her sights on her new best friend's single father. The man may be charming, sweet, and a believer, but Kelly is embarrassed. She extracts a pinky promise from her six-year-old to stop proposing to men on her behalf.

Ian Tomlinson isn't looking for a wife but does need care for his daughter during spring break the week after his move to Riverbend. He hates to ask Kelly — and plant ideas in the girls' minds — but he's rather low on options.

How can two single parents fall in love for real with a pair of mini-matchmakers pushing from both sides — pinky promises or not?

Sweet Serenade

River guide and canoe builder Reed Daniels stands by as his lifelong friends pair off. After all, he's waited this long for the right woman… what's a little longer? But when newcomer Carly shows up at the gang's bonfire, he's mesmerized. Could she be the answer to his prayers?

Water-sport enthusiast Carly Thorbergsen is starting over in Riverbend. Hired as a canoeing and hiking guide, she's ready to focus on work and leave the personal stuff behind. That is until the competition, Reed Daniels, offers her a ride in his cedar-strip canoe. No resisting that!

But no matter how much they have in common, Carly can't erase her past, and Reed is bound to discover the truth. When a date finds Carly and Reed running rapids on the outside of the canoe, they come face to face with the real reasons their new relationship might capsize.

Team Bride

Sarah Jamieson has avoided weddings since a traumatic stint as a flower girl, but reluctantly agrees to stand up for her best friend. Only why does the best man have to be one of those confident, life-of-the-party types? Even worse, why does the bride make her promise to go on one date with the guy? Easy enough to agree, because she'll make sure he never asks.

Corbin Morrissey takes his responsibilities for Team Groom very seriously, but coaxing smiles out of the maid-of-honor is harder — and more addictive — than he expected. To his surprise, she agrees to go out. There really isn't any way a date to the Fall Fair could go amiss. Is there?

Can Corbin convince Sarah he's ready to settle down and make her the head of her own Team Bride, or will their past keep getting in the way?

Merry Kisses

Fired from her retail position for saying *Merry Christmas* to a customer, Sonya Simmons chafes at the over-commercialization of the season and the difficulties of finding a new job. If only she'd actually said *Merry Christmas* instead of *Merry Kisses* to the tall, good-looking man buying enough toys for at least a dozen children. How embarrassing!

It was fun to fluster the pretty toy store clerk, but Heath Collins, the mall's volunteer Santa Claus, hadn't meant to get her fired. When his elf assistant comes down with a bad cold, Heath offers Sonya a few days' work, only to discover she believes Santa is nothing but a liar and a fraud instead of an opportunity to make a difference in children's lives.

Can Sonya and Heath embrace each other — opinions, traditions, and all — in time to share merry kisses for Christmas?

Acknowledgments

I'm so thankful to all the readers who've enjoyed the Riverbend novellas in digital format. You've emailed me, Facebooked me, and tweeted me to tell me what my characters, themes, and stories have meant to you. You are so appreciated!

I'm thankful to my husband, my kids, and my grandgirls, who encourage me every day in the endeavors God has given me. I love your hugs, kisses, and reminders to get outside to spend time together, enjoying the wonderful nature all around us.

Thanks to my street team, my beta readers, and my editor, and especially to you who've placed reviews on your blogs, readers' groups, and online stores. A big thank-you hug to everyone who's recommended one of my books to your friends.

I love my co-bloggers at InspyRomance.com. It's a pleasure sharing tales of Christian contemporary romance with our readers… together.

My deepest gratitude is to Jesus, without whom I would have no stories to tell. Every sentence, paragraph, scene — book — is an act of worship to You, the King of Creativity. May I continue to be a conduit to show Your love, mercy, and hope to all my readers.

Other Romances by Valerie Comer

Farm Fresh Romance Novels

Raspberries and Vinegar
Wild Mint Tea
Sweetened with Honey
Dandelions for Dinner
Plum Upside Down
Berry on Top

A Riverbend Romance Novella

Secretly Yours

Valerie Comer

Chapter One

"Please say yes!" Madison begged.

Lindsey Solberg leaned out the car window and into the freezing wind. Had she ever been as enthusiastic about anything as her sixteen-year-old sister was now? "Madison, I don't know. My boss may see it as a conflict of interest. And I just don't know that I have time to take this on."

Madison dropped both hands to her hips, her long hair blowing sideways. "But we need you. Pastor Nick says we could earn the rest of the funds in one night if the Valentine's banquet does well."

Would she ever hear the name Nick without thinking of the guy from high school? Not likely. But one thing she knew for certain. Nick Harrison wasn't the pastor of any church, to say nothing of how he'd been even more eager to leave the small town of Riverbend, British Columbia, behind than she had.

"Please, Lindsey. At least say you'll think about it."

Lindsey closed her eyes, letting the biting wind cool her cheeks. More like letting it pelt her with icy snowflakes through the open window. "Get in the car, Madison."

Her sister tilted her head to one side. "You'll think about it?"

"Fine. I'll think about it. Now get in."

"Yay!" Madison sashayed around the car as Lindsey raised the window and rubbed her cold hands together.

Several other teens hung around the parking lot beside the church, presumably waiting for their rides home. The winter roads would only get worse in the next few hours. At least when she'd lived in Castlebrook, there had been city transit wherever she needed to go, especially on the occasional wintry days. Being back in Riverbend meant driving everywhere. The town was too long and skinny for walking yet too small for a bus system. She hadn't driven on slick roads in eight years.

She shifted into reverse and gingerly put her foot on the accelerator, but Madison's hand grabbed her arm. "There he is. Pastor Nick is the dreamiest thing ever, don't you think?"

Lindsey glanced at the man's silhouette framed against the brightly lit rectangle of the open church doorway. Kind of hard to tell. She pressed the gas and the tires spun. Great exit. Or lack of exit, as the case might be. She pushed harder and the tires whirred as the rear of the car slid sideways.

Oh, no! Heart pounding, Lindsey removed her foot before she smacked the black Toyota parked beside her. Bare centimeters separated them.

"Whoa, don't hit Pastor Nick's car!"

As though she'd done it on purpose. Lindsey sucked in a deep breath. "It's really slippery."

Madison slumped in the passenger seat. "Want me to drive?"

"Are you kidding me? You only got your learner's permit last week."

"Well, I can drive at least as good as you can."

She probably could, but no way was Lindsey going to test that out. But how was she going to get this old car out of the parking lot with apparently bald tires?

A rush of cold wind and snow blasted in as Madison shoved her door open. "Hey! Give us a push!" she hollered.

Great. All Lindsey needed was a dozen teens making fun of her. And Pastor Nick, of course, though he was probably some balding ancient man and not the amazingly hot guy Nick Harrison had likely turned into since high school.

The group streamed toward the car and leaned on the hood. Someone tapped on her window and she pressed the button to lower it again.

"On the count of three, give it a little gas."

She knew that voice. Nick?

"One."

Harrison?

"Two."

Not a chance.

"Three."

A pastor?

The teens pushed against the hood. Belatedly Lindsey remembered she was supposed to be helping. She jammed her foot on the accelerator and the car slid backwards. Sideways, but backwards. Away from the other car.

Nick Harrison? A pastor? Couldn't be. The name had brought back memories, that was all. Her mind played tricks on her. Not Nick. Not that player who'd tampered with her heart.

In a flurry of icy slush, her car cleared the black Toyota and spun so it faced the street. Now if it would only go forward.

"You should be all right now, but you need new tires." Nick loomed in her wide-open car window.

As if she hadn't figured that out.

Maybe as long as she kept quiet, he wouldn't recognize her. Where was Madison, anyway? After all this, she couldn't leave without her sister.

"I don't believe we've met." Nick peered in. "I'm Nick Harrison, the youth pastor here at River of Life Church."

"I, uh…" Lindsey tapped the horn. Madison needed to come *now*.

Nick pulled back. "Sorry."

Lindsey kept her face turned away. The collar of her coat, the scarf around her neck, and the knitted woolen tuque pulled down over her hair should all help to camouflage her.

"Hey, Pastor Nick! Thanks. My sister isn't used to driving in winter anymore." Madison ran and slid across the icy parking lot toward the driver's side.

Lindsey jerked her thumb toward the passenger seat, but of course Madison couldn't see. Or chose to ignore it.

Her little sister slid right into Nick, who held her upright. "Glad to help." He glanced back at Lindsey. "Drive safely and try to stay off the roads until the sand truck has been by."

She nodded sharply.

"Pastor Nick, this is my sister Lindsey. She's the new chef at the

Water Wheel. You know, that farm-to-table restaurant beside the park. The committee has asked her to cook for our Valentine's banquet!"

Lindsey froze, and it wasn't just the swirling snow.

"Lindsey?" Nick's voice sounded closer. He was looking at her now. Really looking. "Lindsey Solberg?"

"Um, yes." Could she pretend not to recognize him? Would he believe her?

"Wow, long time no see. What brings you back to Riverbend?" He held up a gloved hand. "Oh, wait, Madison just said. So you're a chef now?"

She nodded. "Madison, get in, will you? I want to get home before the roads get even worse."

Madison ran around the car, slipping and sliding like it was some big game.

"Good to see you again, Lindsey. I'd love to take you out for coffee and catch up."

Coffee? No way. Not with Nick. "I'm busy."

He grinned. That same goofy grin that'd had every girl in high school hanging onto every word he said. "You can't work every single day, can you? When's your next day off?"

She bit her lip. "Tuesday. But I'm busy."

Madison collapsed into the passenger seat and pulled the car door shut. She reached for her seat belt.

"Gotta go. Nice seeing you." Lindsey put the car in Drive.

"We'll catch up soon!" called Nick as she slid the window back up.

He hadn't changed a bit, still sure of his charm. But still… a pastor? That was definitely a change.

Nick stuffed both hands in the pockets of his down parka and watched Lindsey's car slide onto Pitoni Street and head north. If he'd guessed the roads would turn so terrible during youth group he'd have canceled. A few of the teens had driven themselves with novice drivers' licenses, the second tier of B.C.'s graduated licensing system. Others lived within walking distance, but many relied on a parent to swing by.

Or a sister.

How could he possibly have guessed Lindsey was Madison's sister when they had different surnames and didn't look a thing alike? Nothing had prepared him for seeing Lindsey again. Ten years ago he'd been at the top of the high school food chain doling out attention only to those he deemed fit to receive it.

Lindsey hadn't made the cut. Two grades behind him, she'd been an awkward girl with braces on her teeth. She'd been on the cheerleading squad. He'd teased her once that she yelled loudest when she yelled his name. She turned beet red and vanished, confirming her crush. He kept on poking fun of her adoration outwardly, but secretly found her fascinating. Fast forward to the end of the year, and he moved on to University of Calgary with a hockey scholarship.

Nobody had ever cheered loudest for him since then.

Didn't look like she was cheering for him now. She hadn't been able to get out of the parking lot fast enough.

Lindsey didn't wear braces anymore. The slightly awkward adolescent was long gone, replaced by a cool, confident woman. The kind of woman he'd like to get to know, unlike anyone he'd met since his return to Riverbend. Had he subconsciously been waiting for her?

He'd give her a day or two, then see if she'd go out with him at least once. Somehow he didn't think once would be enough.

Chapter Two

Lindsey tapped the button to end the call on her cell phone and turned slowly around. A slither of socks in the vinyl hallway told her all she needed to know. Madison had been eavesdropping on her call.

"Madison!"

"Yes?" Her sister sounded breathy as she appeared in the doorway of Lindsey's bedroom. "Who was it?"

Lindsey stared at her.

Eyes wide, Madison casually flipped her hair over her shoulder.

"How would Nick Harrison have gotten my phone number, do you think?"

"Umm…" Madison batted her eyelashes. "I didn't think you'd mind. Isn't he the cutest guy *ever*?"

Lindsey waved her phone under her sister's nose. "Do not assume I want people to have my number. Especially guys. Okay? I have a job to do here, and I don't have time for a social life. Nor do I want one."

Madison tilted her head to one side. "But Nick…" Her voice faded off into dreamland.

"Oh, stop it already. I mean it. No more giving out my number."

"Because he asked you out, and you're going, and you'll marry him, so no one else will ever need it?"

"What on earth, Madison? No!"

Her sister's face fell. "He didn't ask you out?"

Lindsey dropped the phone on her bed and grabbed her sister by both shoulders. "He did, and I said no. Madison, listen to me. Stop meddling. I'm not interested in dating right now."

"You said no? To Nick Harrison?" Madison's eyes grew wide as she fanned her face. "You must be crazy. There's not a girl alive who wouldn't want to go out with him. You don't just turn him down."

"Then I guess I'm dead. Whatever." It wasn't a matter of wanting to or not. Madison was right. Any female with a pulse would want to. That was the whole reason she'd said no.

That and disbelief he'd really changed. A youth pastor? Not the Nick Harrison she'd once known.

* * *

Nick paced the living room of his small apartment. Didn't take that many steps to get from one end to the other. Out the window, early January continued her barrage. The wind carved falling snow into drifts that stretched toward the other side of the street, as though to escape the reach of the street lamps. The temperature had plummeted to fifteen below Celsius since night had fallen.

She'd said no. She hadn't even been overly nice about it.

Probably served him right. High school memories had dimmed due to the partying he'd done for a few years, but somewhere in there he remembered pretending to be interested in Lindsey to get even with her best friend Sarah. Once Sarah had gotten his intended message, he'd ditched them both.

He'd all but forgotten Sarah in the intervening years, but Lindsey's blue eyes, filled with hurt, had lingered.

Lindsey Solberg. A chef. Madison said she'd asked her sister to cater the Valentine's banquet the youth were planning for a fundraiser for their missions trip at spring break. He didn't need to win Lindsey in a day. They'd both returned to Riverbend. Both were single. Madison surely wouldn't have doled out her sister's number if she were married. Besides, Lindsey would have made sure he knew.

So, yes, single. How could he convince her he was different than her memory? That he'd changed? Become a Christian, gone to seminary, and served the Lord with all his heart at River of Life Church?

He'd win her over. Little gifts. Notes. He'd do the whole secret admirer thing while keeping any face-to-face meetings strictly business. For a while.

Now, what could he start with?

* * *

Lindsey trudged up the walk to the 50s-style split-entry she shared with her half-sister and step dad. Every time she'd glanced out the window of the Water Wheel all day long, she'd seen snowflakes fluttering by. The cold gray waters of the Sandon River flowed just beyond the patio that, come summer, would be full of patrons enjoying both the food and the view from the historic building.

All of Riverbend seemed hushed today beneath the half-meter of snow that had fallen in the past few days. The snowplow steadily churned up one street and down the next, pushing the heavy fall into the center of the roadways. It took a four-by-four to make a left turn anywhere in town with that center pile higher than many vehicles.

Perfect days for leaving Greg's car parked and walking to work, though it took a good half hour. She'd be just fine not getting behind the wheel again until spring.

Lindsey pushed the door open and entered the shelter of the drab house. She'd move out of Greg's place in a heartbeat, but she couldn't bear to leave Madison behind again. Not now that their mother was gone. Her sister needed her.

"Hey, there was something for you in the mailbox!" Madison slid down the wood-toned vinyl hallway into view.

That kid ran and slid everywhere. So much energy.

"Oh? What's that?" She unwrapped the scarf and shrugged out of her coat, hanging both on a hook. Then she unzipped her tall boots and wiggled her toes. Frozen, but they wouldn't likely fall off. She shoved her feet into furry pink slippers. Moving back to Riverbend in the dead of winter had been a dumb idea. For many reasons.

"No stamps or postmark, so somebody must have put it there in person." Madison brandished a package wrapped in brown paper and tied in twine from above the railing in the living room.

Reminded Lindsey of the song from the Sound of Music movie. Intriguing. A surprise was definitely one of her favorite things, too. Oh, wait, the music was really playing. She chuckled. "Good choice of soundtrack, Madison."

Her sister beamed. "I thought so. I've been home for over an hour, so I had lots of time to figure out how to give this to you."

Lindsey climbed the few steps to the main floor of the house. "So, are you going to hand it over or not?"

Madison swept a bow, handing the package over. "Here you go, ma'am."

The paper crinkled in Lindsey's hand. Something soft, not in a box. Her name was scrawled across the package with a black marker. Bold. What could it be? And from whom?

"Open it already!" Madison rocked on the balls of her feet.

Lindsey slipped the string off the package and parted the tape along the edge. She pulled the paper back until something pink and fuzzy was revealed. She lifted it up. A pair of cable-knit mittens? That was sweet, but where had they come from?

A piece of paper drifted to the floor, and Madison pounced then unfolded it. Her eyes widened and she clutched the paper to her chest. "Oh, how romantic!"

The drama team didn't know what they were missing without her sister. Lindsey held her hand out until Madison relinquished the note.

The paper appeared to be from a memo pad, pink with red hearts around the edges. She raised her eyebrows. Seriously?

Dear Lindsey,
Cold hands, warm heart.
Secretly Yours.

She turned it over. Nothing. No hint of the sender.

"I bet it's from Pastor Nick."

Lindsey dipped her head to glare at her sister. "I bet it isn't." Nick Harrison wasn't a romantic kind of guy. Not the Nick she remembered, for sure. Get a girl's hopes up, then dash them. Maybe it *was* him. Maybe he was doing it again.

She didn't need to play along.

Chapter Three

All bundled up, Lindsey left the restaurant into another cold, dark evening. If only Greg would put new tires on his old car, but he'd simply dismissed her concern saying she'd just forgotten how to drive. Being as he wasn't completely wrong, she hadn't pushed it. Still, it would be nice to drive to and from work… at least if Greg let her use the car. Yeah, wouldn't happen anyway.

A man in a fluffy down jacket and a knitted toque and scarf straightened from where he'd been leaning against the patio post. "Lindsey?"

The panic disappeared as quickly as it had surged, replaced by wariness. Seriously. What was Nick doing here?

"Can I give you a ride home?"

Half an hour walking down slippery sidewalks, some not even shoveled, freezing to death. Three minutes in a warm car. Walking sounded good.

He chuckled. "Promise I won't bite."

A gust of wind blasted past the edge of the restaurant, whipping her coat and hair.

She was being ridiculous. "Whatever." Whoa. That had been rude. Lindsey took in a long breath and let it out slowly. "Thank you. But why are you here?"

He held her arm as they descended the few steps to the parking area. "I wanted to talk to you."

The nerve. Lindsey pulled away. "I've already said no."

"Madison tells me she's asked you to be lead cook for the Valentine's Day banquet." He opened the passenger door of a compact black car.

Lindsey closed her eyes for a second as she slid into the upholstered interior. He must think her a total idiot. Of course he wanted to talk about the banquet, not about taking her out. She waited until he'd rounded the car and buckled himself into the driver's side. "Yes, she mentioned it. Did she over-step?"

Nick turned the key in the ignition. "Not at all. We'd talked options at our last banquet committee meeting." He grinned. "Your sister thinks a lot of you."

Yeah, and she seemed to think a lot of Nick, too. Plus determined to get them together.

"I did talk to my boss. I was afraid he might see it as conflict of interest." Maybe even hoped it.

He shot her a sidelong glance as he backed out of the parking spot. "And?"

She shrugged. "He wants to approve the menu, to be sure it represents the Water Wheel well. He'll provide ingredients at cost to help with expenses."

"Oh, that's awesome!"

"Yeah. So, I guess we need to talk."

Nick's grin widened as he turned north on River Way.

Great. She narrowed her gaze at him. "About the banquet."

His smile didn't dissipate. "Of course. What else?"

Lindsey's jaw tightened. "I'm not going out with you."

"So you said on the phone."

And he'd accepted it just like that? Then why did he keep grinning? He didn't add up. She brushed her hair from her cheeks with a mittened hand.

"Those look warm."

Nothing showed on his face but a passing interest in a pair of knitted mitts.

"They are." Should she poke a bit more? Why not? She held up both hands. "A gift from a secret admirer."

"No way."

"Yes way." Wind blew snow across the front of the car. A good evening to have a ride instead of walking.

"Well, congrats. I should've guessed there was someone in your life."

"A secret admirer, by definition, is someone I don't know."

He chuckled. "Oh, you probably do know. A pretty woman like you… lots of men must be lined up for your attention."

"I'm back in Riverbend for Madison's sake. Her father—" No. Nick didn't need the family history.

"Condolences on the loss of your mother. It's been hard on your sister."

Of course, he already knew. He was Madison's youth pastor. Too strange. "Thanks. Yes, it's rough for her."

Rough for Lindsey, too, even though her mom had lingered in a coma for months after the accident. And Greg, who'd never been the most stable man, had been floundering ever since. Madison should have been able to count on her father, but it hadn't happened.

"When can we get together and talk about the menu?"

Lindsey's thoughts derailed. Why was she doing this again? To please her sister, right? To help give Madison the opportunity to go on a missions trip. Not so she could see Nick Harrison a dozen times between now and Valentine's Day.

Definitely not that.

"Want to go for coffee and we can talk about it now?"

She shook her head. Too much like a date. She didn't want to be seen in public with him. People would get ideas. She became conscious of his gaze on the side of her face.

"I'm sorry I make you so uncomfortable."

He'd noticed? That probably meant she was being rude, but she hated how unsettled he made her feel. It was disconcerting to think that she'd never gotten over her high-school crush. If she'd been comparing guys to Nick all these years, most of them should have come out ahead. He'd been such a jerk.

He wasn't one now. Probably. She should give him the benefit of the doubt.

"Want to come in for a few minutes? I'm not sure if Greg's home, but Madison's there. We can make some preliminary plans."

"I'd love to."

Yeah, she'd just bet he would.

* * *

Nick held the door for Lindsey as they entered her house. This was even better than he'd hoped. To be here when—

"Linds! You're home." Madison skidded down the hallway and grabbed the banister above to keep from sliding past the steps. "Oh, hi, Pastor Nick." Her eyes gleamed. "Guess what?"

Nick helped Lindsey off with her coat and hung it on a vacant hook. He couldn't help grinning as she tossed the fuzzy pink mittens into a basket.

"What, Madison?"

Lindsey sounded tired. Maybe his idea to ambush her after work hadn't been the best. Well, he'd done it, and he was here now. Invited in, no less.

"You got another package today. See?" Madison held up a brown box.

Lindsey glanced up, her cheeks flushing. Or maybe it was just the chill from the wind outside. "That's nice. Madison, Nick is here to go over the menu for the banquet. Do you have any ideas of what you'd like?"

"Open your gift first."

She shrugged as she ascended the steps. "It can wait."

"No, go for it," Nick said, unable to help himself.

She pivoted on the top step and stared him in the eyes, pretty much at his eye level. "Why?"

Uh. "Don't you want to see what's in it?"

"Come on, Lindsey." Madison shook the box.

"Fine. I'll open it. Please put on water for tea, Madison."

"In a sec. I want to see."

Lindsey took the box, slit the tape, and opened it to reveal a small box of chocolates. She glanced at the pink paper on top then set both on a chair.

Nick didn't need to see the paper to know what it said.

Dear Lindsey,
You are as sweet as candy.
Secretly Yours.

"Ooh, chocolate!" Madison clutched her hands together. "Are those the ones with peanut butter? Those are your favorite."

Ah, something he'd have to keep in mind for another time. Unless that would give his hand away. Hmm.

Lindsey turned to him, box extended. "Here, want a chocolate?"

"Oh, I shouldn't. Those are from your secret admirer."

She narrowed her gaze. "How do you know?"

"Just a guess by the fact you didn't know from whom. Besides, you told me you'd already gotten something from a secret admirer, so it seemed a safe guess."

"Ooh, is it you, Pastor Nick?" Madison batted her eyelashes.

He laughed. "Go put the tea on, girl. Let's sort out this menu." He took a few steps toward the dining room table.

Madison jumped in his path and poked him in the chest with her forefinger. "I bet it is you."

"Hey now, if I wanted to date your sister, I'd just come right out and ask her. No need for games."

"Unless she said no the first time."

Lindsey's voice broke in. "The teakettle, Madison, if you will."

When Madison flounced back to the sink, Lindsey gave Nick a searching look. He must've passed because she grabbed a pad of paper and a pen from the counter and took a seat at the table.

"So, what do you have in mind for the banquet?"

Chapter Four

"Dude, the teens and I have totally got this covered." Jared leaned forward and pressed both hands on Nick's desk. "You don't have to worry about a thing."

"I'm not worried, exactly…" Well, maybe he was. Nick hadn't known the other guy more than a few months, but he was a drama major at the community college, and the presentation was for credit.

"We're doing a little fairytale mash-up. I ran the script past Pastor Davis on Monday, so it's all good."

Nick narrowed his gaze. "Pastor Davis? He's not the youth pastor. I am."

"You weren't in your office. Loosen up, dude. The drama for the banquet is in good hands." Jared pointed at himself with both thumbs. "That would be moi."

If the senior pastor had approved it, Nick supposed it would be okay. Jared still should have run it by him first. "How many kids are involved?"

"Just six." Jared held up both hands, forestalling Nick. "I didn't want to leave you shorthanded for everything else. Some of them will be playing dual roles. We've got it covered."

Nick shuffled the papers on his desk until the top one showed the teens who'd pledged to raise funds for the missions trip. He pushed the sheet to Jared and offered him a pencil. "Who do you have tied up?"

"Let's see." Jared marked off several names and slid it back to Nick.

"Madison? You can't have her. Her sister needs her in the kitchen." Though if anyone were a born actor, it had to be Lindsey's little sister.

Jared shook his head. "No can do, sorry. She's a natural, and the only girl in the group who can pull this off."

"Pull what off?"

"The whole drama thing. Seriously, dude. I need her, or we may as well cancel the event."

"But—"

Jared shook his head. "You can find someone else to plop food on plates, but I need my leading lady."

A trickle of alarm sifted through Nick. "She's sixteen, Jared. Way too young for you."

The other guy laughed. "It's all on the up and up, I promise. I see great talent. I'm not looking for an underage date."

"Okay. You had me worried there for a minute."

"No need." Jared surged to his feet. "When you're finalizing your program, give us twenty minutes. I'll take care of everything else."

Had he somehow agreed to relinquish Madison? Well, he hadn't exactly promised Lindsey to reserve her sister as sous chef. He could see Jared's point, though. Of all the teens doing fundraising, Madison seemed to have the most dramatic talent.

Nick stood and reached across his desk to shake Jared's hand. "Okay. You've got it. But if you have any questions, and I mean even little ones, please ask. It's my name on the line with the teens' parents and the community, and I'd rather be safe than sorry."

"You cause me pain, dude. I know what is appropriate and what is not." The younger guy grinned. "You're looking for a play that will entertain the guests, honor God, and stay on theme. I've got it covered."

It wasn't until the door had swung shut behind Jared that Nick realized the drama major had never even given him the name of the play.

* * *

"I'd like to adapt the Glory Bowl salad recipe for the banquet," Lindsey told her boss, Antonio.

He swiveled his chair to look her over. "Oh? How so?"

"Well, I'm looking for a lighter salad, not a small meal, so I thought I'd go with the mixed greens from Vitality, the hazelnuts, grated carrots and beets, and then the dressing."

Antonio nodded. "That works. What are you looking for in an entree?"

Lindsey hesitated. "I was hoping for some guidance on that."

"What's the budget? How many tickets?"

"That's the problem. Nick says we could get anywhere from fifty to a hundred people. And, of course, the more I charge per plate, the less the youth group makes for their fundraiser."

"Fundraisers." Antonio shook his head. "Only for you, Lindsey. Only for you. The kind of dinner we are speaking of, with a bottle of the best Castle Rock red, would be easily one-hundred-fifty a couple." He held up a hand. "Yes, we would be making good money on that, but we are a business, and we do our job well."

One fifty? Lindsey felt faint. "The wine won't be an issue. It's a church event."

"But it is a gourmet dinner. Of course there is to be wine." He glared at her until he seemed to understand. "A raspberry soda, perhaps?"

She nodded. "That sounds good. Is there anything we can do with lamb within the budget? Or do you have another suggestion?"

"You cannot just *get*—" he kissed his fingers "—enough local lamb to feed one hundred people without months of advance notice."

Yeah, she'd been afraid of that. It had seemed a fair request on Nick's part, but logistically… not so much.

"Also, it is too expensive for a fundraiser unless you are the Ritz." He peered at her over his glasses. "And you are not."

"Right, okay. It was only a question. What do you suggest?"

"Perhaps a roulade." He tapped his pen. "No. Again with the budget. Cacciatore, then."

Hmm. It would still be a flight of steps above the spaghetti dinners they'd put on as fundraisers back when she was in youth group. Memories of congealed pasta and bland meatballs drowned in cheap tomato sauce caused a shudder to run through her.

"No?" Antonio eyed her. "I feel sure it is a good move for you. Ingredients we can get that do not cost the moon. The purpose is to please the guests and to make money, yes?"

"Sorry, yes. I think cacciatore can work." Easier to have her untrained staff help with that than a roulade, for sure. If only Madison hadn't bailed on her in preference for the drama team. Should've been no surprise, but, whatever. "Perhaps we can borrow the pasta maker?"

"Do you have enough sous chefs to pull that off, Lindsey? For you, I would say yes, but I am concerned you bite off too much."

"But it is to be a local meal..."

Antonio waved a hand. "Indeed. This I understand. It is what we are all about here at the Water Wheel, yes? But there is a line of what is sensible and what is not."

Lindsey nodded. "I understand." But there must be a way. She'd promised Nick and, for some reason, the look she was sure to see on his face when she delivered the final banquet meant more to her than it ought to, being as she didn't care a speck about him. Less than a speck.

"That is good, Lindsey. Write out your plan and leave it on my desk. Your banquet is only five weeks away now, and it is time to place some of the orders so ingredients arrive on time."

She knew when she'd been dismissed. "Thanks." She backed out of Antonio's office and nearly ran into one of the waitresses.

The girl kept her platter from falling by the luckiest of moves.

"Sorry," murmured Lindsey. She needed to get her head back in the game, both for the remainder of today's shift and for the upcoming banquet.

"Earth to Lindsey."

She glanced up at Marc as she approached her workstation. "Hey."

"Don't run Beatrix over." He waggled his eyebrows at her. "Got a hot date with her tonight, and she'll need her dancing shoes on."

So... unlikely that Marc was her secret admirer. Not that she'd suspected him. And there really wasn't anyone else. Other than Nick.

Why again was he singling her out? Was it really possible he'd changed since high school? She couldn't imagine Pastor Davis and the elders not doing a thorough check on the guy before hiring him to work with their youth. On an intellectual level, she understood he had to be different. But at gut level? Hard to believe when his smile was just as devastating as it had been way back when.

Chapter Five

Madison cautiously turned the car into the church parking lot and eased to a stop. "There! How'd I do?"

Lindsey let out the breath she'd been holding for the past twenty minutes. "Good." How had she gotten stuck being the designated adult to ride along with a beginning driver? Yeah, Greg sure didn't have patience for it.

Her sister spilled from the driver's seat and thrust both fists triumphantly in the air. "Did you see that?"

A group of teens turned from their hacky sack game near the church door. "Dude, Madison! You're driving?"

Only because there hadn't been any fresh snow in a few days, and the streets had been cleared. Lindsey climbed out of the passenger side and rounded the back of the vehicle to snag the red magnet with the large L on it, signaling to the otherwise unsuspecting world that a newbie was behind the wheel. A car pulled in beside her and she glanced over. Nick.

Lindsey wrenched her attention back to Madison. "I'll be back for you at nine-thirty," she called.

Not that her sister heard her. Madison pirouetted across the parking lot to catcalls from the guys.

Nick laughed. "Kids, eh? Were we ever that young?"

Had she really heard those words from Nick Harrison? The guy who'd stomped across every heart in sight when they were teens? She turned slowly to face him.

He was right there, mere inches from her. Tall, dark, too hot for his own good. He always had been.

"Lindsey?" His eyes darkened, and he took a step closer.

She backed up, but there was nowhere to go. She bumped into the car.

"Lindsey, about high school." His eyes searched hers.

She tried to look away, but his gaze was more magnetic than the L she held in her hand.

"I was a jerk back then. I know that, and I'm sorry."

Lindsey leaned against the car and crossed her arms. Maybe she could pull off nonchalance. "Yeah, you were."

Nick grimaced. "I was full of myself. A kid." He gestured at the teens goofing off on the church steps. "God got a hold of me and changed me from the inside out. I'm a different person than I was then, Lindsey."

"I'm happy for you."

"No forgiveness, huh?" he asked softly.

She shrugged. "Sure. You're forgiven. We've all done stupid things." Nick had been stupider than average, but still. Who was she to hold a grudge?

"So you'll go out with me?"

"I didn't say that."

"But—"

Lindsey forced herself to look him in the eye and not drown. Tougher than it sounded. "Nick, what you're doing here for the youth is great. I'm committed to doing my share to make the Valentine's fundraiser a success. But I'm not looking for a relationship. Okay? Can we just leave it at that?"

He shifted, blocking her view of the teens, and swept her hair away from her face. "What can I do or say to make you understand?"

She sidled toward the rear of the car. "You don't need to do anything."

"Is there someone else? Madison said…"

"My sister talks entirely too much."

He chuckled. "Probably true." The grin slid off his face, and his eyes intensified. "Lindsey, the old Nick Harrison is gone. He's been saved. Washed in the blood of Jesus."

"I'm glad for you. I really am."

Another car pulled into the parking lot, and several teens spilled out then swarmed toward the steps. One glanced over and elbowed his buddy. They both grinned. One sent a thumbs-up.

"I need to go." Wait. Had he said the exact same thing at the same time as her?

She narrowed her gaze at him. “What we don’t need is a bunch of teenagers getting some crazy idea about why we’re out here talking so long, okay? Especially when they’d be dead wrong.”

He opened her car door and she slid inside, tossing the L into the passenger seat. She turned the ignition as he leaned in.

“But they wouldn’t be.”

She shifted into reverse, knowing full well the car door was still open and Nick was in the way.

“Until later,” he said, and swung it closed.

Lindsey bit her lip and made her escape.

“Whoa, Pastor Nick! She’s hot!”

“Need advice for your love life, Pastor Nick?”

“Who is she, anyway?”

“You’re kidding. Madison’s sister?”

“You can’t keep secrets from us, Pastor Nick.”

And that’s what he got for trying to talk to Lindsey just before youth group. Like bees swarming him, incessantly buzzing, as he strode toward the church door.

Someone tucked a hand behind his elbow, and he glanced down to see Madison beaming up at him. “Don’t worry, Pastor Nick. We’re on your side.”

They climbed the steps. He patted her hand, removed it, and managed to get a teen or two between them. That’s what he was afraid of. This gang of teenagers, committed to a cause, could do way more than set a third-world country on fire in an upcoming missions trip. Being the center of their attention could be terrifying.

Nick stifled a groan as they entered the youth room en masse. The whole place was covered with heart, dove, and flower decorations. How was he going to teach the teens about romance and purity God’s way with all this speculation going on around him? He’d just become a personalized object lesson.

God, this one is up to You.

"So, Pastor Nick, she doesn't seem as into you as, you know, you are into her."

Could this get more humiliating?

"I could give you some advice," Aidan said, arm wrapped around his girlfriend of three weeks.

Apparently, yes, it could get more humiliating.

"Yeah, we can totally help you."

"Whoa, whoa, whoa." Nick forced out a chuckle. "I don't need any help here." Except perhaps God's. "You want to talk about love? Hit the carpet. Let's talk." He'd planned for an icebreaker game to lead into the devotional but, hey. The ice was broken. He could adjust.

"There's a few things to learn here." He eyed Aidan as the gang settled onto the carpet. "No PDA, remember?"

Aidan rolled his eyes and shifted a few inches from his girlfriend.

"I want to talk to you guys about God's love for us. It's constant, whether we respond or not. How come we don't always accept it? What reasons might you have for not wanting a boyfriend or girlfriend right now? Do any of those reasons relate to God?"

The kids looked at each other.

"We don't think we need it?" one girl offered.

"Yeah, maybe it's cool to be single. You know, independent."

"Sometimes being part of a couple means you're not as much yourself."

"Maybe we think the other person is too cool to really like us, so we're afraid they're only pretending."

"Yeah, who wants to get hurt? Or feel used."

Nick nodded. "Those all sound valid. But what about God? Can we trust His motives for loving us?"

Groupthink happened again as the kids exchanged looks. Nick could all but see their antennae swivel as they communicated telepathically.

Madison sighed. "Sometimes it all sounds too good to be true. Like a fairy tale. We've seen our parents fight and maybe get divorced."

"I get that. My folks split up when I was in Junior High." Nick grimaced. "And my dad's been divorced again since then. It's hard to believe in love."

"My parents don't fight," a boy put in, glancing around. "Not much, anyway."

"Mine do," someone added.

"God's love is the ultimate." Nick grabbed his Bible. "It shows us what is possible. It gives us a standard to stretch for." Did he really love Lindsey, or was he only intrigued because she seemed hard to get? He'd have to think on that later. "We humans aren't perfect like God is. That means we can't love perfectly, either. We get selfish and proud and impatient, but, if we keep trying, keep praying for God's help to love perfectly, I believe He teaches us to do that."

He flipped his Bible open to 1 Corinthians 13. "I want to read the love chapter to you. We'll stop often to talk about what love really looks like. Ready?"

The kids nodded.

Nick breathed a prayer. Tonight's devo was as much for him as for the kids.

Chapter Six

Lindsey's cell phone rang seconds after she stepped out the door of the Water Wheel. She glanced around, looking for Nick's car, but it wasn't in sight.

Because, yes, that was his ring. She'd assigned one to him in self-defense, so she wouldn't accidentally pick up when he called. Maybe that was dumb. He had a reason to call, after all. The banquet.

By the third ring, she had her fuzzy mitts off and the phone slid on. "Lindsey here."

"Hey! It's Nick."

Um, yeah. She knew that. "Hi."

"I was wondering if you'd like to go snowshoeing tomorrow. It's the annual full-moon event put on by the Riverbend Trails committee."

"Uh…"

"It starts at nine o'clock at the golf course."

Her brain fumbled. "At night?"

"Hence the full moon." His grin was evident in his voice.

How could he possibly know she'd bought a pair of snowshoes at Base Camp Outfitters with her final bonus from Fresh Start? She hadn't even gotten out on them yet.

Madison. That would be how. Lindsey gritted her teeth then forced herself to unclench them. "Right."

"Lindsey, I'd like a chance to show you I'm not the same guy I was in high school. Can we get together? Share a good time? Talk?"

Was she being too hard on him? Didn't everyone deserve a second chance? Well, nearly everyone. She sighed. "Okay, fine. This once."

"Did you say… yes?"

Last chance to retract. "Yes."

"Great! I'll pick you up about eight-thirty. Make sure you dress in layers. Don't worry about snacks. I've got all that covered."

Her head spun. "I can meet you there." Definitely a better idea in case things went wrong.

"Oh, no, you don't. A date's a date, and I'm doing this one right." Nick hesitated. "We could go for dinner beforehand…?"

"Don't push your luck."

He chuckled. "I promise I'll be good."

"You better." She should perhaps summon some graciousness. "Thanks, Nick."

"My pleasure. Until tomorrow, then."

She pocketed the phone and tugged her mitts back on. The icy wind caught her cheeks as she stepped out of the shelter of the restaurant and turned onto the sidewalk along River Way. The town's sidewalk plow had been by a couple of hours previously, and the walkway was still passable.

Maybe on her next paycheck she'd offer to buy Greg a new set of tires. How much did they cost, anyway? Only then maybe he'd drive to work himself instead of catching a ride to the sawmill with a neighbor, and she wouldn't have gained a thing. If he really wanted tires, she was pretty sure he'd have bought them by now.

If she stayed in Riverbend another winter, she'd buy her own car. And, yeah, she had to stay. Madison had three more semesters of high school. Could Lindsey stand living with Greg that long? Not that he interfered with her life, other than randomly deciding she couldn't use his car. He was thankful enough for the groceries she brought in and the meals she fixed. Whether or not he noticed the mold had been scrubbed from the shower tile was anybody's guess. He hadn't commented on the plastic film on most of the house's windows, but he had to be aware the place was less drafty and the heating bill lower.

But all that she did for herself and Madison. Not for Greg. He didn't deserve it.

Just like Nick didn't deserve to be forgiven.

Ouch. That stabbed her heart like the frost tingling her nose. How did she get to decide who deserved what? Wasn't that God's job?

Okay, well, she was giving Nick a chance. The sooner he destroyed it, the sooner she could shove him out of her mind — again — and go back to planning Madison's future.

* * *

"Pastor Nick's here!"

He stood under a small overhang outside the door, the sound of the doorbell still reverberating under Madison's announcement, and shook his head. That girl.

The door swung open, but it wasn't the teen's eager face looking up at him. Nor was it the pensive face of her older sister. Instead, a stubbly middle-aged man about his own height stared back. The guy hitched his thumbs through belt loops on saggy jeans.

"So you're the guy I keep hearing about."

More likely from Madison than Lindsey, sadly. Nick offered his hand. "Nick Harrison, sir."

"Greg Kimball. Madison's father."

"Pleased to meet you." There'd been no handshake, so Nick dropped his hand to his side. "I'm here to pick Lindsey up."

"She's almost ready," yelled Madison. "Come on in."

He would if Greg stepped aside. On the other hand, he wouldn't give the man the satisfaction of waiting in the car, either. If Greg wanted to cool the house down with a wide-open front door, so be it. Nick's honor to Lindsey came first.

"Don't have her out too late."

No wonder Lindsey had a hard time forgetting high school. "I'll keep that in mind."

Lindsey appeared at the railing above. "Greg, we're adults. I'll be back when I get here." She turned to her sister. "Behave yourself."

Greg harrumphed. Madison batted her eyelashes then winked at Nick when Lindsey turned away.

That kid would be the death of him. Nick stifled a grin. But at the moment, Lindsey took center stage. Easy enough. She looked amazing in a turtleneck and slim leggings. Not only that, but this girl knew winter layers.

She pulled on a pair of ski pants, leaving the ankles unzipped, tugged a knitted tuque over her soft blond hair, and slid on a puffy vest. She met his gaze for a second as she reached for her boots. "My snowshoes are just outside the door."

He stepped outside and plucked them from the snow bank.

Lindsey grabbed her jacket and slipped a thin wallet into an inside pocket before following him outside. As soon as she'd closed the door, she leaned against it. "Sorry about Greg. He forgets I'm not Madison's age."

Nick picked up the snowshoes leaning against the steps and flashed her a smile. "It's okay. It's hard for parents to keep track." He wanted to take her hand on the walk to the curb, but thought better of it. She wouldn't let him, anyway. Even if she did, what were the odds Madison watched from the window? A hundred and ten percent.

For now, he'd settle for opening the car door for her and treating her like the beautiful princess she was.

Chapter Seven

It seemed to Lindsey that half the inhabitants of Riverbend must be in the golf course parking lot, strapping on their snowshoes. Which also meant way too many people she might know would see her with Nick. It looked like a date.

Oh, who was she kidding? He hadn't even pretended the purpose was to discuss the banquet. No, he'd invited her on a date and, in a moment of weakness, she'd agreed.

Lindsey stood and took a few steps, testing the fit. The snowshoes felt good. She slid cold fingers into thin knit gloves then into waterproof over-mitts.

From the corner of her eye she saw Nick swing a small pack over his shoulders. "Ready?" he asked.

She nodded and took a deep breath. How had he talked her into this again? But she was here. It would be fun. She fell into step beside him across the parking lot to the entrance to the city's bike trail, covered in at least a foot of snow. They were ahead of most of the group. Some folks had babies strapped to their backs, while others pulled toboggans with young riders. Kids, parents, and grandparents readied themselves together.

Lindsey inhaled deeply. The wind had died down and the temperature was only five below freezing. Practically a chinook. Across the inky depths of the Sandon River, the town's fanciest houses lit up the distance and cast long, weak fingers of light. Brighter puddles from lampposts along the path kept the eeriness at bay.

"This path is the best thing town council did for Riverbend in the past decade," Nick said.

"It's pretty cool." She hesitated. "How far north does it go, anyway?" What had she let herself in for? But then there were all those families with little kids. It couldn't be that bad.

“It goes more than eight kilometers before connecting with the old railway bed. That part isn’t paved, but it’s still great biking and hiking.”

“Uh…”

Nick chuckled. “For tonight, we’ll go as far as you want to. There are buses and volunteers at every crossing ready to take people back to the parking lot if they don’t want to hike back.”

She quickened her pace. He figured she was the weak link? She’d done a lot of walking since returning to Riverbend. He might be surprised at her stamina. Although — she cast a sidelong look at his lean frame — he probably worked out at the gym. If she made this a competition, she’d probably lose.

Around them, voices drifted away as they set their own pace ahead of most of the pack.

“Thanks for coming with me, Lindsey.”

His quiet words broke through her reverie. Not that she’d forgotten the crazy hot guy beside her. How could she? If only she knew if he’d really changed, if he could be trusted. Would she wake up tomorrow morning and find he’d pulled the plug with another *ha-ha, got you again*?

Might as well start looking for those answers. “I was surprised to find you became a pastor.”

“I bet.” Nick chuckled. “It definitely hadn’t been my plan.” A few strides later, he continued. “I went to U of C on a hockey scholarship. I was going to get drafted to a big NHL franchise. Somebody with a good shot at the Stanley Cup. I was going to be the driving force that pushed my team to victory. I could already see my name next to The Great One in the Hockey Hall of Fame. Don Cherry would speak of me with respect, and I’d rake in the goals… and the trophies, of course.”

Of course. That certainly sounded like the Nick she remembered. It hadn’t all been ego speaking. He’d been talented enough to pull it off. She was interested in spite of herself. “What happened?”

“Got sidelined. I’d never been sick a day in my life, but I got run over by the mononucleosis train midway through my first semester. I missed most of my games and nearly flunked out.”

Against her better judgment, a niggle of sympathy worked its way to the surface. “Bad luck.”

“I sure thought so. I was very bitter. All those dreams, crumbling into dust. But things happen for a reason. I'd been ignoring thoughts of God, shoving them aside in my self-worth and busyness. Suddenly I had little time for anything *but* thinking."

Snow crunched under their snowshoes. Lindsey pulled her water bottle out of her pocket and took a long swallow.

"My roommate's brother came to visit at his school's study break. A religious guy, not very athletic. I hadn't given him a second thought before that because, you know, he couldn't help Nick Harrison into the NHL." Nick's laugh didn't seem forced. "I was right about that, but he could help Nick Harrison into the kingdom. He asked me questions and answered mine and challenged me to think deeper, then deeper yet. At the end of the week, I opened my life to Jesus and joined my friend at Bible college the next fall."

"And the rest, as they say, is history?"

"Not quite that simple, but yeah, that's when things headed a new direction in my life. What about you? When did you become a Christian?"

"Nothing so dramatic. My mom took me to church when I was a kid. I guess you could say I drank the kool-aid early."

She could feel Nick's glance, so she increased her speed a little, forcing him to focus on the snowy path.

"That's an odd way to put it," he said at last. "I see God's love and His gift of salvation as the biggest prize in my life. It's what makes everything worth living. Even the Stanley Cup, the Conn Smythe, and the Art Ross rolled into one season finale wouldn't come remotely close."

"You've sure changed."

He reached over and touched her arm. "I've been trying to tell you that for three weeks."

He had. So it seemed he'd done a full one-eighty. Why did she still feel stuck in the middle, with no significant growth in her own life? She hadn't been good enough for Nick Harrison before, and it seemed she still wasn't.

* * *

Nick studied Lindsey's face as they approached the highway. "First chance for a ride back to the golf course," he offered.

Her chin lifted as she glanced at him. "You tired?"

"Just checking if you were."

"I'm good."

The path narrowed as it headed under the bridge. Several fixtures cascaded brightness over the path and into the river beyond. And then semi-darkness loomed again. They were across from Riverside Park now, the full moon glinting off the river.

Nick wasn't going to waste this evening, even if getting any words out of Lindsey felt like a bigger workout than snowshoeing. "Tell me what you've been doing since you left town. What got you into cooking?"

"I waitressed for a year after high school, saving up for culinary school back east. After graduation, I got into a start-up with really fresh, local ingredients. Moved up from there to a larger, more established restaurant in Niagara, but I began to miss the West. When Fresh Start opened in Castlebrook, I put in my resume and got the lead chef position."

"That's really impressive. Fresh Start has a great reputation."

She shrugged. Yeah, of course she knew that. She'd been largely responsible.

"It seems you were all set. Why come back to Riverbend?"

Lindsey stopped in the middle of the path. "Madison. I'd missed so much of her life. She was only a little kid when I left and, honestly, she still seems like one. She's too young to be without a mother."

Nick took a couple of more steps before realizing she'd really stopped. Now he turned to face her. "I'm sorry about your mom."

Was it his imagination, or did her eyes glisten?

"Yeah, it's been rough. Impaired driver, and she was in a coma for months. I came home every chance I could, but she never regained consciousness. Never said my name again."

She was definitely crying.

"Or Madison's." Lindsey's voice broke. "My sister needed it more, and she didn't get closure, either."

Nick angled his snowshoes closer and reached out. He didn't ask permission, just gathered Lindsey in his arms. She didn't fight, but sagged against him, sobbing into his jacket collar. He rubbed the back of her puffy vest, then swept the hair away from her damp cheeks.

He had no words.

Chapter Eight

How had she gotten herself in Nick Harrison's arms? Lindsey sniffled and tried to pull away. With a little extra hug, he released her, but when she dared a glance at him, his dark eyes were lined with concern.

She put on a shaky smile. "I-I'm okay."

"You don't have to carry everything alone, Lindsey."

What exactly did he mean by that? There hadn't exactly been a line of people willing to help. Look at Greg, for instance. She wiped her eyes on the sleeve of her jacket and glanced at the path. Had anyone just witnessed her meltdown? Possibly. The backs of a few snowshoers disappeared at the north end of the visible trail.

Nick reached for her hand, and she let him take it as they started moving again. He studied her. "What I really meant was that I keep giving my troubles to Jesus, and that helps a lot. I know He cares about me. He doesn't give me more than I can handle, but He sure does allow things that make me lean on Him and grow as a believer."

"You have troubles, Nick?" Oops, had the bitterness shown in her voice?

He swung her hand. "Is that so hard to believe?"

Okay, he sounded like he was teasing. She could try to match that. "And here I thought you were born with the golden hockey stick in your hands."

Nick laughed outright, and her heart warmed at the full, rich sound, so different from that of a selfish teen bent on making himself look good at the expense of others. It was going to take some getting used to, this new-and-improved Nick. One who seemed to actually enjoy being with her even when she was such lousy company.

She could change, too. Couldn't she? Like him, she could set the past where it firmly belonged — in the history books — and see where the future might lead. Not just with Nick, either, but with the Lord, too. She'd let that relationship stagnate, forgetting how meaningful Jesus had been to her as a teen.

Lindsey squeezed Nick's mittened hand. "Thanks."

He angled his head toward her. "For what?"

"Reminding me." She took a deep breath. "I've let bitterness eat at me for long enough."

Several steps later, he said, "Bitterness at…"

"You."

"Whoa. So I'm not just a symptom of the problem."

She shook her head. "I was just a kid with a serious case of crush on an older guy. And when you seemed to finally notice me…"

Nick ducked his head and scratched his neck. "I was a jerk."

"Pretty much." But the heat was out of her words.

He turned toward her. "Have I told you yet that I'm really sorry? Because I am."

"You've mentioned it once or twice." A smile tried to lift the edges of her mouth. "I might consider forgiving you."

"You might, eh?" In the dim light, it was hard to tell if his eyes were twinkling or not. He stepped in front of her, arranging his snowshoes so he filled her space. His voice deepened. "What might it take?"

Her first intention was to look him in the eye, grin, and dodge out of his reach down the trail. But that was before the emotion in his gaze captured hers. She stood transfixed, barely daring to breathe as he tipped his head and covered her lips with his own.

This.

She slid her arms around his neck and, for a long moment, kissed him back. His lips, gentle, not demanding, warmed her to the core of her being, clear to the bottom of her size-six boots. But this was hardly the time or place for nonstop smooching. Under a full moon on a cold January night, with other people snowshoeing past.

On the other hand, what was wrong with that?

* * *

Snowshoes didn't make the best footwear for hugging and kissing, something Nick hadn't particularly considered before. He couldn't help the grin that forced its way from his mind to his mouth. Not that he wanted Lindsey to stop. He'd been dreaming of this moment on-and-off for years… constantly for a month.

"What's so funny?" she murmured.

"Trying to decide if I want to keep snowshoeing or simply go somewhere more conducive to, um, doing more of this."

She leaned back far enough to look into his eyes with those baby-blues of hers, catching a glint from the lamppost by the bridge. She looked wary.

He dropped a quick kiss to her mouth. "I mean nothing nefarious by that comment. I've waited years for this moment. I can wait… longer… for more." How much longer, though? How long did he have to wait to put one ring on her finger, let alone two?

"Years?" she asked with wonder.

It took him a second to realize she was addressing his spoken words, not his thoughts. "Years." He grimaced. "I was mean to you. Not *immune* to you."

"Never would have guessed." She tipped her head sideways and bit her lip.

Could he kiss it better? Maybe a bit of restraint would make a better impression when she clearly had something else to say.

"So…" She watched him closely. "This secret admirer thing."

Which way to go? Admit it? Not? He chose the frown. "That chump still bothering you?"

"Yeah. Every few days there's something else. Candy, endearing gifts. A tasty little cupcake a few days ago from Carmen's Cupcake and Confectionery."

"Wow. He sounds like quite the romantic guy."

"I'm not so sure. He's never sent flowers. Aren't roses the symbol of unending love?"

Nick was pretty sure that was a diamond ring. "Maybe it's been too cold for flowers. Ever consider that?"

Lindsey shook her head. "Huh. You think that's it?"

"Just a guess."

She shuffled her snowshoe out from between his. "Race you to the next bridge." She pivoted and took off in a lumbering run.

"Hey!"

She didn't stop.

Nick started laughing. He just couldn't help it. All of the stress of the past few weeks, the angst of whether she'd ever forgive him, all dissolved in that moment of relief.

Lindsey must be halfway to the finish line by now.

Still chuckling, he ran after her, not as easy to do on snowshoes as she made it look. "Hey, wait for me!"

She glanced over her shoulder, tripped, and tumbled into a snow bank, where she flailed to right herself.

The old Nick would have rubbed snow in her face and tickled her while she was down. He wouldn't promise that Nick wouldn't show up again in good fun, but not tonight. Not in their new relationship after all their painful revelations.

Nick reached for her hands and pulled her upright into his arms. "Did you enjoy your run?" he teased.

"You tripped me!" she challenged, her cheeks rosy, her eyes bright.

He burst out laughing. "I was ten meters away. I don't think you can blame me for that one." He ran his fingers through her hair, dislodging clumps of snow. "You okay? Didn't twist an ankle when you went over or anything?"

"No. I'm fine." She glanced up the path. "So, are we finishing what we started or what?"

A wee bit competitive, this Lindsey girl. He wrapped his hands around her cheeks. Also a bit cold. He kissed her, using all his self-restraint to keep it to one short kiss with a hint of promise. "We've started more than one thing tonight. We don't have to finish everything right now."

Her eyes darkened in the dim light. "What have we started, Nick? What is this?" Her gloved hands tangled with the front of his jacket.

The million-dollar question. He knew what he hoped to have started. He'd tried for ten years to get her out of his mind and been unsuccessful at it. He'd prayed for her often since coming to know the Lord, and way more often still in the past few weeks since she'd slid back into his life. She was The One.

She hadn't been waiting for him the way he had for her, so, to her, any declarations of unending love would need to wait. She was worth treating like a princess. Worth the trail of gifts to make sure she understood how much she meant to him. He wouldn't rush in and throw his plans to the winter wind.

"What're you thinking, Nick?"

"What have we started?" He dropped a kiss to those upturned lips and nearly groaned. "We've started what just may be the adventure of a lifetime. I can't wait to see what's around the bend, can you?"

The glimmer in her eyes warmed him to the core. "Pretty sure there's just the same windy, snow-covered trail for, what did you say, a million kilometers?"

Oh, she was going to pretend to misconstrue his words, was she? "There's only five to go. Or we could catch a ride back from the next road crossing." He caressed her cheeks and jaw, holding her face between his hands. She felt warmer now. "What do you want to do?"

She stretched and planted a kiss on his lips.

Nick slid his arms around her and pulled her closer. "I wouldn't mind doing more of that, myself," he murmured against her fluttering eyelids.

Chapter Nine

Saturday morning Lindsey stretched under her down comforter, her sore leg muscles reminding her of every step she'd taken on snowshoes last night. Under a full moon. With Nick Harrison.

All. Those. Kisses.

Who'd ever have guessed he'd been interested in her, praying for her, all those years? Was he… The One?

She squished the teddy bear, the most recent gift from her secret admirer, just as a light tap came at her bedroom door. "Linds?"

"I'm awake, Madison. Come in." Her sister was going to want to know everything. How much info did she want to have going around the youth group? Nick was their pastor.

Her brain hit the brakes. She was absolutely crazy to fall for a pastor. Last night it had been easy to forget, even with his coming-to-Jesus story. But in reality, a pastor's life was way different than, than a chef's. Or an electrician. Or a guy who worked shift at the nearby sawmill. Nick was more spiritual. She… well, she really wasn't.

Madison jumped on the bed. "Was it amazing? Did he kiss you?" She grabbed a pillow from under Lindsey's head — thunk — and settled in, cross-legged and bright-eyed.

Probably half the town had snowshoed past while they were lip-locked. Denial wasn't going to get her anywhere. Lindsey nodded.

"He kissed you?" Madison's eyes grew larger as she pressed a hand over her heart.

"Yup."

Madison collapsed backward on the bed. "He kissed her. They're getting married."

Lindsey tugged the teddy bear out from under the blanket and threw it at Madison. Her secret admirer had to be Nick, didn't it? Not that he'd admitted to anything when she asked. "Not so fast, missy."

"First comes love…"

Lindsey shook her head. “Madison, grab your brain. One kiss does not an engagement make.” More than one kiss. But the principle was the same.

Madison propped herself up on one elbow. “Do you go around kissing every guy you go meet?”

“Of course not!”

“When’s the last time you got kissed?”

As though it was any of her snoopy little sister’s business. Lindsey edged to a sitting position, leaning against the white-painted headboard. “Been a while.” Never like that.

Madison flopped onto her back. “Just as I suspected. Can I be your maid-of-honor?”

Lindsey blinked. “I said put on the brain brakes. Good grief, girl.”

“Well, can I?”

“Um, no, you can’t. You have to be nineteen to sign legal paperwork in British Columbia.” Which brought up an interesting question. Whom *did* she want to stand up for her? Speaking of runaway thoughts…

“Well, that’s a bummer. I can be a bridesmaid, though, right? Don’t forget I look great in pink.”

“I — um — I’ll keep that in mind.”

“You and Nick Harrison…” Madison’s dreamy voice faded dramatically. “Lindsey Ann Harrison.”

Lindsey flipped as much of the duvet on top of Madison as she could before rolling her legs off the edge of the bed. “Want to bake cupcakes with me today? I want to practice some decorations for the fundraising banquet.”

“Sounds fun.” Madison’s voice was muffled by the comforter. “The banquet colors are chocolate brown and cream and pink. And we need hearts everywhere.”

Lindsey couldn’t resist tickling Madison’s bare feet hanging off the edge of the bed. The feet kicked at her before being inhaled under the flipped-over comforter.

“I’ll get a shower then make us some breakfast,” Lindsey said, heading for the door. “Cupcakes after that.”

* * *

"Pastor Nick's here!"

He stood outside, his finger still on the doorbell, as Madison's yell echoed through the house.

Thump. Thump. Thump.

The door whisked open and the teenager beamed at him. "Come on in. We're making cupcakes."

"Sounds like I came at just the right time." He was speaking to air. Madison had already run up the steps and disappeared into the kitchen.

Lindsey poked her head around the corner above. "Hi, there."

That was more like it. He removed his snowy boots and hung up his parka before mounting the steps and making his way into a kitchen that smelled amazingly of molten chocolate. He tried to push back the grin that wanted to erupt when he saw the pink lips-and-hearts covered apron proclaiming, "Kiss the Cook!"

He'd had a lot of gall buying that one last week. Now he just wanted to obey its direct command.

"I'm dying to know if you're Lindsey's secret admirer." Madison's eyes gleamed. "It can't be anyone else, can it?"

"Why not?" Nick tweaked her nose. "Are you saying your sister isn't sweet enough for more than one guy to fall for her charms? There's probably a line down the block."

Madison ran over to the living room window and pulled back the ancient vertical blinds before making a production of looking up and down the street. "No one there. Just your car."

Nick took the distraction to close the distance and obey the apron with a quick kiss on Lindsey's upturned mouth. "So, what's the big occasion for these cupcakes?" A cooling rack with a dozen perfectly browned specimens sat beside a bowl of frothy pink frosting.

She grinned at him. "Practicing for the banquet. We're undecided between the poufy cloud of pink frosting or something more sculpted. What do you think?"

"Hmm. I might have to taste them both to know for sure."

Her eyes twinkled. "The taste is the same. It's the look that's different."

"You can't know that for sure," he protested. "In fact, there's no way to be absolutely certain that every single cupcake tastes the same. There could be a rogue."

Madison slid back into the kitchen, nearly knocking him into Lindsey. Might not be so bad. "These are even better than Carmen's cupcakes."

Lindsey shook her head. "I doubt that. She's a pro. Have you tasted her poppy seed lemons? Uh. Maze. Ing."

Lemon cupcakes. Check.

"Well, you're a pro, too, and I like chocolate better." Madison tilted her head to look critically at the row of confections. "Can we make them look like tuxedoes?"

"Maybe," said Lindsey.

Feet shuffled down the hallway and Madison's father came into view wearing a ragged T-shirt and striped pajama pants. He stopped when he saw Nick, running a large hand across his unshaven jaw. "You here again?"

"Sure am."

Greg's bushy eyebrows disappeared into mussed hair. "Madison says you're a pastor?"

"Pastor of Family and Youth over at River of Life Church."

"And the one Madison has an all-fired crush on." Greg glanced at Lindsey, shaking his head. "Both of them? Awkward."

"Daddy!" Madison's cheeks flushed.

Nick wouldn't have guessed anything could embarrass her.

Lindsey shot her stepfather a piercing glare. "Enough, Greg."

"A pastor. Sure never thought we'd see one of those here." Greg glanced at Lindsey. "I could use some bacon and eggs, sweetheart."

Madison rocked on her heels. "I'll get it, Daddy."

"I asked your sister."

"Madison is perfectly capable, Greg." Lindsey untied her apron and pulled it over her head. "Nick and I were just heading out for a walk. I'll be back in a little while."

They were?

Greg's eyes narrowed at Nick. Yeah, a walk sounded like a great idea. It wasn't that much colder outside than in this kitchen, after all.

Chapter Ten

Lindsey didn't resist when Nick took her mittened hand in his as they turned toward the river. At the end of the block, she blew out a puff that crystallized in the cold air.

"Nick, I don't think this can work."

To give him credit, he simply squeezed her hand. "Why not?"

"You saw Greg." She let out a sharp laugh. "That's just the kind of guy he is."

"I'm not m… dating Greg. It's you I care about."

What had he nearly said? She wouldn't let her mind go there. "He's part of my life. And so is Madison. They are the reason I came home." Okay, the entire reason was to buffer Madison from her father. But still. That didn't change her reality.

"I get that," Nick said. "But you deserve happiness, too. You can't give up everything for your sister."

So he'd seen right through the way of it. "A year and a half, Nick, before she graduates from high school. I-I can't leave her with Greg."

Nick swung her around to face him and gazed straight in her eyes. "Does he abuse her?"

Lindsey bit her lip and shook her head. "Not like that, I'm pretty sure. He's just so selfish and… and needy. But Madison doesn't know what's appropriate. She really craves his love and attention."

Nick cradled her face, his thumbs smoothing her cheeks.

He was interfering with her ability to think. Lindsey stepped back to break contact, and stared down at her boots. "It's not just Madison."

He tipped his head. "Are you looking for validation from Greg? I'm not sure he's capable of delivering."

Lindsey shook her head. "That's not what I meant. I meant… you're a pastor."

He closed the gap, but Lindsey grabbed his hand and started walking again. She could cope with him beside her, maybe, but not that soulful touch that electrified her senses.

"Yes, I am." He glanced toward her. "I was yesterday, too."

"I-I forgot there for a bit."

"But now it's a problem?" He kept his voice even.

"It's just that you're… spiritual. And I'm really not. I forget to read my Bible half the time." There, she'd admitted it.

"Lindsey, I'm not on a pedestal. I'm not perfect. Pastors are real people, too." He slid his arm around her, and she let him. "I'd like to say it's just a job, but that's not completely true. It's a calling. I know I'm where God wants me. I know that, through me, He can make a difference in these kids' lives. Teens like Madison."

"But I come from — well, you saw Greg."

"Greg was your mom's choice, not yours. It's okay. Give me a chance, Lindsey? Even a pastor wants a home, a family. I'm just a red-blooded guy who's been waiting a long time for the woman I couldn't get out of my head. A woman I wronged years ago when I was a selfish, immature kid myself."

Back then, she'd been better than him. Oh, that wasn't a great way to look at it, but it was true. He'd been a jerk. But now he was practically a saint, and she was still Lindsey, still struggling with her self-esteem and no closer to sainthood than she'd ever been. Definitely not pastor's wife material.

Nick might think he loved her, but he didn't really know her. Didn't know how much baggage half a lifetime of Greg could pile on a girl.

"I'm sorry, Nick. I can't do this. I can't be the woman you need."

He reached for her but she stepped back, crossing her arms, closing him out. Kissing would only prolong the agony. She already had enough of those in her memory to run on instant replay for the rest of her life.

Nick ordered a lemon poppy seed cupcake and a latte at Carmen's Cupcakes and Confectionery then took his purchases to a little table near the window. How could he not have seen this pothole coming on his romantic road?

He'd barely slept all night. He'd Googled engagement rings and practically planned the wedding. Debated the merits of buying a house sooner rather than later, and whether Madison would need to live with them.

He took a sip of the latte. Talk about getting ahead of himself. He broke off a piece of the cupcake and raised it to his lips. It tasted like so much cardboard after the tantalizing scent in Lindsey's kitchen.

"Hey, bro. Mind if I join you?" Jared loomed over the table.

"Have a seat." Nick pulled his stuff closer to make room as Jared dropped into the dainty pink chair across from him. Carmen may have been aiming for a clientele of women, but her coffee and baking were so tasty that many guys squeezed into the diminutive seats. Of course, more took take-out.

"Rumor has it you and Lindsey are an item now." Jared nudged Nick's plate. "That the lemon? Any good?"

"Go for it. I'm not hungry after all."

"You sure?"

"Yeah."

Jared shrugged, took a big bite, and nodded. "Wow. Nice." He looked at Nick. "Love didn't give you an appetite?"

"Uh, no. Not really."

"Rumor has it the kissing was hot."

Nick closed his eyes. He'd known people had to have noticed. That someone must have recognized him or Lindsey. Or both of them. "You can't believe everything you hear."

Jared paused, the last piece of cupcake halfway to his mouth. "What happened?"

"She forgot I was a pastor."

"Uh… she forgot this when? Before, during, or after?"

Nick forced out a laugh. "During, I guess. She certainly remembered it this morning."

"Oh, man. I'm sorry to hear that. You're not giving up on her, are you?"

"Are you kidding me? I've been thinking about her for ten years.

Praying for her. While she's single, there's still hope." A bit of hope flared. He still had the secret admirer thing going for him. He'd definitely step that up, plus pray. She wasn't immune to him; that much was obvious. Just struggling. Maybe he'd pushed her. Let his dreams get the best of him.

She'd definitely kissed him back. She'd come to love him if he gave her a bit more time.

"So, Jared, in all your vast experience with women…"

His friend wiped the last of the cupcake crumbs from around his mouth. "Uh, yeah, that's me."

"What's the way to win a woman's heart?"

"If I knew, would I be single?"

Nick grinned. "Maybe. You're still in college. Not a bad idea to get that out of the way before marriage."

"One more semester."

"Before the wedding?"

Jared chuckled. "Nah, that'll be a bit longer. As far as I know, I haven't met *her* yet."

"So when you meet her, how will you win her?"

"You mean besides my good looks and obvious charm?"

"Yeah, besides that."

Jared plunked his elbows on the table and peered into Nick's eyes. "You're really asking, aren't you?"

"Seems so."

"If I really believed she was the one for me, I'd keep doing what I was doing, and I'd ask the good Lord for His help. And maybe that of a few friends." Jared winked. "Can't have too many friends on your side."

Nick could think of a few ways having friends on his side could be a negative, not a positive, but he'd let that go.

"You were going to get her a ring soon?"

How had Jared known his mind had gone there already? And by already, he'd been daydreaming about it for the past month, never mind the sleep he'd lost last night. A half-smile escaped. "Been thinking on it."

Jared slurped back half his coffee. "Buy it," he said, putting his cup down. "Step out in faith. You want to be ready when she comes back around."

Chapter Eleven

For you!" sang out Madison, brandishing a brown package.

Lindsey's heart hiccupped. Was another secret admirer gift a good thing or a bad thing? Maybe it hadn't been Nick after all. But then, who? She'd watched the guys at work, and none seemed to have more than a casual friendship in mind. And besides church on Sundays, she didn't really go anywhere else. She tugged off her boots, set them on the rack, and glanced up at her sister hanging over the rail. "What is it?"

Madison clutched the package to her chest and rolled her eyes. "I didn't open it, silly. It's from your secret admirer."

Lindsey took a deep breath as she climbed the few steps and forced cheerfulness into her voice. "Well, let's see what's in this one." The package felt like a book. She slid the twine off the end and slid her nail under the tape to reveal an off-white cover with raspberry lettering and gold embellishments.

Meditations for a Woman Beloved of God.

She wiped a finger over the embossed cover. Should she laugh? Cry?

"Pastor Nick has got to be your secret admirer." Madison crossed her arms. "Even though he keeps denying it. Who else would get you something like that?"

Had he denied it? "He's never really said. He always turns the subject."

"Hmm." Madison tapped her chin and narrowed her gaze at Lindsey. "Could it be?"

"Enough drama. It doesn't matter." She slid the book back into the paper. "Did you and your dad have supper already?"

"Dad's on afternoon shift, remember?"

Right.

"Wasn't there a note in this one?"

"I, uh, didn't see one. I'll look at it more closely later. So, are you hungry?"

"I'm not a child, Lindsey. I fixed something hours ago. Dad has been on afternoon shift before, you know."

"Sorry." Of course Madison was capable. She was sixteen, not six. It was just that she seemed so much younger sometimes.

"I thought we'd have more fun when you moved back home. Instead you're always worrying about something. Even all those fun gifts don't make you smile."

Was her sister just begging for positive attention? Lindsey narrowed her gaze at Madison. "It's not you pretending to be a secret admirer, is it?"

"Don't be ridiculous. Where would I get that kind of money? And why?"

Lindsey's mind began to add up the probable cost of all the gifts. None by themselves were expensive, but two or three a week over a month must've added up. This wasn't just a game. Someone was very serious about getting her attention.

Meditations for a Woman Beloved of God.

Nick. Why didn't he give up? She didn't want him in her life. She wanted… what? To be a grumpy big sister to the girl she'd given up everything to take care of? To become an old maid with a permanent bun in her hair?

"Sorry, Madison." She reached out and snagged her sister to her side with a quick hug. "You're right. It must be Nick. And I'm sorry for being a grouch. I have a lot on my mind, but I shouldn't be taking it out on you. What do you want to do this evening?"

Madison's face brightened. "I forgive you. Want to do pedicures and a chick flick?"

Not really? "Sure." She'd take a closer look at that devotional later. There was a message there from Nick, whether a separate paper lay inside the cover or not. A woman beloved of God. Was that her problem? Did she think, somewhere deep in her subconscious, that she wasn't good enough for Nick because she wasn't good enough for God? What had happened to the joy in her salvation?

Like a fine coffee, it had cooled and the aroma had dissipated. Would a little book like this help her reheat it? Hopefully the allegory slipped there. A reheated coffee was never as good as freshly brewed.

"What colors of nail polish do you have?" Madison erupted from her room carrying a shoebox. "I'm not sure I'm in the mood for any of mine."

Lindsey peered into the open box. She couldn't hope to have any color not in her sister's repertoire. "Hmm. Let's see. I'll go get mine." She hurried into her room and set the book on her bed before digging in the closet for her collection of more subdued hues than Madison's. Did that prove she was old and out of touch? She laughed to herself. Maybe it proved she'd grown up a little. That was okay, too.

The book caught her attention as she turned for the door. Madison could wait a moment longer.

Lindsey opened the front cover where the now-familiar scrawl simply said,

Dear Lindsey,
Zephaniah 3:17 (The Voice)
Secretly Yours

The Voice? Wasn't that a Bible translation? She didn't have that one. Oh, but her phone app likely did. This would just take a minute. She dropped to the edge of her bed, thumbed on the phone, and searched for the reference.

The Eternal your God is standing right here among you, and He is the champion who will rescue you. He will joyfully celebrate over you; He will rest in His love for you; He will joyfully sing because of you like a new husband.

Whoa. She rocked back. Now that… *that* was love. Did this truly represent how God thought of her?

"Lindsey?" Madison's disappointed voice came from the doorway. "Did you forget already?"

Lindsey shook her head. "No. I've got the nail polish right here. But sis? Come read this."

"Okaaay." Madison plunked down beside her and reached for the phone. A moment later a low whistle slid out. "Wow. That's cool. That's talking about God?"

"Yeah." Lindsey looked at her sister. "I'd kind of forgotten how much He loves me. I mean, I remember the whole He-died-for-me thing, but that's almost cliché by now, you know? It doesn't make sense, but I can think about that without my heart melting. It's like, universal. He loved everybody. Dying for us was His job."

Madison's face was unreadable.

She was bungling this. "I'm not trying to make light of salvation. It's really important and, yes, it shows God's love for us. What's that verse? God isn't willing that any should perish?"

The phone turned itself off, and Madison pushed the button to read the words again. "But this is different. It seems more romantic."

If her sister hadn't ever heard of the Song of Solomon, Lindsey wasn't about to educate her. At least not today. She still remembered the day she'd accidentally found it. She couldn't believe *that* was in the Bible.

Hmm. Maybe she should read it again. Lindsey glanced at the little devotional. Would this book take her there? A woman beloved of God. It was possible.

But first, a pedicure with Madison. A way for a teen to feel beloved by her sister.

Chapter Twelve

Nick sat in his church office with nothing to do. Well, that wasn't entirely correct, but plans for the Valentine's banquet didn't require any immediate attention.

All the tickets had been sold. Every last one of them, filling the missions trip coffers in time to buy everyone's plane tickets.

The guitarists in the youth worship band had been practicing and sounded great. The decorations committee had come up with a plan and bought all their supplies.

Jared had the drama production under control, or so he said. Nick didn't even know what the play was about other than what was listed on the posters. He'd caught Pastor Davis coming out of the practice space half an hour ago. The senior pastor had chuckled and said Jared's group was going to bring the house down. Told him not to worry about it.

Just the fact everyone told him not to worry about it made him suspicious, but that was ridiculous. Why would Jared be trying to pull a fast one? Nick wasn't that important, and what was there to tell? Nothing.

Nothing to tell. Time seemed to have stalled from Saturday morning to Tuesday afternoon. He'd sent a gift book yesterday, and of course hadn't heard anything about it.

Had he been dumb to do the secret admirer thing? Was it too juvenile? How long would he keep it up if she didn't respond? He'd told Jared he'd waited ten years, what was a little longer, but it seemed longer. Harder.

Those Friday evening kisses. Man, he'd been crazy. Crazy for her. He hadn't imagined her response. She'd been kissing him, too.

Nick rested his forehead against the heel of his hand. "Father God? It's me again. Talking about Lindsey again. I hope You know what You're doing here, Lord. It's not looking really good right now. Why couldn't You have gotten her out of my head sometime in the past decade if this was not to be? Why wait until now to crush me?"

As if God didn't have anything more important in the universe to micromanage. Hadn't God promised to give him his heart's desire if he was truly yielded to God? But he was. He had been. Over and over he'd laid this at Jesus' feet.

Had he ever read Psalm 37:4 from *The Voice*? He grabbed the worn paperback from his shelf and thumbed it open.

Take great joy in the Eternal! His gifts are coming, and they are all your heart desires!

All his heart desired. What was that? Was it to make Lindsey his wife? Yes, but it was more. It was to accept whatever gifts God gave him. He simply needed to take deep joy in God.

"Lord, thank You for the reminder that my joy isn't found in any earthly circumstance, but through You. Your love. Your gift. It's all I need."

Did that mean he should stop sending gifts to Lindsey? He thought about it for a long moment. If his gifts brought her joy and helped her find her rest in the Lord — like he hoped the devotional book would do — there was no reason not to continue, at least for now.

A knock sounded on his office door amid the growing tumult in the corridor outside. Jared must've released the drama team.

"Yes? Come on in."

Madison stuck her head around the corner. "Pastor Nick, could I get you to give me a ride home? My dad has the car at work, so Lindsey can't pick me up. And I might've gotten a ride with Parker, but he was sick and didn't come today."

"Of course." The requests happened so rarely from any of the teens that he didn't hesitate. "Are you ready now or do you need a few minutes?"

"Five would be perfect." She beamed at him. "Lindsey gets off work pretty soon."

Uh, yeah. Nick knew her schedule.

"It's only a couple of blocks further to swing by the restaurant. Would you mind?"

He held her gaze steady. "It's not would *I* mind. Will Lindsey?"

The teen shrugged. "It's like twenty below out there, and it takes her half an hour to walk home. She should be thankful."

"Ask her if she'd like a ride."

Madison pulled out her phone and tapped out a message. She angled her head and looked at Nick. "Are you Lindsey's secret admirer?"

He met her gaze. "She hasn't figured out who it is yet?"

"Answer my question, please."

This was too much power to put in a teenager's hands. Especially an impulsive one like Madison.

Her phone beeped, and she glanced at it. "Lindsey says thanks."

Nick's heart sped up. "Okay, great."

"When are you going to tell Lindsey you're the secret admirer?"

"What makes you so sure it's me?"

She gave him a *duh* look. "You're a pastor, so I assume you're an honest person. And you haven't ever flat-out denied it. You've had plenty of chances to. So, it doesn't take any mastermind to figure out it's you."

He threw both hands in the air. "Fine. It's me. But don't you dare be the one to confirm that to her. I have ways of getting even." Okay, that sounded juvenile even to him. He managed a smile. "Please let me do this my way."

Madison studied him. "How much longer?"

A little velvet box already dug into his thigh. Speaking of crazy, he must've been nuts to spend the money when there was no reason to believe she'd relent. But, after talking to Jared, he'd done it.

"Not much longer, Madison. A week or two is all. I promise." He stood and reached for his jacket. "Ready?"

Her eyebrows waggled. "So ready."

Lindsey slid into the comforting warmth of Nick's car. "Thanks for thinking of me." She didn't have to make eye contact, did she?

"No problem. We were practically going right past anyway, right, Pastor Nick?"

"It's true. Besides, Lindsey… I'm always thinking of you."

Madison snickered from the back seat.

Five minutes in a heated vehicle. Thirty minutes with an icy wind. It was all she could do not to pull the door handle, but he'd already put the car in gear and turned north onto River Way.

Besides, the reverse was true, too. She was always thinking of him. Why didn't he give up on her? It would be so much easier when he did. Her heart panged. Okay, maybe not easier. But then she could move on. That's what she wanted, right?

The Eternal your God… will joyfully celebrate over you.

And she'd taken a peek at Song of Solomon, too. Whoa, that had brought up pictures of Nick in a way that made the heat rise in her face. Best not to be thinking of that while she sat in his car.

She couldn't think of a thing to say during the drive. He pulled up in front of the house and Madison bounced out of the backseat. "Thanks, Pastor Nick!" Then she ran up the front walk, unlocked the door, and slipped inside. An instant later the living room lights came on.

What was Lindsey doing, still sitting in the car? She should've been faster to escape than her sister. "Thanks for the ride."

His fingers fanned gently against her cheek. "You're welcome," he whispered. "I'd do anything for you. You just need to be willing to accept it."

She clenched her jaw, refusing to turn and look at him. "Why?"

"Because I love you."

The words hung in the air. "I don't get it."

"You're beautiful and sweet and compassionate. You set aside your own dreams to watch out for your sister."

She brushed her hand to the side. "That's nothing. Anyone would do it."

"Not everyone, Lindsey. But the point stands. Other people have made sacrifices for family members, and it hasn't made me feel this way about them."

Oh, no. She shouldn't have pushed it.

"Lindsey, you're a unique woman, someone God created and has a very special plan for." He hesitated a moment. "You are someone I'm very attracted to. Someone God is passionate enough about to sing love songs to."

He was referring to that verse scrawled in the devotional. Nick was her secret admirer. Of course he was. How could she ever have wondered anything else? Lindsey swallowed the hard lump in her throat.

"Thanks, Nick." She pushed open the car door, and half the Arctic swept in.

His fingers brushed her face once more, causing a tingle that completely counteracted the outside air. "I'm praying for you, sweet Lindsey."

She wanted to lean into his touch. More than that, she wanted to fling herself across the console between the bucket seats and kiss him. But she couldn't do that. Once they went back… there… there was no undoing it. And she needed to be sure.

"Good night, Nick." She climbed out of the car and shut the door.

The car didn't pull away until she'd closed the house door behind her. She heard the engine rev slightly then fade as he drove away.

"And here I thought you'd invite him in." Madison's hands plunked to her hips.

Lindsey shook her head. "Stop interfering." But she couldn't bring any heat to her words. "It's been a long day. I'm going to read for a while then shut off my light. Good night, Madison."

No need to tell her sister exactly what she'd be reading.

Chapter Thirteen

For three days, Nick texted Lindsey at nine-thirty in the evening and offered her a ride home. For three days, she responded with *thank you*. For three days, he'd dropped her off at her house after a few minutes of rather quiet riding.

Friday was youth group again, and the teens had their second to last practice for the Valentine's banquet program. Nick tried the door to the drama room and found it locked. He stared at the unyielding handle in his hand. He was the youth pastor. Shouldn't he be part of what Jared and the teens planned? Small comfort that Pastor Davis had approved it.

Tonight, something different. He stopped the car in front of the house, and Lindsey turned to him. "Would you like to come in? I made some cupcakes this morning before going to work."

No second invitation required. Nick turned off the ignition and followed her and Madison to the door. Madison unlocked the door and preceded them in, flipping on lights and pulling the living room blinds before turning up the thermostat. Whoever had been the last to leave the house earlier in the day had turned that thing way below twenty-one Celsius. It didn't feel much warmer in here than outside, but at least there was no wind. He hung up his coat with reluctance and followed Lindsey into the kitchen.

She stopped abruptly, and he nearly ran her over. Her hands came to her hips. "Well, he did leave some," she muttered.

Nick peered over her shoulder at an open container with two cupcakes in it… and a lot of crumbs.

"I don't know why I even bother." She sounded near tears.

"Oh, man. Did Dad take them all?" Madison shook her head. "Let's have hot cocoa, and Pastor Nick can eat what's left." She peered into the fridge. "Yep, there's milk."

Lindsey stayed where she was for a long moment, so close in front of Nick that he could have wrapped his arms all the way around her without shifting. As it was, her body heat warmed his chest. But he didn't want to move too quickly. Not after the week they'd had.

Lindsey reached for the jug of milk Madison proffered. "Good idea." She got out a pan, poured in some milk then added cocoa, sugar, and salt.

She'd done this before.

Madison ran off down the hallway, her socks swishing as she slid on the vinyl floor.

"How was work tonight?" Nick leaned against the counter a meter away from the stove. Safely out of reach.

Lindsey, whisking the pot's contents, glanced at him. "All right, I guess. The restaurant was pretty busy, but we kept up."

"That's good." Why had she invited him in this time?

"Nick, I'm sorry about the—" She waved her free hand to indicate the near-empty container.

"I don't keep coming by because there might be cupcakes," he said softly, keeping his arms folded across his chest. "I come because there is something else here that is sweet."

Her cheeks flushed as she whisked. "I wasn't fishing for a compliment. I just wanted you to know I wouldn't have invited you in if I'd known."

"Then I'm glad you didn't know."

Lindsey turned the element down and shot a glance toward his mid-section. "Why do you keep doing that?"

"What?"

"You fluster me with the things you say."

At least she noticed. "Flustering you isn't my goal. Not in any way."

"Then… what is?"

"Making sure you know you are treasured. Valued." He wanted to say, "loved," but thought better of it. The time was coming. Soon, he prayed. But not this minute.

"But why? What did I do to deserve this?"

Nick opened his mouth and shut it again. Her question was deeper. It wasn't about him, whether she realized it or not. "Love isn't something we deserve. Any of us. But God gave us an example. He loved us when we didn't deserve it at all. When we were mean to Him and hurled our filth in His face. Still He gave us His greatest treasure, His only son, because He loved us that much."

Lindsey brushed against him as she stretched for mugs on a shelf. He lifted them down for her.

"We can't do anything to pay God back for His salvation, to even the scale. We can only accept His gift with gratitude and bask in the warmth of His love."

"I guess that's why you're a pastor." She ladled steaming cocoa into the mugs then handed one to him.

He held her hand around the warmth of the mug. "I guess it is. God has done so much for me. I just have to share it. Help other people — the teens — turn their thoughts to God's gift. Love is the greatest thing, Lindsey. God loves us with a passion we can only begin to imagine."

Dare he mention the reference he'd scrawled into the devotional? It fit so well, this very minute. Nick lifted his free hand to her face, sweeping back the blond hair that obscured his view. "Imagine God as a guy with a guitar, sitting on the bank of the Sandon River in a meadow strewn with wildflowers, singing love songs to you. Love songs He wrote with you in mind."

She looked up at him with wonder in her eyes. "But God loves everyone. Why should I think of myself as special that way?"

"Because you are." His fingers cupped her cheek. "It's a bit tricky taking on an allegory like that, because it always breaks down. The apostle Paul told men to love their wives as Christ loved the church. He also said to be the husband of just one wife. To give himself for her. Everything on the line."

Her lips were so close to his, it was all he could do not to duck his head a little and close that gap. But it wasn't the time. He'd rushed her last week. He wouldn't let it happen again.

Lindsey pushed the cocoa mug into his hand and took a step back. How could a man talk about God's love like that and still make her feel singled out? Special? Not just as a Christian, but as a woman?

"Cocoa ready?" yelled Madison.

"Yes," Lindsey called back. Her voice sounded unsteady.

"Ready or not, here I come."

Nick chuckled. "She's something else, isn't she?"

Lindsey snuck a peek at his face as he took a sip of the cocoa. "Is it okay? Sweet enough? Hot enough?"

He grabbed her gaze and held it with all the power of an industrial-strength magnet. "It's perfect."

"I'll take this to my room." Madison lifted one of the remaining mugs. "I'm texting with Erica."

"Didn't you just spend all day with her?" teased Nick.

"Yeah, but she's my best friend. We always have stuff to talk about." She disappeared down the hallway, walking rather than sliding for once.

Probably eavesdropping and telling Erica all about it.

"Another facet of love," Nick said softly. "Wanting to spend time together."

She knew about that. Since the moonlit snowshoe the week before, she'd wanted nothing more than to be with Nick. But he scared her. Or maybe it was that she scared herself.

How could she trust love? God's love, or her own? Look at her mom, who'd been married three times and never been happy. Was Lindsey doomed to the same fate?

She wasn't going to let her mother dictate her view of love anymore. Nor Greg.

Lindsey sat on the edge of her bed and picked up the little devotional book.

Not Nick, either. For some reason she'd crammed everything she thought she knew about love in a tiny box. Then into the corners around it, she'd poured her own history and understanding of God's love.

Maybe it was time to reverse that. No, even more radical. Completely throw away the box. Let God's love be big. Be invasive. Let it soak into the fabric of her soul.

Just the thought felt like trickles of refreshing water into the dry cracks of her life. She'd been so busy holding things together, trying to cushion Madison from Greg, trying to be a nice, stable person, she'd forgotten the joy she'd once had in the Lord.

Lindsey turned to a random page in the little book and found a quote of Isaiah 61:10. *I am filled with joy and my soul vibrates with exuberant hope, because of the Eternal my God, for he has dressed me with the garment of salvation, wrapped me with the robe of righteousness. It's as though I'm dressed for my wedding day in the very vest: a bridegroom's garland and a bride's jewels.*

Exuberant hope. Joyful celebration.

Yes, she was ready to open herself to that kind of love. Where that would lead with Nick didn't matter. Right now her soul craved to revel in the fact that God came in like a mighty champion to rescue her, a damsel in distress.

It was enough.

Chapter Fourteen

Lindsey lived for moments like this. Outside the church kitchen, the banquet hall buzzed with murmured conversation and the clink of silverware. Several of the teens perched on high stools, playing a medley of songs on guitars. The room flickered with candlelight that glittered off gowns before being swallowed by the darkness of black suits and tuxes. The teen wait staff carried trays from table to table.

In here, florescent lights illuminated every work surface. The commercial dishwasher hummed incessantly as teens tried to stay ahead of the incoming plates.

Other helpers now busily plated cupcakes, half of them swirled in frothy pink clouds and half tailored with smooth chocolate frosting and crisp pink hearts. Lindsey drizzled a squirt of chocolate syrup over each plate before it went out.

She released a long breath as the last tray disappeared. They'd done it! Suddenly she was famished.

The three kids who'd been at her side since early afternoon collapsed against the counter. Lindsey raised her right hand and high-fived them each in turn. "You guys were awesome. I couldn't have done it without you."

"It was fun!" Madison's friend Erica announced. "Maybe someday I'll be a chef."

"You could be," Lindsey assured her.

The music dwindled from the sound system and Nick's voice came through. "Wasn't that an amazing dinner?" he asked.

A smattering of applause came through the speaker.

The kids grinned at each other.

"I'd like to ask Chef Solberg and her staff to please come out of the kitchen."

Oh, no, he wouldn't. But he had. Lindsey motioned the teens through the door ahead of her. She blinked as a spotlight found them.

"Chef Lindsey Solberg is a Riverbend girl trained at Niagara Falls Culinary Institute. She was the premiere chef at Fresh Start in Castlebrook for several years and is now on staff at the Water Wheel here in Riverbend. Chef Lindsey donated her time to help our youth group raise funds for our missions trip to Mexico during spring break. Thank you so much, Chef Lindsey!"

This time the applause rocked the roof.

Nick listed her helpers before the spotlight turned off. Then he named the local farms and businesses that had offered deals or donations on food and decorations.

Lindsey heaved a sigh of relief. "Let's get our dinner and sit here in the back for the drama presentation."

The kids exchanged glances. "I'll get the plates," offered Erica. "Let me serve you."

"Thanks." It felt wrong, even though she was in charge. Even though her legs had turned to rubber after the rush. She sagged into a chair as Nick introduced Jared and the drama team. Madison had been very close-mouthed about their production. Some kind of fairy tale thing was all she'd said.

The illumination on Nick at the podium faded as the row of spotlights shone on the stage curtains, which slowly drew apart.

"May I join you?" whispered Nick.

"Um, sure." Her heart warmed that he'd sought her out on this busy evening.

A moment later Erica set a plate of chicken cacciatore in front of her. "Did you eat?" the teen asked Nick as she sat down on the other side of him.

"I did. It was incredible."

A few minutes ago Lindsey had been starving at the brink of death. Now, with Nick seated beside her, she wasn't sure she could force down a single bite.

The curtains revealed a divided set with a darker raised portion on the right, evidently the inside of a room with a window to a bright wildflower meadow, trees painted on the backdrop.

Madison, wearing a wig of long braided hair, leaned out the window, her side to the audience. Rapunzel. A familiar enough fairy tale, even though the original was a long way from the Disney princess version.

Lindsey settled into her chair and toyed with her fork. This production would likely be distant from any previous adaptation she'd seen. Hadn't Madison said something about this production being for credit for Jared's college classes? Probably somewhere in this room his instructors watched, grading him on the finished play.

A parade of men in various costumes engaged the princess in her tower. Some begged her to come down with flowery poetry, while others tossed gifts. Madison waved, smiled, and shook her head as the lights very slowly illuminated the tower room. A narrow beam shone on her ankle, and a gasp came up from the audience as they noticed the ball and chain holding her in place. A cackle crackled through the sound system.

That illumination shone straight into Lindsey's soul. This was where she'd been, smiling and waving and pretending everything was okay while being chained in place, unable to respond to love.

A young man knelt at the foot of the tower, head bowed, while the princess fumbled with the bindings on her ankle. Lindsey's heart reached out for Madison. She knew exactly what it felt like, struggling to remove the bondage by herself. She'd battled for years, unable to free herself.

"I can't believe this," whispered Nick.

"What do you mean?"

"This is one of those things God had to orchestrate, you know?"

Her eyebrows pulled together as she tried to see him in the darkness. "I'm not following. You didn't know what the drama team was going to do?"

"No clue." He shook his head. "Jared kept avoiding my questions. Pastor Davis sat in on a practice and told me it was great, and not to worry."

She still didn't understand. Yes, it was uncanny how closely the unfolding story mirrored her life lately, but how could Nick know that? Let alone Jared. She'd only shared a little with Madison, and that in the past few days. Certainly not in enough time to affect the presentation.

The shaft of light narrowed on the ball and chain while Madison shielded her eyes from the brightness. The crowd gasped as the clasp clattered to the stage. Madison raised her hands and pirouetted around her little tower, no longer bound.

The guys with guitars found themselves in the spotlight again as they picked and strummed a song of praise. Free. Only at the end did Madison peer back out of the tower, hoist her skirts — thankfully leggings clad her legs — and jumped out of the window in front of the startled young man. They joined hands and ran off stage.

Lights dimmed and the curtains drew together as the audience erupted. Across the banquet hall, a hundred women and men stood to their feet and applauded the presentation.

Madison and her fellow cast members ran out from the side, holding hands. They bowed to the left and right, then scampered back offstage.

"Hard act to follow," Nick murmured as the audience began to settle. "Pray for me?"

Lindsey's eyes locked on his for a moment before her fingers twined around his. "You've got it."

Nick's gaze softened as he stood. After a moment he broke contact and strode for the microphone at the side of the stage.

"Today on Valentine's Day we celebrate love. Usually we think of romantic love such as a man might have for a woman."

Was he looking straight at her?

"But Jared and his team have reminded us that there is something bigger, something foundational, and that is God's love for us. Embracing God's love gives us a freedom in life that opens everything."

He paused, looking over the audience before pointing at the now-empty tower. "The damsel in distress didn't need a prince in shining armor to come rescue her. The Bible says that God is our champion, our defender. Not only that, but He joyfully celebrates His love with us and sings love songs to us."

Had there been any doubt at all that Nick had been her secret admirer all along? Lindsey's heart swelled with joy as he spoke the words of Zephaniah 3:17.

Across the darkened banquet hall, he alone stood in the light, and he was looking straight at her, though he couldn't possibly see her.

“Have you danced with abandon before Jesus? Have you spread your arms wide and reveled in His love for you? If you haven’t, what are you waiting for? He’s there, ready to undo that ball and chain, to take you in His arms and give you the twirl of a lifetime.”

Nick turned to the wings. “This isn’t in the program, but I’d like to ask the guys to come back out with those guitars. Will you play *Free* again? And then I’ll close in prayer.”

He stepped to the side as the kids trooped back on and settled on the tall stools. The words of the song tumbled through Lindsey’s mind. Free to be loved. Free to be cherished. Free to be celebrated. Free.

Free.

Chapter Fifteen

Nick shut down the main auditorium lights as Jared and the teens filed for the door. The sound system had been put away. The stage cleared. Tablecloths bundled for washing. Tables and chairs loaded on carts and trundled to the storage room. The janitor would do the final cleaning tomorrow in plenty of time for the Sunday service.

The kitchen door was a rectangle of light at the back of the hall, shining like a beacon. If that light was on, Lindsey was still here.

He crossed the space and peered into the kitchen. No one, but the far door was open and a brisk breeze blew in. Several boxes stood in a line on the counter. She must be hauling things out to her car. Greg's car? Must be.

She came in, rubbing her arms and caught sight of him standing there. She stopped, looking straight at him. They spoke at the same time.

"Lindsey, you were ama—"

"Nick, thank you."

He tilted his head. "For what?"

"For the devotional book. For… for all the lovely gifts. For everything. You've been so patient with me."

That crazy heart of his tried to escape out his throat. She knew. Of course she knew. He just hadn't thought it would come in the open here, at eleven at night, while cleaning up behind the fundraiser. He'd envisioned something more romantic.

A man in a heavy parka clomped into the kitchen behind Lindsey. She stepped aside as he grabbed a box then turned and left.

"Greg was here?" he couldn't help asking, despite the evidence.

She nodded. "His sister invited him. And, of course, Madison begged."

"Of course." He grinned. "She did well."

"Yes. I was impressed."

Greg came in for another box. "You gonna stand here all night or give me a hand?"

Lindsey reached for a box but Nick intercepted. As he lifted it, he whispered, "Can I take you home? I'll help you unload later. He doesn't have to."

The closed look was gone from her eyes. "Sure. I'll tell Greg. Madison is staying over at Erica's tonight."

Nick carried the box out to Greg's trunk then returned with the last one. "I'll be bringing Lindsey home in a bit," he told the older man.

"Okay." Greg glanced toward the open door. "What you said about God's love. That true stuff?"

"Absolutely."

"Huh. I'll think on that." Greg jerked his chin toward Nick. "Take care of her. She's a good kid."

"I will." That was all the comment Greg had a right to give, no doubt. Lindsey wasn't his daughter. And yet, hearing the words was balm for Nick's heart. He reached out and shook Greg's hand. "Thank you."

Greg climbed in his car and spun out of the parking lot on bald tires.

Nick headed back to the kitchen, where Lindsey arranged a few things on the counter, no doubt making sure everything was just as she'd found it many hours before. "Ready?" he asked.

She nodded and glanced around then turned toward him.

He opened his arms and she walked right in, resting her face against his puffy down parka. "Tired?"

"Yes." She let out a long breath. "I'm glad it's over."

"Me, too." He steered her toward the door and flipped off the light as he passed the switch then locked the door and pulled it shut behind him. "Pastor Davis is still in there somewhere. He'll set the alarm when he leaves." Nick slid his arm around Lindsey.

She trembled under his touch, leaning against him as they made the way to his nearby vehicle. He tucked her into the passenger seat then rounded the car and started it.

Lindsey leaned against the headrest, her eyes shut.

Tonight wasn't the night. He might feel the urgency of that box in his pocket and believe he'd get a positive answer, but there were ways to do things… and ways not to.

"What're your plans for tomorrow?" He backed the car out of its stall then turned north on the highway.

"Sleep until noon." She didn't even open her eyes to tell him that.

Nick chuckled. "And then?"

"As little as possible. Glad I don't have to go back to work until Monday."

"Can I take you out for dinner tomorrow?"

She opened one eye and squinted at him. "So long as it's not the Water Wheel."

He couldn't resist the poke. "But they have the best food in town."

"Ha-ha. Also, I don't want chicken cacciatore."

"Noted. I'll pick you up at six?"

"I'd like that." She turned to look at him more fully. A parade of streetlights lit her face as they drove up Pitoni. "Nick, how did you know?"

His voice caught in his throat. "How did I know what?"

"What I needed to hear."

"I didn't, Lindsey." He waited a beat. "But God did."

She searched his face. "That's pretty incredible." Then she leaned back to think.

A few minutes later he pulled into the driveway behind Greg's car. "Let me give you a hand with that stuff, and we'll talk tomorrow."

But the trunk was empty. Greg had hauled everything inside.

Lindsey stretched her toes under the luxurious down duvet. By the daylight shining in her window, she wasn't far off her wish to sleep until noon. She yanked her hair into a ponytail, pulled on her bathrobe, and padded out to the kitchen.

Greg looked up from the table, where he sat with a cup of coffee. "Something for you there," he said with a poke of his chin.

A take-out container shaped like a brown lunch bag sat on the counter. She peeked in to see a lemon poppy seed cupcake and a slip of paper. A little grin toyed with the corners of her mouth as she tugged out the heart-lined note.

Dear Lindsey,
Lemons are tart, but you are sweet.
Secretly Yours.

She laughed. That Nick. Would he ever stop romancing her? She hoped not. She poured herself a coffee. "I'm going to have a bubble bath, Greg."

He nodded. "I'll be out for a while. My bonus came through at work. Gotta get some tires on that car."

Lindsey stopped and looked at her stepfather. Really looked at him. "Sounds good. That will make it a lot safer for all of us."

"Yep." He dashed the rest of his coffee down and pushed back his chair.

She started the tub filling as she examined her closet. Going to dinner with Nick was definitely a dress-up affair.

The doorbell rang.

Who could that be? Lindsey peered out her bedroom window to see a van with Petals written across it in large flowing script. A man came up the walk with a large bouquet bundled in plastic.

Bathrobe or no bathrobe, she couldn't let those flowers get nipped by frost.

"Lindsey Solberg?" the man asked when she opened the door.

"That's me." She thanked him and accepted the bouquet before opening the wrap. Whoa. A dozen pink roses mixed with white lilies? The fragrance enveloped her like a feathery kiss from Nick. She found the card.

Dear Lindsey,
Roses are red, but these are prettier. Like you.
Not-so-secretly Yours.

The rumble of the filling bathtub caught her attention as she chuckled. She ran for the bathroom and got the tap turned off before the bubbles overflowed.

Lindsey lowered herself into the steaming bubbles, the devotional book and the cupcake perched on the porcelain edge.

She'd wear the pink dress tonight. It matched the bouquet.

Chapter Sixteen

"Thanks for the flowers, Nick." Lindsey sat across the little table from him at Sala Punjabi, dressed in a stunning pink the exact color of those roses. It looked great on her.

He couldn't resist teasing. "Did I give you flowers?"

"Didn't you? Maybe I'm out to dinner with the wrong man."

He caught her hand on the lacy white tablecloth. "You can't be, because then I'd be here with the wrong woman." He rubbed his thumb across her palm. "And I know for a fact that I'm here with the absolute right woman for me."

"Is that some kind of secret?" Her blue eyes gleamed in the candlelight, capturing his.

"It's not a secret anymore. Everything is out in the open."

She tilted her head to one side. "Everything?"

No way was she going to rush the setup for this evening. He hadn't reserved this table tucked inside the fireplace alcove and made all his arrangements for nothing. He grinned at her. "Sure. I'm an open book."

"Your appetizers," the waiter said, lowering a plate between them.

Lindsey examined the irregular golden shapes. "What are these?"

"Broccoli bajji. See the bits of green peeking through?"

"Deep fried broccoli, Indian style?"

He grinned and nudged the plate closer to her. "Basically. Try one."

Her eyes widened as she took a bite. "Wow. Those are great."

"I love Indian food. I'm glad you do, too."

"It's certainly different than what we serve at the Water Wheel."

He held her gaze. "I try to do as I'm told. There's no cacciatore in sight. Though that was amazing last night." Not just the dinner itself. The whole evening. The good-night kiss.

A few minutes later the remains were whisked away and replaced with bowls of butter chicken and a basket of naan. Feasting his eyes on Lindsey was better than the food, delicious as it was. He managed to keep some small talk going as the waiter cleared the dinner plates. Nick's heart hammered and his palms turned sweaty. No holding her hand at the moment. He wiped his on his pants under the tablecloth.

The waiter returned with two dessert dishes, each lit by a sparkler. From the corner of his eye, Nick caught the waiter's nod and grin. The glimmer from the flame reflected off Lindsey's eyes. Then they widened as she noticed the crowning touch.

"Nick…" she breathed.

He rounded the table and got to one knee before plucking the diamond ring from its tiny pedestal amid the rose cookies. "Lindsey, I love you. I don't want to keep it a secret anymore. Not from you, not from anyone." His voice caught. "Will you marry me?"

She flung herself into his arms, nearly knocking him flat to the floor. "Nick, yes!"

He braced himself with one hand then got the both of them in balance. Somehow he got to his feet with her wrapped around his neck.

A murmur of well wishes and soft applause from the wait staff faded into the distance as he gazed into Lindsey's eyes, bright with unshed tears. "Really, Nick? You want me?"

"More than anything in the world." He kissed her, and that took a few minutes. Then he rested his forehead against hers. "I want to spend every single day that we have on this earth cherishing you. Celebrating you. Loving you as Jesus loves the church."

"Will you make up love songs for me and sing them by the river?"

He pressed a quick kiss to her lips. "You might want me to pass on that. My singing is no better than my poetry."

She sighed against his lips then kissed him again.

Nick sat and pulled her into his lap then held the ring up for inspection. "What do you think?"

"It's beautiful," she breathed.

"I just want to be sure..." He hesitated. "Are you okay with me being a pastor? It's what God's called me to be."

She nodded. "I'm not sure how much help I'll be, but I'm willing to learn. I loved working with the teens on the banquet." She held out her hand, and he slipped the ring onto it.

Secretly his?

Not anymore. Now the whole world would know.

The End

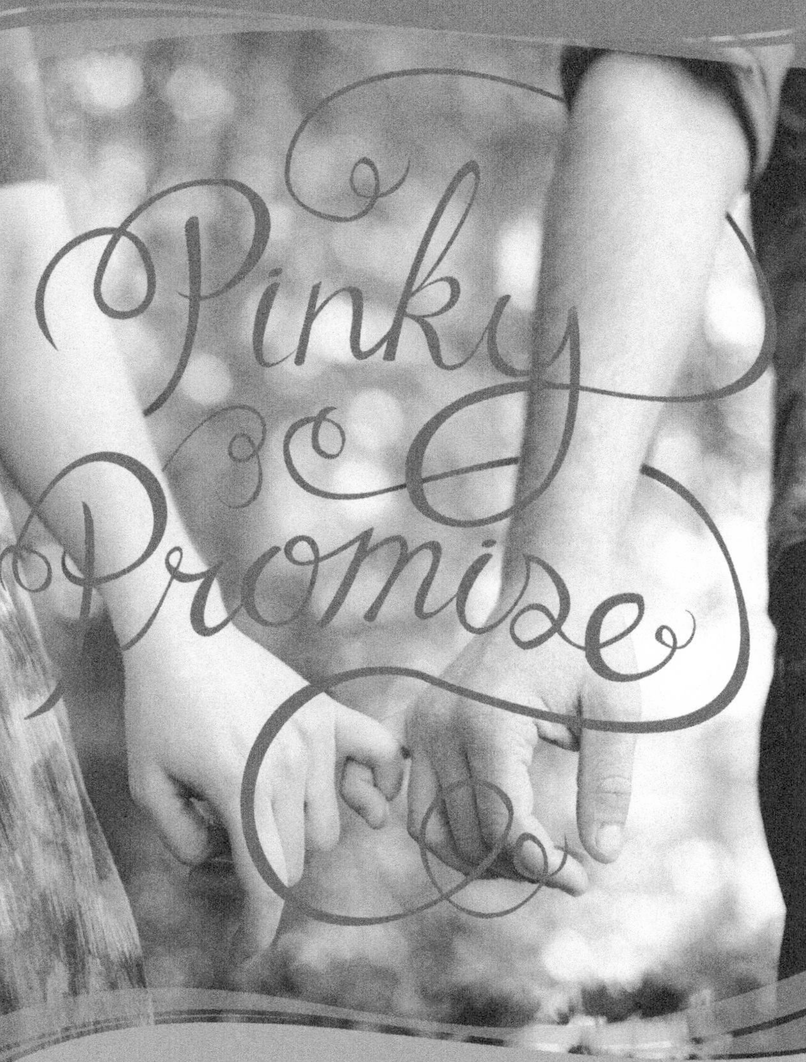
A Riverbend Romance Novella
Pinky Promise
Valerie Comer

Chapter One

"Hi, Mommy!" Elena ran across the schoolyard, her long curls streaming behind her. "I met my twin sister today."

Kelly Bryant knelt and braced herself for the collision. "Did you now? That's interesting. I never knew you had a twin."

Wham. The sturdy little girl hurtled into her arms. "But I do! Miss Jamieson said so. She said, why look at you two. You have the same birthday and the same cute noses. You must be twins."

Time to explain how it worked… or not? Kelly hugged her daughter. "That's great. I'd like to meet her."

"Well, good, 'cause she's right over there. See her, Mommy? She's waving. And she has a daddy but no mommy. Why don't I gots a daddy?"

"You don't *have* a daddy." Kelly smoothed Elena's tangled blond hair, wild from swinging and climbing and sliding, and followed the pointing finger to see a little girl with a brown bob clinging to the hand of a tall man. The pair turned and looked at them, and the girl jumped excitedly, pointing back.

Looked like Kelly was going to be a victim of childhood matchmaking. Temporary victim. "Okay, baby girl, let's go meet them."

"Yay!" Elena tugged Kelly to her feet and dragged her forward a few steps before abandoning her to run into the other child's arms. "Sophie!"

Kelly trailed along. Sure, she wanted to meet a great guy. Most single moms probably would. But the older Elena got, the more demanding she got on the subject. The girl was certain all that mattered was the daddy part. But a man who'd cherish them both? Like that was going to happen.

"I don't gots a daddy." Elena planted both hands on her wee hips as she tilted her head up at the tall guy.

"Elena. The word is have." How many times had Kelly tried to break her daughter's habit? And never more embarrassing than the present moment. "You don't *have* a daddy."

The man chuckled. "They say it like they see it, don't they?"

Kelly shook her head and tried to smile. "Apparently. I'm Elena's mom, Kelly Bryant. Your little girl is Sophie?"

He nodded. "I'm Ian Tomlinson. Sophie and I just moved to Riverbend. I'm the new Public Works Manager for the town."

It got better and better. That made him the new boss she'd heard was coming. "Um, welcome. I'm one of your serfs." And not one who would be seen trying to climb the town ladder by schmoozing her boss. Not that she was interested, anyway. He wasn't *that* good looking. Just because he was tall with broad shoulders and brown hair that curled around his ears, brushing his collar. Just because he had an adorable grin turned on all three females in his presence. Just because he caught her staring, and the grin grew a little wider, crinkling his eyes. No, she'd never be attracted to a guy like that.

Right. She pushed out a smile. "Welcome to Riverbend. Maybe we'll see you around. Come on, Elena, time to go home."

Elena's lip protruded. "But I want to play with Sophie. Can she come to our house?"

Ian angled his head to one side. "Wait a sec. What do you mean, one of my serfs?"

Kelly shrugged as she reached for Elena's evasive hand. "I work in your department. This time of year I'm in the greenhouse growing the flowers we'll be planting in the parks when the danger of frost is past."

"Cool. Can't wait to see the results. One of the things that attracted me to Riverbend was the whole doing-things-from-scratch attitude, rather than just ordering a truckload of flowers from some big grower."

"Yes, our parks are always pretty and homegrown. Elena, time to go home."

Two little girls clutched each other's arms and turned pouty faces in Kelly's direction. Since when did Elena blatantly disobey like this?

"Hey, I have an idea," Ian broke in. "Sophie and I were heading down the street for ice cream. Maybe you two would like to come along? My treat." He pointed to Glacial Creamery several blocks away toward the river.

"Yay!" shouted Elena.

"Thank you, Daddy!" Sophie blasted into Ian's legs, rocking his balance.

Kelly took a deep breath and let it out slowly before meeting Ian's gaze. She forced a smile. "I guess I'm outnumbered. Thank you."

The two little girls ran ahead hand-in-hand, a Cinderella pack bouncing on one back and Elsa on the other.

Ian glanced down at the woman walking beside him. "Sorry for putting you on the spot. I didn't mean to make it awkward."

"And I'm sorry about Elena. I keep trying to teach her that there are things you just don't blurt out to everyone on the street, but it's like changing the flow of the Sandon River." Kelly's blond hair curled slightly against her shoulder blades. She was cute in a casual way, dressed in jeans and a purple hoodie.

Yeah. He'd moved to Riverbend to *un*complicate his life, not add to it. But he and Kelly could be friends, right? She worked in his department — which obviously bugged her — but the little girls couldn't be more bonded if crazy glue were involved. Wasn't it important to set aside his personal issues for Sophie's sake? Sure it was.

"I guess she misses having a father figure," he said carefully. "It's tough on a kid when all her friends seem to have an intact family."

"Elena is constantly trying to take matters into her own hands. I don't know how many men she's proposed to on my behalf. Many of them already married."

He couldn't help chuckling at the mental image that created. "Maybe we shouldn't encourage their friendship. I'm not sure I want Sophie to learn that from Elena. Could get embarrassing."

Was it his imagination, or was she walking more quickly… and further over on the sidewalk than she'd been? *Way to put your foot in your mouth, Tomlinson*. "Uh, that was meant to be a joke."

"Yes, I know."

The girls stopped at the tree-lined intersection ahead. "May we cross the street, Daddy?" called Sophie.

Ian stretched his stride. “No, we’ll cross together.”

A few minutes later, they all stood under the white-and-black awning, obviously intended to look like a Holstein cow. The little girls took five minutes changing their mind about which flavor they wanted. In the end, both chose bubblegum, and the server began to scoop small cones.

Ian turned to Kelly. “What would you like?”

She peered into the case and pointed at a multi-brown swirl.

And he’d been thinking butterscotch ripple, as usual. Why not live a little? “I’ll try the same,” he told the server. “Double scoops on both.”

Two minutes later Ian steered them to a table in the sun. Mid-March was definitely too early in the season to be seeking shade. He took a lick off his cone. Hmm. Banana. Peanut butter. Chocolate fudge swirls. A bit of the butterscotch he liked. He usually preferred things separate. Distinct. In order.

He watched Kelly savor her ice cream for a moment. “I’ve been meaning to ask someone.”

She glanced at him. “Hmm?”

“Our move here happened rather suddenly. I saw the ad, interviewed, and moved in just a few weeks.” He took a deep breath. It had been an absolute whirlwind, and he still couldn’t believe he’d done it. But moving out of Calgary had seemed necessary since Christmas. “There were some things I didn’t have time to plan out.”

“Oh?” Kelly swirled her tongue across the mottled brown surface of her cone. “Like what?”

Ian jerked his attention back to her eyes. “I went online and enrolled Sophie in school before we moved, but I didn’t take time to really examine the calendar. Imagine my surprise when I learned there was only one week of classes before spring break. I thought I’d have more time to figure it out.”

She glanced at the two little girls with their heads bent together at the other end of the picnic table. “So you don’t have daycare lined up for Sophie. Is that what you’re saying?”

He scratched his head and nodded. “Yeah. Can you recommend anyone? What are your plans for Elena?” He probably shouldn’t ask. No doubt Kelly had a relative who pitched in for her daughter.

“I’ve booked the week off as vacation time.”

"So you're off on a Disney adventure cruise?" The girls were discussing which princess name was best for a horse of which color. A horse? Who was getting one of those? Maybe the other household. Certainly not him.

Kelly laughed with no humor. "Not so much. My mother kept her last year, but my grandmother's health is failing, and Mom's all but moved to Castlebrook to be at her side. I asked around, and the daycares were full. So I booked the week off work, and then my church decided to run a full-day program that week Elena would've qualified for. Of course my vacation time was already locked in. Bernie wouldn't change it."

Bernie. Wasn't that the guy over in human resources? Ian frowned. "Do you want me to talk to him? Get it overturned?"

"No, thanks." Kelly's eyes narrowed at him. "I'm not looking for special favors."

Ian felt a flush creep up his cheeks. "That's not how I meant it." He stopped before trying to explain further, because he'd likely dig a deeper hole. This dating someone in his department could get awkward. Whoa. Was he seriously considering that? Just because two little girls had formed an instantaneous friendship? Or — he glanced at Kelly, whose ice cream was now level with her cone while his was about to drip all over — or was he actually attracted to the young woman across from him? Whether he was or not didn't matter. A relationship wasn't an option. Was it?

"So." Ian took a deep breath. "Which church has a program planned for spring break? I guess I'd better look into it."

"River of Life, south of the highway."

"I'll give them a call." This single-parenting gig never got easier. He couldn't very well bring Sophie to the office every day if this didn't pan out.

Kelly popped the tail end of the cone into her mouth. "Thanks for the ice cream. Elena? What do you say?"

The little girl turned to examine him. "Thank you, Sophie's daddy."

She wore blue ice cream everywhere. "You're welcome, Elena." He reached into his pocket, pulled out two packets with pre-moistened wipes, and tossed one to Kelly. "Looks like you could use one of these."

Kelly gave him a strange look. "C'mere, baby girl. Let me wipe your face."

Ian beckoned Sophie closer. "It's amazing how far one scoop of ice cream can spread, considering I'm sure they ate most of it."

Kelly smiled, keeping her grip on her child. "Elena and I are happy to have met you, but we're heading home now."

Elena's eyes brimmed with tears. "But—"

How could Kelly stand up to that? Ian wasn't sure he could.

"You'll see Sophie again in school tomorrow, baby girl. Time to go."

"Okay." Elena's lips trembled. "Goodbye, Sophie."

Seemed like all of them were sad about the parting. All except maybe Kelly. *Get her phone number*. The thought was so strong the words nearly came out of his mouth as she turned away, her daughter's hand in a firm grip. But they worked together and the two new best friends went to school together. He'd see Kelly again.

Chapter Two

"Kelly!" Her coworker, Vanessa, greeted her the next morning when she walked in the Public Works Department's entrance to Town Hall. "They've called a staff meeting first thing."

Sound casual. "Oh? What's up?"

Vanessa leaned closer, lowering her voice. "Have you seen our new head? Girl, that man is a splendid specimen."

"A *what?*" Not that Kelly hadn't noticed. She chuckled. "Only you would use those words. So he's not some graybeard here to put in the last few years before retirement?"

"Are you kidding me? Wait until you see him." Her co-worker glanced around and whispered, "Dibs."

Nice try. No way was Ian Vanessa's type. "Aren't we a being a tad bit possessive this morning? Over someone we just met?" Kelly eyed her friend. "If you've even met him in person yet."

Vanessa shivered. "You'll see." She looked past Kelly's shoulder and her eyes widened. "There he is now."

Did she have to play this game? Either way, it was about to get embarrassing. She'd worked in this department for two years, keeping her head down, staying out of trouble, and doing her best for Elena. Surely no one could fire her for having met her new boss... and having their daughters hit it off. She groaned, earning her a worried look from her friend, before turning to glance over her shoulder.

"Kelly! Good to see you this morning." Ian strode toward her, a cute smile creasing his face.

Vanessa's elbow found her ribs. "You've already met?" she whispered. "I'm so gonna get even with you for this, girl. Letting me blather on."

“Good morning.” Should she call him Mr...? Man, she couldn’t even remember his surname at the moment. Her mind totally blanked at the warmth in his brown eyes. A sharp elbow in her back jogged words out of her. “Have you met Vanessa yet? She works with me on the landscaping crew.”

Vanessa slid past Kelly and took Ian’s hand. “Pleased to meet you, Mr. Tomlinson. I’m sure things will run smoothly in Public Works with you in charge.”

Ian chuckled and quirked a grin at Kelly. “Well, I hope so. It will take a bit of time to settle in and get my bearings. I won’t keep everyone long for the meeting. I know you all have plenty to do.”

Yeah, she did. And it didn’t involve daydreaming about her new boss. Feet on the planet, head out of the clouds — that was the way to keep her and Elena grounded. She’d been doing just fine for seven years.

Thankfully, Ian turned to greet some of the other employees in their division and gestured everyone toward the lunchroom. That meant he wasn’t witness to Vanessa standing in front of her, hands on her hips, eyebrows raised. “When did you meet him?”

Kelly sighed. “I don’t know why you’re making such a big deal of this. For all you know, he’s married.”

Vanessa leaned closer. “Is he? Then he sure shouldn’t be looking at you like that, girl.”

“No, he isn’t.” Not that Kelly knew his precise situation.

“Which is it?”

“He’s not married, but you didn’t know. You practically threw yourself at him.”

“Did not, girl. That’s just my way.” Vanessa winked. “But, you know, if he were interested, I wouldn’t turn him down.”

Nearly everyone had filed into the lunchroom by now. Kelly stepped around Vanessa, but her coworker held her arm in a tight grip. “Not so fast,” she said in a low voice. “How did you meet him?”

“When I picked up Elena after school yesterday. He has a little girl in the same class, and they hit it off.” Wowza, that had been more than hitting it off. “He was there to get his daughter. The girls introduced us all around.” No point in mentioning the ice cream.

“Well, isn’t that convenient.”

"Maybe it depends on your point of view." Kelly removed her arm from Vanessa's grasp. "Come on. Let's get this meeting over with so we can transplant petunias."

* * *

Ian had a hard time keeping his mind on learning the ropes of his new job all day. Town maps covered his wall, marked with various legends. A group of streets near downtown were due to be paved this summer and contractors needed to be confirmed.

His secretary, a middle-aged woman named Rhonda, walked him through his day with utmost patience and probably two packs of gum. All the minty fresh he could handle.

When she took her coffee break, he stayed in his office to look up the church's number and made the call.

"River of Life, Jessica speaking. How may I help you?"

"Hi, Jessica. I've just moved to town and understand you are running an all-day children's program through spring break. My daughter is in first grade, and I'd like to enroll her."

"Hmm."

He heard a chair roll across a hard surface then a few clicks.

"We don't have any openings for that age group. I'm sorry."

"But—" Now what was he supposed to do? "I'm sorry to hear that. I was thrilled when a friend mentioned this to me as a possibility."

"Most years we have more openings, but our youth pastor and a group of teens will be away on a missions trip next week, and that cuts our staff in half. Without the appropriate leadership ratio, we simply can't add more children."

"I understand." And he did, but it still didn't help him any. "Do you have any other suggestions? Anyone in the church run a private daycare that might have space, for instance?"

"I'm sorry, sir. I don't know of anyone."

Ian managed not to sigh deeply into the phone. It wasn't Jessica's problem. "Thank you for your time."

"I hope to see you at River of Life on Sunday morning. Church starts at ten-thirty, and we have a terrific children's church for your daughter's age group."

"Thanks. I'll consider it." More than consider it, if that's where Kelly and Elena attended, even though he felt a bit disgruntled at the moment. He set the receiver down, ending the call.

Back to square one.

The teenage girl next door was happy enough to come over mornings when he left for work to help Sophie get ready for school and walk her over on her way to the high school, but she wasn't going to be around for spring break. Ian wondered if she was going on that missions trip.

It took little time to call the daycares registered with the town and be told they were full, as Kelly had said. Unlike her, he didn't have any vacation time coming to simply stay home with his daughter. What did Kelly do with Elena over summer vacation?

Maybe he'd been overly hasty moving away from his parents. His network. He sank his head into his hands. "God? I'm sure you led me to Riverbend. Please don't let my daughter suffer for this. Help me find a place for her with someone I can trust."

Wait a minute.

He surged to his feet and strode over to the window. What would Kelly say? He definitely couldn't ask her in front of the girls or she'd have no chance to make her own decision. But he knew where to find her, at least from seven to three-thirty.

"Splendid specimen headed this way," Vanessa said in a low voice.

Kelly resisted the urge to glance up. She'd always found her coworker's fixation on men amusing. Until today. "Otherwise known as our department head, or have you discovered a new splendid specimen in the last eight hours?"

A manly chuckle came to her ears. That was so not Vanessa.

Heat exploded up Kelly's neck and across her face. No stinking way. Had she really said that out loud? And he'd overheard her? If the trowel in her gloved hand were a spade, she could dig a hole big enough to sink into in no time flat.

"Good afternoon, ladies."

Definitely Ian.

She turned slowly, staring at the ground, fervently wishing — praying — this was a dream. But no. Brushed suede shoes stood on the gravel base of the greenhouse. Tan slacks with a brown leather belt. A beige and tan striped shirt, open at the collar. A mouth upturned in a grin. Brown eyes crinkled with amusement. "Hi."

Off to the side, Vanessa's eyes danced as she covered her mouth.

Ducking her head, Kelly shot daggers at her friend. Not that anything would suppress Vanessa.

"So, this is the Public Works Greenhouse." Ian glanced around him. "Care to show me the operation?"

The man was perfectly groomed, and Kelly could be certain dirt smudges on her face matched those on the knees of her jeans. "I'm sure Vanessa would love to."

He quirked a grin. "But you're the team leader, according to the personnel lists." He swept a hand toward the entrance, his gaze still locked on hers. "If you'd be so kind."

There really wasn't anything to explain. Weren't the banks of seedlings evidence enough?

"I'll be over in C," Vanessa murmured, brushing past them.

That left her with Ian, a still-burning face, and an awkward silence. Did she have to look at him?

"Splendid specimen? Can't say I've ever been called that before."

Kelly's humiliation was complete. "That's what Vanessa calls half the men she sees. I was just mimicking her." She scuffed the toe of her boot into the gravel.

His voice lowered. "I think you're very pretty, too."

The temperature on her face rose another ten degrees. "Uh, thanks." What else was she supposed to say? Had he really come down to the greenhouses to flirt with her? During work hours? Wait, he'd asked for a tour. Good change of subject. She took a deep breath. "We have four greenhouses here, growing all the flowers for the baskets downtown and in beds at the various parks."

When he didn't reply, she snuck a glance up. Man, he was tall. And looking straight at her with a bemused expression.

"Kelly, I have something to ask you."

No. Too soon. Way too soon.

"I called the church this morning, but they don't have any spaces for kids Sophie's age."

Had she really thought he was going to ask her out? Well, he *had* said she was pretty and kept looking at her strangely. Time to get her head in the real direction he was going. "I'm sorry to hear that."

"I double-checked with all the daycares, and none of them have room, either."

She nodded, still caught in his gaze.

"I'm a wee bit stuck here, Kelly." He hesitated, searching her face. "I know it seems very forward being as we just met, but is there any chance you could watch Sophie next week with Elena? I'm happy to pay you the going rate for child care."

This was a slippery slope. He might not be asking her for a date, but this was almost more serious. The way those two little girls had latched onto each other, somebody's heart was likely to get broken if she said yes. Possibly multiple hearts, including hers.

Yet how could she decline, knowing he was out of options? It would be far easier to have a buddy for Elena than have her moping around the house by herself. And a bit of pocket change would not go amiss.

Dear God, how did I get in this situation again? Is this really the right thing to do? I don't need a broken heart.

"I'm sorry to ask, Kelly. I fully intended to get to know you more slowly. Take our time."

He said *what?* Oh, man. He was attracted to her. The slope was more than slippery, and the toboggan was poised at the top. "Ian, I don't know what to say."

He bit his lip but kept his gaze steady.

"If I didn't work here—" she swept her hand around the greenhouse "—it might not be an issue. But you're my boss. It all seems so awkward. I don't want anyone to have reason to think I'm trying to... you know."

"I scanned the town employee guidebook this afternoon."

She blinked. “Pardon me?”

“There is nothing in there saying two town employees can’t date each other. Uh, not that I’m asking for a date.”

Talk about a mixed message. “Oh.”

“At the moment.”

She heard the grin in his voice and glanced back up into his warm eyes.

“Today’s question is about Sophie, though. I’d probably be asking you about next week regardless of the dating question. It’s separate. Intertwined, maybe, but separate.”

Kelly opened her mouth and closed it again. Everything in her screamed a protest at being pushed. No, he wasn’t asking for a relationship. It was much, *much* too early for that. And yet, wasn’t this the first step? She’d get to know his daughter. She’d see him every day away from Public Works.

Was this wise? She wasn’t responsible for Sophie. She should tell him no. Surely he’d be able to come up with a different solution.

“I think we can make it work.” Apparently her mouth — and heart — had made the decision for her brain. “I know Elena will be delighted.”

Relief was evident on his face. “Thank you. You have no idea how much this means to me.”

“I think I do.” She shrugged. “I’m a single parent, too.”

Chapter Three

"Can Sophie come over and play? Pleeease?" Elena batted her pretty little eyelashes and clutched her new best friend's hand.

Kelly clenched her teeth. "Not today."

"But, Mommy, she's my bestest friend. And she's my twin."

Sophie nodded.

This wouldn't be so bad if Ian wasn't standing right beside them at the edge of the school sidewalk. But he was. Kelly crouched down. "Look at me, baby girl."

Elena rolled her eyes then obeyed.

"We have a rule, remember? You don't get to tell Mommy what to do. You ask me, in advance, and don't nag. If you nag me, I get to say no without any other reason. That's our rule."

"I'm sorry, Mommy."

"So, the answer for today is no."

Elena's face fell, but she stayed silent.

Kelly could ignore the tear wending its way down the freckled cheek. She glanced up at Ian, who gave a quick hand spread and raised his eyebrows. Hopefully that signaled it was up to her whether she mentioned the deal right now or not. But there was little to gain from putting it off.

She put a hand on each little girl's arm. "You know next week is spring break, right?"

Two little heads nodded.

"And Elena, remember Mommy is taking next week off work to spend time with you?"

Another nod.

"How would you like it if Sophie came to our house every day next week while her daddy is at work?"

Elena squealed and threw herself in Kelly's arms. "Really, Mommy? Really truly?"

"Really truly. Is that okay with you, Sophie?"

Sophie looked up at Ian, who nodded. "Yes, thank you," she said in a wee voice.

"Okay, it's settled then. Now, today is Tuesday, and it is a long time until Monday. Six days. I know that's a really long time for you two to wait to play together, so how about if Sophie and her daddy come for a little visit Thursday after school? That way they'll see where we live." It also gave her time to tidy their place. Two days wasn't long enough to get rid of shabby, but it would help.

The girls twirled in circles together.

Probably putting them together all of spring break was a bad idea. But she couldn't be that mean to Ian or the girls just to guard her heart. She was an adult. She'd deal with it, one way or another.

"Thanks, Kelly. I look forward to visiting."

She let out a long breath and looked up at Ian. Did he have to be so good looking? And so nice? She smiled. "No problem. It will be fun." She reached for Elena's hand. "Time to come home now, baby girl."

"Okay." Elena squished Sophie. "Bye, Sophie."

"Bye. You're my favorite twin."

Kelly dragged Elena down the sidewalk, purposefully not glancing back to see which direction Ian went. He had probably driven over from the office, unlike her.

"Mommy?"

"Yes?" She peeked over her shoulder. No Ian in sight. Whew.

"Sophie would really like a mommy, and I'd like a daddy. Can you be Sophie's mommy?"

"Baby girl, this isn't something kids decide. For kids to get a mommy or daddy, their parents have to get married. That means they have to love each other a lot. They can't become a mommy or daddy for someone else's daughter without loving each other first."

"But—"

That didn't sound pouty. Kelly glanced down to see her daughter chewing her lip, obviously thinking things through.

"How about if you love Sophie's daddy?"

Kelly dropped to her knees on the sidewalk and gripped Elena's shoulders. "Listen to me, sweetie. I just said this is something for grownups. Kids can't decide this for their parents. It takes a really long time for grownups to fall in love and get married. Even grownups can't always decide who that other person will be."

She knew that all too well, plus the pain of going too far, too soon, and dealing with the consequences. Not that she could ever regret Elena.

It was like her daughter read her mind. "Did I have a daddy before?" she asked wistfully.

How to answer? When was it time to talk about the birds and the bees? "What is a daddy?" Kelly asked instead.

Elena dipped her head and scowled. "You know what a daddy is." She poked her toe at the edge of the sidewalk.

"Tell me."

"A daddy is somebody, like a man, who plays with his daughter. Maybe he takes her on bike rides and gets her ice cream, like Sophie's daddy. And he tucks her in at night and reads her stories."

Kelly's throat closed. "Then you never had a daddy," she whispered. "But your mommy does all those things for you. I love you very, very much, baby girl."

"I love you, too." Elena wrapped her arms around Kelly's neck, her shoulder digging into Kelly's throat. "But I still want a daddy."

"There is something you can do."

Elena pulled back, a hopeful expression on her face. "What?"

"You can ask Jesus for a daddy."

"Will He give me one?"

Kelly lifted a shoulder. "I don't know. Sometimes He says yes to prayers, and sometimes He says no. And sometimes, like Mommy, He says to wait a while. Like when you wanted Sophie to come visit, and I said not until Thursday."

Elena nodded thoughtfully. "I'll ask Jesus *lots*."

A vision of Elena running around the playground at school and shouting out her prayers popped into Kelly's mind. "There's another rule. I've told you that you can talk to Jesus anytime, anywhere, and He'll always hear you. But this is a special kind of prayer, and you're only allowed to pray it out loud at bedtime. Otherwise it has to be a quiet prayer in your head."

"Why?"

"It just does. And one more thing."

Elena sighed. "*What?*"

"Remember when we talked about pinky promises?" Kelly held up her hand and stretched out her little finger. "I want you to pinky promise me you won't talk to Sophie's daddy about it. That you won't ask him to be your daddy."

"I don't want to pinky promise that."

"I need you to."

"But—"

"Elena, please obey me."

How could such a small body come up with a sigh the size of an elephant? Elena twined her finger around Kelly's. "Pinky promise."

* * *

"Elena is my bestest friend in the whole world, Daddy."

Ian smiled at his daughter as they walked toward the Jeep. "I'm glad you made a friend so quickly, Sophie. I know you were sad to leave Willow behind."

"I like Willow, but Elena is my twin."

Who could argue with that logic?

"Can I really go to her house every day?"

"During spring break, yes. I couldn't find anyplace else for you to go, so I asked her mom."

Sophie clung to his hand and skipped. "I'm glad. I don't want to go anywhere else, except maybe heaven."

Ian's heart clenched. "We can't visit heaven. When we move there, like your mommy did, we can't come back here and visit." Sophie was only two when her mother passed away. She didn't even remember Maria. Only a few photos tied them together. If Ian could help it, it would be a long time — if ever — before Sophie found out her mother had left them months before she died in the plane crash.

"Can you get me a new mommy?"

He'd bet anything Kelly and Elena were having a similar conversation. Those little girls were both plenty determined.

"Maybe someday. It's not quite like going to the store and picking out a new pair of shoes. It's more complicated." Although, he wouldn't say no to a few dates with Kelly to see where things might lead. Wasn't that like seeing if the fit was comfortable?

"Why?"

He blinked and shook the vision of dating Kelly out of his mind. "Why what?"

"Why is it com-pul-cated?"

"It's a grown-up thing, Sophie."

"Everything grown-up is com-pul-cated."

He chuckled. "You got that right. But I'm glad you made a friend. How about the other kids in your class?"

"There's a boy who makes faces at me and sticks out his tongue."

Aw, young love. Ian bet Sophie didn't see it that way. "Any other girls?"

Sophie shrugged. "Gracie is nice, but Elena is my twin."

Ian would like to sit Miss Jamieson down and talk to her about putting ideas in these kids' heads. Did the teacher have any idea what she'd turned loose with her simple words?

"Is it a long time until my birthday, Daddy?"

A calendar blinked into his mind. "Uh, not very long. Not quite two months."

"And then I'll be seven? And my twin will be, too?"

How the years had zipped by. He shook his head. "Seven. Yes, I guess you will be. You're getting so big."

She giggled. "That's because you feed me good, Daddy. And I eat my veggies."

"That's right." He grinned down at her as he opened the Jeep door for her.

"When I turned six you took me and my friends to the zoo. Can we go again?"

"No, I'm sorry. We moved, remember? There isn't any zoo nearby that we can go to. We'll have to think of something else."

"I'll think hard."

"You do that." At least she'd forgotten her quest for a mother, if only for a moment. He'd have to be careful not to ask her what she wanted for her birthday, at least in public. He could just hear the answer now.

"Did you have fun at work today, Daddy?"

"I did. I had a meeting and talked to all the people who work in my new office."

Sophie snapped the buckles on her harness. "A meeting doesn't sound fun."

"A meeting is fun if you like the people who are there with you." And he did like one of them quite a lot for someone he'd just met. He already knew he wanted to get to know Kelly Bryant much better. If only he could do that without planting ideas in Sophie's head.

The kid was too observant for her own good.

Chapter Four

Elena and Sophie ran off down the sidewalk, holding hands, leaving their parents to walk along behind, *not* holding hands. Of course they weren't. But this was weird. More purposeful than when they'd gone for ice cream on Monday.

When was the last time Kelly had invited a man over? Never since Elena's birth, that's how long. Telling herself this was a daycare arrangement wasn't helping. She knew that wasn't why her heart was skittering and her hands clammy. She was far too aware of the tall, good-looking guy beside her. Having his child in her home — getting to know and love Sophie — was only going to compound the problem.

If only a certain handsome man hadn't kept her awake the past few nights. She needed all her wits about her to keep from saying the wrong thing, and lack of sleep wasn't helping.

"Tell me about your church."

Kelly blinked. Not the question she'd expected, but she'd rather talk about that with him than work. "It's great. Pastor Davis has a way of making the Bible interesting and practical. There's a broad range of ages, too. Lots of young families, teens, middle-aged folks, and seniors."

"Sounds good. I think Sophie and I will give it a try Sunday."

"It starts at ten-thirty, and there's children's church during the service. Elena loves it."

"Then I'm sure Sophie will, too."

Because the two were practically joined at the hip like real twins. Whatever one voiced, the other immediately approved, like an echo. Was Kelly really up for this?

The girls waited at the street corner. “Can I push the crosswalk button, Mommy?”

“Hang on a minute.” Kelly glanced up at Ian. “Waiting is not Elena’s strong suit.”

A dimple creased his cheek as he winked at her.

“She has strong opinions. About everything.”

He bumped her arm. “Does she get that from anyone I might have met?”

Kelly’s face flushed. “Maybe. I guess I should ask my mother how she taught me tact. And appropriateness.” Given with whom she was speaking at the moment — and what they were saying — maybe her mom hadn’t managed to teach her anything at all.

“Kelly, we don’t need to let those kids bully us into anything. They’re just being children and don’t understand what they’re asking.”

Did that mean Sophie was begging him the way Elena was begging her? Oh, man. How embarrassing.

They arrived at the corner, Elena pushed the button, and the girls dashed across and down the block, once again leaving Kelly with Ian.

“I guess what I’m trying to say is, all they see is their own wants.” He shrugged. “They aren’t bad wants, of course, but the girls are only six. They don’t understand the entire scope of what they’re asking.”

Kelly wasn’t so sure about that. “It’d be easier to derail them if we could convince them their schemes had no hope.” She felt his gaze on the top of her head, but no way was she looking up. It wasn’t a lack of interest, but it *was* too much, way too quickly, and he knew nothing about her. She’d always thought this impulsiveness in a relationship was in her distant past and that she’d learned her lesson. That one day, maybe, she’d meet a wonderful man and he’d court her and shower her with gifts and sweet words and eventually they’d marry. By the lack of her daughter in that daydream, she’d obviously assumed it would happen after Elena left home.

Elena and Sophie skipped around the corner at the end of the block, holding hands.

“This is a nice established neighborhood,” Ian said. “I can’t wait to get Sophie and me into a house again. I rented an apartment as there was no time to look before our move.”

As they turned the corner into the cul-de-sac, Kelly pointed to the blue and white bungalow a few doors down. “That’s where we live.”

“Nice!”

Once again, she could feel his gaze. Once again, she didn’t look up. Time for full disclosure, lest he think she was richer than she was. Though of course he could look up her salary with just a few clicks at the office. Maybe he already had. “I rent the basement suite from an older lady. She’s happy to let us use the backyard, so it works out well.”

“Sounds good.”

She tried to see the 1960s-era neighborhood through his eyes. Obviously he was used to something nicer. Newer. Or maybe she was inventing thoughts for him.

The girls ran up the empty driveway and through the gate at the back of the house.

“Where do you park your car?”

Kelly took a deep breath and let it out slowly. “I don’t have one.” This time she sneaked a peek. “That’s one reason we live in this part of town. Close enough to walk to work, school, shopping.” Everything but church, really. That was clear across town.

He looked thoughtfully around.

“Look, if it’s not a good enough neighborhood for Sophie, I understand.” *Or if* I’m *not good enough.*

Ian touched her arm. “Kelly, I wasn’t thinking any such thing. I’m not a snob.”

She looked up into his brown eyes, bracing herself for pity, but it wasn’t there. He was looking at her, not her house. Not her lack. Both his hands rubbed her upper arms.

Kelly pulled away. Not in the middle of her street, where any of her neighbors might be peering out from behind their curtains — and probably were. Like Mrs. Consuelo across the street. Yep, her drapery shifted a little when Kelly glanced over.

Awkward.

If Kelly hadn’t planned to stay on the straight-and-narrow before, the realization that every single neighbor would know exactly when Ian came and when he left would keep her there.

* * *

Ian followed Kelly into the backyard where both girls, squealing with glee, already played on a swing set reminiscent of his own childhood. The lawn, still brown with a few lumps of snow in shaded areas, looked well tended. A flowerbed along the patio was thick with green shoots and the fuzzy heads of developing crocuses. Looked like Kelly worked in the right department with the town.

"Want coffee or tea?" Kelly clicked the gate behind her. She headed down a set of steps that descended from the patio to a blue door.

"Sure. Whichever you're having." Should he follow her or not? The patio contained a small round table with two chairs. Maybe that's where he should wait, where he could keep an eye on the girls.

She paused with a key in the door, glancing up at him. "It's okay to have an opinion."

He grinned. "Is it equally okay *not* to have one?"

"Men." She rolled her eyes. "Tea it is. Just for that, I should serve yours in an antique porcelain teacup." She opened the door before seeming to realize he hadn't followed her. "You're welcome to come in, if you like. The girls will be fine. Elena knows not to open the gate without asking."

A quick glance was hardly needed, as both girls were singing *Jesus Loves Me* at the top of their voices, not quite in time to the creaking swings.

Ian hoped that old set was well anchored, but he couldn't see any of the six legs lifting off the ground, so he had to assume someone had installed it well. He followed Kelly down the stairs and into her home.

The walls were covered with 60s-style wood paneling sheets, but someone — maybe Kelly? — had painted them a pale blue. The entry immediately opened up into a kitchen with the living room beyond. A vintage table and vinyl-covered chairs separated the area. Although nothing was new, the space seemed incredibly welcoming, and even homey with a stack of magazines and a child-size easel. Nothing like his bare space.

Kelly pulled an electric kettle from a lower cupboard, filled it with water, and plugged it in. Then, leaning against the sink cabinet, she turned to look at him.

"This is a great apartment you have here. Did you paint the walls?"

She nodded, still seeming wary. "It was beyond dingy when we moved in two years ago. I could barely stand it."

"Then why choose this place?" He probably shouldn't have asked.

"Limited budget." She shrugged. "The owner is a friend of my grandmother's, and she's given me a good deal. And location, like I said."

"Makes sense. It sure isn't dingy now. It has a lot of personality." Kelly's, no doubt. A personality that exhibited itself all across the space, from the robin's egg painted cupboards with crisp white trim to the white TV stand and bookshelf combo running the length of one living room wall. No, it wasn't as tidy as his place, but maybe he shouldn't have aspired to sterile.

"Thanks. I love fixing up old stuff. Paint is my best friend."

He quirked a grin. "Not Vanessa?"

Her face flushed. "Not so much, no. She's a fine person to work with, but we don't hang out after hours." She glanced at him then away. "There's not a lot in common besides landscaping."

"Where do you find your projects? Kijiji? The antiques mall?"

"More like garage sales or people emptying basements." She opened an upper cupboard, revealing a jumble of boxes and tins. "What kind of tea? Black? Green? Herbal?"

"Uh..." He'd been going to say, whatever she wanted, but she probably didn't keep any varieties she didn't care for. He crossed the room as Kelly started to step out of his way, but he braced his hands on the counter on either side of her, hemming her in. The top of her silky hair came nearly to his chin, and her back warmed his chest. He shifted slightly closer, reveling in the fruity fragrance of her shampoo. He could definitely be interested in this woman.

"Ian?" Her voice sounded a little strained, but she did not turn to look at him.

He slid his hands a bit closer together, so his arms brushed hers. "Hmm?" The impulse to gather her up, turn her around, and enfold her in his arms was nearly irresistible.

"What kind of tea?" But her voice was faint, breathless. Maybe the attraction was mutual.

"How about this?" Ian plucked a box of chai out of the cupboard and set it on the counter, his hands daring to meet in front of her, not quite cradling her. "Do you like it?" She could answer that any way she pleased.

He heard her swallow hard and felt a deep, shuddering breath through the contact. "Maybe?"

"How about this?" He set his hands on her arms and slowly turned her to face him.

She stared at his shirt. "I'm not sure?" she whispered.

Ian tucked a finger under her chin and raised it until her gaze bounced off his. "I'm not trying to rush you," he said quietly. Although he could certainly see where it might come across differently. "I'm attracted to you, and I'm thankful to two little girls for introducing us."

She sucked in her lips.

"All I want to know for now is, do you feel the same way? Or do you think I'm some weird guy you can't wait to get rid of, but are too polite to tell me because I'm your boss?"

"Not that weird." Her gaze flicked to his eyes then away.

Ian fanned his fingers across her cheek. "Can we see where this attraction goes?" Why he needed to know today, right this minute, was beyond him. But somehow it was all that mattered. A chance to win her.

If he hadn't been touching her face, he might have missed her nod, it was so tiny.

"Thanks," he whispered, sliding both hands around her back and tugging her just a little closer. He became aware of silence from out in the yard just as it was broken.

"Hey, Sophie! Your daddy is hugging my mommy. Want to come see?"

Uh oh. Ian was pretty sure the girls couldn't see the quick kiss he planted on Kelly's hair. He took a step back and rubbed his hands against her arms. "Guess I've given them fuel. Sorry about that."

"Coming!" called Sophie, her footsteps skittering down the concrete steps.

Kelly shook her head, but she was smiling. "Secrets are impossible around here." She met his gaze for an instant. "It's time for tea and cookies."

Chapter Five

Years of starting work at seven meant Kelly slept in but still had time for a shower and her quiet time before she heard Ian's SUV in the driveway. "Elena! Time to get up. Your friend is here."

Elena emerged from her room rubbing sleep from her eyes just as the knock sounded.

Kelly opened the door to see Sophie yawn. She squatted in front of the little girl. "You must have stayed up too late last night, like Elena."

Ian chuckled as he set down her backpack. "She was too excited to sleep. All she could talk about was playing with her twin and how much fun they'd have." He bent and helped Sophie with her jacket and shoes.

"We'll have so much fun!" Elena took Sophie's hand. "Come see my room."

"Make your bed," called Kelly as the girls disappeared. Now she had no excuse not to look at Ian.

"Thanks so much. This means a lot to me." His brown eyes searched her face.

Kelly took a step back. "I know. It's okay. It will be nice for Elena to have someone to play with. Maybe I'll hear a bit less of *I'm bored*."

"She seems like she makes her own fun wherever she goes. Sophie is a bit quieter."

"It doesn't take much to be shyer than Elena."

His face crinkled into a grin. "I should give you my cell number in case you need to reach me, and I'm not in the office."

"Right." Kelly plucked her phone off the kitchen table and thumbed it on. "The number?"

He held his phone out to her. "Probably less chance of a mistake if we put our own numbers in each other's phone. Allow me?"

"Um, sure." She took his cell and added her name and number to his contact list.

A second later he offered her hers back. "All done." He gave her a lopsided grin. "I guess I'd better be going or I'll be late. Have a good day."

"I'm sure we will. I forgot to ask if Sophie has any food allergies or anything like that I should know about."

Ian reached for the doorknob. "Nothing I know of."

"Okay. Have fun at the office."

He grinned and waved as he left.

A moment later she heard his vehicle start up and drive away. Now for those girls. Kelly walked down the short hallway to Elena's room. The door was slightly ajar. Surely eavesdropping was appropriate?

"My daddy said I couldn't ask your mom to be my mommy."

Kelly sagged against the wall, her knees nearly giving out. Both of them? She and Ian were dead in the water. There'd be no way to have a casual friendship with these two around. They would either have to separate the girls, or... She kind of liked the sound of *or* but hated the feeling of being so out of control. This pair would just keep pushing.

"I know. My mommy even made me pinky promise not to ask your dad the same thing."

Kelly should've made her pinky promise not to tell anyone that, too.

"What's a pinky promise?"

"It's when you do this." There was a second of silence. "And then you make a promise you have to keep *or else*."

"Or else what?" asked Sophie.

Kelly imagined Elena's shoulders doing her ever-so-dramatic shrug. "Or else your baby finger breaks, and that would hurt a lot."

"But I like your mommy."

"She's nice. I like your daddy, too."

Silence. The girls were probably staring at each other and thinking hard. No good could come of this. Forewarned was forearmed, right? Kelly had to listen to the rest of the conversation.

"My mommy says that grownups have to decide stuff like that. They have to love each other."

"Like kissy stuff? You said my daddy was hugging your mommy, but

I didn't see it."

Right. Because Ian had stepped back after Elena's announcement, and they'd all had some of those chocolate chip cookies she'd baked the night before.

"Yeah, kissy stuff, I think. If they do that, then your daddy will be my daddy, too."

Kelly put her hands to her cheeks. She'd known she and Ian needed to be careful around the girls, but good grief. The two of them were practically planning their flower girl dresses. Whoa. Now where had *that* thought come from?

"How do we make them do kissy stuff?" asked Sophie.

"I don't know. We'll have to think about it. Do you want to play princess? My grandma made me some dress-up clothes."

"Yes!"

Kelly took a deep breath and tapped on her daughter's door before sticking her head around it. "Elena, want some breakfast? Sophie, are you hungry?"

The two little girls glanced at each other and nodded before joining hands and following Kelly back to the kitchen. She didn't know whether to laugh or to cry.

Ian turned the corner onto Kelly's dead-end street just in time to see a pink bicycle tip over in the driveway. The child was wearing a helmet and Sophie's clothes. He pulled in a sharp breath. Was his daughter okay?

Kelly extricated Sophie and gave her a high-five, which Sophie returned with little enthusiasm, pointing at her knee. Kelly crouched and kissed Sophie's knee as Elena, also wearing a helmet, righted the bicycle and pushed it to the top of the barely sloping driveway.

He pulled to a stop at the curb. On the one hand, Kelly hadn't asked about teaching Sophie to ride a two-wheeler. On the other hand, the image of Kelly pressing a kiss to his daughter's knee would be forever imprinted in his memory.

Sophie ran toward him as he exited the Jeep. "Daddy! Did you see? I can ride a bike."

He scooped her in his arms and nuzzled her little neck until she giggled. "I saw you take a tumble. How's your knee?"

She squished his throat with her hug. "It's okay. Kelly kissed it better."

There she stood, halfway up the driveway, watching him, casual in faded jeans and an untucked flannel shirt, her hair pulled back with a tie. How had Sophie managed to get the first kiss from Kelly's pink lips? It hardly seemed fair, even if it was a scraped knee. He smiled at Kelly, and she waved at him before turning back to her daughter. Suddenly his entire day brightened.

"Okay, Elena. Make sure there are no cars coming then give it a try."

Elena straddled the bike and pushed off. She pedaled down the driveway and turned onto the street without toppling, the beaded spokes clickety-clacking as the pink handlebar streamers rustled. She turned carefully in the roundabout, the front wheel wobbling until Ian was sure there'd be another casualty.

"Keep pedaling!" called Kelly. "Go faster so you don't fall."

Elena rode past Ian and onto the driveway before sticking both feet on the pavement to stop the bike. "I did it, Mommy! I did it."

"You sure did. Good job, baby girl." Kelly looked at Ian, a grin on her face. "I guess I'd better quit calling her that. She's growing up so quickly."

Sophie slid from his arms and ran to Elena. "Is it my turn?"

Ian followed her. "I can't believe how quickly time is going by." He also couldn't believe how short a time he'd known this mother and daughter. Was it really only a week?

"I guess I should have asked before letting Sophie ride Elena's bike. I promised Elena weeks ago that we'd work on it during spring break. She wants to ride to the park one day soon."

"Looks like I should find a bike for Sophie, then." He hadn't even thought about it before. In Calgary they'd lived in a high-rise with no safe riding place nearby. He couldn't even remember the last time he'd ridden. Probably if he got one for Sophie, he should consider buying one for himself. Small towns were different. He needed to adjust.

Kelly nudged Sophie's head as Elena wheeled the bike to the top of the driveway. "This time go faster, and you won't fall over. You can do it."

Ian's hands twitched with the desire to cushion his daughter, but if she was game even after hitting the pavement once, how could he hold her back? Kelly was right. Sophie was growing up. Instead of trying to stop it, he needed to give her a safe place to fail.

Sophie grabbed the handlebars and swung her leg across the bike. She narrowed her gaze and bit her lip. Nothing if not determined, that one. She gave a little push and began to pedal.

"Go, Sophie, go!" shouted Elena.

When she lost control, she got both feet on the ground instead of falling. Ian caught the set of her jaw as she balanced then pushed off again, this time more successfully. Wow.

"Good job, Sophie!" called Kelly. "Keep pedaling."

Ian should probably be watching his daughter as she mastered a new skill. Instead, he found himself gazing down at the blond head beside him.

Kelly's ponytail flipped when she turned and glanced up at him. "She's doing well."

"Yeah, she is." He was totally caught in her clear blue eyes. "Thanks for teaching her."

Time held still for a long moment before she pulled her gaze away and back to the street. "Okay, Sophie, keep going. Can you make it all the way around the circle? Go faster!"

That seemed to be today's mantra from the bike-riding lesson. *Don't stop, or you'll fall over. Keep pedaling.* Could he apply that to Kelly? There was danger in rushing their relationship, for sure. The faster he pedaled, the more it would hurt when he fell. But if he took it too slow, the danger of falling and getting hurt was just as great. Either way, it wasn't just he who would be hurt. It was Kelly, too, and both little girls.

Sophie and Elena were already in so deep he couldn't protect them from the potential pain. Maybe they'd be lifelong friends even if nothing came from his... friendship... with Kelly. Kids were resilient. They'd get over it.

Ian shifted closer to Kelly as Sophie circled and pedaled back, her entire face lit up beaming.

"I did it! I did it!"

For half an instant, the girls were focused on each other. Ian took the opportunity to tuck Kelly against his side and whisper into her sweet-smelling hair. "Thank you."

She pulled away immediately, but glanced up with a little smile. "Enough bike-riding today."

Elena pouted. "But I wanted to—"

Kelly gave her the *mom look.*

Ian managed not to snicker.

The little girl's shoulder slumped, but she took the handlebars and pushed the bike to the back gate, Sophie at her heels.

"Have time for a snack?" Kelly looked up at him. "I promised the girls, but we stayed outside longer than I expected."

"Sure." He'd swing by Canadian Tire on the way home and pick up a bike and helmet for Sophie. It might not be her birthday yet, but the time had definitely come for wheels for both of them.

Remembering his plan to pedal faster, he looped an arm over Kelly's shoulder as they walked toward the gate. She didn't shrug away.

Chapter Six

"Are you getting anything done inside?" Ian teased Kelly when he found her sitting on the front lawn for the fourth afternoon in a row. Those two girls now rode up and down the block with ease, pretending their bikes were horses.

She turned off her tablet and laid it on the grass. "Not much, but I've certainly caught up on my reading."

"Oh?" Ian lowered himself beside her, brushing his shoulder against hers. "Fiction? Nonfiction?"

"Fiction." Her face flushed.

Interesting. "What genre do you like?"

When she didn't respond right away, he leaned closer, nudging his elbow against her arm. "Must be romance novels."

She bit her lip.

Ian chuckled. "Nothing wrong with that. Reading is good. I like to read epic fantasy, myself."

Still no answer.

"So, tell me about the one you're reading now. What makes it interesting?"

Both hands were clenched in her lap. "We can talk about something else. Did you notice how well both girls are riding?"

"I did." Ian extricated one of Kelly's hands and caressed it with his own. "Being interested in love and romance is a good thing." Unless she was reading the explicit kind, but he couldn't imagine that. He nuzzled her hair. "Romance itself is a pretty good thing."

"Ian..."

Keep pedaling. Don't stop or you'll fall off. "Kelly," he said softly.

"I — why are we talking about this?"

"Because I'm attracted to you even more than my daughter is. And that's saying something. Do you know she talks about you as much as she talks about Elena when we get home?"

He felt Kelly take a deep breath and let it out slowly. She pulled her hand away and shifted so they weren't touching. "Ian, what happened to Sophie's mother?"

Had a cloud covered the late-March sun? Seemed the warmth and brightness had disappeared. "Her name was Maria. We got married too young and too soon after we met." Ian hoped there wasn't a lesson in that second part. "It was a mistake from the start. Maria didn't want to be a mother. She blamed Sophie for losing her figure and, generally, wasn't very nurturing. She left us when Sophie was a baby, and died in a plane crash not long after."

"I see." Kelly glanced at him, her face unreadable. "That must've been rough."

"I wasn't a very good husband. I figured Maria should be happy taking care of the house and Sophie, but she wasn't. I never stopped to figure out what she wanted. In retrospect, what she wanted had nothing to do with me or our child." He sighed deeply. "I regret a lot of things, but I don't regret Sophie. She's a good kid."

"You've done a great job with her. She's well-adjusted and fun to have around."

Ian's heart swelled with pride for his daughter. "Thanks. She makes it easy."

Kelly nudged him. "Don't sell yourself short."

He took the opportunity to clasp her fingers again. Hey, she'd touched him first this time. "While we're having confession, what about Elena's father?"

Kelly stared at the girls so long that Ian checked to make sure they were okay. If calling bikes Philippe and Maximus and pretending they were horses was fine, so were the girls.

"Brief college romance gone sour," she said at last. "Needless to say, the pregnancy was unexpected. He thought I should terminate. I believe life is God-given. He said he wanted nothing to do with the situation. I came back to Riverbend, took another semester of college courses online, gave birth to Elena, and took a minimum-wage job in retail when she was six months old. I don't know what I would've done without my mom's support."

He studied her profile, but she didn't look at him. "Sounds rough. When did you start with the town?"

"Two years ago. I heard about the opening through the friend of a friend of a friend. All this—" she waved her hand at Elena "—is not how I planned my life when I was growing up."

"I bet." He tucked a strand of her blond hair behind her ear.

"I did a lot of things wrong," she said at last, firing him a quick glance. "And I hated having her in daycare as a toddler. Without government subsidies, I couldn't have done it. It's easier now that she's in school. But even so…" She shook her head. "I can't imagine my life without her. She brightens every day."

"I know what you mean." Ian needed to choose his words carefully... but not stop. "Being a single parent is a tough job, however a person gets there." He rubbed his thumb around the palm of her hand. "Someday your prince will come."

She glanced at him, biting her lip.

He couldn't resist running the thumb of his free hand across her lips. Maybe he was here already.

Kelly felt herself drowning in Ian's dark eyes. That touch reminded her what else her lips could do. Not that she needed any reminding. She'd been thinking of little else but a kiss from Ian all week. It wouldn't take much encouragement from her at this moment. She only needed to lean a little closer, and he'd take it from there.

"Is that kissy stuff?" asked Sophie in a stage whisper.

"Shh," Elena replied. "Almost."

Ian's eyes crinkled in amusement as his hand swept Kelly's face. Then he reached out and snagged Sophie around the middle, tumbling her into his lap. "What's all this talk about kissing?" He nuzzled into his daughter's neck with several loud smooches.

Sophie giggled and squirmed, but he didn't release her for a long moment.

"Now that's all the kissy stuff you need to know about," he said when Sophie struggled to her feet, shrieking with laughter.

Kelly's gaze latched onto Elena's wistful expression. Oh, man. Life was totally out of control.

Ian reached for Elena. "C'mere, you." He pulled her to his knee and wrapped one arm around her. "Do you need some kissy stuff, too?"

Elena melted against him with a little nod.

He gave her a smack on each cheek, rubbing his short stubble against her soft skin. Elena grabbed his face between her two little hands. "Mr. Ian, would—"

Kelly cleared her throat. "Elena." When her daughter sighed and looked at her, Kelly held up her baby finger and wiggled it. "Remember."

Elena gave her a sour look and leaned back against Ian's shoulder. Sophie launched onto her dad's lap, and Ian snuggled a little girl with each arm.

Longing filled Kelly. Could this be a reality? Could she and Ian and their daughters become a real family?

Too soon. She wasn't ready to give her heart away yet. Only, maybe her heart had already done a flying leap just like Sophie.

* * *

"Daddy, I'm hungry." Sophie's elbow dug into his knee.

"Me, too." Elena flopped back onto the grass, her arms spread wide.

Ian glanced at his watch. How had it gotten to be five-thirty already? No wonder the girls were starving. Kelly probably had something planned for her household, and he'd overstayed his welcome. Or had he?

Kelly scrambled to her feet. "Wow, the afternoon got away from me."

Maybe he could redeem this. "Why don't I order in pizza?" He watched Kelly closely as Elena bounced to her feet, grinning. "Unless you have other plans."

Kelly shot him an unreadable glance, and he raised his eyebrows. "Please?" he mouthed.

"Yay! Pizza!" Sophie grabbed Elena and they danced in a circle.

"Sounds good." Kelly shook her head.

That didn't add up. He probably shouldn't have asked in front of the girls. "What kind do you guys like?"

"Hawaiian!" yelled Elena.

Sophie pulled away and looked at her friend in horror. "That's yucky."

Finally something the two didn't have twin-brain about. "I can order plain, too, Sophie." He turned to Kelly. "How about you?"

She chuckled. "Hawaiian is good for me, too. Or anything that doesn't have hot stuff or anchovies."

He couldn't resist. "Not a fan of heat?" He pointed at her tablet lying on the patio table nearby and waggled his eyebrows.

"Ian Tomlinson, has anyone ever told you you're a brat?"

He winked. "Not since I was ten, but you can tell me anytime you like."

"Oh, you. Once again, I see I'm outnumbered. Why don't I put together a tossed salad while we wait?"

"Sounds good." Ian tugged out his phone and tapped the Panago Pizza number on his favorites list. He'd placed Kelly's number there, too.

Kelly's hands dropped to her hips. "How often do you get pizza, anyway?"

Ian held up his hand to silence her as he recited the order and gave Kelly's street address. He slid the phone back in his pocket. "Uh... it's a working single dad's best friend?"

"You get off work at three-thirty," she pointed out. "You have plenty of time to make a real dinner."

She had a point there. "I cook on weekends," he offered. He glanced at Sophie. The kid knew exactly how often he was in the kitchen. "Sometimes, anyway."

"My daddy makes yummy pancakes," announced Sophie. "And bacon and eggs. And he hardly ever burns the toast."

"Hey now." Ian tickled his daughter to silence her. "Don't give away all my secrets."

"I like pancakes." Elena looked from one to the other.

"One of these days I'll make you some."

Kelly shot him another one of *those* looks. "Come on inside, girls. Wash your hands and you can help me make salad. What kind of dressing do you and your daddy like, Sophie?"

"We like ranch." Sophie tucked her hand inside Kelly's as they went down the steps to the door of the basement suite.

"Then it's handy we have some in the fridge." Kelly grinned down at Sophie.

Elena ran down the steps behind them.

Oh, yes. Ian could totally get used to this. The door shut behind the threesome, and silence descended on the backyard. He looked up at the blue spring sky, where a few fluffy clouds scuttled across as though they were in a hurry to go somewhere. Like if they stopped moving, they'd fall.

"Lord?" whispered Ian. "I do want You to guide Kelly and me. Don't let me pedal so fast I don't hear Your voice. You know how much she warms my heart. How attached Sophie is getting already. I commit everything to You, Lord. But can I just say please?"

Chapter Seven

Ian's vehicle pulled into her driveway at eight on Saturday morning. Kelly peeked through the curtains to see his new bike mounted on a rack. He'd likely be taking Sophie's wheels home with him at the end of the day as spring break was over. He opened the back door, and Sophie slid from her booster seat onto the pavement. Both of them reached into the Jeep for grocery bags then headed toward the gate.

"Mommy? Is Sophie here?"

"Yes, baby girl. They just got here. Run, put on your clothes. Remember we have a busy day planned."

She'd hit the shower at five-thirty, as usual. Too bad she couldn't sleep in a bit on weekends, but Elena had cured her of it as an infant and she'd never gotten back into the groove. But it was only in the past week or two she'd had trouble sleeping. A certain man — tall, dark, and handsome — kept invading her dreams.

The same man now stood at her door, knocking.

How had Kelly agreed to let him make breakfast in her kitchen? One of these days she needed to see his place, but hers was closer to the park. The girls weren't up to long bike rides yet.

Kelly opened the door wide. "Come on in!" She knelt, and Sophie walked into her arms for a hug.

"Where's Elena?" asked the little girl after hugging her back.

"Getting dressed. She'll be out in a minute." Kelly glanced up at Ian then back at Sophie. "Are you helping your dad cook?" She couldn't let her eyes linger on Ian. All week he'd arrived after a day at the office, dressed in business casual. Today's jeans and Vancouver Canucks T-shirt looked good on him. Too good. All she needed was one more Ian to parade through her dreams with the others.

Sophie shook her head. “I don’t know how.”

Kelly squeezed her. “We’ll find you a job.” No wonder it was easier for Ian to get take-out. Kelly enlisted Elena’s help every day. There was always something a six-year old could do, even if it was just setting the table. She’d been flipping pancakes at three.

Ian set his bags on the kitchen table. “Do I get a welcome hug, too?” His dark eyes danced.

Sophie rolled her eyes. “Daddy needs lots of hugs.”

“Oh, does he?” Kelly straightened. “Scoot and tell Elena to hurry.”

“I’m right here, Mommy,” said Elena from the hallway. “I’ll give Mr. Ian a hug if he needs one.”

“I sure do.” Ian squatted as Elena pitched herself at him. He picked her up in one arm and strolled back to Kelly, eyes fixed on hers. “Good morning, beautiful.” He pulled Kelly into a side hug.

Elena leaned between them, peering into Ian’s face. “Did you call my mommy beautiful?”

“I did. It’s true, isn’t it?” Ian’s hand rubbed Kelly’s arm.

The little girl tipped her head. “Yes. Mr. Ian, will you—”

“Elena.” Kelly clipped the one word, and her daughter sighed.

“Will I what?”

“I can’t say.”

Kelly pulled away and cupped her hand behind Sophie’s head. “Why don’t you two wash your hands, so you can help in the kitchen?”

Ian set Elena down and the girls ran down the hall. In seconds, splashing water could be heard. He stepped closer to Kelly, his dark eyes intensifying. “You look great today.”

The space between them seemed to buzz. “So do you.”

His eyes twinkled. “Canucks fan?”

Kelly grinned. “I wouldn’t admit it if I wasn’t. Not anywhere in British Columbia.”

“Good girl. Now you know why I had to move to Riverbend. I couldn’t cheer for the Calgary Flames anymore.” He tugged her into his arms and planted a kiss on her hair. “I’m looking forward to spending all day with you and Elena.” Then he let go and grimaced as the sound of running water ended. “Time’s up, I think.”

Two little girls ran into the room.

Kelly laughed. “You’re right. Now, what have you got there? What can we do to help?”

Ian hesitated. “Fixings for pancakes. Bacon. Butter. Syrup. I wasn’t sure what all you had, so I brought everything. At least, I hope I did.”

She peered into one of the bags. Organic, whole-grain pancake mix. Of course he didn’t cook from scratch. What had she been thinking? It did look a step up from generic, though. “I’ll get out my electric frying pan and set it up here at the end of the counter. That way the girls can flip pancakes.” Kelly had cleaned everything off the counters to make room. She pointed to the other side of the sink. “That’s a good spot for mixing. There are bowls in the cupboard below. And, oh.” She opened the drawer under the stove and pulled out a cast iron skillet. “This is good for bacon. Anything else?”

“Uh, no. I think I’m good.”

The girls clasped hands. “Do you know how to flip pancakes?” Sophie whispered.

“Yeah, don’t you?” Elena whispered back.

Sophie shook her head.

“Today’s a great day to learn,” announced Kelly. She opened the under-stair storage space off the hallway, the perfect place for bulky things like electric frying pans. She brought it back, set it on the counter, and plugged it in.

Ian measured pancake mix into one of her stainless steel mixing bowls. The girls stood in the middle of the floor and watched the kitchen invasion.

Kelly shifted from one foot to the other. Shouldn’t someone start the bacon? She set the one remaining grocery bag in the sink. “Here, girls. I’ll get the plates down and you can set the table. By the time you’re done, it will be time to start cooking the pancakes. Okay?”

They nodded. A few minutes later the table was set and the frying pan hot. Elena dragged a kitchen chair to the counter and pulled a flipper from the jar at the back. “I’m ready, Mr. Ian.”

Sophie copied Elena with a second chair.

Ian shot Kelly an indiscernible look before handing her the mixing bowl. “I was planning on doing everything.”

"And spoil their fun?" she replied lightly. Had he always been this controlling and she only now realized it? Kelly got a third-cup measure out of a drawer and handed it to Sophie, being as Elena had the flipper. "Here's what you do. You put four scoops in this pan, okay? One close to each corner. Be careful not to touch the pan. It's hot."

Sophie pulled back a little and shook her head.

"Do you want Elena to do this part?"

The little girl nodded.

Elena took the scoop and plopped batter off to one side. A few drops dribbled along the way. She frowned and reached for the flipper. "I wanted it in the corner."

"You can't move it now, baby girl. Not until it's brown on the bottom, remember?"

"But I can't fit four."

"Three is fine this time. Don't worry." Behind her, the bacon began to sizzle on the stove.

Elena bit her lip and dropped another load of batter, then another.

"That doesn't look like pancakes." Sophie peered from a safe distance.

Kelly braced her foot on the chair and leaned closer, encasing Sophie. "They will. Give it a minute. Do you remember how to tell when they need to be turned over?"

Elena frowned. "Bubbles?"

"Right. Bubbles all over." They waited a minute, while the aroma of cooking bacon wafted over the kitchen. She glanced at Ian, but his back was to her as he stood at the stove. "Smells good, Ian."

He glanced at her with a little grin, but it didn't seem to reach his eyes. Was he really so perturbed she and the girls were helping? That didn't seem right.

"Can I turn them over now, Mommy? Look at the bubbles."

Kelly nodded. "You can do two of them. Then Sophie can do one if she wants. Remember the pan is hot."

Sophie shook her head and backed closer to Kelly. "You do it."

Elena's face scrunched in concentration as she got the flipper under the first misshapen pancake. It landed partly on top of one of the others. "Oh, no."

"It's okay. Flip the other one. Then we can scoot this guy over and turn his buddy." Kelly became aware of Ian close behind her. She glanced up as he watched Elena, a little crease on his forehead. She leaned back a centimeter until she touched his chest.

He massaged her shoulder — the one furthest from Sophie — and gave her a little smile.

"I did it!" announced Elena.

Kelly turned her focus back to the pancake-making operation. "Good job, baby girl. I'll get a plate you can put those on, and you can start the next pan-full. Want to try this time, Sophie?"

Ian's hand stopped rubbing.

Whatever. She stretched to reach a plate from the cupboard above the frying pan then set it on the counter.

Elena transferred the pancakes to the plate with a satisfied glint in her eye.

Kelly's back chilled. Ian had returned to his spot by the stove. "Okay, now more batter. Can you get them closer to the corners this time?"

Her daughter set her jaw and nodded. Blobs of batter landed more-or-less in the pan's four quadrants.

"Good job!" Kelly raised her hand and high-fived Elena.

Ian cycled at the back of the parade. He tried to focus on the two wobbly little bikes single-file in front of him, but it was hard not to stare at Kelly's trim backside as she leaned over her handlebars and led the pack.

He liked his life orderly. The most spontaneous thing he'd ever done was move to Riverbend, and that hardly counted because he'd been looking for an opportunity like this one for a couple of years. Especially recently.

Kelly was not orderly, but she was a lot of fun. Oh, it wasn't that her place was dirty, but it certainly looked lived in. Maybe that's because it was, compared to his. Ian suspected it wasn't just that she'd been home over spring break and that he'd barely moved in. It had that lived-in look the first time she'd invited them over.

She was so good with little girls. Sophie had even gotten up the nerve to flip the last pan of pancakes with Kelly's hand guiding hers. Not a single one of them were close to a circle. That hadn't affected the flavor. Why had he kept thinking Sophie was too young to help? Maybe perfection wasn't as necessary as he'd always thought.

His mind veered from that thought. Not perfection, exactly. But talent for detail and order were necessary for his job.

Kelly made free-form look appealing, but how would he feel about it in a year or two? A sudden shot of insight rocked him. Would he squelch spontaneity in Kelly as he had in Maria? He'd known the kind of mother, housekeeper, and cook Maria should be — which hadn't matched up to her own vision of herself.

No wonder she'd left him.

Chapter Eight

The girls ran from the swings to the monkey bars to the slide.

Kelly glanced over at Ian. He seemed to be keeping a bit more distance than he had all week, but that was likely because they were in full public view. She was just as glad. A person never knew whom they'd run into at Riverside Park on such a beautiful late-March day. While she was fine with introducing him to people, she didn't want anyone she knew jumping to conclusions.

Elena and Sophie had done all the jumping anyone needed to. Okay, maybe she'd been guilty of it herself, even while trying to hold Ian off a little. Or was it their daughters making everything feel claustrophobic? Did she and Ian even have a choice, or were the two little matchmakers so bent on success true romance wasn't an option?

There was always a choice. Heartbreak for Elena now was better than heartbreak for both of them later. Kelly had to be sure. The merry-go-round the girls now rode pushed bodies outward with centrifugal force. The merry-go-round her life had become shoved her closer to the center with similar unrelenting power. Closer to Ian.

She stole another peek. He sat with arms looped loosely around pulled-up knees, watching their daughters. He had thick biceps for a guy with an office job. Brown hair curled close to his T-shirt's ribbed neck and around his ears. Was it soft or wiry? She didn't even know. She'd never touched it.

He must've felt her gaze on him, because he turned to her. This time he seemed to truly look at her with more dispassion. Not as Elena's mom, not as Sophie's caregiver, not as a woman to flirt with, but as though he'd seen her for the first time.

It nearly chilled her. What was he thinking? That he'd been crazy to spend so much time with her this week? That he couldn't wait for spring break to be over and normal life to resume?

"Ian?" She didn't realize his name had escaped her lips until the question hung between them, all but visible.

The lines around his eyes crinkled as a slow smile curved his lips. He shifted position, bracing himself on an arm that angled behind her. Not quite touching, but she could feel the warmth from his body. This was what she wanted, right? To be closer to him?

"Hey, beautiful."

Her heart warmed along with the side of her that was nearest him. She quirked him a grin. "Hey." She couldn't bring herself to give him a nickname. Not yet. And even though she didn't feel beautiful when she looked in the mirror, she didn't doubt he said what he saw.

Now that she had his attention, she couldn't think of a thing to say.

The girls ran back to the swings. Several other children from their class trooped alongside them.

"I've been thinking about their birthdays," Ian said in a low voice. "What kind of party do you usually do for Elena?"

Was he expecting a joint celebration? Well, it only made sense as they shared the day, and Sophie was new to Riverbend. Kelly's heart squeezed. In just over a month, her baby girl would be seven. How had so much time gone by already?

"I don't usually do anything big," she replied at last. "We invite a few little friends over. Last year they played dress-up while I made pizza and cake in front of a Disney movie." She studied his face. "What do you usually do?"

Ian shrugged. "Last year I took Sophie's friends to the zoo for a Canadian Wilds party. Sophie wants to do that again, but Calgary is too far for a day trip."

Kelly kept forgetting that Ian's job paid probably double hers. She could only imagine what an event like that might run.

"You and Elena ever been there?'

She shook her head. "No, but I'm sure she'd love to go sometime." As would Kelly. When was the last time she'd been to any zoo? She'd been just a little kid, probably not much older than her daughter. "The closest thing we've got around here is a farm where they offer parties. If you can pretend farm animals are zoo animals, it's all good."

"Oh, that sounds fun. Do they offer horseback riding?"

Kelly frowned. "I think so. I'm not sure. You'd have to look them up online. It's Holiday Hobby Farm."

Ian poked his chin toward the girls. "If there are horses, those two will be thrilled, don't you think?"

She shouldn't have mentioned it. Even a party at Holiday's was out of her price league, and she couldn't assume Ian would happily pay double. Besides, that wasn't fair. He could do what he wanted for Sophie, and she'd do the usual for Elena. It wasn't like they were a family.

Maybe someday? But she couldn't hope too much, no matter what his eyes said. He didn't really know her. Something was bound to scare him off sooner or later. With most men she'd met, that was Elena. She stifled a grin. Well, that certainly wasn't the case this time around.

"What are you thinking?" He nudged her shoulder with his arm. "I saw that smile."

He'd said something before that. Her brain scrambled to catch up. Right, horses. "Yes, Elena is into horses. Most little girls their age seem to be. She talks about le..."

"Lessons?" prompted Ian. "Great idea."

She'd done it again. She took a deep breath. "Ian, I can't afford riding lessons for her, nor can I drive her out there every week. In all honesty, I probably can't afford a party at the hobby farm, either."

"I'd be happy to cover the party."

"Don't you see? I can't be beholden to you. I can't let Elena expect that sort of thing all the time. It's simply not our reality."

* * *

Ian glanced at the playground to see Sophie follow Elena out onto the monkey bars. He blinked. That was a first.

"Kelly, I think what you've accomplished is amazing. Part of the proof is right over there. Your daughter is happy and well-adjusted." He nestled in a little closer, his chin nearly resting on her shoulder.

"Well adjusted? She asks men to marry me."

Ian couldn't suppress the chuckle. "It's not wrong for a kid to want a dad. You and Elena are a package deal. A man who doesn't love her can't possibly love you." Ian could do it. He filled his senses with her nearness. He could definitely love them both.

Kelly shifted away from him then clambered to her feet. She cast an unreadable glance his direction then strode toward the girls without saying another word.

What had he said? Was he rushing her? The past two weeks had been like hurtling through space. She had to feel something similar. Maybe instead of pedaling faster, he needed to hit the brakes or at least let things coast a bit. What did he have in common with Kelly, really? Besides the girls, of course. They both loved the Lord, both worked for the town but, beyond that, how well did he know her?

Ian scratched his head, watching her.

Kelly lifted Sophie to a higher swinging bar than his daughter could reach on her own. Sophie grabbed hold and gave a tentative pump of her lower body. Fear crossed her face and her lips moved as she said something to Kelly.

He couldn't see Kelly's face, but her hands stayed close to his daughter's sides. Not touching, it didn't look like from Sophie's movement. She must've said something calming, though, as Sophie nodded and gave another tentative swing before letting go. Kelly easily caught her and lowered her to the ground.

Ian dared breathe again. Kelly took so many chances with Sophie — without asking him — but no more than she took with her own daughter. But the girls had such different personalities. Was it good for Sophie?

Was it good for *him*?

Chapter Nine

"Coming?" Kelly glanced over her shoulder as she cycled down the edge of the street. The girls followed with Ian bringing up the rear.

Elena, in a bit of daring, wove her bike from side to side. They were on a residential street with no traffic in sight, so Kelly bit her tongue. No harm would come from it.

"Can you do this?" shouted Elena.

Kelly glanced again in time to see Sophie try to mimic Elena, but with less confidence. Sophie's front tire caught the edge of the curb, pitching the bike over.

Sophie wailed, Kelly hit her brakes, and Elena ran into Kelly but managed to remain upright. Kelly jumped off her bike, letting it spin where it landed as she sprinted the few steps to Sophie.

Ian got there first. He picked up his daughter and cradled her. "You okay, baby?" he crooned. "Where does it hurt?"

Kelly bit her tongue. Babying Sophie wouldn't help, but she was Ian's child. Not hers.

"My finger hurts!" Sophie's sobs continued unabated as she clutched her right hand to her chest.

Elena reached for Sophie's wrist.

Ian turned away, and Kelly put her hand on Elena's shoulder. "Let her daddy take care of her," Kelly whispered.

"I just need to know which finger." Elena crossed her arms.

Ian glanced at Elena sideways. "Why does it matter?"

"Because if it's her baby finger and it's broken, she—"

Whoa. Kelly put a hand over her daughter's mouth. She knew exactly the trail Elena's thoughts were on. "It doesn't matter which finger. Are you okay, Sophie? Can I have a look?"

Sophie shook her head and burrowed harder against Ian's T-shirt, her crying escalating rather than abating.

Now what? They were four blocks from the cul-de-sac, and it didn't look like Sophie would be riding any minute soon. Nor could they leave their bikes lying at the edge of the street.

Kelly hated the helpless feeling pulling at her gut. This wasn't a decision she could make. It was up to Ian, but how long was he going to sit on the curb listening to his child cry without making an attempt to even look at the damage? Sophie probably had nothing but a scrape. She hadn't fallen far or hard. "Hey, Sophie, let's get back on our bikes and ride to our house. I've got some ice cream in the freezer. Want some?"

"Yeah!" Elena bounced from one foot to the other. "I want ice cream. Is it bubblegum?"

"I was asking Sophie. And, no, it's chocolate."

Elena sighed heavily. "Come on, twin. Let's get ice cream."

Sophie shifted slightly, and Ian captured her wrist, holding up her hand.

Uh oh. Even from here, Kelly could see the pinky finger at an awkward angle. Oh man. Was she somehow to blame?

Elena plunked both hands on her hips. "What promise did you break?"

"Elena!"

"It's her baby finger. That's how they get broke. You told me."

Ian frowned, his eyes chilling as he glanced at Kelly. "You told her *what?*"

"Nothing. It's not relevant."

Ian rose, Sophie still in his arms. The little girl clung to his neck, legs wrapped around his middle. "I need to get her to E.R. Can you manage the bikes back to your place?"

Now she was superwoman and could ride two at once? "I'll lock your bikes to that light post. Elena and I will take ours home and come right back for yours."

He nodded. "That works." He strode off down the sidewalk.

Kelly stared after him. What was going on here? Something sank in her gut. She'd known he was too good to be true. He seemed to somehow blame her for Sophie's injury. Or maybe it had been Elena's words that caught him wrong.

Either way, she'd just as soon get back to the house after they'd left in the Jeep. They'd both be in a better frame of mind once that finger had been taken care of and they returned for their bikes. She hoped.

* * *

Ian hovered over his daughter as she lay on their crisp gray sofa. "Can I get you something else, baby?"

She shook her wan face, and he smoothed the short brown hair off to one side. "Why did Elena say that to me, Daddy?"

Good question, and one that had been running through his mind for the past two hours, all the while they'd sat waiting in emergency for a doctor to tend the finger and splint it. He sat on the ottoman by Sophie's head. "I'm not sure. Do you know?"

"She told me about pinky promises." Sophie held up her other hand and wiggled her fingers. "She said her mommy makes her hook their baby fingers together sometimes and make a promise."

Ian nodded. But there had to be more to it than that.

"Her mommy said that if you don't keep your pinky promise, your finger breaks." Tears welled in Sophie's eyes again. "But I didn't. I promise I didn't."

What kind of things did Kelly fill her child's mind with, anyway? "It's okay, baby. Sometimes things happen. You fell off your bike, and that's how your finger broke. It had nothing to do with promises."

Though it had to do with Elena being a daredevil — again — and encouraging Sophie to do things she wouldn't normally have the nerve for. A few days ago that had made him smile. Now, he wasn't so sure. Why shouldn't Sophie be timid? It was her personality, how God made her.

"Her mommy made her pinky promise not to ask you to be her daddy."

A sharp chuckle managed an escape. That would account for Elena's cut-off questions a time or two. Ian inhaled and let the air out slowly. "Do you like Elena and her mommy?"

Sophie nodded. "Except Elena was mean to me."

Hard to deny. "How about Kelly?"

Sophie's serious brown eyes met his. "I like her. Is she going to be my new mommy?"

Stall, Tomlinson. "Do you want her to be?"

"I think so. Would we live at their house or would they live here? Because my room isn't very big, and Elena's room is full of princess stuff."

"Is that good or bad?"

"I don't know. Could we have bunk beds like at Grandma's house?"

Should he laugh, cry, or change the subject? "We'll go to Calgary over Easter, and you can sleep in your bunk bed at Grandma and Grandpa's house."

Sophie narrowed her eyes, thinking. "With Elena?"

"No, baby." Though yesterday he couldn't wait to bring Kelly to meet his folks. "Just you and me." Maybe that was best, anyway?

He looked around the small modern apartment. It hadn't taken long to unpack. He wasn't into extra stuff. Kelly's home swam into his mind. Her place wasn't cluttered, exactly. But it was full of color, full of stuff she seemed to use. Vibrant, like her. Why hadn't he noticed it as a huge lifestyle difference? Could he live with so much going on around him, 24/7? Could Sophie?

She was asleep. The pain meds the doctor had prescribed must've finally kicked in.

Ian edged across the space and into his bedroom, where a pale two-toned comforter covered his bed. Maria had loved bright colors. Why did he only remember this now? Had he pushed Maria into a mold she was ill fitted for? Would he do the same to Kelly?

No, Kelly was different. Self-contained. She wouldn't put up with that from him or anyone.

He hadn't been looking for a relationship, though. Not at all. She'd snuck up on him and he'd fallen. Hard. He'd let his defenses down.

Now what?

His cell chirped with an incoming text. Kelly. He took a deep breath and thumbed his phone on to read her message. Should he call her? No. He didn't know what to say after all the twists and turns of the day.

Safer to answer her inquiry by text, the same way she'd asked.

Home a few minutes ago. Doctor splinted Sophie's finger. Long day. Will get bikes tomorrow.

He stared at the words for a few minutes then stabbed send.

Chapter Ten

"Sophie played with Gracie again at recess." Elena plunked her elbows on the table, her face forlorn.

"I'm sorry, baby girl." It seemed mother and daughter both suffered broken hearts. Kelly hadn't seen Ian except from a distance. He hadn't sought her out once. Not like he'd done that first week.

He'd texted he'd swung by for the bikes when no one was home. That had been two weeks ago. Why was he so chicken?

"I told her sorry about her pinky. That you told me they can break from falling on them." Elena sighed heavily. "Not just from breaking promises."

Could the whole situation really be a result of her daughter's accusation? It broke Kelly's heart to see how much Elena suffered.

"I miss Mr. Ian, too. I thought you were going to love him and make him my daddy."

Kelly's heart clenched at the thought. "It takes longer for grownups to fall in love than you'd think, baby girl. And sometimes things don't work out the way we hope." *Get used to it, sweetie. Life is rough.* Now if only she could convince herself that it was just a speed bump. But two weeks didn't lie.

"Are Sophie and her daddy going to Calgary at Easter?"

Kelly sighed. "Last I heard, yes."

"Maybe they're going to the zoo. How come I can't go to the zoo, Mommy? Sophie said there are bears and giraffes and even red pandas. I want to see them."

Kelly, too. But not as much as she wanted to see Ian. See his eyes crinkle at the sight of her. Feel his gentle touch when the girls weren't looking. Hear him call her beautiful. She tried to keep her voice bright. "We'll have four days at home, just the two of us. Won't that be fun? I bet you're up to riding across the bridge to the long trail by the river. We could take a picnic."

"I want Sophie to come." Elena angled a glance at Kelly. "And Mr. Ian."

Kelly forced a chuckle. "But you already told me they won't be here."

"I want Sophie to be my twin again."

So did Kelly.

Her mother's ring tone chimed. They hadn't talked often lately with Grandma so sick over in Castlebrook's nursing home.

"Hi, Mom."

"Hi, Kelly. How are my two best girls doing?" She sounded tired.

"We're good." And lying was acceptable. "How about you? How's Grandma?"

"Not well. The head nurse pulled me aside today and told me to prepare for the end."

"This isn't the first time."

"No, I know. But when I think how she looked even a week or two ago, I have to agree. Is there any chance you can come this weekend? It will probably be the last chance you have to say good-bye."

The thought of cooping Elena up for hours or even days in a dim, quiet nursing home room was not appealing. Kelly thought longingly of the sunshine outside, the daffodils and tulips blooming beside her sheltered back door. Or the zoo in springtime. "I'm not sure, Mom. I don't even know how I'd get there."

Her mother sighed. "Surely you know someone whose car you could borrow, or who is coming to Castlebrook sometime this weekend. Once you're here you can drive my car, if that helps."

Ian would be going right past on his way to Calgary. Uh… no.

"It would mean a lot to me, Kelly. The end is near. I can feel it."

Kelly didn't want to think how her mother knew that, or if she really did. Seemed freaky. "I hear you, Mom. But I still have Elena to juggle. Does your friend have room for us?"

"Yes, you both can stay with Lorraine. She has a double fold-out bed in the basement."

Sounded comfy, especially since Elena tended to sleep sideways. "I'll see if there's a car I can borrow and come over for the day at some point, rather than the entire weekend."

"Kelly, please..."

Kelly's eyebrows rose. It would help if her mom would meet her halfway. "I'll see what I can do."

"She's the only grandparent you have left."

Nice guilt trip. Kelly had great memories from when she was a child, but Grandma had a stroke five years ago. It had been a rare visit since then when her grandmother had recognized her, let alone Elena. Yeah, she'd still be sad if Grandma died, and she hadn't said good-bye. She hadn't been over since just after Christmas.

"I'll let you know what I can arrange. Take care of yourself, too, Mom."

When the call ended, Kelly turned to Elena, who sat slumped in a chair beside the table, with a scowl on her face. Kelly knew how her daughter felt.

"I don't want to go see Great-grandma."

"I know you don't, baby girl." She didn't, herself. "But sometimes we have to do things even if we don't want to." Like calling Ian… or giving up on him? Which would it be?

She wakened her tablet and searched for the local car rental place, dreading whatever the price would be. Terrific. They weren't accepting one-day reservations over Easter. She'd have to take a car for four days or not at all.

Not at all was the winner. Even one day would tax her carefully-constructed budget. She wasn't going to jeopardize Elena's birthday for a trip to see Grandma. She simply couldn't do it.

Her elderly landlady had sold her car last year when she'd failed the vision test for her driver's license. Who else? Someone from church? Vanessa?

Kelly couldn't do this. A person didn't randomly phone everyone she knew asking to borrow a car. But just because her mother was a professional guilter didn't mean Kelly shouldn't go. The truth was, Kelly hadn't seen her grandmother in nearly four months. The truth was, closure would be good.

The truth was, Elena would go crazier than the Mad Hatter sitting quietly in that nursing home for hours every day. Kelly could download some new games and picture books to her tablet, but that wouldn't hold her daughter for long. Besides, she'd want the tablet herself sometimes. She was still in the midst of that great Farm Fresh Romance series.

Which brought her back to Ian's teasing the other day. If only he'd talk to her anymore. Teasing would be great. She'd hand him her tablet and let him read for himself.

Ian. He was driving right through Castlebrook, probably after work on Thursday. Day after tomorrow. Surely he'd give her and Elena a ride if she simply asked, regardless of how things had been left. Maybe this was the chance she'd been waiting for to break the deadlock.

Lord, I was so sure you were leading us together. Please help me know, one way or the other.

A light tap sounded on Ian's office door, which he'd left ajar. Rhonda seemed to think she couldn't disturb him if it was latched, and he couldn't convince his secretary otherwise. He stared at the white rectangle. In today's frame of mind — all twisted up with the little girls' spat and how he felt about Kelly — he probably should have made sure it was shut.

He sighed. "Yes? Please come in."

But it wasn't Rhonda's fake-red hair that peered around the door.

Ian sprang to his feet. "Kelly!" Man, she looked good. He feasted his eyes long enough to note her long blond hair braided from the top and the dark circles under her eyes. His heart clenched. Those had not been there before. He'd caused them. He and Sophie.

She bit her lip. The one he had not yet kissed. "Hi. Sorry to bother you in the office, but I needed to talk to you." She met his gaze. "I wasn't sure you'd pick up your phone or reply to a text."

Ouch. But if it wasn't work-related, she might be right. What could he say? He knew where to start. "I'm sorry."

Kelly came the rest of the way in, shut the door, and leaned against it. Hurt shone in her eyes. “For what?”

He made a helpless gesture. “For everything. For Sophie. For not calling you back.”

“Why, Ian? I know Elena spoke out of turn, but don’t you think she’s been punished enough?”

Ian pulled to his feet, only then recognizing the overwhelming desire to cross the space and gather Kelly in his arms. No. He couldn’t do that. He raised the mini-blinds of his office window, but the view of the Sandon River blurred. He took a deep breath and turned back to face her.

“It’s Sophie. She’s my first responsibility. Really, my only one.” He pleaded with Kelly with his eyes.

“You’re telling me that it’s because she is still angry with Elena? Two weeks later? Kids don’t usually hold grudges, Ian.”

Ian straightened the phone and day planner on the corner of his desk then moved the pen caddy a little to the left. He squared Sophie’s framed photo.

Kelly’s hands appeared in his view. She tipped the pens and they skittered across his desk. “If Elena and I messed up your orderly life a bit too much, just say it like a man. Tell me why we went from… from flirting and hanging out together to a brick wall.” She placed both hands on the back of his desk and leaned forward.

Right into his view. Right where he wanted her forever. He shot a glance at Sophie’s image.

Kelly reached over and turned the frame on its face.

“Hey!”

“Listen to me, Ian Tomlinson. What are you teaching Sophie? That you deal with problems by retreating and blocking them out? How about teaching her to be forgiving? How about teaching her to respect the feelings of others? How about teaching her that life is all about give and take and doing her part to live in harmony with others?”

Her finger jabbed toward his chest, but he took a step back before she connected.

“If those are your family values, then Elena and I are better off without the both of you.”

Ian took a shuddering breath. Were those accusations true? Was he modeling a non-Christ-like attitude for his daughter? Maria had called him rigid. Unbending. Were both women right?

"Never mind." Kelly spun on her heel and headed for the door.

"Kelly, wait." The words came out past the lump in his throat. "You're right."

She paused, her back to him and her hand on the doorknob.

"I've gotten so wrapped up creating a safe place for Sophie that I've messed up everywhere else." He rounded the desk and stopped. He choked on his words. "I'm sorry. Can you forgive me?"

Kelly turned slowly, her eyes searching his. "I want to." She bit her lip.

"But…?"

Moisture pooled in her blue eyes. "I have to forgive you, don't I? Otherwise I'm doing what I just accused you of. Keeping you at a distance to protect myself. To protect Elena." A tear trickled down her cheek. So vulnerable. He'd caused that pain.

"Kelly." He crossed the space between them in a heartbeat and wiped away the tear with his thumb. "I'm so sorry. I've been miserable, but to know how much pain I've caused you breaks my heart. Can we try again?"

Her lips trembled. "What about Sophie?"

He touched her lips with his fingers. Cradled her face in his hands. "I'll talk to her. I'll be an example to her. Today."

Kelly took one step closer and slid her arms around his waist.

Ian clutched her to him. Would she look up at him again? Would he kiss her if she did? Too soon. Not until this turmoil was solved. He rested his cheek against her hair. "Thank you, Kelly. Thanks for caring enough to confront me." He gave a slight squeeze and stepped back, releasing her.

She searched his face. "Is this a bad time to tell you I had an ulterior motive? Well, maybe not ulterior, but a reason that pushed me to talk to you now instead of later?"

He kept his hands firmly at his sides, no matter how much they itched to touch her again. "What's that?"

"Are you still going to Calgary this weekend?"

He nodded as his heart leaped. Did she want to go, too? It was too early to introduce her to his parents. Or maybe not.

"My grandmother is in a nursing home in Castlebrook. I think I told you my mom has been over there most of the past few months to spend time with her." She watched him. "Grandma is failing quickly, and my mom really needs me to be there. Both Elena and me. But I have no car."

"Do you need a ride? We're leaving shortly after work tomorrow. I have plenty of room for you, and, as you know, it's not out of the way."

"Will it be okay with Sophie?"

"I'll make it be okay. It's time for her to face what her hurt is doing to Elena. To you." He closed the gap once again, grasped both Kelly's hands, and brushed his lips across her forehead. "Thank you for perspective. For a second chance. I've been praying for a way through this."

* * *

Sophie poked her toe at the edge of the patio behind Kelly's house. "I'm sorry I was mean to you."

"I'm sorry I said that about breaking a promise." Elena watched Sophie, who didn't look up. "I missed playing with you."

"Me, too." Sophie peeked up. "I like Gracie, but she's not my twin."

Kelly dared breathe. Dared to meet Ian's gaze from where he stood behind Sophie, both hands on her shoulders. Kelly crouched. "Can I get a hug, Sophie? I've missed you, too."

Sophie nodded and shuffled forward a few steps.

Kelly encased the little girl in her arms and snuggled her until she felt the small body relax. She kissed Sophie's forehead and reached for Elena. Cuddling both girls, she looked up.

"Is there room for one more?" Ian's face wore a look of longing. "I could use a hug."

Elena nodded and launched at him. He caught her and swung her up then reached for Kelly and Sophie. A moment later they stood, arms holding each other up.

Like a family. Was this what God had for them? Kelly could only hope and pray.

"Time to start driving," said Ian. "Do you girls want to talk or watch a movie?"

Elena leaned over to look in his eyes. "Is it a princess movie?"

He grinned at her. "Is there any other kind?" He released both girls to the patio. "Let me buckle in your booster seat so you two can get settled. Ready?"

Kelly caught her breath as Ian's gaze lingered on her face. Ready? Oh, yeah.

* * *

Ian glanced over at her now, leaning back against the headrest, her eyes closed and long lashes fanned against her cheeks. Blond hair flowed past her shoulders in gentle waves. Her pert nose slightly raised. She was wearing his favorite of her outfits, the well-worn jeans and fitted purple hoodie.

"Eyes on the road, buddy," she said without moving.

Ian chuckled. The highway was fine. He'd looked often enough, even though there was a fair bit of holiday weekend traffic. "So you're watching me watch you."

A muscle twitched in her cheek as though she prevented it from smiling.

He wanted to see that smile spread across her face in the worst way. Wanted to see her blue eyes dance as they met his. "It seems forever since we've spent time together." He hesitated. "Are we okay?"

She nodded slightly. One blue eye opened and looked at him. "When we first met, and Elena asked you to be her daddy…" Kelly's voice trailed off.

Ian swallowed hard. "I remember."

She turned to face him. "I told her kids don't get to decide things like that. Only grownups can decide."

Ouch. He deserved that. "Sophie's been my entire world for most of her life. I lost perspective. I'm sorry you and Elena suffered while I learned." He reached across the console and laced his fingers with hers. "I'd do anything to take back the last two weeks."

"Your daddy is holding my mommy's hand," whispered Sophie.

Kelly turned in her seat, letting go of Ian's hand. "Is it a good movie?"

Elena grinned. "Yep. I hadn't seen this one yet."

Kelly settled back in her seat, a small smile twitching her lips.

Those lips. Ian wrenched his gaze back to the highway and took a long breath. "Can I take you on a real date soon? One without two little chaperones? I can get a sitter for both of them."

The little smile grew until her dimple deepened.

How could he wait until next week to have her to himself, if only for a few hours? If that talk went well, he'd kiss that dimple. Kiss those eyelids. Those lips. He swallowed hard. "How about Friday?" He'd heard the food at the Water Wheel by the park was excellent. That was still eight days away, but Easter weekend would take up the first half of it.

"Friday's good."

What was she thinking as she looked at him? Did she find him as attractive as he found her? His gut tightened as her gaze trailed over his face. Maybe she was thinking about kissing, too.

Their eyes caught for a few seconds before Ian realized he'd passed a sign to lower the speed. They were entering Castlebrook. He gave her a lopsided grin he hoped was a promise for more to come. "Where in town are we going?"

She blinked and looked around. "Turn right on Forest, but that's not until the other side of the mall."

"Mommy? I don't want to go to Great-grandma's."

"I know, baby girl, but we're doing it anyway."

Ian glanced over. It wasn't going to be an easy weekend for either of them.

"I want to go to the zoo with Sophie."

"Elena. Enough."

Elena heaved a sigh from the bottom of her lungs.

He bit back a grin. He couldn't interfere, couldn't fix everything within a day of finally getting over the hurdle. But what had happened to pedal faster so he wouldn't fall? Oh, man. He'd fallen, all right, and he liked it that way.

Kelly gave directions until they pulled in front of a small bungalow in a residential neighborhood.

"I thought she was in a nursing home?" he asked.

"Tomorrow is soon enough," Kelly replied. "Mom's been staying with her friend Lorraine. Her car is here."

Ian shut off the motor. How he wished he could do something. Anything. But he knew he couldn't. It wasn't time.

The front door of the house opened, and a middle-aged woman ran out. Eyes rimmed with red and clutching a tissue, she reached for Kelly almost before the Jeep door opened.

"Oh, honey, you missed her. Grandma passed away an hour ago."

Kelly hugged the woman. "I'm sorry. I came as soon as I could."

"I know. Where's my munchkin?"

Kelly turned to open the back door and released Elena.

"Hi, Grandma." Elena hugged her grandmother.

"Look at you! You've grown even in the past few weeks." Then the woman's eyes seemed to notice him and Sophie. "I don't believe we've met?"

He wouldn't meet Kelly's mom while seated in his vehicle. He'd probably already made a poor first impression by not getting Kelly's door, but the sight of her sobbing mother had distracted him for those precious seconds.

Ian exited the vehicle and opened Sophie's door. She could use a stretch before the next, much longer, leg of their journey.

"Mom, this is Ian Tomlinson and his daughter, Sophie. They're headed to Calgary this weekend. Ian, this is my mom, Roberta."

"Pleased to meet you." Ian put on his best smile and reached to shake the woman's hand.

"The girls are best friends," Kelly told her mother.

He noticed she said nothing about their own relationship. Time. He needed time.

"We're twins," Elena informed her grandmother.

"Oh, are you?" Roberta's gaze flicked between the girls. "Well, that's nice." She turned back to Kelly. "I'm so glad you're finally here. We have all the funeral arrangements to make, and I need you."

Wasn't that going to be a bit tricky across a long weekend? Ian's heart went out to Kelly as she swallowed hard and glanced at Elena. The little girl stood with head downcast, clutching Sophie's hand.

Maybe there was a solution. It wasn't perfect, but it might do. "Can I speak with you a moment, Kelly?"

She looked from him to her mother. "Sure." She followed him to the back of the Jeep. "What's up?"

"You're going to be even busier this weekend than you thought, aren't you? More stressed?"

Kelly nodded, grimacing. "I'm sorry I didn't get to say goodbye, but this is probably for the best."

He lowered his voice. "May I take Elena with me to Calgary? My parents will be fine with it, and it would be good for the girls to get their friendship back on track." He searched her unchanging face. "Please? I know I can't do anything for you here, but this would make it easier for you, wouldn't it?"

Her gaze met his. "Really? That seems like such a big deal."

"It's not. You know how well they play together. It would be an honor to do this for you. For Elena."

"Are we going too fast?"

Ian twined his fingers with hers. Surely their hands were out of sight of Kelly's mom and the girls. "It can't go too quickly for me."

Chapter Eleven

Kelly worked beside her mother the next afternoon, packing the personal items from Grandma's room into cardboard boxes. This wasn't how she'd envisioned spending Good Friday. A group from a Castlebrook church led an Easter service in the residents' lounge just down the corridor. Listening to *The Old Rugged Cross* from a distance wasn't the same as attending River of Life Church, but it would have to do this time around.

Meanwhile, she peeled sticky-tack off the backs of dozens of photos that had been attached to the wall by Grandma's favorite chair. Photos of Elena and her second cousins.

"Tell me about Ian," her mother said at last. "You've never mentioned his name before, but all of a sudden he's a good enough friend to take Elena for the weekend? Are you sure he can be trusted?"

"We have a few things in common. He works for the town, for one." No need to mention that he headed her department. "The girls share a birthday, and that bonded them the first day Sophie came to Riverbend Elementary. Plus, Ian is a Christian." The other thing they had in common was that they'd pretty much instantly fallen for each other, but Ian's twinkling eyes and strong hands were not something Kelly was about to mention to her mother.

"Just be careful, honey. Don't let him take advantage of you."

Kelly shot a glance at her mom. "He's not that kind of guy."

"You can't know that."

"Actually, I can." From the bit of distance the past two weeks had provided their relationship, she was more than certain. "His daughter loves him and respects him, and he is always a gentleman. He's not a closet serial killer or child molester."

"That's not what I meant, honey."

Kelly grabbed the packing tape dispenser and sealed a box then labeled it with a black felt marker. "Ian treats me like a princess, Mom. He treats Elena the same way. He's more than safe." Sure, the powerful instant connection had scared her a little at first. Her heart hadn't seemed safe, but that had changed. Now Ian seemed the safest cradle.

"It's unusual to see a man with custody of a child."

If only Mom could ask about Ian without accusation, this would go a lot better. "His wife died when Sophie was two." No need to mention they'd been separated at the time. "He's done a great job raising her." And would do a better job now that he'd considered the messages he'd sent to Sophie.

"I just don't want you hurt, Kelly. He's probably angling for a mother for his child and taking advantage of the fact you're single, and your daughters are friends."

Kelly straightened and reached for her mother's shoulders. "Look at me, Mom." When her mom obeyed, Kelly went on. "Please stop talking about Ian this way. You don't even know him, and you're jumping to all kinds of wrong conclusions. Ian just might be the very best thing that ever happened to me. Could you believe I have better judgment than I did eight years ago, and try to be happy for me?

Mom's blue eyes, etched with worry lines, searched hers. "Are you sure?"

"Not one hundred percent. And he's not pushing me. Trust me, Mom. I know I only moved out of your house two years ago. I know you still think of me as... as Elena's age, but I'm twenty-six. I'm old enough to know my heart and to make decisions about my future. About Elena's future." She finally had her mom's undivided attention. "I'm so grateful for your support and help with Elena. I don't know what I'd have done without you, but things have changed. Please give Ian and Sophie a chance."

"Does he love you? I mean, truly love you?"

They hadn't said the words to each other, but there was no doubt. "Yes, Mom. He loves me, and I believe God brought him into my life."

"Just take it slow."

"Mom. Trust me."

"I'll try."

* * *

"So you're happy with your move to Riverbend, then?"

Ian and his father strolled down the walkway at the Calgary Zoo behind his mom, who had a small girl by each hand. His folks had taken to Elena immediately, and it had been mutual.

"Very much so. There have definitely been some adjustments to small-town life, but it agrees with both of us."

"Sophie cried for two days before you left," Dad reminded him.

"She did. But her very first day at school she met Elena, and there's been barely a whisper about missing Calgary since."

"I guess sometimes you know when you've met someone you click with, right, son?" Dad's elbow caught Ian's side.

Ian laughed. "Yeah, sometimes you do."

"So tell me about Elena's mother. Kelly, you said?"

Where to start. "She's beautiful. Amazing. And you can tell what a good mom she is by watching her daughter."

Dad chuckled. "So it wasn't my imagination. There's something going on then? Already?"

And that was the problem. He'd known Kelly not much longer than a month, even though his mind and heart had agreed weeks ago that she was what they'd been waiting for. "You think it's too soon?"

"I don't know. Is it?"

He glanced into his dad's dark eyes. "I'm not sure I trust myself after Maria."

"Are they anything alike?"

Ian's head was shaking before his dad's question was complete. "Not in any way that counts."

"Son, if you were on the rebound, I'd be concerned. But you've made a life for yourself and Sophie. You've been content to raise her by yourself, if need be. I know you've avoided women who tried to get close to you since Maria's death, though it didn't seem there was a shortage of willing candidates."

Ian winced. There had been plenty of opportunities, including the woman who'd sent him scurrying for Riverbend.

"But no one caught your eye. So, I repeat. What's different with Kelly?"

"Those two little matchmakers started it." Ian poked his chin toward Sophie and Elena. "Kelly is pretty self-contained. She was definitely not on a manhunt. Just the opposite."

Dad chuckled. "So she presented a challenge. I hope there's more to it than that, for your sake."

"The biggest challenge is not letting those two push too hard and fast. They decided from the beginning that we were destined to be one big happy family. The girls share a birthday, you know. So they decided they're twins."

"Kids are a poor reason to get married. I guess that was sometimes a valid motive in pioneer days, but not now. You've done very well with Sophie on your own."

Kids might be a poor reason *not* to get married, too. "Having your support made a big difference, but you're right. Kelly had to drop out of college when she got pregnant. I respect her for taking classes online while caring for a baby and working retail, but she wasn't able to complete her degree. She got a much better job with the town two years ago, but she still needs to live frugally. And she does."

"Sounds like your mother and I need to meet this paragon of virtue."

"That would make her laugh. She's not perfect, Dad." Though at this instant it was hard to remember in what way she might fail that test. "You guys are coming to Riverbend for Sophie's birthday, right?"

"Your mother wouldn't miss it for the world. Especially if it means meeting the woman who stole our son's heart."

"We went to the zoo today and there were lions and giraffes and, Mommy, you should have seen the hippopotamus! His mouth is sooo big!"

Kelly clutched her cell phone Saturday evening. When had Elena stopped saying hippotamus? It had been so cute. Her little girl was growing up and experiencing things without her. Things like the zoo, and lots of time with Ian.

"Did you have fun with Sophie and Mr. Ian?" Kelly's own Saturday had been far from entertaining. Even though Good Friday was in the rearview mirror, many of the services needed to prepare a funeral would remain closed all weekend in a town this size.

"I did! And Sophie has her very own bunk bed at her grandparents' house. I slept on the top, and I didn't even fall out."

Kelly's throat closed. "Is Sophie's grandma nice?" Maybe she was really asking what Ian's mom thought of him bringing home a stray. What had he told his parents about her and Elena?

"She is a nice grandma. She came to the zoo, and so did her grandpa. Then we went to Pete's Drive In and had a milkshake. Mr. Ian got me a whole chocolate shake all to myself!"

The zoo and a milkshake sounded better than spending the day with her mom, who alternated between guilting Kelly and crying on the phone with her sister. These few minutes hiding in Lorraine's basement talking to her daughter were the brightest part of the day.

"Mr. Ian wants to talk to you, Mommy."

Maybe the day had brightened even more. Kelly heard distant voices then the Calgary phone clattered to the floor. "Sorry," said Elena.

Ian's deep, rich voice came on the line. "Kelly?"

She leaned back against her pillows. "Hi."

"I sure missed you today. It was strange showing Elena all our favorite places when I really wanted to be in Castlebrook with you. To be there *for* you."

If only he had been. "Elena elsewhere and having a good time makes all the difference." Maybe not all, but a lot.

"My pleasure. You doing okay? When will the funeral be?"

About that. "It will be next Friday. I'm sorry, Ian. I tried to get Mom to pick Thursday instead, but with this being a holiday weekend, we couldn't get all the arrangements made. When out-of-town family insisted on Friday, my mother agreed."

“It takes time to arrange everything. Would you... would you like me to come with you, or will being surrounded by your family be best?”

“Ian...” She choked on his name. How could she say the words she wanted to? Tears flowed down her cheeks.

“It’s okay, sweetheart. Cry if you need to.” He paused for a moment then his voice cracked. “I wish I were there to hold you. I hate that you have to go through this alone.”

She clutched the phone even tighter. “I wish you were here, too.”

“Kelly, I’m putting on my town hat for a minute. Do you need this week off work? You’ve got two days of bereavement leave coming to you.”

“Just Friday,” she whispered. “My aunt will be here Tuesday from Toronto, and she and my mother can handle things all week.”

“Okay. Do you want Elena to come to the funeral?”

“I don’t think so. I know some will say she’s old enough, but I don’t think it’s necessary.” Her voice broke again. “I don’t know how to do this, Ian.”

“I’ll arrange for someone to meet the girls after school and take them to either your place or mine. And — unless you really don’t want me — I’m coming with you. Giving you a ride and being there for you.”

Meeting all her relatives. Maybe that was okay. Ian was a keeper.

Chapter Twelve

"How are you doing?" Ian asked Kelly in a low voice. She seemed to be flagging after the funeral, the graveside service, and now a lengthy luncheon at the church her grandmother had attended.

She cast him a wan smile and squeezed his hand. The thrill that gave him wasn't lessened by the number of times it had happened that day.

"We can leave anytime," she whispered. "I just need to say goodbye to my mom."

He was a fan of leaving the chilly church basement and getting Kelly to himself. Feeling a wee mite daring, he put his hands on either side of her waist and steered her between groups of chairs to where Roberta Bryant and her siblings sat together.

Kelly bent closer to her mother, and Ian feasted his eyes on his beloved, also not for the first time. She looked incredible in a calf-length black dress and a string of pearls she'd said her grandfather had given her for her sixteenth birthday. With blond hair swept into an up do and a bit more makeup than she normally wore, she looked older than the twenty-six he knew she was. While he was honored to escort this version of Kelly Bryant, he preferred the woman in faded jeans and a fitted T-shirt. The woman who was casual, rode a bicycle, fixed tea, and tickled little girls. Thank the Lord they'd had time for all those things this past week.

Roberta's gaze flicked to Ian, and she rose, stretching out both hands. "Thank you for bringing Kelly. It was wonderful to get to know you a little, even at such a sad occasion."

Clasping her hands meant letting go of Kelly. He could probably stand that for a few seconds if it would charm her mother. "My pleasure.

Your daughter is a lovely woman, and I'm honored to accompany her." He'd heard a bit of whispered speculation throughout the day from various relatives. A thumbs-up directed to Kelly from one of her female cousins had caused a grin he'd needed to swallow.

Roberta smiled and air-kissed both his cheeks. "I'll be back in Riverbend next week, and we'll get to know each other better then."

"I look forward to it." Maybe his first impression had been uncharitable. He'd give Kelly's mom the benefit of the doubt. After all, her mother had just passed away. "You'll be back before the girls' birthdays?"

"I wouldn't miss Elena's seventh for anything."

"And my parents are coming from Calgary for Sophie's. I'm sure we'll all see plenty of each other then."

Roberta searched his face then glanced at Kelly, whose baby finger had already snagged his. "That sounds good."

She didn't sound completely convinced, but he could hardly blame her. She'd been so busy with her own mother in the past month it was not shocking she hadn't been able to keep up with his relationship with her daughter. *He* could barely keep up, even with the two-week gap. He knew his parents would love Kelly but, in some ways, it was more important that Roberta find room for Sophie and him in her heart. After all, she lived in Riverbend, not far from Kelly's place.

"Kelly and I are headed out now," he told Roberta. "See you soon." He nodded around the small circle of Kelly's aunts and uncles. "Nice meeting you."

"Drive safely and give my munchkin a kiss for me."

Kelly leaned over and brushed her lips on her mom's cheek. "Will do." She waved at the others then tugged Ian away. "Whew," she whispered when they were out of earshot. "Let's get out of here."

Ian was happy to oblige. Happier still that her finger remained tangled with his as they wended their way to the exit. Once outside, he slipped his arm around her waist.

Kelly turned to face him within the curve of his embrace, giving him the opportunity to lock both hands behind her back. He gazed down into her blue eyes, choking up at their intensity. "You're amazing."

A smile creased her cheeks. "You are more."

Ian grinned but shook his head. "Impossible." He pulled her closer, and she didn't resist, but laid her cheek against his shirt. Then her arms slid around him beneath his suit jacket.

This. He wanted it, every single day for the rest of his life. He knew it with blinding certainty. He rested his cheek against the top of her head, but prickly pins from her bun stabbed his face. "Allow me?" he whispered, lifting his hands.

She chuckled. "Go for it. I'm all done being formal."

Ian released her hair and tucked the pins in his suit pocket before wrapping her tight once more. This time the waves of her hair lay soft beneath his cheek. Much better. "I think this is where you belong," he whispered. Amazing as it was to hold this gorgeous woman, it was equally amazing to do so without two pint-sized matchmakers high-fiving each other around the corner. He couldn't help chuckling.

"What's so funny?" she murmured against him.

He caressed her back and dropped a kiss to her hair. "The girls would have a heyday with this."

Kelly tipped her head back to look at him with dancing eyes. "They would. It didn't take them long to get back in stride, so it's a good thing they're not here."

He bent toward her slowly, giving her plenty of time to send signals. The only ones he needed were her languid-lidded eyes and parted lips. He covered her mouth with his, gently, and tightened his arms around her. If only he didn't ever have to release her again. Of course, a church parking lot might not be the best place to hold her forever. But he could certainly think of a worse place to start.

Ian glanced over at her from the driver's seat of his Jeep. "Want to talk about the girls' birthday?"

This was a place Kelly's misgivings had found a resting place before. "We can talk," she replied cautiously.

His fingers twined around hers against her thigh. "Will you allow me to do something special for both of them together?"

She swallowed, staring down at their hands. What should she say? She hated being dependent on anyone. It had taken her years to create an income she and Elena could live within. But Ian... well, didn't he change everything? *Yes!* But was she sure? "What do you have in mind?"

"You suggested the hobby farm. I looked it up, and it seemed reasonable. I think they'd both enjoy it." He glanced her way then back at the highway. "They have a package deal for up to fifteen kids. Is that enough? We can add a few more, up to twenty total."

"Ian... I don't know." She pulled her hand free and tucked her hair behind her ears.

"Why not?" His jaw tensed, but he didn't look at her.

"I don't know how to give up control," she whispered. He probably knew a bit about that himself.

Ian snapped on the turn signal then swerved into a roadside pullout. He put the Jeep in Park before giving her his full attention. "You've carried a heavy burden by yourself for years."

She bit her lip. "So have you."

"But I was able to finish college before Sophie was born." He ran his fingers through her waves of hair. "I want to make it up to you."

"I-I don't understand."

"Okay, that was a bad choice of words. I know I can't undo your past, or mine either." His fingers found her chin, turning her face toward him. "All I can offer you is a future filled with love and respect."

What did he mean by that? She lifted her eyes and saw his rueful grin.

"I'm bungling this. For right now, I'd be honored if you'd allow me to bless you and Elena with a birthday party." His brown eyes darkened as his fingers fanned across her cheek. "There's more I want to say — much more — but this isn't quite the moment."

She swallowed hard, unable to tear her gaze from his.

"Soon." His eyes promised her the world as he undid his seatbelt and leaned closer, kissing her thoroughly across the console. Time held still, the promise in his words demonstrated in his caress.

Kelly was safe with Ian. Her heart was safe in his hands. "Okay," she whispered when he gave her a chance to breathe.

"Okay what?"

She grinned. "You've forgotten your question?"

"Straight out of my head."

"The birthday party."

"Oh, right." Ian's gaze held hers as surely as did his hands. "I'll take care of everything. Thank you."

She trailed her fingertips across his face. "No, thank *you*."

He caught a ragged breath then touched her lips with his again with a slight groan. "I think we'd better head home."

"You're probably right." All those promises. There'd be time to bring them to pass. She'd been self-contained and patient for the better part of eight years. She could manage a little longer.

* * *

Ian set the Jeep back on the road to Riverbend. He'd come so close to asking her to marry him. She had to know those words had nearly spilled out. But that wasn't a question to blurt out without careful planning, without the perfect ambience. Even so, he could barely think of anything else to talk about, and they still had an hour to drive.

He glanced her way for the millionth time, memorizing her features, imprinting them on his mind. "I don't think I ever asked you what you were taking in college."

Kelly gave a half-hearted chuckle. "I wanted to be a teacher."

"You'd be good at it. What grades?"

"Lower. K through four. Before they get as much attitude and lip as older kids." She shrugged. "Public Works is good to me, though. Decent pay and benefits."

Ian couldn't keep his fingers away from hers, but gave them a squeeze. "Would you go back to college?"

She laughed. "In a perfect world."

Maybe he could make her world perfect.

"I'm okay with reality," she went on. "It looks a lot better than it did for a few years."

"You're welcome."

Kelly gave him a startled glance. "I didn't mean—"

"I know." He couldn't help laughing as his thumb caressed her palm.

"Teasing you. But I hope it's at least a little bit true, even so."

She met his gaze for a second then shook her head and grinned. "Yes, you've helped make my life better, too. Is that what you wanted to hear?"

"Only if it's true." Oh, she was distracting, this one. It was hard to keep enough attention on the road.

"It's true."

"Kelly—"

She put her finger on his lips. "Don't. Today's not the day, remember?"

He caressed her finger with his lips for a few seconds before she removed her hand. This might not be the right day, but it had better be soon. He needed her in his life every day, to wake up beside her and pamper her like a princess.

Chapter Thirteen

Kelly couldn't take her eyes off her daughter as Elena spun in a slow circle at Holiday's Hobby Farm. Elena clutched Sophie's arm. "Look! Baby chicks!"

Sophie grabbed her back. "Horses! Are we going riding, Daddy?"

"Good choice of venue," Mom said to Ian as he nodded at Sophie.

He smirked at Kelly. "This is right up their alley."

Kelly held up both hands and laughed. "You were right. Of course you were." He also knew why she'd resisted... and why she'd relented.

Sophie's grandparents were here, too. They'd come for the weekend to celebrate both girls' birthdays. Ian's mom, Joyce, had been none-too-subtle in making sure Kelly knew Elena's joy in her day was just as important as Sophie's. Kelly had felt welcomed within minutes of meeting both of them. Now her mom and Joyce were thick as flies as they herded a dozen first graders toward the hay-filled wagon that would give them a tour of the farm before the horseback riding.

Ian tucked his arm around her. "Do you know what our mothers are cooking up?"

"Hmm. Should I be worried?"

"I would say… no."

She peered up at him, safe in the shelter of his embrace. "That's not comforting at all."

He grinned, checked the whereabouts of the girls, and dropped a brief kiss on her lips. To her amazement, neither child had caught a glimpse of the many quick moments shared in the past three weeks. Or, if they had, they hadn't said a word. Kelly couldn't imagine that being the case.

"Your mom invited my parents and Sophie over for the evening. She said something about pizza, popcorn, and a movie."

"Let me guess. A Disney princess movie."

"Close." He winked. "Something with horses." He leaned closer. "Nobody invited either you or me, but I'm not overly offended. It sounds like date night to me. What do you say?"

She'd barely seen him without the girls — other than at work — since the day of Grandma's funeral. "I'm pretty sure you can talk me into it. But date night has an official sound. Should I get dressed up?"

The hay wagon pulled out of the farmyard to the squeals of a dozen children.

"Do you want to?"

This wasn't how this conversation was supposed to go. "You tell me."

He nuzzled her hair. "Then how about that pretty skirt with the flowers. It draws out the color in your eyes."

It did? She'd worn it to church a few times and noticed his admiring look. But then, he hadn't worn any other expression around her recently. "Okay. What time?"

"We'll be done here about four, and I think we can get everyone settled at your mom's by five. How much time would you like to get ready?"

She sagged against his arms. "Bubble-bath without interruptions," she said with a sigh.

Ian laughed. "I was thinking of having the date before midnight, if it's all the same to you."

Kelly swatted his arm. "Okay, fine. How long do I have?"

"How about six o'clock?" He rubbed his nose against hers for a second. "I can't wait."

Suddenly, neither could she.

* * *

Ian walked around the Jeep in the parking lot of the Water Wheel Restaurant and opened the door for Kelly. He caught her in both hands as she slid out of the vehicle. In those heels she was much closer to his height.

"How did you get reservations here on such short notice?" she asked, eyes widening.

Should he tell her he'd called it in several days ago? That this babysitting gig by the older generation hadn't been an impulsive decision this afternoon? Maybe later. Now he was too enthralled with Kelly's beauty and charm to make any verbal detours. He laced his fingers through hers. "I have my ways."

"You must."

The May evening was pleasantly warm. A slight breeze lifted off the Sandon River beyond the restaurant, riffling through Kelly's hair.

"We have a few minutes before they can seat us. Come for a little walk." He glanced down at her footwear. "At least, if you can in those shoes."

"Oh, watch me," she said with a chuckle. "Do you want to see all the flowers Vanessa and I have planted out here in the park in the past two weeks?" She swept her hand around the tended flowerbeds.

"They look great, but they're nowhere near as gorgeous as you are." He couldn't take his gaze off her, but that was nothing new. "The hanging baskets around the gazebo are impressive. Those are the same style that will be throughout downtown?"

She nodded. "That's next week's plan."

They strolled toward the gazebo, arms wrapped around each other. When they stood in the very center, he turned and cradled her close. Then he lowered his lips and savored the taste of her.

She clutched him and deepened the kiss.

He pulled away with a groan. "Oh, Kelly. I love you more than I ever imagined possible. I can hardly stand to be apart from you. Will you marry me?" He'd meant to wait until after dinner, but... why? Why, when they had this part of the park to themselves? Why, when more sustenance would come from the answer to his question than from the meal?

Kelly slid her hands around his neck and tangled them in his hair. Her clear blue eyes looked straight into his.

Why didn't she speak and put him out of his misery? Why toy with his heart lying on the line?

"Ian." She stretched to kiss him.

He rested his forehead against hers. "Please, Kelly?"

"I say yes." She swallowed hard, her gaze fixed on his. "I also say, when?"

"Soon," Ian whispered. "The sooner the better." He hated to release her even a smidgen, even for a second, but it had to be done. He reached into his pocket and tugged out a small velvet box.

Her eyes widened. "You planned this."

"Of course I did." He winked and pulled her into his lap on one of the gazebo's benches. "Here, want to see?"

"Um, yes?"

Ian opened the lid and angled it so the sun glinted off the diamond nestling between two smaller emeralds.

Kelly sucked in a sharp breath as her finger slid across the three stones. "The girls' birthstones. How beautiful."

"What do you think?"

"I think yes, Ian. Didn't I already tell you that?" She kissed his nose, which was a bit awkward since she didn't stop looking at the ring.

He pulled it out of its nest and slid it on the third finger of her left hand. Then he raised her hand to his lips and kissed the palm.

"It's stunning," she breathed. "It makes my heart melt you thought of the girls." Then she glanced at him, a glint in her gaze. "There is something wrong, though."

"Does it need adjusting?" He twisted it on her finger. It might be a little loose. "We can take it in Monday."

"That's not it."

"Then what?"

"It looks so lonely. How soon can you place another band beside it?"

The girls had spent the night at Kelly's mom's house. Ian didn't see Sophie again until after church on Mother's Day when the children's church attendees came into the main service and offered each mom a little pot of pansies. Both Sophie and Elena had handed theirs to Kelly, and she'd hugged them both equally, pressing a kiss to each soft cheek.

Now they were down at Riverside Park again with Chinese take-out. His treat for the three moms in his life: Kelly, Roberta, and his own mother. He and Kelly had talked to their parents last night, telling them of their engagement, and asking for their temporary silence.

Roberta, spreading a tablecloth on the picnic table, could barely take her eyes off the sparkling ring on Kelly's finger. Ian's dad winked and mouthed "congratulations" at him.

Ian grinned and held out his hands to his girls. "Let's go for a walk down to the playground while your grandmothers unpack the food."

Elena pouted and crossed her arms. "Mommy won't let me climb the monkey bars in this dress."

He chuckled. "Come on. I have something to show you."

Both the seven-year-olds latched onto his hands before he could save one for Kelly, but the look she gave him over Sophie's head showed she was fine with it. The four of them strolled toward the playground. When he reached the teeter-totter, Ian leaned against it.

"What, Daddy?" asked Sophie.

"I've seen this old playground before," Elena complained.

Ian's eyes filled with the vision of Kelly. He nodded to her, and she squatted between the girls. Then she held out her hand.

Elena tipped her head and examined the ring. "That's pretty."

Clearly she had no idea what it meant.

Sophie looked from the ring to him. "Grandma has a ring like that, but not with green bits. She says it's her wedding ring."

"The green bits are called emeralds. They represent two little girls who have birthdays in May."

Elena's eyes grew wide as she turned to Ian. "Are you going to be my—?" She choked off the word with both hands over her mouth. Her eyes begged Kelly for an answer.

Kelly held up her hand and wiggled her baby finger. Elena hooked hers around it. "I release you from your pinky promise."

Elena whirled and flung herself at Ian so hard he nearly toppled. "Are you going to be my daddy?"

"Would you like that?"

"Yes, because then Sophie is my sister, not just my twin. Right, Sophie?"

Sophie nodded, her eyes fixed on Kelly.

"C'mere, little girl," Kelly whispered, and Sophie walked into her arms.

Ian twirled Elena in a circle, her feet flying out. But each revolution gave him a glimpse of Sophie snuggled up against Kelly. His heart was full. So full.

"What does that ring mean? I want to see it again," asked Elena when he set her down, grabbing her mom's left hand.

"It's a promise," Ian said. "It means I promise to marry your mom and that the four of us will be a family."

"Or else what?"

He frowned. "What do you mean?"

Elena shook her head and plunked her hands on her hips. "What happens if you break your promise?"

"I won't."

"But what happens if you do?" She glanced at Sophie. "Real promises have con-se-kanses. I think you should pinky promise."

Dangerous words. He managed to keep the laughter from bubbling all the way up to his face. "Okay, it's a deal." He squatted down and held up both little fingers. Elena took one, and Kelly the other. The circle was completed when Sophie hooked Elena and Kelly's fingers.

"Pinky promise I will love you and your mommy forever. Okay?"

Elena stared at him. "Or else your baby finger will break, and it will hurt."

"Remember fingers can break other ways, too," Kelly cautioned.

"I'll accept that punishment if I break my promise." His gaze met Kelly's, and a slow smile spread across her face. He leaned over and caressed her lips with his own. Let the girls watch. "But I won't."

"Kissy stuff," said Sophie. "I think they mean it."

The End

A *Riverbend* Romance Novella

Sweet Serenade

Valerie Comer

Chapter One

"Please tell me today was better than the rest of your week."

That might require lying. Carly Thorbergsen rolled her shoulders and shook her head at her cousin. "No wonder Neil Maddrey couldn't find anyone local to fill the position at Base Camp Outfitters. Everyone in Riverbend knew he was an idiot, right?"

Brittany plucked her phone off the table and swiped it on.

"Just the fact you're ignoring me proves I'm right." Carly sighed. "I'll survive until I can find something else." Or move on. That was definitely an option. That's how she and Dad had survived for years. There was always more to see in Canada's west.

"Okay, the man does have a bit of a surly reputation. I'll grant you that. But the job itself sounded right up your alley. Taking tourists out on Sandon Lake in a canoe. Leading day hikes into the mountains. You won't spend much time with Neil once your orientation is done."

Hopefully. Carly crossed the small living room into the apartment's galley kitchen. Good, there was still some of the sun tea she'd made yesterday. "Want a glass?"

"You put honey in that, didn't you? I'll grab a diet cola, thanks."

Because a zero-calorie diet coupled with a gym membership and a jog every day was healthy? Brittany couldn't be more than a size two.

Carly's idea of a good time didn't mesh with her cousin's. Eat healthy and play outside a lot was Carly's motto. Let the chips fall where they may. Which meant sometimes consuming actual chips from actual potatoes. Oh, the horror.

Brittany reached past her for a cola and a container of chicken breasts. "These have been marinating all day. I'll grill them and we can put them over salad. Sound good?"

Carly'd been paddling all day in the hot sun, not sitting in an air-conditioned library. She could inhale an eight-ounce steak and a baked potato without blinking. "Sounds good. Mind if I make myself a sandwich while you cook?"

"Be my guest."

Weren't they past the guest stage? "Hey, I bought some groceries." Even though she was sleeping on the living room floor until she could get her own place. If she stayed in Riverbend.

"I know, I know." Brittany carried a pair of tongs and the chicken to the patio door then stepped out onto the third-floor balcony. "This will be really good. I promise."

Carly didn't doubt it. It sounded great, but not enough. She headed into the kitchen, slathered peanut butter on two slices of sourdough, and followed her cousin out to the tiny balcony. In the distance, the Sandon River flowed southward, curving around the town of Riverbend. Hills crowded the horizon. The locals called them mountains, but they were nothing like the glacier-clad peaks in the Rockies near Jasper. She could make out gaps between the hills where other creeks and rivers joined the Sandon. Farther up the valley lay the lake.

She closed her eyes. Traffic was muted this far from the busier streets. A hummingbird zoomed to the feeder at the neighbor's balcony. The chicken breasts sizzled on Brittany's portable grill. A gentle breeze loaded with the fragrance of mock orange caressed her face. Peace. She could almost taste it.

"A bunch from the church's singles group are getting together tonight. Want to go? Meet some people?"

Carly glanced at her cousin. "Um, maybe? What's the scene?"

"Swimming in the river. Bonfire. S'mores. Guitars."

With every word, Carly relaxed a bit more. "Oh, that sounds awesome. My kind of night out." She had to admit it didn't seem to match Brittany, though. Her cousin would hate to break a nail outdoors.

Brittany shot her a look. "Yeah, it would be. Not that many unattached guys, but what do you expect in a town this size? Sometimes I think I should've gone to college in Calgary or even Castlebrook instead of staying here."

"Why didn't you?"

Her cousin shrugged. “Because Joseph was staying. And then we broke up anyway.” Brittany grinned and arched her perfectly-plucked eyebrows. “But I hear he’s back in Riverbend for the summer.”

“And you want to see him.” Carly drained her glass of iced tea.

“Of course. But my gang often does this on Friday nights in summer. You’ll like them. Just stay away from Joseph. Oh, and forget Reed Daniels. He’s the hottest looking guy and ice cold in every other way.”

Check. And check. “What time is the get-together?”

“You’re seriously into this.”

“Why not? I like rivers and s’mores. Unless all the guys wear pants pulled up to their armpits and taped-together glasses, it should be fun.”

“Evan says bring chips and pop.” Brittany scrunched her nose. “No junk food for me, but I’ll take a few cans of diet cola along.”

Right. Must preserve that size two at all cost.

Reed Daniels leaned against the open tailgate of his pickup, watching his friends jump into the river. Why was he here again? Right, to scope out the competition. He allowed himself a small grin at the thought. Not the other fellows crowding around the girls, but to see if Brittany brought her cousin.

Probably a bad idea. If Maddrey’s new hire was anything like her cousin, Reed would stay clear of her. But, wow, he’d caught a glimpse of a gorgeous young woman out in a canoe with Maddrey the other day. Evan, his business partner, had said she was Brittany’s cousin. Coming to Friday’s bonfire, he’d added, as though he knew everything.

Was it so wrong to want to meet her in person? Probably a bad idea in front of this bunch. They were hungry for blood.

Reed averted his eyes from the deep pool where several couples were wrapped in each other’s arms. Rumors abounded about who’d slept with whom. It made his gut hurt. These were kids he’d grown up with, gone to youth group with, made purity pacts with. Sometimes he felt like the last man standing.

Brittany’s white Mazda picked its way down the dusty road, avoiding the biggest rocks and deepest potholes. She had a passenger.

Reed wiped clammy hands on his navy swim shorts and prayed he wouldn't make a fool of himself as the Mazda angled in among the other vehicles and the doors opened. Brittany's cousin exited the vehicle on the far side, red-gold hair pulled back into a ponytail. No orange life vest now, just a soft green tank top and darker green mid-thigh shorts.

She glanced his way, caught his eye, and smiled. She had the most beautiful, genuine smile he'd ever seen.

He couldn't help the grin that spread across his own face. He'd never started a conversation with a pretty girl in his life. There was a first time for everything.

Brittany glared at Reed and hooked her arm through her cousin's, pulling her toward the river. Her cousin glanced back.

Yep, he was going to do this if it killed him. He sauntered closer. "Hi, I'm Reed Daniels. You must be Brittany's cousin."

She pulled away from the tight grasp. "Pleased to meet you. I'm Carly Thorbergsen."

Her hand gripped his with more strength than most girls. But then again, what man went around shaking hands with pretty girls? Had she noticed the sweat on his palm against her long fingers? His gaze snapped to her face, to eyes that hovered somewhere between blue and green, framed with long lashes that didn't seem heavy with mascara, her face more tanned than made-up.

Brittany leaned close to Carly and whispered something. Carly shrugged as she released his hand. Brittany tossed a plastic grocery bag onto his truck's tailgate on her way past then pulled her tank top off to reveal a bikini. That was one of the problems with this kind of party. A lot of skin. In Brittany's case, a guy could count every rib.

Words. He needed to find some. "So, um, hi. What brings you to Riverbend?" Man, he was tripping all over. This was amazingly unsuave, even for him.

She smiled at him. Amazing smile. "Brittany told me Base Camp Outfitters was hiring, so I applied online. I got the job, and here I am."

His guess had been correct. "I think I saw you with Neil Maddrey out on Sandon Lake in a canoe Wednesday." At 3:41 p.m. near the north shore. He'd sound like a stalker if he said *that* out loud.

Her face lit up.

Oh, man. She was cute enough without that extra glow.

"Not sure if Maddrey mentioned it to you or not, but a grizzly was sighted up that way last week."

She angled a look at him. "A grizz? Not a black?"

Ah, she knew her bears. Good girl.

"It's true we don't see many in this area, but I trust the person who reported it to know the difference. A big silver-tip, he said. Distinct hump."

"Neil didn't say anything, but thanks for the warning. I'll make sure to watch for it." She nodded as though filing the information. "But that was you? In the cedar-strip canoe? I have such envy. Paddling around in a red floating cooler like Base Camp's rentals is almost enough to make me quit my job before I've barely started."

Reed's spine straightened of its own accord. "You like it? It took me months to build." He couldn't keep the pride out of his voice.

Her mouth formed an o as her eyebrows rose. "*You* built that gorgeous canoe?"

"Yeah." The interest in her eyes made him look down at his sport sandal scuffing the dirt on the path. But it was way easier to talk about bears or canoes than about himself. "Cedar-stripping fills winter hours when I can't be on the water."

"A bit of an addict, are we?"

He glanced up again at the teasing tone in her voice. "Just a bit."

"My dad and I used to talk about building one together."

What message was he supposed to get from that? "But something always came up, eh?"

"Like cancer."

"Oh." Now he felt like a heel. "I'm sorry to hear that."

"He fought for six and a half years. For a while we thought he had it beat. Anyway, he's gone now."

Reed searched her face, hoping she could see the sympathy in his eyes. "It must be tough to lose a parent." He still saw his nearly every day. Yeah, he'd moved out of the house—all the way to the apartment he'd built above the boat-building shop on their property.

Her pensive gaze shifted to the river behind him. "Two for two."

Carly's words were so quiet he wasn't certain he'd heard them. "Your mom?"

"Died when I was eight."

"Oh, man. I'm so sorry."

She bit her lip and glanced at him. "Sorry to overload you when we only just met. So, uh, what temperature is the water?"

Reed turned to watch his friends splashing in the deep eddy. Evan climbed up on a rock and cannonballed in. They'd been swimming here since they were kids. Everyone knew where the water was deep enough for a dive. "Pretty cold," he said at last, eyeing her at an angle. "It's glacier-fed. The snow is still melting in the mountains."

"Those aren't mountains." Her eyes gleamed. "Jasper has mountains. These are like little bumps in the ground."

Reed laughed. "Then maybe you'll find the river like bathwater. Jump in and see."

"You know, I think I'll do just that." She tugged her tank top over her head then stepped out of her shorts, leaving her clad in a one-piece racing swimsuit. She tossed her clothes in the back of the Mazda and kicked off her sport sandals. "I notice you haven't been in yet. Bet I'm wet before you are."

Carly sprinted across the rocky beach.

Reed gave his head a shake and took off after her, but she was right. She ran straight up that rock and cannonballed off of it. He was five steps behind her when she resurfaced and shook the water off her face.

"Cold!" she yelped.

He was grinning as he hit the river.

Carly settled on a fallen log near the bonfire. She'd pulled on jeans and a T-shirt once her swimsuit had dried, as had most of the group. Several of these twenty-somethings had been quite friendly. She might even make some real friends in Riverbend. Those had been hard to come by thus far in her life, as often as she and Dad had drifted on.

Evan dropped down beside her, holding out a can of cola.

"No, thanks. I've got water." She lifted the stainless steel bottle nestled by her sandals then set it back down.

"Oh, don't tell me you're one of those." He bent the tab, and the can fizzed.

She stiffened. "What do you mean?"

"Won't drink pop, won't drink bottled water."

"And that's a problem how? Notice I didn't judge your choice." She had, internally, but he didn't need to know that.

He looked at her speculatively.

Yeah, well, she wasn't interested in him, anyway. He was the life of the party, telling jokes nonstop. She preferred being a wallflower. Not a combo made in heaven. Across the fire, a guy sat down with a guitar. His fingers drifted over the strings, but she could barely hear the picking above the chatter.

From the shadows behind the strummer came the haunting melody of a harmonica. She hadn't heard one of those in years, not since she was a little kid.

One of the girls began to sing along with the worship song. Others joined in. Evan added a strong baritone and winked when she did a slight double-take. He grinned at her.

Carly knew this chorus and joined in softly. This was what her soul had needed. She could put up with Neil at work if she had friends who upheld each other this way after hours. She closed her eyes and laid her hands palm up on her knees.

After a few choruses—Carly lost track of how many—the music faded away. In that quiet moment, she knew she'd come home. Riverbend was the right choice, regardless of her job.

Evan nudged her knee. "Hey, want to go out with me tomorrow? See a movie?"

She opened her eyes and turned toward him, but caught Reed watching her from beyond the dancing flames. She stared back for a few long seconds before meeting Evan's gaze. What could she say? "Not this time, thanks." Probably not ever, but that would be rude.

Chapter Two

Reed picked up his guitar and plugged it into the amp. Around him, the rest of the worship band arranged sheets of music and adjusted microphones. No mike for Reed. Instrumentals took all his focus.

Evan stepped up to the lead mike. “Good morning, and welcome to River of Life Church. Please stand and join us in worship.”

Was Carly here? Reed searched the congregation as everyone rose. There she was, beside Brittany and several others from their group. Brittany whispered with the girl on the other side of her, but Carly focused forward. A little grin poked at his cheeks as she recognized him and gave him a discreet thumbs-up.

He fingered an A chord as the first song began. Carly closed her eyes and as she sang.

Was she the woman he’d been waiting for? The thought froze him. He’d been waiting for someone? Of course he had. What man wanted to grow old all by himself? But he needed someone who loved the Lord as he did. So many of the group had drifted in their faith. Sure, most came to church, but more as a way to connect with each other than to connect with God. And since he didn’t play that way, they thought him rigid.

Whoa. He’d better pay attention to the quick chording or he’d fumble. But it was hard to worship while watching a pretty girl. With all the thoughts about her that had churned through his mind since meeting Carly Friday night, centering himself in Jesus this morning was vital.

* * *

The pastor's benediction still rang in Carly's ears when Brittany nudged her.

"Didn't I warn you about Reed Daniels? I caught him staring at you all through the singing. If you're going to date one of my friends, I can recommend someone a whole lot more fun."

Thanks, cuz. Way to break the mood. Carly took a deep breath and turned to Brittany. "Thanks for caring, really. But I'll pick my own dates." As far as she could tell, Joseph was way too smooth. Most of the guys the other night had spent more time looking her up and down than meeting her eyes and actually talking to her.

Except Reed.

"Take Peter, for example. The boy can sing like an angel, but he knows how to have a good time."

"Why doesn't Reed sing into a mike?"

Brittany shrugged and picked up her purse. "Who knows? Probably too shy. Or maybe he squawks."

Carly doubted that. Not the way he played. She glanced toward the platform, where Reed rolled microphone cords. "He didn't play Friday night." What had been the name of the guy with the guitar that evening? Had that been Peter?

"Oh, he played, just not the guitar. He was on the harmonica. Says it's a dying art." Brittany rolled her eyes. "As it ought to be."

Joseph leaned over the back of the pew and whispered something to Brittany. She turned his way.

Carly glanced back at the platform. They'd put nearly everything away, which spoke of experience as a team. Her gaze followed Reed as he zipped his acoustic into a case. What did Brittany have against him, anyway? He seemed to be the nicest guy she'd met—certainly in Riverbend, and probably anywhere else.

Brittany called him hot and ice cold. He was definitely swoonworthy with that thick dark hair grazing his collar. Dark brown eyes that glinted with humor when he'd challenged her to jump in the river. A hint of a dimple in his cute face. She was going to hang around long enough to see that dimple come out to play—at least if he'd talk to her again. The man seemed so shy.

The chilly part? She hadn't sensed that in Reed. Brittany might be right, but she might also be wrong. It would be okay to be around a man who kept his hands to himself. Like Joseph's weren't doing. His hands slid just below Brittany's hips as he kissed her.

In church.

Okay, after church, but still in the sanctuary. Hardly the time or the place. Carly grabbed her Bible and purse and exited the pew at the other end. She'd find her cousin later... or find her own way back to the apartment. Riverbend wasn't that big.

She smiled and nodded at people of all ages as she edged around the crowded foyer to the great outdoors. Wow. Corporate worship was great, possibly even necessary, but give her a secluded lake or a majestic mountaintop anytime. That's where a gal could really feel close to God.

Families crossed the parking lot, little kids dancing as they showed off the projects they'd made in children's church. Cars started up and drove out onto the street. No sign of Brittany yet.

Carly wandered along the sidewalk to a well-tended flowerbed near the building's corner. Sweet fragrance from the blossoms surrounded her as she inhaled. A red pickup with a cedar-strip canoe mounted on a rack was backed up to an open door.

Reed had been leaning on a red truck with an empty rack the other night. This must be his truck. More importantly, this must be his canoe. Narrow strips ran the length of it, the various hues of cedar wood gleaming beneath a coat of Kevlar. Probably a bunch of protective coats. That craft was a thing of beauty with its graceful lines and uptilted bow. A sixteen-footer, if she didn't miss her guess.

No one was around. Sounds from the parking lot dimmed as she strolled closer, gaze fixed on that canoe. She reached up and touched its satin finish.

If only Dad hadn't died before they had a chance to build their own. They'd had so many good times together in their fiberglass seventeen-footer—a better length for all the distance tripping they'd done. So many memories.

She missed him.

Something heavy thumped into the pickup box, and Carly jumped back. Reed's face appeared peering out from beneath the canoe. "Hey."

"Hey. Sorry. I was just admiring your canoe." She dared to run her fingers across the smooth wood of the gunwales.

"Sometime I'll have to take you down the river." A flush seemed to appear on hs cheeks. "I mean, if you want to."

"Oh, that'd be awesome. Neil said something about a few good whitewater sections to run, but he didn't have time to show me last week." Her boss seemed reasonably adept on the placid lake, but she doubted he had the chops for fast water.

"Uh, yeah. Sometime we'll have to do that."

The guy was a mystery. At times he seemed interested in her, but now he had a perfectly good opportunity to set a time for a date—or at least a paddling excursion—and he backed off? Was that the cold her cousin had mentioned?

"There you are, Carly!" called Brittany from the parking lot. "A bunch of us are going to the park. Want to come?"

Carly's gaze snagged on Reed's. It seemed they both waited for the other to respond first. "Sounds fun," she called back.

"Near the grandstand?" Reed looked past her to Brittany.

By her cousin's expression, the invitation hadn't really included Reed. More and more interesting.

"Yes." Brittany could put chill in her voice. "If you're coming, bring something for lunch."

"Will do." Reed gave her a half salute then focused back on Carly. His brown eyes darkened.

She could drown in them, like molten chocolate. Drown and die happy. That was crazy talk. She'd only just met the guy. But it was the beginning. Who knew of what?

"I warned you about Reed Daniels." Brittany grabbed the take-out bag of fried chicken, French fries, and coleslaw from the backseat.

Carly reached in for the jug of tea and colas they'd picked up from the apartment on the way by. "What do you have against him? Is he some kind of abuser or addict?"

Brittany's lips tightened. "Nothing like that."

"Then why? What's the big deal? Just because he's not your type doesn't mean he's not mine." Carly narrowed her eyes. "Or did you have a crush on him and he wouldn't pay attention to you?" Bet anything she'd nailed it. That'd burn Brittany through and through.

"Oh, look! There's Joseph and Peter." Brittany pressed her key fob and the locks beeped. She strode off across the grass.

Carly shook her head as Reed's red pickup pulled into a nearby parking spot. Did she dare wait and walk over with him? Why not? Just because he seemed a bit shy didn't mean she had to pretend she was. She waved at him as he swung out of the truck.

He grinned and waved back as he crossed the asphalt toward her, carrying a paper bag.

"What did you bring?" she said when he neared.

"A couple of sandwiches from Loco-To-Go. You?" He glanced at the drinks in her hands.

"Crazy to go?"

"I think they meant it as a play on local. It's a little deli and bakery beside that mini-mall just off the highway serving locally-grown and sourced food."

"Neat. I'll have to check them out sometime." She lifted the jar of tea as she fell into step beside him. "Mint sun tea."

He nodded but said nothing.

So that left her to keep conversation going if one was to be had. "This is a nice park." Okay, so she wasn't going to win awards for dialogue starters. Since when did a cute guy tie her tongue?

"It is. The town takes pride in its green spaces. They even grow their own flowers from seed in those greenhouses."

She followed the direction he pointed and nodded.

"Not much in them this time of year, though. Everything's been planted out."

"I like it here. It seems like a town normal people live in, not just folks who work for Parks Canada or run tourist-oriented businesses." She was one to talk, here for the express purpose of showing visitors the local sights.

"Tourists keep a lot of wheels greased in Riverbend, too. Yours," he pointed out. "Mine."

"Oh? Where do you work?"

His mouth pulled into something that might have been a grin as he glanced down at her. "I'm part owner in Sandon Adventures with my uncle."

She was supposed to infer something from those words? "What is Sandon Adventures?" It sounded like...

"Neil Maddrey's chief competition. We guide whitewater rafting, kayaking, and canoeing trips. Single and multi-day." He watched her for a response.

Carly pulled her eyebrows into a frown. "That seems like peripheral competition. Base Camp only offers one-day canoe outings and day hikes. Sounds like there should be plenty of room for both."

"You and I might think so, but your boss doesn't look at it that way. All he can see is where the two overlap, and it makes him see red."

"Red like the floating plastic cooler he calls a canoe?"

Reed's full-throated laughter caught Carly by surprise. She glanced up to see his brown eyes dancing above a deep dimple in his left cheek. Oh, man. She was such a sucker for dimples.

"I knew I liked you for a reason." The gleam disappeared from his eyes. "Sorry. Shouldn't have said that."

Had she missed something? Oh, wait. Had he admitted he liked her? As in, *liked?* She grinned up at him. She might have to be a bit more forward than usual to get anywhere with this shy guy. "I like you, too. And not just because you have the prettiest canoe in Riverbend." She waited a beat. "But it helps."

Chapter Three

Carly couldn't get Reed out of her mind. Last time she'd been on Sandon Lake, he'd been out here, too. But there was no sign of a cedar-strip canoe anywhere on the water this morning.

She angled the canoe north along the shore. Her clients, Garret and his tween daughter Drea, wanted the guided tour, and she'd give it to them.

"I see something moving on the bank!" the girl said. "Is that a bear?"

Carly scanned the shoreline. "Nope, much too small. Maybe a beaver, though. Stay really quiet, and let's see how close we can come."

"I've got my phone ready to take a picture," Drea whispered.

If she thought she'd upload that straight to Instagram or Snapchat, she'd be sadly disappointed. Carly would hazard a guess they were a dozen kilometers from the nearest cell phone tower. Just the way she liked it. Out here a girl could see the hand of God, experience some serenity, and get some perspective. Just breathing in the fir-scented June air and feeling the gentle breeze against her face relaxed her. Yet at the same time she felt more alive than ever.

The smooth wooden paddle in her hands could propel her anywhere she wanted to go with only the gentlest tinkle of water droplets dripping between strong strokes. She could pull the canoe up close to wildlife slowly and silently...

"It *is* a beaver! I see the tail!" yelled the girl.

Thwack.

With a smack of its tail on the water, the animal disappeared. In seconds, only a ripple remained.

"The guide told you to be quiet." Garret turned and glared at his child.

"I'm sorry. It just caught me by surprise. I didn't even get a picture." Drea sounded chagrined.

"Maybe if we wait, it will come back up for air," Garret said. "They can't hold their breath forever, can they? Beavers are mammals."

"Beavers don't need to come to the surface to find air." Carly scanned the shoreline before pointing out the telltale signs of construction. "That's its den over there, which has an underwater entrance. No doubt the beaver is already inside, taking a break until we're long gone."

Carly turned the canoe along the shoreline and began to paddle again. "If we're quiet, we may see something else."

"Are there any bears?" Drea asked. "My friends would be so jealous if I saw one."

Reed had mentioned a grizzly sighting at the north end. That would be something. Sure, bears could swim, but, if she kept the canoe at a good distance, there'd be no problem.

"There might be. You never know. Keep an eye out along the bank. You never know what you'll see, a grizz or something else. Maybe some loons or a white-tail, even."

She paddled for nearly an hour, Garret assisting as he could in the bow. He didn't have much previous experience, but he was more help than hindrance. Drea, sitting not far in front of Carly, sank into her life vest like a turtle. Dozing, if Carly didn't miss her guess.

An object loomed at water's edge in the distance, but they were still too far away to make out its identity. Definitely an animal, as uniformly dark as it was. Probably not a bear, though. Wasn't that a bit of daylight she could see beneath it? Long legs, then. Black. It had to be a moose.

"Okay, stay really quiet. Get out your binoculars and focus on that dark spot ahead of us where the waterline meets the trees. See it?"

Garret laid his paddle across the bow and lifted a pair of binos. "A moose..." he breathed, adjusting the eyepieces.

"Let me do the paddling from here on in. It will take a while to get there, but you should get a really good look at it if we don't spook it first."

Drea straightened. "Dad, can I see?"

Her father handed the binoculars back.

"Way cool! But I thought moose had those funny antler things."

Carly shrugged, not that the girl was looking behind her. "Bulls do, but the females don't."

"Oh."

Drea lifted her phone and zoomed in the camera app. It wouldn't be enough at this distance but, if the moose left the scene before they got closer, this might be her only chance.

Carly increased the power of each stroke, keeping the canoe pointed in a straight line. Twenty minutes later, they coasted into the lily-pad-clogged section of the lake where the moose browsed.

"Can we get closer?" whispered Drea.

"This is plenty close enough. She can move an awful lot faster than you'd think."

"What's that in the rushes?" asked Garret quietly.

Carly caught her breath. "A calf moose. Good eye. Do you see it, Drea?" She sculled the canoe sideways half a meter to provide a clearer view.

"Awesome." The girl dragged the word out, her eyes fixed on the sight as she raised her phone and snapped a few more images. "My friends are never going to believe this."

Carly grinned. And that's why she loved sharing the wilderness.

He hadn't seen Carly since Sunday. Was it too much to hope she'd be at the bonfire tonight? If she was, he was going to ask her out. Really. He'd almost done it Sunday but couldn't force out the words. His palms on the truck's steering wheel grew sweaty just thinking about it, but he'd find the nerve somewhere.

It'd been five years since he'd last said those words to a girl. "Want to go out with me?" And he'd regretted it less than an hour into the date. Brittany had expected... Well, he didn't know exactly what she wanted. All he knew was that it had been more than he was prepared to give.

Carly seemed nothing like her cousin. They didn't appear to be close friends, judging by how little they'd talked at Sunday's picnic. Or maybe Brittany steered clear because Carly was near him. Might have even looked like she was *with* him.

Dear God. Reed parked the truck with his friends' vehicles beside the river. *I sure could use some wisdom here. Should I stretch out of my comfort zone for Carly, or should I leave things alone before I get hurt?*

Now that was a crazy prayer. He wasn't afraid of pain. Not physical pain, anyway. He'd broken bones taking chances with his bicycle as a kid and with his kayak three years ago.

Emotional pain scared him more. Other fellows bounced in and out of love every week if the changing couples by the bonfire were any indication. Okay, give the gang some credit for maturing. They were in their mid-twenties now. Changes were less frequent. More like monthly or seasonally these days, with occasional wedding bells. Still, why was he the only one to fear the pain of commitment and breakup equally?

The Mazda parked beside him. His heart clenched and he wiped his hands down his swim shorts as he slid out of the truck. *Buck up, Daniels. How will you ever find The One if you can't even talk to a girl without practically passing out?*

It was so junior high of him. *Here goes, Lord.*

He didn't have to fake the grin once his gaze met Carly's over the top of the compact car. Her face lit up at the sight of him, her beautiful mouth spreading into a generous smile.

Man. He was a goner.

Brittany shot him an aggravated look then elbowed past him on her way to the river. He hadn't been in her way. Would it have killed her to avoid him? But thinking about that distracted him from Carly.

She approached around the back of the car. "Hey."

He swallowed hard. "Hey." Did a man tell a girl how pretty she was? He could hardly think about anything else. "You look great. Did you have a good week?"

Smile lines crinkled around her blue-green eyes that matched her tank top. "I did. I took a few tourists out on Sandon Lake. We've seen a moose and her calf at the north end several mornings."

This he could talk about. "That's a beautiful spot. I haven't been up there much yet this season. Evan and I did a multi-day rafting trip with a youth group from a church in Castlebrook most of this week."

"Oh, that sounds fun. On the Sandon?"

"Yes, further north." He took a deep breath. "Done much paddling in rapids?"

Carly nodded. "Yeah, some."

From the faraway look in her eyes it seemed her mind had wandered. He'd have to get that story from her sometime.

He took a deep breath. Here went nothing. "Want to run the rapids at kilometer fourteen after church next Sunday? They're a lot of fun this time of year." He'd done it. Now it was up to her.

Her face lit up. "Canoe?"

"Or kayak." He dared breathe. "I could nab two of our rentals."

"Oh, man, I'd love to. But if it's doable in open craft, I should try that first. Then I'll have a better idea for work."

Reed's hand reached up to rub the sleek finish of his canoe on the overhead rack. "We'll take the cedar-strip, then."

Carly's eyes shone. He'd like to think a bit of that was for him, not just for his canoe. But whichever way, he'd take it.

She glanced past him to the river. "Going for a swim?"

"Yeah, figured on it." He grinned down at her. "The water hasn't warmed up much in the past week."

She smacked his arm. "Oh, you."

"Hey, don't say I didn't warn you."

"You tried to, but I wasn't listening." Her intense eyes caught his. "I'm listening now."

She might be listening, but he had nothing to say. He wasn't going to be the man who rushed into a relationship with a girl he barely knew. They were going to take this nice and easy and give both of them plenty of room to back away.

Wait. Was her hand still on his forearm? He pulled his gaze from her eyes and glanced down. He watched his own hand come across and rest on top of hers as though it belonged to someone else. A little squeeze. That was all, then he stepped back and broke contact.

Nice and easy, eh, Daniels? Leave room to not get hurt?

Yeah. Tell that to his heart.

Chapter Four

Give me words, Lord.

Reed glanced at the woman in the passenger seat of his truck as they jounced up a mountain road. In the brief time he'd known Carly, he'd figured she was quiet. Introspective. He liked that. But she seemed quieter than he'd expected. Never before had he felt like he needed to be the one to carry a conversation.

"It's sure a beautiful day." Like that. Who talked to a gorgeous woman about the weather? The great conversationalist Reed Daniels, that's who. Yeah, he was pathetic.

"Is this typical for June?"

Well, if she was going to go along with it... "We usually get a lot of rain this time of year. That and the heat get the mosquitoes hatching in droves." Again, like she didn't know.

"At least they're not usually a problem out on the water."

"True." One benefit of paddling as opposed to backpacking. "There's a picnic area up a few kilometers. I figured we could have lunch there. After that it's not far to the put-in spot for the rapids."

Carly smiled at him, her eyes gleaming, probably with curiosity about what kind of picnic a guy like him would pack. "Sounds good."

She had the most stunning smile he'd ever seen. Wide and generous. He'd never spent any time looking at a woman's lips before, but hers deserved some consideration. He shifted in his seat, suddenly uncomfortable. Thinking about lips meant thinking about kissing. And that was crazy. They'd barely met. All his friends figured him to be the slowest mover on the planet. If they could only see inside his brain right now, they'd amend their opinion in a hurry. It was too early to fall in love, for sure, but he was definitely sliding headlong into like.

* * *

Carly watched Reed spread a red-checked tablecloth on the picnic table and set a wicker basket on the end of it. Just when she'd thought she couldn't be more impressed by this quiet man he went all out on something like this. Their first date. Frankly, she'd expected bags of take-out from a drive-through.

He shot her a glance as he lifted two plates from the basket.

"Can I help?" she asked.

His devastating dimple creased his left cheek. "I've got it. Have a seat."

Carly straddled the picnic bench. "This looks really good. Impressive."

Had his face just turned a wee bit pink under his tan? "I didn't make it myself. And besides, it's not really as fancy as it looks. Loco-To-Go offers picnics like this for a deposit." He arranged a sandwich on each plate.

"That's awesome."

Reed gave her an apologetic grin. "Mind if I say grace?"

"Please do."

He ducked his head. "Lord, thank You for this beautiful day and for this great food. I ask for safety on the river today, and thank You for the chance to enjoy Your great outdoors with Carly. In Jesus' name, amen."

Short, sweet, and to the point. She could like that in a man.

Plus good taste in food. The whole-grain bread was amazing and once filled with sprouts and thinly sliced ham and cheese, even better. Sugar-snap peas had never tasted so good. Maybe she'd never had any this fresh before.

But when Reed assembled two strawberry shortcakes from biscuits, a jar of sliced berries, and another of whipped cream, Carly knew she could love this man forever. He slid the plate across the picnic table toward her and handed her a fork. Just the brush of his fingers against hers sent her insides spinning.

His gaze met hers. Eyes such a deep brown, but with a glimmer of something else. A little smile curved his mouth, punctuated by that dimple.

Carly turned her fingers to clasp his, the utensil sliding to the tablecloth. “Reed, thank you. This picnic has been amazing. No one has ever done anything like this for me before.” Not even close.

Reed’s thumb rubbed the back of her hand. “It’s my pleasure. I-I haven’t done this for anyone before, either.”

“Then I’m even more honored.”

The silence stretched between them for several more seconds. Then Reed let go, picked her fork off the table, and handed it back to her. “I think you’ll like their version of shortcake. Give it a taste.”

Her fingers felt chilled where his touch no longer rested. But, yeah. She couldn’t sit and stare at him much longer. She pierced through the layers of the dessert and popped a bite into her mouth. Reed was right. This was beyond amazing.

Reed parked the truck among the trees at the put-in spot. He hurried around the vehicle to open Carly’s door for her, and she rewarded him with a smile from her gorgeous mouth. He needed to stop noticing that.

She slid out of the truck and strolled over to the riverbank. Looking downstream, she shaded her eyes.

Good girl. She didn’t blindly trust his expertise in the canoe but expected to do her part. “Want to walk the trail first and get a feel for it?”

Carly nodded. “Good idea.” Then she slid her hand into his.

Reed’s heart nearly stopped before his fingers tightened around hers. Oh, man. It was going to be a very good thing they’d be sitting a meter or two apart in the canoe, plus they’d be keeping busy if they intended to stay dry. Otherwise he’d be insanely distracted.

He led her down the portage trail, pointing out the rocks they’d need to avoid and places where the water churned beneath the surface. Enough red osier dogwood and taller trees crowded the bank that Carly sometimes seemed unable to see where he was pointing. He found himself with his arm around her and his head close to hers as she followed his finger.

This was kind of a lot like bliss. Her floral scent mingled with the aromas of willows and water. Her red-gold hair was just as soft against his cheek as he'd dreamed about.

He was in trouble, and he didn't want to get out. Forget that whole going slow thing. He liked her, and he was pretty sure she liked him back.

Running the river had been a dumb idea. All he wanted to do was talk to her and hold her close like this. Not exactly like this, but with her gazing back into his eyes, not craning her neck to see the next section of rapids.

Time. They had lots of it. Reed took a deep breath. He was going to spend as much of it with her as he possibly could.

Carly stepped out of his encircling arm and reached for his hand again. For a second their eyes met and the universe stopped turning. Then she smiled. "Looks like a challenging set of haystacks around the bend."

Haystacks. Right. Time to get his head back in the game if he didn't want to spend the afternoon banging into rocks, damaging either his canoe or his skin. "We run this section on the east side." He pointed out the rock formation. "We'll need to back ferry over after that V to nail the chute."

She nodded. "Looks doable. The next section just looks fast. What's after that?"

They walked the kilometer-long portage path and talked through the strategies they'd need for running the rapids.

"Ready to give it a try?"

Carly swung his hand. "Absolutely." She beamed up at him. "I'm so glad God made rivers, aren't you?"

Reed chuckled. This was his kind of woman. "Yep. And I'm also thankful for the guy who invented the canoe. Rivers and canoes are made for each other."

Their eyes caught for a long moment. He hadn't meant to send the message he apparently had. But what was in his heart had surfaced, if only a little. He managed to grin. "Don't you think?"

"Oh, yes." Her voice was barely louder than a breath. "No fighting it."

Chapter Five

Carly pressed her paddle across the bow of the canoe as she stepped in and knelt against the braces. The river looked different from this position than up on the bank, but she was used to that. Dad taught her to read rivers a dozen years ago. This one looked like a good run. She glanced over her shoulder as the canoe shifted.

Reed settled against the stern seat, kneeling rather than sitting to keep the center of gravity low. He flexed his shoulders as he picked up the paddle, and his eyes gleamed. "Ready?"

"Oh, yeah! So ready."

The current caught the canoe in seconds. Carly pried deep on the left as Reed brought the craft in line with the flow. They'd let the river do most of the work, just interfering enough to keep from crashing on the jagged rocks.

Sounded like a plan.

They veered left of the main channel to get past a partially submerged tree then back before the first set of haystacks.

The river filled Carly's senses. The scent of icy water drowned the fragrance of the nearby trees. Water splattered her as it boiled over rocks mere inches away, cooling her skin and pounding in her ears with God's drumbeat.

A pry of the paddle here, a pull there. The bow rose as they entered the chute then lunged downward, taking on a little water before leveling out. Reed knew what he was doing in the stern.

The next set of boulders loomed, and she strained to pull the paddle to her right, seeking the deepest channel. They shot through the rolling water and into the eddy below.

What a rush! She lifted the paddle high with both hands and hollered into the sky. "Yes!"

Above the churning water she heard Reed's answering shout. The canoe slid toward the bank, and Carly drew the bow closer. As soon as it touched the riverbank, she leaped out and held the craft for Reed's exit then looped the towline around a sapling.

She leaped at Reed as he straightened. "That was awesome!"

Wait. She'd jumped straight in his arms, and he'd caught her. Her arms clung to his neck and her legs wrapped around his waist. Oh, man. She hardly knew him.

He twirled her around once, looking deep into her eyes, his eyes mirroring her thrill. Then he set her down and disengaged her arms. "That was a great run." His jaw twitched.

Carly wasn't quite ready to let him go. She gripped both hands. "Thanks so much. I haven't had this much fun since, well, since last summer." But never with a partner like Reed. His expertise made him one of the best she'd ever paddled with. Other than Dad. But this racing heart wasn't only for an exhilarating paddle. It had a lot to do with the man who held her hands with the same ferocity she gripped his. The man with the glimmering brown eyes, the devastating smile, and the dimple that was just now starting to reappear.

"Want to do it again?" he asked.

It was all she could do to not fling herself at him again. "Oh, yeah."

"How are you in the stern?"

Seriously? Carly jiggled with anticipation. "I think I can handle it, but we'll need some weight to keep the stern low." Not that he was all that heavy, but he still outweighed her by probably eight or nine kilos.

"There's ballast in the truck."

"You're on!"

Reed grinned, leaned over the canoe, and hoisted it into the air. He settled the yoke on his shoulders. "Lead the way."

Carly knew better than to ask if he needed a hand with the carry. It was a dozen times easier to carry one alone as he did than for two people to lift and carry. She'd done it herself many a time, but she'd bet her Kevlar craft was lighter than his cedar-strip. Even though his was infinitely more beautiful. She'd rather walk behind him so she could admire the canoe's lines. Really. It wasn't like much of Reed beyond his sport-sandal-clad feet would be visible from the back. But he'd asked her to lead, so she would.

Was it so he could keep an eye on her? The thought warmed her more than the summer sun streaking between the trees.

Ten minutes later he twisted the canoe back to the ground near his truck and flexed both shoulders.

"Sore?"

"A little." He shrugged. "It's early in the season. The muscle memory hasn't come back yet."

She knew all about that. "Here, let me help." She hopped up on a rock behind him and put both hands on his shoulders. In seconds her thumb dug into the knot by his right shoulder blade.

"Ouch." He winced. "You found the spot."

"Uh, yeah. I've met it before." She massaged a few minutes longer then patted his shoulders and jumped down. "That better?"

"Yes, thanks." He sat down on a log. "Where'd you learn to paddle?"

Memories washed over her. "My dad. He wrote adventure books in the off-season, and we canoe-tripped all summer for several years."

"Just you and him?" Reed's gaze studied her.

Carly nodded as she settled beside him. "It was after Mom died. We paddled the North Saskatchewan nearly from the headwaters to Hudson Bay. We paddled the Nahani the summer I was thirteen."

Reed's eyebrows rose. "That's some serious tripping."

Campfires. Mosquitoes. Cast-iron frying pans and canvas tents. Three changes of clothing to match the weather. "It was a great way to grow up." If only Dad hadn't succumbed to the cancer. They'd had so many more rivers they wanted to run. So many more memories to make. Dad had so many more novels he wanted to write.

Reed must've read her mind. "What kind of books did he write?"

"Stories about the outdoors and survival for boys."

"Sounds like the kind of thing I would've enjoyed as a kid. Maybe I even read some of them in between all the playing outside I did in every type of weather."

"He had nine books out." Carly poked at a pinecone with her toe. "I still get a small royalty check from his publisher twice a year."

"That's cool. You going to write books, too? Or maybe you already do."

"Me? No. I can't sit still long enough. And besides, I don't really know how normal kids think. My upbringing was far from average."

"Kids these days are glued to their computer games. If they get outside, it's for organized sports. So few are even curious about God's handiwork." He swatted a mosquito. "They think nature is only about bugs and dirt. They don't get how much more there is out here. How close to God it brings a person."

Carly inhaled the forest air. "I know. I feel closer to God here than in a church building. Creation shows me His love as surely as anything else."

"You shall go out with joy and be led forth in peace."

She glanced at him with a grin. "The mountains and the hills shall break forth before you."

His eyes focused on hers. "And all the trees of the fields shall clap their hands when you go out with joy."

"Isaiah fifty-five. I love singing that chorus." She began humming the tune.

Reed dug into his pocket and came out with a harmonica.

Really? He carried it with him everywhere? As he played the familiar worship song, she reveled in the moment. This would be a memory right up there with the best from her canoeing trips with Dad.

* * *

"Ready?" Reed stood at the canoe's bow watching Carly. This business of letting someone else control his beloved craft was new... and more than a bit terrifying. Everything about Carly was terrifying... and exhilarating.

She stood in a few inches of water with the canoe between her knees. "Go for it."

He pressed his paddle across the bow for balance as he climbed in and settled himself, knees against the braces. As soon as he held the paddle in hand, he felt the shift as Carly pushed off and climbed in. Seconds later they were in the middle of the current, shooting downstream.

Everything looked different from the bow. Upfront and personal. He used his blade to help guide the canoe around the rocks and through the deepest water, but most of it was up to Carly. He could only hope she hadn't puffed her experience.

He began to relax a little as they blasted through the chute. She might not be as familiar with this river as he was, but she knew what she was doing. As long as she was strong enough to pull the canoe out of the current and into the eddy at the bottom.

Carly was plenty strong. The memory of her jumping into his arms would never leave him. Was there a chance this could become something more than a mere friendship? He hadn't known he was looking for someone like her but, now that they'd met, he knew with certainty that he had been. She'd be a match for him in every possible way, loving the Lord and loving the outdoors as he did.

Too late he saw they were a little too far into the current to make that eddy. He hollered and set his paddle into a brace position. He could sense the canoe begin to turn with Carly's strong stroke. Too late. They'd be shooting the next bit of river as well, a section he'd run before but hadn't even shown Carly. Man, he hoped she was a quick thinker.

Carly yelled as they swirled past the take-out, but there was no time to turn and reassure her. No more daydreaming. Reed needed to make every movement of his paddle count to ensure they nailed the next chance to get ashore. Beyond that, the rapids went from Class Two to Class Three, and he had no desire to run them in an open craft. In the kayak, perhaps, but it was a canoe beneath his knees.

With exhilarating speed they careened over several haystacks and rounded a bend. A tree had fallen across part of the waterway since last time he'd run this section, its branches sweeping the river. Reed applied as much power to the paddle as he could, fervently wishing he were in the stern and not the bow. Praying Carly could get them past the sweeper.

Not quite. The tip of the tree tangled the canoe and sent it sideways, where they hit a rock broadside.

The next thing Reed knew, he was kicking to the surface and sputtering for air, still clinging to his canoe. But where was Carly? He frantically searched the turbulent water in every direction before he caught sight of her hanging onto the tree that had swept them into the boiling water.

Reed clung to the overturned canoe with all his strength as the current carried him downstream. He forced himself to think about getting himself and the craft ashore. Only then could he go back and rescue Carly from the undertow of that tree. His legs bashed into a rock under the water, then another. Man, he was going to have some bruises. Hopefully he wouldn't break a bone. For half a second the current stilled, and he shoved the canoe into shallower water with all his remaining strength. His feet found the rocky bottom and dug in as the current twisted, all but wrenching the canoe from his grasp. No. This was his boat, and he wasn't letting go.

After an eternity, he was able to swing it toward the shore and slip out of the current. He hoisted the canoe up on the rocks with strength only God could have given him and clambered up behind it. He looped the towline around a log. If only he could sit down and catch his breath. But not with Carly still in the water.

Reed grabbed the rescue bag with its long rope coiled inside, climbed the rest of the way up the bank, and ran back the way he'd come, jumping over rocks and logs, searching the river for her orange vest. He rounded the bend. She was still out on that tree. He cupped both hands around his mouth and shouted her name.

Her head swung toward him.

Good, she was conscious and she'd seen him. Now how was he going to get to her? The tree she clung to had been rooted on the far bank, and there was no bridge for several kilometers up or downstream. Still, could he really advise her to let go and mimic his own trip? He'd had the canoe for buoyancy. She had nothing to hold onto.

He'd only have one chance to get the throw bag to her. Even then, she was going to swim. Didn't look like there were any options eliminating that.

A limb cracked, and Carly bobbed under the water then back up. Her face was set more with determination than fear. Good girl.

Reed wrapped the tail end of the rope around his fist, wound up his pitcher's arm, and hurled the rescue bag toward her, rope playing out as it flew.

Carly let go of the tree and surged toward the bag as the branch she'd clung to floated free.

He swallowed his panic, forcing his mind to clear and his hands to hold that rope.

She caught the rescue bag and yelped as her body slammed against a rock. He remembered that one with a wince. She flipped herself into a water-skier's ready position. Good thinking. Her feet and bent legs should cushion the worst of upcoming impacts. There'd be a few. No getting around it.

Reed gathered the rope as it slackened, leaping back along the rocks downstream. He had to give her just the right amount of leeway and help pull her in when the channel opened for that split second.

Eternity rolled around again before he knew she'd make it. Seconds after that, she collapsed at his feet against a log.

He jumped into the water, gathered her into his arms, and lifted her to the waist-high rock beside the canoe. "Carly. You okay?"

"Man, what a ride. I don't think I broke anything. Is the canoe okay?"

He kept both arms wrapped around her. "The canoe is fine."

"I'm so sorry I missed that pull-out. I didn't get a deep enough draw at the end of the chute."

"All that matters is you're okay." He held her, rubbing her back.

"I can't believe that happened. You must think me an absolute greenhorn. And then the sweeper caught me off guard. I should have been ready for that."

This had to be adrenaline talking. A bit of hysteria.

Reed did the only thing he could think of to silence her.

He kissed her.

Chapter Six

Reed's lips on hers turned off her words. She'd overturned his canoe, sent him for a bone-rattling swim, panicked him out... and he kissed her?

Carly didn't normally go around kissing guys she'd met only a few weeks before, but this was Reed Daniels. Reed who saw God in creation, who loved the river, who'd let her control his beloved canoe. And look what she'd done to it.

She considered releasing his lips to apologize again, but thought better of it. That could wait. For this moment, his nearness—his comfort—were all that mattered. Carly wrapped both arms around his neck and kissed him back with all her pent-up emotion.

All too soon Reed released her and took a step back. His dark eyes seemed more alive than ever as they searched her face. "I-I'm sorry, Carly. I shouldn't have done that."

A chill that had nothing to do with the icy dunking wound around her heart. "Shouldn't have—?"

"I shouldn't have kissed you." His Adam's apple bobbed, and he looked away. His gaze darted back to meet hers then settled somewhere around his feet.

Understanding seeped into Carly's mind, and with it, a flush crept up her face. "You kissed me to shut me up."

He lifted a shoulder slightly without looking up.

Oh, man. And she'd kissed him back like she thought he really meant it. Like she'd been waiting for him to make a move. Truth? She had been.

"And because I wanted to."

His words were so quiet against the roar of the river she almost missed them, but fierce hope surged again. Maybe she really wasn't to be trusted right now. The adrenaline was still there, close to the surface.

"Reed?" She waited until he met her eyes again then she grasped both his hands. "Thank you."

Reed sucked in his lower lip as he searched her face. "For what?"

For kissing her. But she couldn't say that. "For rescuing me."

A little smile poked at his cheek, but not enough to invoke that deadly dimple. "You mentioned that already."

"I'm not normally into that whole damsel-in-distress thing."

"Most wouldn't think of me as a knight in shining armor."

Carly leaned forward and brushed her lips across his. "I will always think of you that way." She heard his breath hitch as she pulled back. "Thanks."

Reed removed his hands from hers and, looking at his canoe, ran his fingers over its wooden strips. "Maybe we should head back to the truck."

"Probably a good idea." Carly swiveled on the rock and drew her legs up under her. She inhaled sharply. Oh, the pain. Her legs felt like they'd been through a blender. She peeled off her life vest and tossed it into the open canoe beside her.

"You okay?"

"I think so. Just battered. But no more than you, I'm sure." After all, he'd swum the rapids, too. The sight of him clinging to that canoe, bouncing from rock to rock away from her, was permanently etched in her brain.

She rolled to kneeling then to standing and looked down at her legs. Some abrasions and cuts, but no blood to speak of. Bruises would be sure to surface within a day or two.

Reed, still standing on a lower rock, brushed the side of her left knee. "I bet that one hurts."

His touch tingled.

"Honestly, they're all the same right now. I'll let you know tomorrow."

He angled his head and looked up at her. "You'll still be talking to me tomorrow? After all this?"

Carly frowned. "Why wouldn't I be?"

"You'll never think of me without reliving getting caught in the sweeper. You'll have nightmares from that."

She needed him at eye level. Wincing, she sat back down. Ah, the perfect height. "Reed, I won't have nightmares. These aren't the first rapids I've swum. I'm pretty sure they won't be my last." She searched his eyes. "I'm a river rat from way back, remember? I'm not saying that ricocheting off rocks with my bare legs was my favorite part of this afternoon, but it's inevitable sooner or later unless a person never ventures into dangerous territory."

Carly was in dangerous territory right now. "Life is full of risks. Some people sit in their recliners, eat chips, and watch other people do things on TV. I'm not that kind of person. I'm a doer, not a watcher." Somehow their hands were gripped together. Had she reached for him, or had he taken the initiative? She pulled him closer, against the rock between her knees. "Reed, life is worth a few risks, don't you think? Isn't that when we know we're truly alive?"

She wasn't talking about the river anymore. Had he noticed the shift? She moved her hands to his shoulders. When he didn't resist, she slid them all the way around and held him against her. Gently. Loosely.

A few seconds later his arms encircled her waist where she sat, and he rested his forehead against her shoulder. "You might not have nightmares," he murmured. "But I will. I was struck with terror that the undertow of the sweeper would... would pull you right under. That I'd lose you before I even really knew you. I promise you I'll wake up in a cold sweat more than once in the next week or two."

Carly rested her cheek against his damp hair, allowing one hand to play with the tapered edge on the nape of his neck.

Reed's grip tightened. "Carly."

She smoothed the strands of hair. Would he kiss her again?

"Carly, I—" He tipped his head to meet her gaze from mere centimeters away.

Her breath caught on the emotion in those deep brown eyes. "Yes?"

"I-I like you. I like spending time with you. A lot." He swallowed hard, and his hands moved against her hips. "I'll be really honest. I want to kiss you again." His gaze flicked to her lips. "But I need to wait. I respect you too much. I need to know what we're feeling isn't just relief at surviving that dunking with little more than scrapes and bruises."

She nodded slowly. A thousand thoughts tumbled through her mind. She was pretty sure her attraction to him had little to do with the river, but he was right. So many guys would just take advantage of the situation. Respect was kind of nice.

Although she could really do with another kiss.

Reed watched Carly's face. Had he said too much? Scared her off by saying he wanted to kiss her again? Because, man, he was desperate to, and if he stood here much longer with her fingers in his hair and his hands pressed to her hips, he was going to do it, no matter what he'd just said.

He pulled in a deep breath and stepped back, releasing her. "Can you give me a hand hauling the canoe up to the portage trail?"

Carly nodded. "I can do that." She clambered to her feet, wincing.

He hated that she hurt. Hated that it was his fault. He tossed his life vest into the canoe. The beauty had a few more dings than she had a few hours ago.

Carly lifted the bow, and Reed hoisted the stern. They set the canoe on a higher set of rocks, then again. The third time, they rested it on the riverside trail. Reed rolled the canoe onto his shoulders with one well-practiced swing. Oh, man. He was going to feel those impacts every step back to the truck.

"You okay?" asked Carly.

He pushed a grin to his face. "Close enough."

"I can carry it at least part of the way."

"After what you went through? I don't think so."

"You went through the same thing. I bet some of those rocks have both of our DNA wedged in their tiny crevices." At least she'd started walking while she argued.

"I had the canoe for buoyancy. You had nothing."

"I'm not sure that saved your shins any."

She was probably right. But it was his canoe. He was able to carry it, and he would.

"I've portaged a canoe before. Plenty of times."

"I'm sure you have. Tell me about paddling the Nahani." Anything to get her talking about something else. Anything to take his mind off watching the back of her as she hiked the trail ahead of him. Thankfully, she'd slung a life vest over each shoulder, obscuring her curves. He didn't need to see them to remember them.

"I was thirteen that summer. Dad wasn't one for guided tours or anything like that, but we caught up to a group led by Paul Mason. Have you heard of him?"

Paul Mason. Paul Mason. Reed shook his head then remembered she couldn't see. "I don't think so."

"His father, Bill, wrote several books about canoeing and wilderness tripping. They were kind of my dad's bibles. Dad and I watched their instructional videos over and over when I was young. Anyway, it was a real honor to meet Paul. We paddled with his group for a few days, through the canyons."

"It must have been amazing."

"Yeah." She fell silent for a few minutes.

Reed watched her walk. Already her green shorts looked dry. She didn't seem to be favoring one leg over the other, though she was breaking no speed records as she'd done on their previous carry. Somewhere in the current she'd lost the tie holding her braid. Now her red-gold hair fell tangled against her shoulders.

They passed the eddy where they'd taken the canoe out on their first run.

"The mosquitoes on the Nahani were horrific. But we left the fly off the tent lots of nights to watch the aurora borealis."

"We don't see the northern lights often this far south." Reed's shoulders ached with the weight of the canoe, and he shifted it slightly. No way was he going to call a halt and have her insist it was her turn to pack it. A girl—a woman—would never carry a canoe on his watch. Not while he was able.

"Strike one against Riverbend." Carly chuckled. "Maybe I'll have to move north again."

"I've only seen them in color once, when I was a kid. Evan and I lay out on the trampoline and watched the skies dance." Reed allowed the memory to ripple over him. "After that, you couldn't convince me God didn't exist."

She turned and glanced at him. "I hear you. Nature is so amazing, but there isn't anything quite as enchanting as the northern lights. The reds and greens, all dancing together to a music all their own. One night they covered most of the sky, coming together above us in an apex. I closed my eyes and listened to them crackle."

Reed had never seen them like that. Never heard them at all. "If you move north, I'm coming, too."

The words hung in the air.

"Thought you were a Riverbend boy, born and bred." Her voice carried a hint of teasing.

Whew. She was going to let that slide. "It's true. But Canada is a big country, and I haven't seen much of it. What you're describing is something I've longed to experience since that night when I was ten."

They entered the parking lot, and Reed leaned the canoe against the rack on his truck. He flexed his shoulders, unable to stop himself.

"Let me." Carly stepped behind him and kneaded his shoulders, once again going straight for the tender spot.

The cure was as painful as the knot, but he endured the massage for the delight of feeling her hands on him. After a moment, he turned and slung one arm around her. "Thanks."

"You're welcome." She hugged him back, turquoise eyes looking into his.

Why had he said earlier he wouldn't kiss her again? All he wanted was to gather her against him and kiss her senseless. His words, however, had been true. He wasn't a man who went around kissing girls. He never had been. Before he kissed Carly again, he was going to know for sure she was the woman for him.

He was pretty sure that time was coming.

Chapter Seven

Neil's already sour face deepened into a full-on frown when his gaze fell on Carly's legs Monday morning. "What happened to you?"

She'd thought about wearing long pants to work, but it was well over thirty degrees Celsius. Way too hot for covering her legs, especially if she was out on the water with clients. She tried for a casual shrug. "Took a spill."

"Off what, a roller coaster?"

In a manner of speaking. "Not exactly. What's on the agenda today?"

Neil's arms crossed over his chest. "What happened?"

He wasn't going to let it go. "I found myself on the wrong side of a canoe. I'm fine. Really." Carly fingered the stack of brochures on the counter of Base Camp Outfitters.

"Where were you? Don't you know you should have a guide when you're running a new river?"

"Yes, I had one."

Neil shook his head. "Someone wasn't paying attention."

Carly's fuse was ready to blow. "Neil, it was my day off. Today I am here, at work, ready to get started, and well able to do my job." She turned her back to him as she rounded the counter. "What do I need to know?"

He glowered at her. "You've got a middle-aged couple for a tour of Sandon Lake at ten. I hope they'll believe you can keep them on the inside of the canoe. The looks of you doesn't inspire much trust at the moment."

Carly gritted her teeth and smiled. How was Neil at reading the rest of her expression? "Pretty sure no one will go swimming in the lake unless they want to."

"See to it."

Good grief. Like she had a magic wand. Even Neil's plastic tubs were tippable. More so than a good canoe, actually. Carly remembered trying to dump her parents' Clipper with a friend when she was seven. It'd been unbelievably difficult, but they'd finally succeeded. Then Dad had made them bail the water out. She'd never tipped a canoe on purpose since.

Back to her boss. "Anything else on the agenda today?"

"Yes, you have a hike with four people at two o'clock. Remember Miner's Rock?"

"Uh, yeah, but we didn't hike all of it last week."

Neil shrugged. "It's well-marked. Have a look through the brochure at the map and historical info, and you'll be good."

The same brochure the tourists had access to, no doubt.

"There are some First Nations' pictographs just past where I took you." Neil shoved a printout with diagrams on it across the counter. "The drawings are faint, and who knows what, exactly, they were actually trying to draw? But tourists love that kind of thing."

Carly nodded. What else could she do? It's not like she had time to run the trail. The lake tour wouldn't end until noon. Maybe she could grab a sandwich from Loco-To-Go and try to get at least as far as the pictographs during her break.

Her thoughts drifted to Reed like a compass swung north. He'd said he'd text her tonight. She took a deep breath and exhaled. He was definitely something to look forward to.

Reed found himself downtown at five-thirty. He usually avoided Riverbend's core as he would a rock in the river, but not today. He tried to convince himself that he'd only needed to swing by the bank for some cash, but that didn't explain why he'd parked the truck several blocks away and nearly across from Base Camp Outfitters. From here he could see both front and back doors as well as the parking lot. He realized he didn't know what kind of vehicle Carly drove, so he couldn't be certain she was inside.

A few minutes later the back door opened. Neil came out and held the door for a middle-aged woman and Carly.

Reed's heart sped up. Texting. He'd said he'd *text* her, not stalk her. But he couldn't let more than twenty-four hours go by without seeing her. Even from here the bruises on her legs were visible. He had a matching set.

Neil locked up and headed for his pickup. The woman got into a car. Carly took a few steps alongside the stone building before noticing him.

Was it his imagination or did her face light up as their eyes met?

Maddrey drove out of the parking lot and stopped in the middle of the street beside Reed. "What are you doing here? Spying?"

"Nope. Not a bit of it." The truck blocked Reed's view of Carly.

Neil's eyes narrowed. "If you think you're going to steal my new employee, don't even get started."

Reed stared at the older man. "Steal her?"

"She's *my* hire." Neil jabbed his thumb against his own chest. "Stay away from her."

Carly rounded Maddrey's vehicle and crossed to Reed's truck. "Neil, you don't own me after hours."

The man's eyes narrowed. His mouth opened and closed a couple of times with no sound.

Reed would not grin, though it took all his self-control. "Like Carly says, she's her own person. She's your employee. After hours, she and I are friends." He flicked a glance at her, wanting to gaze at her longer in the worst way. Hopefully once he'd gotten rid of her boss.

Neil mumbled something about consorting with the enemy before peeling away.

Reed's full attention swung to the beautiful woman standing just outside his truck window. "Did you walk to work? Can I give you a ride?"

She gave him a slow smile. "I'd like that, even though it's not very far." She rounded the truck and climbed in the other side.

Man, he should have jumped out and opened it for her. He'd totally missed a great opportunity. He knew where Brittany's apartment was all too well, but he didn't want to drop Carly off in under five minutes.

Should've had a plan, Daniels.

"Uh, want to get ice cream and go to the park for a bit? Or did you have something else..." He allowed his words to trail away.

"Sounds good. My cousin won't be home for another hour." Carly grinned at him. "Not that she has any more right to tell me what to do than Neil does."

Reed scratched his neck as he turned the key in the ignition. "About that."

"Don't worry about it. He's been a bear all day. It was just one more tangent for him to go on."

"It's none of my business where you work. I'm not trying to get you to come work for us." He shoulder-checked and put the truck in gear.

"Is that a possibility?"

He shot a look across the console. "Is what?"

"Guiding for Sandon Adventures instead."

"Uh, we don't have any openings right now." But wouldn't it be something, working together? He'd be tempted to fire Evan just so he could. In half a flash, his future stretched out before him, full of adventures with Carly in his bow with several tots in the canoe between them.

Steer in those thoughts, Daniels.

"I wasn't really asking." Carly stared out the side window.

He'd blown it. "Tell me about your adventures today."

"Took a couple out to the lake this morning for a paddle. No moose, though."

"No grizzly either, I take it."

"No." She turned to look at him. "You were serious about one being in the area?"

"That was a while ago. No one's reported seeing it again."

He parked on the street by the black and white awning of Glacial Creamery then hurried around to open the truck door for her. He wasn't going to slip on that one again. Especially not when he saw the smile curve her lips as she took his hand, not releasing it as they wandered toward the display window.

She pointed at chocolate ice cream embedded with bits of brownies while Reed chose maple walnut.

"Want to walk to the park? It's not far." Reed handed her the waffle cone with two chocolate-loaded scoops.

"I've love to." She fell into step beside him.

He couldn't help but notice she held her ice cream cone in her left hand. Was it too daring to take her right in his own? New territory for him, this whole dating thing. He'd always figured he'd get married someday and have kids, but then he'd realized that required talking to girls long enough to find the right one. That had been a challenge since before puberty, and turning twenty-five hadn't tipped the balance.

Feeling like his canoe was poised at the top of the chute—and him wearing no life vest—Reed snagged Carly's fingers with his.

She rewarded him with a grin and a slight squeeze before taking another lick of her cone.

Reed ran the chute in his mind's eye and did a victory salute with his paddle at the bottom. *Please, Lord, don't let me do something stupid and wreck this friendship.* This new friendship he hoped would turn into more. He wasn't done running the river yet. He hoped he never would be.

Carly felt like a brazen woman as a flush stole up Reed's tanned neck. So many guys wouldn't think twice about holding a woman's hand, but, to Reed, it obviously was a big deal. He'd apologized for kissing her yesterday, but hadn't made it sound like a negative, even so.

"Thanks for coming by after work. I wasn't looking forward to a lonely evening at the apartment watching so-called reality TV with Brittany." She swung their joined hands a little, just to catch a glimpse of them in her peripheral.

"Me either. I mean I don't like to watch TV when I could be outside. I didn't mean I watched it with your cousin."

How cute was his blundering? Carly nudged his arm with her shoulder. "No?"

He met her gaze, and his fingers tightened around hers. Those deep brown eyes held untold mysteries.

For a second Carly forgot to breathe. Then a drop of ice cream dribbled onto her hand. She sucked in a deep breath and ran her tongue around the edge of the cone.

Reed's eyes watched as though mesmerized.

She nudged him again. "Yours is dripping, too."

He seemed startled as he lifted his cone and looked at it. "You're right."

"Of course I'm right. Don't forget."

"I'll keep it in mind." His grin returned, and so did that dimple. He turned his attention to his ice cream.

Right. They'd been walking. Carly tugged him into motion again. A few minutes later they wandered onto a paved walkway in Riverside Park. Rose bushes bloomed all around the crisp white gazebo, and well-tended flowerbeds lined the walkways with petunias, marigolds, and alyssum.

Shouts of happy children sounded from nearer the river. Carly pointed. "What's going on over there?"

"Riverbend's newest attraction. Swimming ponds."

"You mean outdoor pools?"

Reed pulled her in that direction. "Not exactly. These aren't chlorinated and pristine." He grinned. "You could say the river runs through them."

"This I have to see."

And a few minutes later, she did. A little waterfall tumbled into a large round pond, a sandy beach reaching well beyond the water level. Another manmade stream tumbled into a second pond and from there into a third, where the water returned to the river beyond.

"Amazing."

Reed leaned closer, pointing. "The top one is the shallowest, and the bottom one the deepest."

Which would explain why the top level was full of parents knee-deep in water pulling toddlers on floatie toys. And why the pond farthest away had tween boys engaged in a battle of epic proportions with water guns. She narrowed her eyes as she scanned more closely. "No lifeguards?"

"Didn't you see the posted sign? Use at your own risk. Riverbend assumes no liability for anyone using these ponds."

"I think I'd rather swim in the river, myself."

Reed's grip on her hand tightened. "That could be arranged."

Carly nestled against him, pulling their joint hands behind her. By the surprise on Reed's face, he hadn't expected her ploy. They stared at each other from mere centimeters apart. "Want to?" she whispered at last.

He swallowed hard. "Maybe not tonight."

Chapter Eight

"You're a million miles away." Evan sculled his canoe closer to Reed's.

Reed blinked, bringing the tourist in his bow back into focus. Paying customers should get his undivided attention. What he wouldn't give for a few river-rafting gigs right now, though. There'd be no time to daydream about Carly while riding a flexible bronco down the river.

"You been seeing Carly?"

He shot a furtive glance at his buddy. What would he see? Mockery? Jealousy? No, only mild curiosity. That was a help. "Yeah. Some." Every evening after work all week.

Evan chuckled. "You've got it bad."

Reed shrugged, dug his paddle in harder, and pulled away from Evan. This was all so new. So unexpected. What did he really know about Carly? She'd lost both parents, had a lot of experience canoeing, loved the outdoors, followed Jesus. Oh, yeah, and they shared some radical chemistry.

It was the chemistry that scared him. It pulled him out of his shell and made him think he was invincible. But stuff with girls could flip a man into churning icy water in no time flat. It was hard to remember when she gazed at him trustingly with those sparkling blue-green eyes and smiled at him with that tempting mouth.

Reed shouldn't have kissed her on Sunday, but she'd been in shock and the kiss catapulted her out of it... and slung him in. He wasn't sure the trade-off was worth it. She'd have eventually regained control, and he wouldn't have been left with the memories of her lips under his.

"This is so peaceful," one of his canoe's inhabitants murmured.

She wasn't privy to the inside of Reed's head.

* * *

Friday at last.

Carly couldn't quite wrap her brain around why Reed had said he wanted to go swimming, but they hadn't headed to the river any evening this week. Instead, they'd wandered the park for hours, kicked water at each other in the shallow ponds, and enjoyed a couple of picnics from Loco-To-Go.

He obviously wanted to spend time with her. Was obviously as attracted to her as she was to him, but something held him back. His words after their dunking last weekend filtered through her mind. How could a man say he respected her too much to kiss her?

She'd met guys that could have respected her more, but that was in her past.

Last week, Reed seemed to make sense. Sort of. But now, nearly a week later, he still side-stepped—sometimes literally—her efforts to snag another kiss. Even a brief one. But she wanted more than that.

Carly glanced at Reed across the console of his truck cab as he maneuvered the vehicle around the deepest potholes on their way to the swimming hole. She'd count this more of a victory if it were just the two of them, but the whole gang was meeting at the river. Brittany was ahead of them riding with Joseph. She'd been out with him a lot lately.

All Carly cared about was Reed. It wasn't that she wanted to push him too far, but kissing didn't have to go too far.

He looked so good tonight... not that that was any different from any other evening. Short dark hair she'd love to run her hands through more often. A chiseled jaw. A slim physique, but that was misleading. She knew the strength in his wiry muscles.

Reed glanced her way, and a smile curved his mouth upward until that dimple appeared. His gorgeous eyes glimmered, and he laid his right hand palm-up on the console.

See? There had been progress. Carly slid her hand into his, and their fingers tangled together with a strong grip. Maybe taking it slow was okay, so long as they were moving forward. There couldn't be anyone else in his life, the way he looked at her.

The truck lurched, and Reed withdrew his hand. “Sorry. I guess I should be paying more attention to the road.”

She grinned back. “Maybe. So will tonight be like the other times?”

“Mostly. With maybe one difference.”

Carly tipped her head to the side. “Oh? What’s that?”

He shot her a dimple-filled smile. “I’d rather you sat beside me than beside Evan.”

“Um...” She tapped a finger to her jaw as though it required a great deal of thought. “That could possibly be arranged.” She filled her gaze with his face. “So you don’t mind if everyone sees us together?” Probably word had already reached the group. Carly was pretty sure Brittany couldn’t keep a secret to save her life.

“I don’t mind a bit. What about you?”

Carly shook her head. She reached for his hand again, but the tires hit a deep rut and required his attention. She waited a second, but he didn’t look at her. “I do have a question, though.”

“Oh?” He glanced over, eyebrows raised, then back at the road.

Her heart hammered. “Does this mean... we’re a couple?” Man, she wasn’t used to being this brazen.

Reed’s jaw flexed as he swallowed. A moment later the truck veered onto the grassy verge. He shifted into Park and turned to face her, brown eyes searching her own as his hands stretched toward her.

She wasn’t launching over the console without knowing that’s what the invitation was for. She placed her hands in his, and his thumbs rubbed over them.

Oh, the intensity in his eyes. “Carly, this is such new territory for me. I’m sorry if I’ve been sending you mixed signals. That’s never been my intention.”

What was she supposed to think? Carly bit her lip but kept her eyes on him. That’s how she noticed his gaze slid to her mouth, but only for a second.

A sideways grin pulled up his dimple. “Carly, going out together sounds so... so high school. But I do like you.” He swallowed hard. “A lot. I’m just not a man who goes making promises he can’t keep. I value you far too much for that. More than I’ve ever cared about a woman before. I'd like to keep moving forward, praying about our relationship and letting God lead us."

Her hands were going to be numb for a week if he tightened his grip anymore.

"I don't know what your experience has been in... in love. In dating. I'll be the first to tell you I haven't ever been attracted to a woman. Not like this." So much more came through his deep brown eyes.

"I've dated quite a lot." She grimaced. "But nothing remotely serious in the past few years. As for the attraction thing, yeah. You're something new for me, too."

He untangled one hand and reached for her face. Cupped her jaw.

Carly leaned into his hand. It was too much to hope he'd lean that little bit further and kiss her but, for now, she had her answer. She could be patient, knowing he cared about her, knowing he wanted to be sure. That was admirable, really.

Reed's fingers caressed her cheek.

The honk of a passing SUV broke the spell. A girl leaned out the passenger window and waved, grinning.

"Guess everyone will know now, for sure." Carly winked.

His slow smile squeezed her heart. "Guess so."

* * *

Reed sat on the ground near the fire, leaning against the log between Carly's knees. He reveled in the brush of her legs against him, of her hands massaging his shoulders. She must have figured out the strength of her thumbs, because she wasn't digging in as deep tonight. More like lazy circles.

He'd kept her close to his side while the gang dived and splashed in the swimming hole, and received furtive winks and thumbs-up from some of the other fellows. He didn't much care whether they approved or not, but at least they'd respect him and not try to push between him and Carly.

Across the fire, Peter began plinking on his guitar. Eli challenged him a moment later with Dueling Banjos. The segues rolled back and forth between the two guitars with increasing speed until everyone was laughing.

Reed leaned back against Carly and closed his eyes as the music headed into a set of rousing praise choruses. His fingers itched for his harmonica, but he didn't want to move. Didn't want to leave the comforting awareness of Carly's nearness.

She sang along softly with about half the songs, probably the only ones she knew. Her pleasant alto washed over him, adding to the ambience of the campfire's crackle.

He never wanted this evening to end. How much more perfect could it be? They'd openly acknowledged their attraction to each other and been recognized by the gang as a couple. The cold river had washed away the heat of the day.

Next to Carly, Evan cleared his throat. "Anyone have something they'd like to share? What's God been teaching you lately?"

Peter shifted seamlessly into a backdrop of fingerpicking.

"God's teaching me patience." That was Steph from the worship team. Had Carly met her yet? "Used to be I wanted patience right now, you know what I mean?"

Several chuckles sounded around the fire. Carly's hands stilled on Reed's shoulders.

"But the more time I spend in the Word, the more I realize God's got it. I don't need to worry about stuff and try to make it happen."

"I totally get that," Eli said. "I wanted to move back home in the worst way. Well, not with my parents, but you know what I mean. Back to Riverbend. This place really grows on a person."

Carly's fingers tangled in the hair at the base of Reed's neck. He felt the warmth of her breath as she leaned closer. "It sure does," she whispered.

He tilted his head all the way back into her lap and looked up at her in the light of the fire.

Carly touched his face as her gaze locked on his.

His gut tightened. What had Steph said about patience? Reed didn't want patience. He wanted to gather Carly up in his arms and kiss her. He wanted more than that. A lot more.

Evan began singing *While I'm Waiting.* As the songwriter said so poetically, there were many things to do while one waited. Keep serving God, keep moving forward... but still waiting.

Reed reached up and touched Carly's face, hoping she could see the promise in his eyes. She knew why he was holding back. He didn't want any regrets between them. No regrets of any kind.

Several of the group members sang along as Peter and Eli played, fixing John Waller's words in Reed's memory. What was Reed going to do with his life? Would Sandon Adventures and building canoes provide enough time and a steady income for a family?

He searched Carly's face as she stared into the fire.

Was he crazy to have such thoughts? No. Better to think things through before kissing her. Before making promises he couldn't keep.

"Hey, Daniels!" called Peter. "Got your harmonica along tonight, or are you just gonna listen to music the rest of us can't hear?'

A few people snickered.

Thankfully no one could see the heat he felt rising in his cheeks as he straightened—but not before catching Carly's little grin.

"It's in the glove box in my truck."

"Lemme get it for you, dude."

A minute later his harmonica dropped into his lap. Maybe the music in his head would come out where he could share it with everyone.

Especially Carly.

Chapter Nine

"Can't believe it's July already." Carly angled a glance at Reed. How could this man possibly look better every single time she saw him?

He grinned down at her and tightened his fingers around hers. "It's been nearly a month since we met."

Her heart skipped a beat. Twenty-six days, to be precise. It seemed like much longer. She'd never been more comfortable around a guy. Well, more comfortable might not be the right term. He also unsettled her like no one else ever had.

On how many of those twenty-six days had they spent the evening together? Wandering the park, taking his canoe out to the lake, or hanging out with the group? Most of them.

Now Carly squeezed through the crowd at the farmers' market, clinging to Reed's hand. "There must be eighty vendors here. They've got everything."

He leaned closer so she could hear him. "The Sandon Valley is one of the few pockets of agricultural land in the interior of BC. We do grow practically everything. Haven't you been to the market here before?"

She shook her head as they found an eddy in the stream of people. "I've worked Wednesdays and Saturdays when the market is on, but I didn't know what I was missing."

"Nice of Neil to give you Canada Day off, and handy it's a Wednesday this year."

She swung Reed's hand, barely missing the head of a kid dashing by, hot on the trail of who-knew-what. "He's just too cheap to pay me double time to work on a holiday. We had requests for tours today." She eyed Reed. "Didn't you guys?" Sometimes it was weird knowing he worked for the competition. *Was* the competition.

"My uncle has no trouble saying no. He's on the committee that organized the Canada Day events."

"It looks like they kept busy with their planning then. The day's agenda looks jam-packed."

"And for that we need sustenance." Reed winked and grinned.

That dimple. She reached up and slid her finger across the crease of it. The crowd drifted away in a gray fog.

Reed's intense eyes burned into hers for a long moment and his fingers tightened their grip on hers. Then he blinked and broke the spell. "Yellow Bus has great food. Hungry?"

Carly swallowed hard and looked down. What had just happened there? "Sure. Sounds good." Even her voice came out a little shaky.

She'd wanted to trace that dimple for the longest time. Probably twenty-six days. Why had she gone and done it here on the edge of a crazy busy farmers' market, with live music blaring over the crowd's chatter and a million jumbled aromas swirling past them? Where half the population of Riverbend surged by on their way in or out of pathways lined with white tents tucked beneath tall trees?

"You okay?" Reed's voice came through a long tunnel.

Barely. She wanted to kiss this man, right here, right now. Crowd notwithstanding. Twenty-six days. He was right, though. They knew each other a lot better than they had, but it was all still so new. Maybe she'd have the rest of her life to kiss him. Now that was a daring thought to have about someone she'd met less than a month ago.

One of Dad's favorite stories had been how he'd seen Mom sitting across the classroom from him in twelfth grade English Composition. He'd taken in her red hair tied up in a ponytail and her bright happiness with her friends. Then she'd glanced his way and time held still. Right then and there he'd decided this was the girl he was going to marry. Yeah, they'd waited three years out of high school, but he'd known.

Could Carly know Reed was the right man? If her dad's story was true, she could have known it at the very first bonfire.

"Here's a spot in the shade, Carly. Sit down and catch your breath. You sure you're okay?" Reed's concerned face swam back into view as he slid an arm around her.

She leaned against him. "I'm fine." *I think.* "Lunch sounds good. Where's the Yellow Bus?" She looked around. Duh. Right across the street at the edge of the parking lot sat a bus. It was yellow and had a sign above an open service window. "What do they sell?"

"They serve a variety of sausages from Clark's Custom Cuts in buns from the bakery downtown. Their bratwurst is to die for."

She nodded as her tummy murmured. "Sounds good."

A few minutes later they'd selected their combinations and sat cross-legged under a tree nearby, knees touching.

Reed bowed. "Thank You, God, for this good food and that Carly and I can spend this beautiful day together." He hesitated. "Please guide us in Your will. In Jesus' name, amen."

"Amen," Carly whispered. Reed felt it, too.

Reed settled against a tree near the grandstand at the south end of the park nearest the trans-provincial highway. Semis and RVs poured over the bridge beyond, all in a hurry to go somewhere else, east or west, like columns of clamoring ants.

He had no desire to go anywhere else. Not with Carly nestled between his knees where he could wrap both arms around her and feel her soft hair against his cheek. His life was perfect right here, right now, like an oasis in a desert. Like an island in the ocean. Like an eddy in the river.

His arms tightened, and Carly looped her elbows around his knees and pressed back against his chest. He felt her through every fiber of his being. It was crazy having such strong feelings for someone he hadn't known for long.

But his heart knew hers. The conviction flooded him with absolute certainty. Reed rested his cheek on Carly's soft hair and closed his eyes. *Dear Lord, help me to know for sure before I do something stupid. If this, this* feeling *I have is just physical attraction, please take it away. I want*

Your will more than anything. I really do.

It was more than a physical attraction. He knew that.

Reed was dimly aware of music striking up from the grandstand as a local band took the stage. Then people stopped in front of them, and he glanced up. Brittany and Joseph stood locked in a tight embrace, kissing each other like there was no tomorrow.

Through their shared contact, he felt Carly's sharp inhale more than he heard it.

She stretched her toe to nudge her cousin's leg. "Yo. You're blocking the view."

Brittany broke the kiss and glanced down at them. "Oops, sorry."

She didn't look a bit regretful or embarrassed. Reed knew they'd dated before, but they'd only gotten back together in the last week or two. Wasn't this a bit early for practically swallowing each other's faces?

Joseph winked at Reed. "We'll join you guys." He tugged Brittany to the ground beside them.

Great. Mood broken. All Reed wanted was to be alone with his girl but in the midst of people to help him remember to keep things in line. Obviously public smooching didn't bother some people, though. Joseph started right in again where he'd left off, one hand fondling Brittany's bare thigh.

Reed shifted slightly, trying to put his back to them without making it obvious. He didn't want to watch or even catch it in his peripheral. Not when it made him long to do the same thing with Carly regardless of his pledge. Regardless of the people who would see.

Carly reached up and slid her arm around his neck. She tilted her head back against his chest so he could see her eyes. They begged to be kissed. Oh, she hadn't said the words again since the day in the rapids, but he knew.

He pressed his lips to her forehead and her eyes closed. "Carly," he murmured against her sweet skin, but he couldn't say more for fear of saying too much. Words he wasn't ready for. Words that would rush their precious relationship.

They weren't ready to run that river yet. The bruises might be gone, but he distinctly remembered the pain of bouncing off rocks in the torrent of water from running a river before they were ready. He wouldn't do that with Carly again. For the moment, burying his face in her hair, feeling her breath against his forehead... that was going to have to do.

* * *

Brittany and Joseph had stuck to them like leeches through the remainder of the day. Carly had never been so sick of spending time with her cousin. Not that Brittany had said more than a dozen words to her. Most of the time, her mouth had been too busy to talk. And her hands...

Carly was half fascinated and half repelled. Had her cousin no shame? But the half-fascinated part dreamed of doing the same thing with Reed, and having the scenario played out less than a meter away kept the vision strong in Carly's mind.

After all these hours—weeks—she finally understood why Reed didn't succumb. It wasn't because he didn't want to kiss her. His tender touch, his glimmering gaze, and that dangerous dimple told her everything his words didn't. Everything his lips didn't.

He respected her too much.

Did that mean Joseph didn't respect Brittany? Carly knew they had a history but, still, things had moved pretty rapidly since they'd gotten back together. She could only hope they wouldn't cross the line anymore than they'd done already. But if this was their public side, what did they do in private? Did she have any right to talk to her cousin about it?

The day had been full of music and speeches and the gigantic Canada Day cake served to everyone. Hyper children had dashed around with painted faces, balloons, and cotton candy. Now the sky darkened and the crowd gathered on the riverbank to watch the fireworks.

Carly nestled into the safety of Reed's arms as the first rocket screamed into the air then shattered with a deafening pop. More and more sparklers lit the sky, one after the other. She pulled his head closer between pops. "The northern lights are prettier. And quieter."

He chuckled against her cheek.

Another rocket soared and exploded. Another and another. This was what Brittany and Joseph were like. Flashy. Loud. Fill the sky for a glorious moment then disappear. Maybe her cousin had found something that would last. Hard to tell, just yet.

But what she and Reed had was more like the aurora borealis. Instead of an instant, it lasted much longer. Flickering and dancing, swelling and subsiding, hushed and awe-inspiring.

Carly's heart swelled. Deep, quiet love? She'd take that over a blaze of passion, for sure.

Chapter Ten

"I think you could do better than Reed Daniels." Brittany eyed Carly across the little dining table in their apartment a couple of weeks later.

Carly stared at her cousin. "Why on earth would you say that?" Wasn't she the one who said he was the hottest guy in the group? Right. But also the coldest. Brittany had been wrong, wrong, wrong about the chill.

"Cute only goes so far. He seems to have a commitment phobia."

"A *what*?"

Brittany rolled her eyes. "You guys have spent a lot of time together since you moved here, but seriously, has he told you he loves you? Has he even kissed you?"

"We've kissed."

Her cousin's eyes brightened. "Ooh, do tell."

Carly should absolutely not have said anything. That long ago day when they'd spilled the canoe didn't count, even though she replayed that kiss a dozen times a day. "I don't want to talk about it."

"Oh, come on. Is he a good kisser?"

"Look, forget I said anything, okay?" Carly stood and picked up her nearly empty plate. Any appetite had disappeared like a wisp. "I'm up for dishes tonight."

"Not so fast, cuz. The whole gang has been speculating about you guys, and you're holding back info? I don't think so. Tell me all about it."

Reed wasn't into random dating. Everyone must know that things between him and Carly had progressed beyond that. They held hands in public, even a bit of casual snuggling.

Brittany wasn't a person to trust with secrets. Carly's dinner sank with a thud to the bottom of her stomach. She could just imagine what would happen when Brittany told the gang. There'd be an explosion rivaling the Canada Day fireworks.

Reed would be furious. Well, no. She couldn't imagine that. But disappointed, for sure. Would one careless admission to her cousin cost Carly his regard? Unless she could somehow convince Brittany to keep the secret.

One glance into her cousin's glittering eyes dispelled that thought. Her best bet would be to minimize it, but could she do that without lying? Because, in truth, that kiss had been amazing. Had sustained Carly for over a month.

"It was the day we capsized the canoe in the rapids. I was kind of hysterical when I got safely to shore, and he kissed me to shut me up." Man, that had totally worked. Her lips had been far too busy for a while to be used for speaking.

Brittany began to laugh. She clutched her arms around her middle and bent over, howling.

It wasn't that funny.

Carly set the plates in the sink and waited for Brittany's other shoe to fall.

"Oh, that's hilarious," Brittany gasped. "I never would have thought to try that tack, but Reed does love peace and quiet. To think Mr. Goody-Two-Shoes would kiss a girl to keep her from talking." She wiped her eyes.

Babbling, more like. Carly wrenched the hot water faucet on and stabbed the plug into the bottom of the sink. But he hadn't kissed like he was too good for her. Just the opposite.

Brittany elbowed her. "What happened next?"

"What do you mean, what happened next?" Carly squeezed the dish detergent bottle over the sink.

"You know."

Carly swiveled to face her cousin. "No, I don't. We carried the canoe back to the truck and came back to town. He dropped me off here. The next day we went for ice cream and took a long walk at the park. You know what's happened since then."

Brittany tipped her head and raised her eyebrows. “Uh huh? You’ve been together an awful lot.”

“Are you asking if we’ve had sex?” Carly reached back to turn off the tap. “Because that’s the only thing I can think of that your question is leading to. And the answer is no. We’ve only kissed that one time, and there definitely hasn’t been any sleeping together.” She stared into Brittany’s eyes. “How about you and Joseph?”

Her cousin shrugged. “We’ve been careful.”

“What on earth is that supposed to mean? Have you, or haven’t you?” But deep inside, Carly knew even before Brittany nodded.

“It’s not that big a deal, Carly. Everyone does it.” She quirked an eyebrow. “Well, *almost* everyone.”

What Brittany didn’t know wouldn’t bite Carly back. “But you know better. You were raised in the church.” Carly had been raised all over, at least after Mom died. Not in church so much.

“Oh, relax already. Times are different than when the Bible was written. Sure, it’s a great ideal to wait for marriage but, in reality, no one does. It’s like the whole ‘all have sinned and fallen short of God’s glory’ thing. We can try to be perfect even while knowing it’s not possible. The Bible even says we can’t be. We can always ask God to forgive us, and He will.”

“So that means it’s okay to do whatever we feel like? We can sin knowingly then ask forgiveness, and it doesn’t matter?” In Carly’s experience, that didn’t ring true. She rubbed the sponge across her plate so hard the floral pattern was in danger of flaking off.

“Pretty much. Society is inundated with sexual temptation. It’s too much to expect people our age to withstand it.” Brittany elbowed Carly again. “Besides, sex is fun.”

Not always. She’d never been more thankful for Reed, and his commitment to being her friend first. To his desire to know her as a person, not a sex object. She hadn’t fully appreciated his commitment to purity until right this minute. Still, she had to choose her words carefully. “Knowing my husband has never had sex with anyone before me sounds mighty good to me.” Hopefully no one needed to know the reverse wasn’t true.

“Ha. You think you’ll marry Reed? You might, of course. I’ve never seen him give any girl the time of day before. But you might break up and marry a guy who's been around like—I don't know—Joseph. What would you think of that?"

Like puking? "And that's a good enough reason to act like a tramp now?"

Brittany rolled her eyes. "You think you're so much better than me."

"I don't think I've said anything of the kind, actually. I feel sorry for you, if you want to know the truth. If Reed weren't... well, Reed... I might have drifted into a wrong relationship, too." She had, in the past. "It wasn't me who was strong. It was him. But, honestly, right now? I'm perfectly good with waiting. He's worth it in every way."

"Even if he ditches you?"

Carly stared into her cousin's eyes. "*Especially* then. Then I wouldn't have given an irrevocable part of myself to someone I wouldn't be spending the rest of my life with."

"But you'd have great memories."

"I'd rather have a great relationship than great memories."

Brittany shook her head. "You're such a prude. No wonder Reed likes you. Good luck getting him to commit."

* * *

"You're kind of quiet. Something wrong?" Reed studied Carly in the twilight as they strolled toward the Friday evening bonfire.

Her beautiful mouth quirked sideways into half a smile. "I'm good."

She didn't look it, but she tangled her fingers with his.

He squeezed back and nudged her shoulder with his arm. "Anything you want to talk about?"

"Not really. It's just been an interesting week with Brittany."

"Oh?" Reed resisted the urge to glance toward Joseph's SUV where the windows were a tad steamed up. Hopefully they'd join the group soon. "What's up?"

Carly shook her head and pulled him toward the log they usually sat on.

Seemed nearly everyone had paired off over the past few months.

Couples sat in close embrace all around the fire. It was getting rather awkward, if he were honest with himself. Sometimes he didn't know where to look. Resting his eyes on Carly wasn't always the best option, because that filled him with longing, too.

How long, Lord?

Tonight she sat on the ground in front of him. Reed gathered her hair and let it slide between his fingers, feeling the softness, smelling the fragrance of her shampoo. He leaned closer, wrapping both arms around her shoulders and drawing her against him. He nuzzled the curve of her neck, hair and all.

Carly's hands caught his in a firm grip but, instead of relaxing against him as she usually did, she shifted slightly away. Not far enough to break contact, but enough to be noticeable.

Had he done something wrong? Said something he shouldn't have? They hadn't seen each other the night before. Carly had texted and said she had a headache and wasn't feeling well. He'd hardly known what to do with his long, empty evening.

"Still have that headache?" he whispered.

She shook her head. Still no relaxing. Okay. He wouldn't push her.

"Hey, Daniels! Want to play my guitar tonight?" Peter hollered from across the fire, his arm around his girlfriend.

Reed could make a guess why Peter didn't want to play. Same reason Reed was content to sit back and feel the closeness of the girl he loved. Yes, loved. Less than two months since they'd met, but he knew that much.

Carly tilted her head back at him.

He grinned at her. "Mind if I play tonight?"

She sat up straighter. "Go for it. I'd like to hear."

Reed looked at Peter. "Sure. So long as no one expects greatness."

"Funny, Daniels. You can outplay me any day of the week, and you know it." Peter disengaged from his girl. He reached for the guitar leaning against a stump and carried it around to Reed. "Here you go. No head-banging stuff, okay?"

Reed chuckled. "I'll keep that in mind."

Carly shifted from between his knees to beside him as he gave an experimental strum and adjusted a tuning peg slightly. There. That was better. He caught her gaze as he began to fingerpick a song he'd been writing. Someday he'd sing the words to her, but definitely not in public.

It didn't take him long to pick his way through a bunch of old favorites and into worship choruses. Some of the group began to sing along. Joseph and Brittany slid in beside Peter across the fire.

"Holy, holy, holy. Lord God almighty..." he sang, strumming along. Sometimes he simply needed to focus on God and not on circumstances. Not on Carly. Tonight he'd fill his mind with thoughts of God's worthiness.

"Where were you guys?" he heard Peter ask.

"None of your business." Brittany sounded smug.

A few people, including Peter, laughed.

Reed was singing alone now. He allowed the vocals to drift away and focused on the chording.

Beside him, Carly shifted. His knee felt chilled where her touch left him. His gaze dropped to her, but she was staring into the fire. Or maybe across it?

"I do have news you guys will be interested, though."

Reed glanced at Brittany. Why was she looking at him? Even in the semi-darkness, her eyes seemed to glitter. A shaft of unease pierced him, but that was silly. He'd done nothing wrong. He bent his head over the guitar, listening to minor chords that didn't seem to belong to any song he knew. Waiting for Brittany's news, like everyone else.

"Reed's not as high and mighty as you'd think, for all his talk of waiting."

He jerked a little. She made waiting sound like a communicable disease. But where was she going with this?

A couple of girls tittered. A few of the group looked his way. Carly drew her knees up to her chest. She was definitely staring at her cousin and not looking all that friendly about it.

Uh oh.

"Apparently the boy does know how to kiss." Brittany's voice dripped poison. "Who'd have believed it?"

Carly surged to her feet. "That's enough out of you."

"Oh, come on. You're the one who told me he was pretty good." Brittany fanned her face.

Reed's heart was trapped by a blizzard. Frozen. Unmoving. Carly had said that to her cousin? Over the years, Brittany had managed to get most of the fellows in the youth group and, later, the college and careers group to date her. To kiss her. And more, in some cases.

Reed glanced at Joseph. Likely in his case, too.

"Whoa, Daniels. That true?" Joseph asked with a laugh. "You've been off smooching in the bushes and telling everyone else to hold back?"

"Kind of a double standard, sounds like," mumbled someone.

Reed couldn't make out who'd said that.

"I never said that to you." Carly stalked around the fire until she was nearly blocking his view of Brittany. "You're blowing what I said way out of proportion. Reed respects me, and I respect him."

"Respect." Brittany waved a hand past her nose as though the word had a bad odor. "It only goes so far."

"I'd much rather have respect than what you've got."

Silence reigned for a long moment.

"What do you mean by that?" Brittany demanded.

"Do you really want me to spell it out here?"

Reed sucked in a long breath and tried to restart his heart. The guitar slid to the ground.

Carly whirled around. "Most of you have known each other for years. I haven't, but I thought when I joined in with a group of people from the church that you guys believed in waiting. That you'd hold each other up to a high standard instead of making fun of someone who lives that ideal quietly."

"Yeah, but did he kiss you?" asked one of the other girls.

"What is a kiss compared to what I'm talking about here?"

"From Reed? Practically the same."

"It is not the same. Don't be so stupid. Just because he values a kiss more than some of you—not naming any names—value your virginity doesn't make it the same thing."

They'd been speculating about him and Carly? Oh, man. And why was she taking the brunt of this? What was going on between her and her cousin, anyway?

"I really thought I'd found something special with all of you." Carly turned slowly. “Good friends who had each other’s backs and would challenge each other to a better life.” Her gaze caught on Reed’s for a second before she looked at the next person. “I no longer want to be associated with any of you.”

“Feel free to move out,” Brittany said.

“I’ll be gone by morning,” Carly shot back. “You won’t even notice.”

Was Reed one of the ones she no longer wanted to know? That couldn’t be. He got to his feet, carried the guitar around the fire, and leaned it on the stump behind Peter.

“Want to head back to town?” he asked Carly quietly, reaching for her hand. He might as well have shouted it with so many eyes focused on the two of them.

She crossed her arms in front of her and stalked over to his truck. He reached for the door handle, but she elbowed him aside and opened it herself.

Looked like it grated on her to even accept a ride from him. Sorrow and anger pierced Reed to the core. How could this possibly have come between them? There must be more. Had to be.

Reed rounded the vehicle and climbed into the driver’s seat. He turned on the ignition and glanced her way as he shifted into Reverse. “Want to talk?”

“Not really.”

“Serious about moving out?”

“Never been more serious in my life.” Carly all but spat rocks.

“Where are you going?” After all this, she must know he couldn’t provide an option.

“A hotel tonight. Then I guess I’ll quit my job tomorrow and see what happens. I’ve had it, Reed. I can’t handle this.”

Reed’s words failed him.

Chapter Eleven

"How can every hotel in town be full?" At least the ones Carly could afford. She growled with frustration. Even worse was that Reed would not leave her until she found a place. If he would only go away, she'd sleep in her car. By sleep, she meant sitting and staring into the darkness, remembering all the reasons she wasn't good enough for him.

"The cherry festival is getting more popular every year." Reed stood beside her under the hotel's neon sign. "I have an idea. Let me call Steph."

"I don't even know her."

"Come out to my pla—"

"Yeah, right."

"I'll pitch my tent over in my folks' yard. You can have my apartment to yourself."

"Reed, stop." Her heart was going to break. Again.

She'd lost count of how many times he'd tried to hold her hand since the blow-up. How many times he'd slid his arm around her. Once more, she stepped out of easy reach. She couldn't stand the disappointment in his eyes, for everything. "How can you be so nice to me?"

"Carly."

She stared at his sports sandals.

"Carly, I-I love you."

Her heart stopped. "But you can't."

"Why? Just because Brittany is making a big deal about the kiss? I wouldn't take back that kiss if I could."

Somehow his hands caressed her arms, and she hadn't dodged away in time. "She said..."

"I've known your cousin most of my life. She says a lot. Whatever she thinks will get her her own way. Some of the others jumped on her bandwagon tonight, but they'll regret it."

He didn't sound vindictive or like he'd make them be sorry. Just that they'd wake up and realize.

"Carly, don't block me out." He rested his forehead against hers, but she couldn't make herself look into his gorgeous dark eyes. "Don't let Brittany ruin what we have."

At that she pulled away and wrapped both arms around herself to keep the sudden chill at bay. "She doesn't need to."

"What do you mean?"

"Reed, why can't you just be angry with me? It would make things so much easier."

He was quiet for so long she snuck a peek. His eyes were closed. Probably praying. He did that more than anyone she'd ever known. Brittany was absolutely correct. Carly wasn't good enough for this man. No matter that she'd felt closer to God in the past few months than she ever had. It was a sham. *She* was a sham.

Which would hurt more? Pushing him away, or telling him everything and him pushing her away? It was a toss-up. Either way, the end result would be the same.

Why had Brittany been so mean? She wasn't the easiest person to get along with at the best of times, but she'd gone out of her way this time.

"About your cousin." Reed sighed heavily. "She's always been a bit boy-crazy. She had her sights set on me for a while."

Carly's imagination had no trouble picturing that in living color.

"Remember I told you I took her out once? We went to a movie, maybe five years ago."

Brittany had missed telling Carly that part.

"She couldn't keep her hands to herself. She tried to kiss me, and more." He took a deep breath. "I walked out of the theater and left her there. Later I heard she'd had a bet with her girlfriends."

"I-I didn't know." Not that it changed anything. After all, he'd resisted.

"It seemed she'd grown out of that phase but, after tonight, I'm not so sure. Anyway, that's probably why she said all those things. She finally saw a chance to get even with me."

It might explain part of it.

His hands caught her shoulders again. “Can you forgive me?”

Carly stared at him in shock. “For what?”

“I don’t know. For even looking at her for five minutes.”

“Five minutes five years ago? There’s nothing to forgive. I wasn’t in the picture.”

Reed’s hands tangled in her hair. “I don’t want anything between us. Full disclosure seemed like a good idea.”

He was wrong about that.

She fixed her gaze on his. “Are you really a virgin?”

“I am.” He could swallow her with his eyes. “I’m saving sex for the woman God wants me to marry. I—“ His words broke off as his hands pulled her nearer.

He couldn’t possibly love her that much. Carly pushed his hands down. Away. She took a deep breath. “I didn’t.”

* * *

Reed’s brain scrambled to keep up. “You didn’t... what?” She couldn’t possibly mean...

She stood just out of reach, hands shoved deep into her shorts’ pockets. The hotel light silhouetted her, and he couldn’t make out her expression.

“I’m not a virgin, Reed. I’ve done it several times with two different guys.”

Why had he assumed otherwise? He’d always believed purity was worth everything, and that God would reward him with a bride who felt the same. Did that mean Carly wasn’t the woman for him after all? Or had he set his sights on unrealistic expectations? *God, what am I supposed to do now?*

“Yeah, I knew what your reaction would be.”

She sounded close to tears, but after all the times she’d pushed him away this evening, reaching for her now would be just as useless.

God? I could use the right words here this very second. The moment is slipping away.

But there was no voice from heaven. He was on his own. "Carly, there's nothing God can't forgive."

"Apparently He can forget, too, but we're not God. Now that you know my dirty little secret, you won't forget. You may not air it to the whole group the way Brittany would if she found out—"

Thank God for small mercies if Brittany didn't know.

"—but it's between us all the same. I'm sorry for leading you on into thinking I was pure. It's all in the past. A long way in the past, but it happened."

He moved closer, but she stepped away, like they were in some weird dance. "Carly..." What to say? *God? Help a man out here.*

"Reed, I'm sorry." Her voice broke. "I should've known better than to fall for a sweet Christian guy. I'll remember this summer for the rest of my life."

"Carly."

She fished her car keys out of her pocket. "Don't. Deep inside, you know we can't get over this. I'll go to work tomorrow because I have an early client, and then I'm leaving town." Her voice hitched. "I'll never forget you."

"Carly, don't give up on us." *Don't tear my heart in half.* "Please."

His feet rooted to the asphalt parking lot as she walked away. She rounded her car and unlocked it then looked across the roof toward him. "Goodbye, Reed."

He stood and watched his life, his hope, his future drive away.

Empty.

Carly parked her car in the Riverside Park lot. The full moon hung high in the sky, casting a long, glittering band of light over the Sandon River. There was no way she'd get any sleep that night. She might as well walk the park.

A bitter laugh erupted as she locked the car. Riverbend was such a safe town she didn't even need to worry about some stranger mugging her. Her own cousin had done a good enough job.

It wasn't Brittany's fault. Sure, she'd been the catalyst, but telling the group Carly and Reed had kissed wouldn't have created this disaster if there hadn't been more underneath.

Carly crossed to the gazebo, where the aroma of roses filled the night air. She stood inside, elbows against the railing as she stared out at the river.

"God?" she whispered. "What do I do now? Where do I go from here?" She'd moved from Jasper to leave her past behind, but it had followed her. It would be her constant shadow for the rest of her life. She could give in to it, like Brittany. Just accept that people had sex, and it wasn't a big deal. But Reed...

Two months of dating Reed had spoiled her. She'd learned what it was like to put God first in a relationship, to talk and spend time together without the pressure of the physical. To be cherished. To feel such a deep attachment—love—and allow it to grow organically.

Would things be different this minute if he'd tried one more time to take her into his arms there in the Best Western parking lot? Would she have let him?

Carly stumbled out of the gazebo, following the path to the river.

The fact was, he hadn't tried again. He hadn't followed her when she left. Yeah, she'd turned south off the highway—in case he watched her taillights—before crossing north again a few blocks over.

She'd done a good job of pushing him away. Should she have listened to him? Let him keep saying the words he'd started to say? Never before tonight had he said, "I love you." She'd longed to hear those words, but deep inside, she'd recognized that the longer he waited, the more real the sentiment.

But they seemed like a sham. It wasn't the real Carly he loved, but the woman she'd pretended to be.

She dropped onto a bench overlooking the Sandon. Yes, the stream of light glinting off the river was solid even while it wavered on the edges from the current. Peaceful on top, but barely concealing the turmoil beneath the surface.

Like her. She'd almost kept it all together. Would she ever have told Reed, or would she have kept her secret all the way to the grave? She'd put on a good cover with barely a ripple. But underneath...

Her phone chimed with an incoming text, and her heart leaped. Would he give her another chance? Was it even wise?

She fumbled as she pulled the device from her pocket, dropping it in the grass. A little more force and it would have tumbled into the river. She steadied her breath as she picked it up and swiped it on.

Brittany. *Where are you?*

Not Reed. Of course, not Reed.

She tapped out a message. *Don't worry. I'm out of your way.*

A text chimed back. *Don't take everything so seriously.*

Yeah, her cousin had liked having help with the rent. Brittany should've thought about that before cat-fighting in front of everyone. Carly stared at the screen and swiped it off without replying.

It pinged again. *You'll thank me later.*

How much later? Fifty years? No, she was done with her cousin. Done with Riverbend. Done with Reed.

Another text. It took all Carly's willpower not to heave the thing in the river. Only the thought of paying for a replacement without a job stayed her hand. She shoved it back into her pocket and dropped her head into her hands. "Jesus? Do you really care? I'm at the end of my rope."

Reed paced his apartment above the boatbuilding shed. He'd texted her three times with no reply.

He'd blown it.

If God could forgive and forget, what made him think he could hold back from Carly? He wasn't better than her. There were a bazillion ways to break God's commandments, and he'd done a bunch of them. Just because they were a different set than Carly was no excuse. God didn't put sin in categories.

The Carly he knew was beautiful inside and out. Over the past two months they'd talked so much. He thought he'd known the significant stuff in her life. They'd read scripture together. Prayed together.

Fallen in love together.

Reed stared out the window toward the river. The moon gleamed across the watery surface. Carly was out there somewhere, maybe driving away from Riverbend. There'd been no available room. Maybe she'd spend the night in her car.

Would she get any sleep? He knew he wouldn't.

He'd been debating when to ask her to marry him. How he'd do it. What he could offer her for a future. If he should buy a ring first or let her pick it out.

Reed crossed the apartment. Out the other side, the trees filtered the moonlight, allowing weird-shaped streaks to light the lawn. He went to the tap for a glass of water. Back to the window overlooking the river.

Were all his hopes and dreams to be dashed in one wicked wave of Brittany's hand? But that wasn't all. Carly had had sex. Willingly, by the sounds of it. But it was past. God had forgiven. Reed could, too.

He could.

Only, where was she? He stared at his phone, where his texts lay unanswered.

Where was she?

Chapter Twelve

Dawn still came mighty early, even at the beginning of August. She'd dozed off a little over the hours and wakened when the first hint of light warmed the sky. Carly stretched, trying to relieve the stiffness that seized her. It wasn't just the wooden-slatted bench to blame, but her heavy heart. It was tied in a knot, and all her muscles had joined it.

She ran her fingers through her hair several times then French-braided it loosely. The wildlife photographer she'd be meeting in a few minutes wouldn't care if she'd had a shower this morning. Last evening's swim in the river would have to do.

Reed, cannonballing off the rock, creating a wave that soaked everyone. He'd been so carefree. So happy. Until—

No. Carly shoved his image out of her mind and strode back to the car across dew-soaked grass. She drove down to Base Camp Outfitters and pulled into the back lot, her headlights catching the company van. Good. Neil had loaded the canoe for her.

A car pulled in beside her and a 40-something woman got out.

Carly pulled on her professional face. "Ms. Daughety? I'm Carly Thorbergsen, your guide today."

The woman took her proffered hand. "Please, call me Linda. Nice to meet you. Thorbergsen is an unusual surname, but I've heard it somewhere before."

Carly unlocked the van and double-checked that paddles, life vests, and bottled water were in the back. Linda loaded her gear and they hit the road.

"You may have heard of my dad, Erik Thorbergsen. He wrote a bunch of adventure novels for boys ten or fifteen years ago."

Linda's face brightened. "Yes, that's it! My son loved that series. I always wished there were more books."

"My father died of cancer about six years ago."

"I'm so sorry to hear that."

Not as sorry as Carly had been, for sure. Would she have made fewer stupid mistakes if her parents had lived? No way to know. She turned the vehicle onto the gravel road toward the lake.

She glanced at the woman in the other seat. “You know there’s no guarantee we’ll see the moose this morning.”

Linda nodded. “I know. But it’s been sighted so many times from what I hear that it’s worth the chance. Besides, it’s going to be a gorgeous morning with terrific light. I’m sure I’ll get some great shots no matter what we see.”

Carly offloaded the canoe to her shoulders in the parking lot, remembering once again how good Reed looked carrying his cedar-strip. She needed to stop that. She set it down at waters-edge with a twist that reminded her how tight her muscles were.

Half an hour later, she finally began to relax. Linda wasn’t given to much conversation and was a fair bow partner. The canoe skimmed across the glassy surface of the lake as the first streaks of true dawn shafted through the trees lining the east shore.

She heard the roar and the answering bellow long before her eyes could make out the figures in the distance. “Get your camera ready, Linda. Don’t worry about the canoe. I’ll bring us in.”

“What’s going on, do you think?” The photographer’s voice hitched with excitement as she rested the paddle across the gunwales.

“Not sure. But we’ll be careful. I’m not taking any risks for a glory shot.”

“That’s what telephoto lenses are for.”

“Good.”

The bellow had to be the moose. The roar? It sounded like a bear. The elusive grizzly? Could they be lucky enough to see both in one tour?

She drew the canoe through the water with the barest of ripples. She wasn’t going to miss Neil Maddrey when she gave her notice later today, but she was certainly going to miss this lake. The river. Reed.

Focus.

Linda had her binos trained on the shoreline ahead. She gasped and dropped them. Her hands shook as she lifted her camera and fiddled with the adjustments.

“What do you see?” Carly whispered.

"A bear just took a swipe at a moose. I've never seen such a thing."

Carly strained her eyes. There was enough daylight now to make out two distinct creatures up ahead, still too distant to see clearly.

The camera began to click. "You never know when it will be the last chance," Linda murmured. "Something could spook them out of the water and up into the trees."

The last chance. Carly'd had that, and failed. But she'd make sure Linda got hers.

She was out on this lake somewhere. Unless it were Neil. Reed had driven up to catch some much-needed tranquility before going to work. The Base Camp Outfitters vehicle had been a powerfully welcoming sight.

He paddled along the shore, knowing Carly loved the north end. But it depended on what her client wanted to see. There'd been no red dot visible to give him an indicator before he started out.

The distant sounds of angry animals filtered into his awareness just as he caught sight of the red canoe in the same direction. Surely Carly knew to give wildlife a wide berth, especially if something was going on out there.

He bent to the paddle. How quickly, how efficiently could he cut through the still water and catch up? The roars and bellows increased in volume as the canoe grew larger. Reed squinted. Bear. Moose. Fighting in the shallows. The red canoe moving like an arrow toward the scene.

Carly was smart. She was no newbie in the wilderness. He could trust her to make wise decisions, but he couldn't help himself as he powered across the water, stroke after stroke. Yes, he wanted to be certain of her safety. Yes, he wanted to witness the battle himself... from a safe distance. But mostly, he just wanted to see her again. Client or no client, he wasn't going to let her walk — or paddle — away from him again.

"This is close enough," Carly said to Linda, just above a whisper. "Both moose and grizzlies can swim, and I don't want to give them any reason to turn their anger on us." She lifted her binoculars to get a closer look as the cow moose lashed out with a front hoof and slashed the bear's shoulder. The grizz screamed and charged, but the moose gave no ground.

Carly frowned and scanned the area. Why would the moose be so determined to keep the grizz away from the shore? She'd expected to see the bear attacking the moose, not the other way around. Her binos caught something in the rushes. "Linda..." she breathed.

Click. Click. Click. "Hmm?"

"The moose is protecting her calf. See it?"

Linda drew her breath in sharply. She angled the camera over and twisted the lens. Click.

The moose splashed sideways, blocking Carly's view. Probably Linda's, too. "I'll get us farther over. Hang on." Carly sculled the canoe over, not lifting her paddle out of the water until the angle cleared.

Click. Click.

The moose's head surged up, her gaze focused on the red canoe. She bellowed.

"I'm getting us out of here." Carly back-paddled a few strokes, not daring to take her eyes off the wild animals.

Click. Click.

The bear rushed the moose, claws raking its shoulder. The moose screamed in rage and pain.

Too close. Carly turned the canoe and paddled as deeply as she could while keeping one eye out over her shoulder. Only when she'd gained a hundred meters of open water did she breathe again.

A sixth sense warned Carly they were not alone. She looked around with something akin to panic, only to see a cedar-strip canoe skimming closer.

Reed. Relief warred with last night's pain.

He spun his canoe sideways with a well-placed brace and came up beside her. "Are you okay?"

Did she look like she wasn't? Carly straightened. "Fine, why?"

"I heard the battle and saw the red canoe. I was terrified."

Linda turned in the bow seat. "Carly is a good paddler. We were never in any danger."

Okay, maybe a little, but she wouldn't tell the photographer that. The canoe had been close enough to distract the moose. If that had been enough to allow the bear access to the calf, she'd never have forgiven herself.

Carly shot a glance back to the battle. The moose seemed to be holding her own.

"I agree about Carly. You're perfectly safe with her."

She would not meet Reed's eyes. She couldn't, not when last night's sorrow was still so raw.

"Then why were you afra—" Linda's gaze swung back and forth between them, and her lips lifted slightly. "Never mind. I think I can fill in the blanks."

"Need any more photos?" asked Carly abruptly. "We can come in from the east a bit if you want to try that angle."

"Sure, so long as we don't get much closer than we are now. My lens can handle the distance."

Carly nodded and plied her paddle, not looking at Reed.

"We need to talk. Carly, I love you."

Had she really heard those quiet words? Did they matter?

Her heart cried, "Yes."

* * *

Reed sat in his truck across from Base Camp Outfitters. He wasn't taking his eyes off Carly's car until she returned to the parking lot to claim it.

Neil glowered at him through the front window.

Whatever. Even the town bylaw officer couldn't make him move.

Half an hour later, the canoe-laden SUV turned into the lot and parked. Reed slid out of his truck, stuck his hands in his pockets, and crossed the street.

The photographer waved at him. "I got some terrific shots! My editor will be very pleased."

"That's great! I hope you'll let Carly know when the magazine is for sale so we can have a look."

The woman glanced at Carly as she came up beside her. "I definitely will. This was the experience of a lifetime. Thanks so much."

"My pleasure." Carly wiped her hands down her shorts.

Reed filled his vision with her petite figure in the blue tank top and khaki shorts. Her lithe, tanned limbs. Her loosely braided red-gold hair swung below her shoulders. Her sweet face that made him want to forget everything he'd ever said about kissing.

What had he said, anyway? He raked his memory. That he wouldn't kiss her again unless he knew she was the woman for him. He was definitely free to make a move.

Reed couldn't help the grin that erupted over his face as relief flowed through him. It was time. He had his answer.

He reached for Carly's hands as the photographer retrieved her equipment.

"Carly." He searched her face. Would she think he was crazy for the big smile he wore? He couldn't help it.

She met his gaze, but then her eyes slipped downward slightly. She disengaged one hand. Her fingers reached up and traced his dimple.

Reed swallowed hard at her tantalizing touch. This was the Carly he'd grown to love over the past two months. He captured her fingers and pressed them against his lips.

Her breathing hitched.

Reed gathered her in both arms and cradled her close. After a few seconds, she relaxed against him, and he could breathe again. Her hands slid around his back until she held him as securely as he held her.

Thank You, Jesus. "Carly?"

She angled her head back and met his gaze.

Reed dipped his head just the slightest until his lips brushed hers with an electrifying touch. "Carly," he murmured then deepened the kiss.

They broke apart a long moment later, staring into each other's eyes.

"I thought you didn't want to kiss a girl until you married her."

He shook his head, never letting her gaze slip. "That's not what I said. I needed to wait until I knew she was the one for me." His fingers traced the side of her face. "I love you."

Chapter Thirteen

The sunset shot fiery shafts across Sandon Lake, the still water casting a near perfect reflection.

Reed packed the empty picnic basket from Loco-To-Go back to the truck and gathered a few more cut logs for the small fire he'd built on the beach.

Neither he nor Carly had said much since he'd picked her up after work, nor had he kissed her again. She waited. He waited. The evening sky seemed to wait, too. Several bats zoomed from nearby trees, hunting mosquitoes. They were welcome to them.

In the distance, a loon called out. The north end of the lake was too far away to tell if the moose and bear were still at it.

By silent accord they held hands and strolled down the beach, stopping on a rocky knoll. Reed stepped behind her and wrapped both arms around her, nuzzling his face into the hair that swept her shoulders. She relaxed against him. It felt like coming home.

"It's beautiful here. So peaceful," she said quietly.

"I know how you feel."

"Brittany called me this afternoon."

"She did? What did she have to say for herself?"

"That she was sorry. That Joseph broke up with her because she was selfish and vindictive."

Hard to argue with that.

Carly looked up at him. "She's worried she might be pregnant."

"Oh, no." *Play with fire, and you might get burned.*

"I don't know what to do, Reed."

He pressed his cheek against hers. "About what?"

"I didn't give my notice today. Neil was in a bad enough mood as it was."

Reed's heart soared. "I'm glad you didn't. Sorry about Neil." He'd hold his bit of news tight a little longer.

"Brittany wants me to move back in."

"Will you?"

"I don't know, Reed." She hesitated. "I don't know where we are going."

He turned her in his arms. "The we that is you and I?"

She nodded, those blue-green eyes fixed on his.

Reed lowered his head and brushed his lips against hers.

She quivered in his arms, and he deepened the kiss, reveling in the taste of her mouth under his. Finally he pulled away just far enough to whisper, "Does this answer your question?"

Brittany's fingertips on his dimple made his knees week. "Kind of?"

He'd already forgotten what she'd asked. He kissed her again, more thoroughly this time, as their lips and hearts melded together.

Are You good with this, God?

The setting sun caused Carly's face and red-gold hair to glow like a blessing. His probably did, too.

"I brought my guitar," he said when he was finally able to stand the thought of releasing her for even a moment.

She blinked. "Your guitar?"

He nodded. "I know you've mostly heard my harmonica except at church, but at home, I pick up the guitar a lot. I've been working on a song."

Her eyebrows rose, and he kissed them.

"May I sing for you?"

"Okay." Her voice sounded uncertain, but she allowed him to lead her back to the fire and seat her on a nearby rock.

Reed braced his hands on the truck door before reaching for the guitar. *This is it, Lord. We're in Your hands.* He brought the guitar and perched on a stump where he could see Carly's face as he tuned up.

Her head tilted in concentration. "You played this the other night."

He grinned and nodded, thrilled she recognized the finger-picked tune. After a few more measures, he cleared his throat and started into the lyrics he'd written.

Love is like a rushing river. Love is like a churning sea. It's like jumping in an eddy. It is the epitome.

Carly sat on both her hands. Her gaze never wavered from his as she listened to all the ways he'd been able to think of to describe his love for her. Not all five verses rhymed that well. He'd planned to take longer and polish the words and chording until the whole thing was a perfect unit.

But he wasn't perfect. She wasn't perfect. It didn't matter. All that mattered was their love, their devotion to each other and to God.

He focused for a moment on the bridging chords he'd arranged to segue the song into the final verse.

You are all my heart desires. You are more than life to me. You are everything that matters. You are the epitome.

The final strums faded into silence. Reed stilled the strings and stared out at the water. The sun was long gone, and a few stars shone their reflections on the lake's surface. He held his breath. This was his heart. Open, vulnerable, on the line.

"Reed, you—I-I don't know what to say. That's the most beautiful thing anyone has ever sung to me. Said to me."

He laid the guitar off to one side in the sand. "I meant every word. I love you, Carly Thorbergsen." He rose and pulled her to her feet. He held her close, feeling her heart beating against his chest. "Carly, I love you so much I can't even describe it."

She took a shaky breath. "I think you described it very well."

"Will you marry me? I'd planned to wait a bit longer to ask. I don't have everything figured out—"

Her lips silenced him. It was awfully hard to talk while kissing, and after a second, he gave up trying. Maybe with the song, maybe with the kiss, maybe there was some way to make her understand the depth of his love.

"Reed Daniels," she whispered at last. "I love you."

He kissed her again, his heart soaring.

"Do you really think you can put up with me and all my issues? I wish I could come to you pure."

"Carly my love, God has more than covered that. I'm not perfect, either. I should be asking you the same thing. Can you put up with me and all *my* junk?"

"It would be my privilege. My honor."

He kissed her nose. "Is that a yes?"

"Yes, Reed, I'll marry you. Tomorrow, if you like."

Reed chuckled, and her fingertips found his dimple unerringly even in the dark. "I hear it takes a bit longer than that to plan a wedding. And I don't even have a ring for your finger yet. Would you like to come with me Monday to pick it out?" He captured her fingers with his lips and lifted his hands to cradle her face.

"I'd love to."

He was torn between kissing her and watching the firelight reflected in her eyes. Or was there more? Reed turned toward the north and caught his breath. "Carly, look."

A long band of green flickered slightly just above the treetops. Several flares shot upward then retracted. The entire northern sky came alive with dancing lights.

"Oooh..." Carly nestled against him.

"The heavens declare the glory of God, and the sky proclaims the work of His hands," Reed murmured into her hair.

"Do you think God sent the heavens dancing just for us?"

"I think He must have. Shall we join them?" With that he began to sway to the unheard music with the woman he loved in his arms.

The End

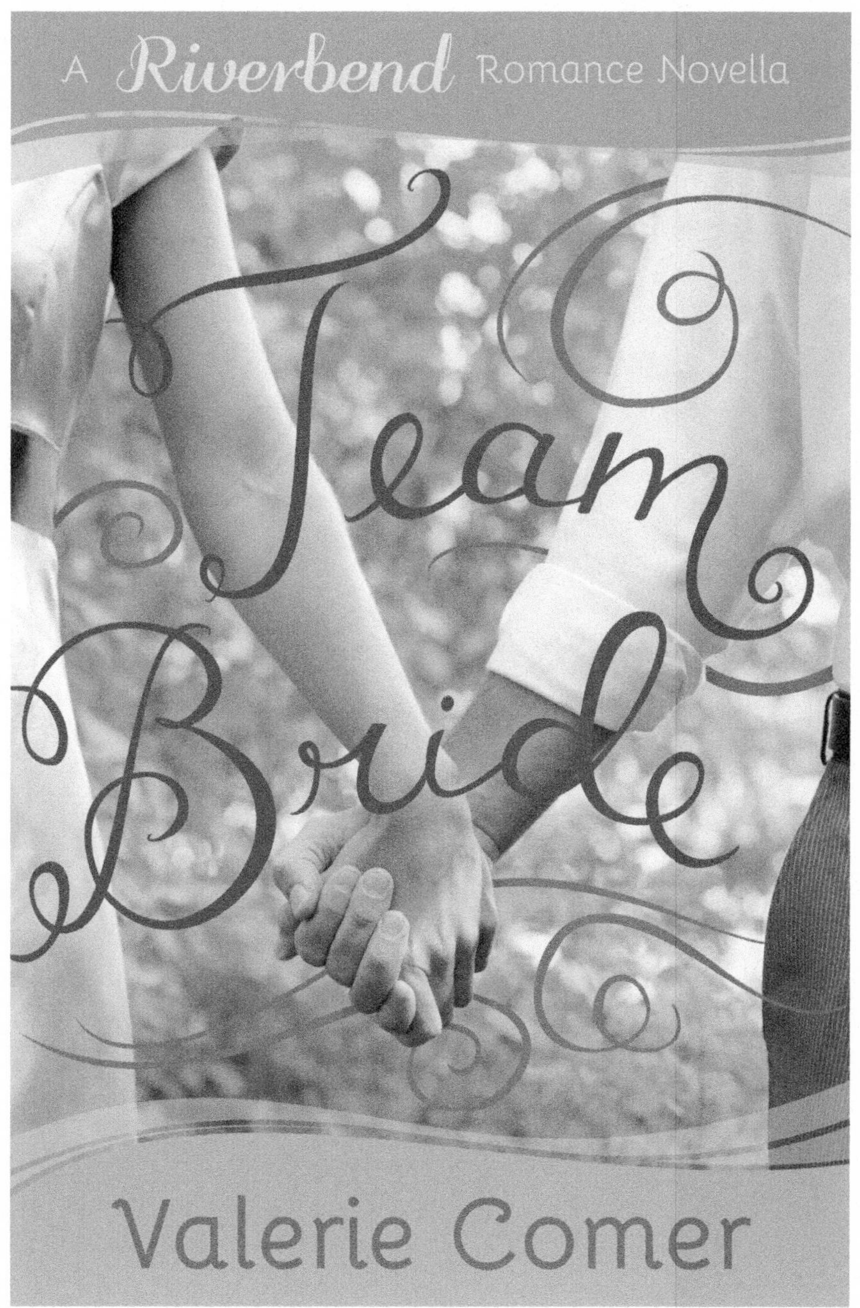
A Riverbend Romance Novella
Team Bride
Valerie Comer

Chapter One

The wedding rehearsal was about to start without Sarah Jamieson.

Thankfully, it wasn't *her* wedding, but that didn't mean her best friend wasn't going to kill her. As maid of honor, Sarah had responsibilities. She tapped her fingers on the car's steering wheel and craned her neck to see why traffic was stopped on the bridge across the Sandon River.

She'd counted on twenty-one minutes to get from her apartment to the River of Life Church. That's all it ever took. With only eight stoplights, the small town of Riverbend, British Columbia, was no metropolis. Also, she hadn't seen any need to get there early. Not with the way she felt about weddings. The things she did for her best friend. At least she'd talked Lindsey out of a flower girl.

Sarah opened the car door and crossed to the sidewalk on the other side of the bridge along with several other drivers. Oh, no. A semi had flipped on the bridge's access, blocking both lanes. This could take a while.

She slid back into her car and tapped the Bluetooth on her dashboard, selecting Lindsey's cell. It went straight to voicemail. A bride too busy to answer her phone at two minutes to rehearsal? Imagine that. Maybe the groom was carrying his. It was worth a try. She scrolled through the list and found Nick's number. It rang three times.

"Corbin Morrissey of Team Groom. How may I direct your call?"

She rolled her eyes as she craned to see if there was any action getting the eighteen-wheeler moved yet. A few sirens wailed in the distance. "This is Sarah. I'm stranded in the middle of the bridge because a semi-truck flipped over, blocking both lanes. I'll be there as soon as I can."

"Sarah from Team Bride?"

She narrowed her gaze and stared at the Bluetooth display. "Lindsey's maid of honor."

"Team Bride affirmative. Expected time of arrival?" He chuckled. "Besides late."

Where had Nick found this guy, anyway?

Sarah leaned out her open car window as sirens approached. "Sounds like the RCMP are here. Tow trucks. And a woman in a safety vest coming this way stopping at every car."

"So you'll know what's up in a minute. We might as well keep talking until she gets to you. Tell me about yourself, Sarah. Have you known Lindsey long?"

She shook her head as she settled back in her seat. Some guys had all the confidence. She preferred them quiet, herself. Not like... Corbin, he'd said his name was? "I've known her since we were kids. We've been best friends since third grade then lost touch until she came back to Riverbend last year."

"So you must have gone to high school here. Did you know Nick?"

Sarah wasn't going there. She had memories of the groom in high school she'd rather forget. Good thing he'd changed. "Yeah, some. How about you? Where did you meet Nick?"

"Bible school, actually. I've lived near Riverbend for a couple of years now."

The woman in the safety vest was still a few cars away. "So are you a pastor now, too?" There were other churches in town. Maybe he worked for one of them.

"I'm a farmer."

Seriously? He said it with some kind of pride. "You went to Bible college to become a farmer?" Now there was a waste of four years.

Corbin laughed. "Not exactly. But God had His reasons."

The woman approached as Sarah glanced out the window. "They expect to open single-lane traffic in under an hour."

"Thanks."

"Whoa, Team Bride is losing this competition. Huzzah, Team Groom is rocking it."

Did that require a reply? "It sounds like I'll get there when I get there."

"Try the bridge down by Arrowsmith?"

"That's another thirty kilometers south. Besides, I don't think the car behind me left enough room to turn around. No, I'd better stay put."

"Your call. So you know, the pizza just arrived, and it smells awesome."

Sarah's stomach growled as she glared at the Bluetooth.

Corbin chuckled. "What's your favorite kind?"

"If it's Panago, the correct answer is Mediterranean with olives and extra feta."

The sound of other voices and laughter became louder. A few glasses clinked. "Yup, there's one of those. You must have an in with the bride. Want me to save you a piece?"

How about saving half a pizza? She hadn't eaten since breakfast.

He lowered his voice. "We could sit out on the fire escape later and share it. Get to know each other."

Um, right. Nick should have left this bozo out in the chicken yard where he found him.

"Who are you talking to, Cor?" Nick's voice. "Is that my phone?"

"Yup, it rang, so I picked it up. Talking to Sarah from Team Bride."

"Well, give it here already." The phone switched hands. "Sarah? Where are you? The food arrived."

"Stuck on the bridge. A semi turned over just a few vehicles in front of me. The tow truck is trying to clear it enough for one-lane traffic now."

"But rehearsal..."

Like she didn't know.

"Right. Well, I guess I don't need to tell you to get here as soon as you can, eh?"

She drummed her fingers on the steering wheel. "I have that part figured out, Nick. There's not much I can do at the moment."

"I'll tell Lindsey you called."

"Thanks. I tried her cell first but she didn't answer." Neither had anyone else. She could wish no one had answered Nick's, either.

"Okay. See you soon, I hope."

"Hey, pass the phone back here."

Corbin? Like she wanted to sit and chat with him any longer? Not a chance. She reached over and tapped the screen to end the call. That'd fix him.

Where was the maid of honor? Being second-in-command of Team Groom wasn't all that much fun without a witty counterpart facing Corbin across the church platform. He was bored already.

The groomsmen would gather in the pastor's office. Check.

They'd stride down the side aisle single file behind Pastor Davis. Nick first, then him, then Jared, then Heath. Check.

The music would change. Everyone in attendance would stand up and turn to the back of the church, blocking Corbin's view of Team Bride as they entered. Check.

Pastor Davis would talk about marriage, and Corbin would *not* be reciting *The Princess Bride* in his head the whole time. Possibly check.

He'd pull Lindsey's wedding band from his pocket and place it on the pastor's open Bible when told to do so. Man, he had to do all the work. Why couldn't Nick and Lindsey have conscripted a ring bearer? Uh, right. Not everyone knew a cute little kid like he'd been back in the day. Check.

Eventually, Nick and Lindsey would be declared married, people would clap and cheer as they waltzed back out to the foyer — were folks in this church allowed to waltz? — and Sarah from Team Bride would tuck her hand in the crook of his arm, and he'd escort her to the photo shoot and reception.

Pastor Davis cleared his throat. "Corbin?"

He blinked to attention and saluted. "Yes, sir?"

"The ring."

Oh, man. Daydreaming again. As he reached into the pocket of his cargo shorts, movement at the back of the dimly lit sanctuary caught his attention. A sprite of a woman with long blond hair paused in the doorway, licking her fingers. Sarah? She must have nabbed a slice of pizza on her way in.

"There she is!" He pointed. Too bad he hadn't gotten a firm grip on that ring first. It flew to the platform steps and bounced on down. Thunk. Thunk. Thunk.

Oops. Not the presentation he'd meant to make at all. He sprang after it and scooped it into his hand.

"Hey, Sarah! Come on up," called Lindsey. "Or should we start over, Pastor Davis?"

But the man was staring at Corbin. He hadn't managed to hide that literal rock taped to a metal washer quickly enough, apparently. Corbin grinned and waggled his eyebrows at the pastor, who shook his head. But there was a glimmer of a smile, so that counted for something.

"Sure, let's start again at the beginning." Pastor Davis shut his Bible and waved them away. "I doubt either of you needs any practice with the *you may now kiss the bride* part. That seems to come more naturally than the correct tempo for the bridal march."

Nick snagged Lindsey and gave her a noisy smooch as he slung his arm around her and steered her toward the back. "That was my practice," he tossed over his shoulder.

Corbin would gladly give up his position in the last four Team Grooms — or was that Teams Groom? — to have found the woman of his dreams and be the guy getting married himself. His gaze lingered on the maid of honor as he made his way toward her.

Sarah Jamieson. Hair streaked in several shades of blond swung past her shoulders, curling slightly at the ends. A cute pixie face, tanned as though she'd been on the farm all summer, became animated while she chatted with Lindsey. Her hands did a tumbling motion, perhaps to demonstrate the accident that had made her late.

How did they both live in the Sandon Valley yet hadn't met before? He'd remember that pretty face anywhere. He bumped Lindsey's shoulder with his arm, keeping his gaze fixed on her friend. "Introduce me?"

* * *

Tall, dark, and handsome. Whoa.

He'd annoyed Sarah so much on the phone there was no way she planned to like him. Teams Groom and Bride, indeed. The entire wedding party was here to make Lindsey and Nick's wedding day into everything the couple had dreamed of, not to create a competition between girls and guys.

But hey, those killer blue eyes didn't belong with such dark brown hair, and Corbin Morrissey was awfully cute right down to his sport sandals. Smile lines crinkled around his eyes as a grin poked at his cheeks. A bold one, looking straight at her with a wink.

Sarah blinked and clenched her hands together lest she accidentally fan her face to dissipate the heat she felt rising.

His grin widened. "Sarah Jamieson? I'm Corbin Morrissey, at your service." He swept a bow.

"Oh, you." Lindsey jabbed her elbow in the guy's ribs. "Must everything be a dramatic affair with you?"

Corbin straightened but kept his eyes on Sarah. "Have you seen your best friend, fair lady? She is beautiful and definitely deserving of having a knight in shining armor at her beck and call."

Shining armor? Sarah couldn't help the smile that had begun playing with her lips. Shorts with a dozen pockets ended just above his knees, and a bright yellow T-shirt proclaiming *If You Ate Today, Thank a Farmer* clung to his upper body. No shining armor anywhere in sight.

"Okay, let's get rolling again or we'll be here until midnight," called Pastor Davis.

About that. "I'm sorry."

"Not your fault, young lady. You girls—"

"Team Bride," supplied Corbin.

"—take your place in the ready room at the back. Men, please join me in the office. Musicians, are you ready?"

Corbin was wasted on a farm, unless the chickens thought he was funny. Sarah's first grade class would totally lap him up.

The guy grinned at her. "See you at the front."

What a flirt. Sarah tried to wipe the smile off her face, but failed.

Chapter Two

Corbin rocked on his heels. "Team Groom is all over it. Right guys?"

Heath high-fived him. "I'll get a ladder."

Yeah, Corbin attended church over in Castlebrook. It wasn't much farther to drive than Riverbend. At any rate, he had no clue where River of Life kept mundane equipment like ladders. He jogged over to Sarah where she stood on a chair holding a bundle of autumn leaves against the wall. "Your knight in shining armor," he quipped as he stretched up. "How high do you want this?"

She glanced down at him, closer than she'd been since he'd escorted her out of the sanctuary after rehearsal. What kind of perfume was she wearing? Not that he knew one from the other, but this was a pleasant kind of tickle. Or maybe not so pleasant.

He dropped the leaves and averted his face just in time to aim his sneeze at his shoulder instead of on her. Oh man. Way to make an impression. He buried his nose in the crook of his arm before two more sneezes erupted in rapid succession.

"Excuse me," he gasped. This could not be happening. Cutest girl in forever, and he was allergic to her? Well, her perfume. How did a guy politely ask her to leave that at home? And what about when he married her and her home was his? Could she forego scents forever?

Corbin pinched the bridge of his nose and backed away. His thoughts might be as recalcitrant as pigs escaped from the pen, but hey, it never hurt to daydream a little. One day, surely, he'd meet the right woman. Why not today?

Achoo.

"You okay?" Sarah's pretty face puckered into a frown.

"Fine." He backed up another step.

"Are you coming down with something? If you were one of my kids, I'd make you stay home for a day or two."

One of her *kids?* No. Couldn't be. She was the maid of honor, not the matron. She was too young to have kids that would be going anywhere.

She burst out laughing, the sound as pleasant a burble as a hen who'd just laid an egg. "I'm a teacher, Corbin. If you could only see your face."

He never could hide anything he was thinking. "A teacher, eh? That explains it. You had me wondering for a minute there." His nose twitched, and he took another step back. Not good. So not good.

"Dude. You all right?" Heath stood there with a stepladder and a concerned expression.

"Sort of."

"You allergic to something?" Heath glanced around. "Autumn leaves? Pretty girls?"

Sarah grinned.

Corbin had to say it. "Perfume."

The smirk wiped off her face. "Mine?"

"I think so. Sometimes I can handle scents okay, but some really seem to irritate more than others."

"So you're saying common sense is fine..."

Corbin blinked and stared up at her. Was she punning?

Heath slapped his hand to his leg. "Good one, Sarah."

"Thanks." She smirked at him, eyes twinkling. "I try."

Hey, she was supposed to be looking at Corbin that way, not the guy with the ladder. Unless maybe they were already an item? But then Nick and Lindsey would have paired them together in the wedding party, wouldn't they? He shook his head. Enough speculating.

"Hey, I'm sorry. I'll leave it off for the wedding tomorrow. The school is a no-perfume zone, so I'm used to not smelling nice." Sarah eyed him uncertainly. "Maybe I get carried away when I get the chance to spritz some on."

Corbin couldn't help it. "And here I thought teachers had to have sense."

Heath high-fived him.

"Can we get those leaves up, guys?" called Lindsey. "Some of us would like to get some sleep yet tonight."

"Yeah, 'cause you sure won't get any tomorrow." Corbin laughed then looked around at the shaking heads. "Well, it's true. Er, I imagine it must be true. I've never had a wedding night—" Time to shut his mouth. It had a habit of running on without him. He glanced at Lindsey's red face. "Never mind."

Heath climbed up and secured the autumn leaves while the women stacked the rest of the decorations on a few tables.

"Thanks for getting the stuff that needed a ladder," Nick said. "The church women will be in first thing in the morning to set up the rest. They couldn't do it earlier because of the Golden Agers luncheon here this afternoon."

"There's still some pizza and pop in the ready room, if anyone's still hungry." Lindsey grinned at Corbin. "Or is hungry again."

"That'd be me." Corbin looked at Sarah. "I think you promised to have pizza with me out on the fire escape."

She planted both hands on her slender hips. "I said nothing of the sort. Besides, being near me makes you sneeze."

"I can live with it if you can."

Sarah tilted her head to one side. "Trying to enjoy pizza while sitting next to someone who sneezes every thirty seconds? Excuse me if that doesn't sound like my idea of a fun time."

Ouch. And he tried so hard to be the life of the party, too.

"You can wash off enough of it that he can handle it, Sarah." Lindsey hip-checked her friend. "Seriously. Who wouldn't want to hang out with Corbin? Especially on the fire escape. Sounds like a hot date."

"Only if there's a fire." Heath managed to keep a straight face.

"Thanks, dude," Corbin muttered.

"Any time. And besides, Sarah, there's a good breeze out there. Sit upwind of Corbin, and you should be fine."

"And exactly why would I want to do that, anyway?"

Lindsey laughed. "Isn't there some kind of tradition about the best man and maid of honor getting together?"

One of the bridesmaids giggled. "I thought that was the ring bearer and the flower girl. Did you see that darling video on YouTube about how they met years later and got married?"

"I've been a ring bearer a time or two. Some of those flower girls were pretty cute."

"Bet you made a move on them, too, Corbin." Lindsey laughed. "I doubt you've changed all that much since you were five."

"Hey now. I resemble that remark. But it's hard dating when your parents have to drive you, and you're too short to get on the good rides at the fair."

Too bad that joke didn't make Sarah smile. He leaned closer. "Were you ever a flower girl?"

She stepped aside. "Once. Not so fun."

"Bridesmaid?"

"Corbin..." Lindsey gave him a look meant to quell.

But why? He looked back at Sarah. "A gorgeous woman like you must've been on Team Bride a dozen times."

She narrowed her gaze. "I don't know where you get that name from."

"Does it matter? I think it's fun. One for all and all for one and all that."

"You're crazy."

"Thank you. I'll take that as a compliment." Wait. Had she diverted the conversation away from past weddings? A mystery. "What do you say, pizza on the fire escape?"

"And you don't give up."

He quirked his eyebrows. "Also true." If she ditched her perfume, he'd be happy to focus his attention right here for the rest of his life.

He took a step back. *Whoa, Morrissey. Really?* But why not? He was ready, too. Ready to take his spot at the head of Team Groom and then never join another one.

The River of Life Church actually had a fire escape. Sarah guessed she'd never been around the entire building. Sure, there was a four-story wing back there with offices and meeting rooms and all. She'd never looked out the windows or wondered about where that door led. The wide interior staircase worked just fine.

She glanced at the tall guy sitting beside her. She'd agreed to this *why*? Because he wouldn't take no for an answer. She'd even tried to remove some of the perfume so he wouldn't sneeze. Seemed to have worked.

Corbin held out a napkin with a slice of pizza on it. "I know you didn't have time to get much earlier."

"Thanks." Sarah accepted it. "True. And I skipped lunch."

"You're not fat."

She pulled back and stared at him. "What?"

"Isn't that why women skip meals?"

"I was on playground duty and had a bully to keep an eye on."

"Oh. Sorry. I guess I jumped to conclusions."

Yeah, she guessed he did. Good grief. "Healthy appetite here, no worries. I'm not a health freak. I ride my bike a lot because I enjoy it. Plus I like real food." She held up the slice. "I can't believe Lindsey let Nick do pizza."

Corbin laughed. "I don't think the bride is supposed to cater rehearsal dinner even if she's a chef, so she had to give Nick some freedom. I'm pretty fond of real food myself. I can even cook. Maybe I should swing by the school and bring you lunch when you're on playground duty."

Did the guy's mouth never stop? "I usually take a lunch, but the teacher who was scheduled for playground had a migraine, so I took her place. On the one day I'd planned to sneak over to Loco-To-Go for a sandwich." She took a big bite of the pizza and closed her eyes with a sigh.

"Here. Let me."

She felt something wipe at her chin, and her eyes sprang open. Seriously, the guy was mopping up a drip of tomato sauce? She couldn't even eat neatly. "Um, thanks."

"You're welcome. You get something at Loco-To-Go often? I'm one of their suppliers."

"Really? That's cool. What do you sell them?"

"Chicken. Eggs. We can never decide which comes first." He tipped his head to one side.

"I'm always looking for places to take my class on field trips."

His grin remained stable. "I'm sure there are more interesting places. Want me to think of some?"

She reached for the bottle of pop. "Do you never give up?"

Corbin leaned a bit closer. "Not very easily."

"Well, I'm a happy single, okay?" She took a swig of pop. "Not looking for a relationship at the moment, either permanent or temporary. Sorry to disappoint."

"You're not looking at the moment? I can wait. You might change your mind by tomorrow."

Seriously? Sarah wadded up her napkin and slammed the lid of the pizza box. She surged to her feet on the narrow fire escape. "Thanks for keeping me company while I ate."

"My pleasure."

He didn't even bother following her up the stairs. She reached for the handle, but there wasn't one. The door was securely shut. She whirled. "You knew this would happen."

"Knew what?"

"You don't need to sound so smug. You know what I mean."

"It's shut? I stuck a sandal in it to keep it open."

Sarah glared down the metal steps. "Sure you did. The door's locked."

Corbin lifted a sandaled foot then a bare one. "Promise."

"Great." Sarah glanced at her watch. Already ten-thirty, and she was due for hair and makeup at seven in the morning. "Well, wave your magic wand then. This isn't funny."

He tugged his cell phone out of his pocket and looked at it. "Oops. Dead."

And hers was in her purse in the ready room. How much better could this night get? She looked out at the huge field behind the church. Likely no one lived within yelling distance, and the escape stopped a story above the ground. If she sprained her ankle jumping, she'd be hobbling at the wedding.

"Kidding."

Sarah stared down at him. "What do you mean?"

He flashed her a grin. “It’s not dead. I was just messing with you.” He punched some buttons. “I’ll give Nick a call. I’d rather bug him than Pastor Davis, and I’m not sure who else has a key to the building.”

Even from half a flight of stairs away, Sarah heard Nick laughing through the cell. Corbin swiped the phone back off. “He’s still in his office and will rescue us in a minute.”

Sarah narrowed her gaze and tapped her foot. “Sounds suspicious. Do you think he took your shoe out of the door?”

“Oh, now you believe that I wasn’t that thoughtless?”

She was thankful the darkness covered the burn on her face. “Um, I guess. You’re stranded, too.”

“But I admit to not minding being stranded with a pretty woman.”

“Stop flirting. Just turn it off already.” A metallic click came from behind her and she whirled as the door opened.

“Everything all right out here?” Nick’s head poked around.

“Fine now, thank you.” Sarah brushed past him and down the corridor.

“Dude,” came Nick’s voice. “I give you a golden opportunity and you can’t even keep her from getting mad at you?”

Great. All she needed was to be ganged up on. She jogged down the stairs to get her stuff and go home. Knight in shining armor indeed. He’d needed someone else to rescue him.

Chapter Three

Somehow Corbin got through the ceremony. Sarah avoided eye contact while she strolled down the aisle looking like a million bucks in that burnt orange knee-length dress. She'd given him enough space to herd a dozen chickens through while watching him sign the register as a witness to the marriage. When he'd rested his hand on the back of the chair while she was writing her name in a neat script, she'd leaned forward, well out of easy reach.

But Nick and Lindsey had just spent five minutes kissing at the front of the church and been declared married. They faced the audience, beaming and waving. The recessional march began, and the newlyweds strode toward the back of the church.

This was the moment Corbin had been waiting for. He marched the three steps toward the center aisle and held out his bent elbow for Sarah. She took it without meeting his gaze. He tightened his arm against his side and leaned over. "You look great."

Sarah's chin came up slightly. "Thank you."

The musical cue came and they stepped off the platform toward the back of the church. The rustle of fabric and muffled footsteps behind him assured him that the other two couples were right behind them. As acting leader of Team Groom, he needed to know that.

They swished through into the foyer where Nick and Lindsey had resumed kissing. Corbin glanced at Sarah, who seemed to be watching the newlyweds. "Aren't you going to tell me I clean up good?"

Her jaw clenched. "Well. You clean up *well*."

He chuckled. "Good to know. You should be a teacher." He snapped his fingers. "Oh, wait. You are."

She whirled to face him, her dress flaring around her knees, and pulled her hand away from his tightened hold. "Can you please stop this right now? How many times, in how many ways, do I need to tell you I am not interested? Can we simply be here for Lindsey and Nick today and then forget we ever met each other?"

Was he really that annoying? On the other hand, was she really such a spoilsport? "Can't you simply play along and have a good time for a few hours? Is that too much to ask?"

"If you mean, will I pretend an attraction to you, the answer is *no*. That's not in my skill set."

He crossed his arms over his chest. "Meet me in the middle?"

"Hey, everyone, get in line. The ushers are letting the guests out now. Time to play nice and pretend not to hate each other." Lindsey glared daggers at him.

"No hate here." Corbin touched the small of Sarah's back to direct her to her spot in the receiving line.

Sarah stumbled into Lindsey's arms and they hugged for a minute, rocking back and forth. Lindsey's narrowed gaze met Corbin's over Sarah's shoulder. "Be nice," she mouthed.

He shrugged. He was doing the best he could.

Nick's parents and Lindsey's step dad joined them, and the group spread into a line as they'd practiced last night. Soon Corbin had been hugged by at least forty middle-aged women, many of them smelling extravagantly floral and having exceedingly large bosoms.

He leaned closer to Sarah when there was a gap. "Remind me to elope."

"Have fun with that." She shifted away.

"What do you mean? You can't seriously want a big hoopla like this. Think of all the perfume that could have been poured on Jesus' feet instead of worn here."

She actually met his gaze for a split second. "You haven't been sneezing."

"No, I took a double dose of allergy meds to forestall the worst of it."

"Good thinking."

He allowed a slow grin to spread across his face. "That sounded suspiciously like a compliment."

"Get over it." She rolled her eyes. "Look, the crowd seems to have thinned out. Now I guess we have two hours of photos before the reception."

Two hours of posing beside Sarah for posterity. How tragic. He could stick a photo in a frame on the wall for a while, then the batch would go in his Team Groom box where mementoes from weddings gone by resided. Twice a ring bearer, twice a groomsman, now twice a best man.

Oh come on, Morrissey. Shove the dark thoughts aside. One of these days you'll meet the one, and you'll both know it.

Too bad it wasn't Sarah, though. She had plenty of spunk when she chose to show it. How had he gotten off on the wrong foot with her again?

The photo shoot and sit-down reception dragged. At least during the meal Sarah sat between Lindsey and her teenage sister, Madison, who was totally thrilled to be a bridesmaid even though she'd really wanted a pink dress, not deep orange. Sarah heard about the drama of it all. And the bride, of course, was understandably distracted by the dashing man seated on the other side of her.

Just a few more hours, and it would all be over. So far it hadn't been as horrible as she'd feared. The zipper on her dress hadn't split open. She hadn't tripped in the aisle and fallen. She hadn't dropped the bouquets or Nick's wedding ring. No one had had any reason to stare at her. Or laugh.

So why couldn't Sarah enjoy the result of all the hard work she'd done with Lindsey? It was all Corbin Morrissey's fault. But even that was silly. She barely knew him, and it wasn't even his fault they'd been locked out on the fire escape last night.

No, they'd gotten off on the wrong foot when she'd been late for rehearsal and had to listen to his cheerfully grating prattle while she waited half of forever on the bridge. He really wasn't that awful. Just a little full of himself. Confidence wasn't a bad trait in a guy, was it?

So that made it all *her* fault.

Lindsey leaned over. "You okay?"

Sarah dredged up a smile and pressed her shoulder against Lindsey's. "I'm fine. Sorry for making you worry about me."

"Thanks so much for standing up for me. I really appreciate it."

"That's what best friends are for."

"Once you get used to Corbin, he's a great guy. A lot of fun. I thought you'd really like him."

Sarah fixed the smile in place. What positive thing could she say? "He's really cute." Because that was no lie. Tall, dark, and handsome was the tip of the iceberg. Twinkling blue eyes, athletic frame, a quick smile. Easy to look at, for sure.

"He is, isn't he? You guys are adorable together."

"Don't even start, Linds."

"Oh, humor me." The bride lowered her voice a little and leaned closer, shoulder pressing against Sarah's. "Promise me something?"

Sarah narrowed her eyes. "What?"

"If he asks you out, accept? Just once is all I ask. I bet that will be enough."

There was no way he'd ask, not after she'd pushed him aside a dozen or two times today. But it was remotely possible a decent guy lived inside that hunky body, well hidden behind the annoying mannerisms.

"Please? I'll text you every day and ask you if he asked you for a date yet."

"On your honeymoon?" Sarah raised her eyebrows. "I think you'll have other things to think about."

"So you wouldn't want to be responsible for distracting me."

"You're crazy."

"Promise. Then I won't have to be distracted."

Sarah couldn't help the laugh that bubbled out. "Okay, fine. One time. I promise. But don't you dare plant the idea in his head."

Across Lindsey and Nick, Corbin glanced at her, his smile warming when he caught her eye. Uh oh. She was in trouble now. But Lindsey was right. He couldn't be that rotten a guy and still be Nick's best friend and the man who led Nick to Jesus. Could he?

"Ready?" he mouthed.

For what? A date? No. It didn't matter if she'd just promised Lindsey. She needed time to get used to the idea. Like a year or two.

Corbin pushed back his chair and approached the mike.

Oh. Ready for speeches and toasts. Yeah, as ready as she was going to get. If Corbin ever got done telling story after story about his and Nick's days in Bible school together. The friends and family surrounding two dozen round tables lapped it all up, laughing in all the right places. Pretty much nonstop.

He was a hard act to follow. Well, she wouldn't even try. She got through her sentimental speech about Lindsey and thanked Nick for coming into her best friend's life. For the second time. But she didn't talk about the jerk Nick had been in high school. Corbin would likely have found a way to spin that into a funny story. Too bad. Sarah proposed a toast and retreated to her seat.

Several other friends came up to the mike and shared stories. Finally the emcee decided it was time for the cake to be cut, and Sarah and the wedding party helped pass around slices to the guests.

Corbin sidled up beside her with a loaded tray. "How's it going?"

"Fine." She turned to the next table with a plate of cake in hand.

Soon the evening would be over, and she'd be back in her cozy apartment across the river curled up in her bathrobe with a mug of tea and a good book. Maybe she'd set aside the romance novel for now and start a whodunit. It might be easier on her nerves.

She held the comforting vision in mind as she smiled, nodded, and avoided Corbin.

A few minutes later, all the single women were invited to gather for the bouquet toss. Sarah slinked to the back of the room until Lindsey caught her eye and flicked her chin toward the group. Oh, man. Whatever. She'd stand behind someone who was eager to catch it. Not a problem.

"Me!" yelled Lindsey's sister. "Throw it here!"

Like Madison. She'd be perfect. Except when the bouquet flew, someone's elbow caught Madison's side and the flowers thunked Sarah in the chest. Her hands automatically grabbed to prevent them from falling.

Great. Sarah had caught the bouquet.

"Yay, Sarah!" yelled Lindsey. "Your wedding will be next! Let me know the date and time, and don't forget to ask me to be your maid — um, matron — of honor."

Sarah narrowed her eyes as a few other people cheered and Madison glowered. But could Lindsey really have set this up?

Behind the bride, Nick and the groomsmen grinned. Corbin sent her a thumbs-up. Sarah buried her nose in the fragrant flowers. She might have no desire to get married any time soon, but that wouldn't stop her from enjoying the gerbera daisies and white mums as long as they lasted.

The tide turned a few minutes later as Nick gallantly seated Lindsey on a chair while the unmarried men gathered behind him. Nick grinned at his bride as he slid her dress up over her knee and reached underneath to remove the garter. He tossed it over his shoulder without looking then bent to kiss Lindsey.

With growing horror, Sarah watched the blue-trimmed garter fly end over end and land directly in Corbin's outstretched hand. The guys cheered. More than one pair of eyes swung over to her.

If only the floor would open up and swallow her on the spot. Instead, Corbin strolled over to her, waving the garter over his head like a lasso. He tucked an arm around her while clapping intensified.

"Looks like we're destined to be together, fair lady," he whispered into her hair. "What do you say we start with a first date tomorrow?"

Lindsey's hopeful expression caught Sarah's gaze.

She'd promised her stupid best friend. "Not tomorrow. I need some recuperation time," she murmured.

"Friday then? I'll get your phone number before we leave tonight."

Sarah closed her eyes for one brief moment. If there was anything she hated worse than feeling manipulated, she couldn't remember what it was at the moment.

Chapter Four

Sarah shouldn't be this nervous. It wasn't like she hadn't gone on a date before. And frankly, every other time, she'd actually had a crush on the guy. Unlike Corbin Morrissey.

She was only doing this because she'd promised Lindsey. She'd do the obligatory date and then tell him *no thanks* for another one. Easy peasy, right?

That didn't explain why she changed her outfit five times. Why she'd put her hair up, then down, then up again. Which would go better with the one-step-up-from-casual pants and cowl-neck sweater she'd finally decided on?

The doorbell rang. Her heart beat faster. She wiped her clammy hands on a towel, glanced at her reflection in the mirror one more time then tugged out the pins holding her up-do together. She swung her head a few times and her natural waves settled around her shoulders.

Out of time. *Please, Lord, help this evening not to be too horrible.*

"Hi, Corbin. Come on in." Hopefully the smile on her face looked halfway genuine as she swung the door open.

She'd only seen him in shorts or a tux. He stood in front of her in dark wash jeans and a long-sleeved polo shirt the same intense blue of his eyes. The eyes that warmed as he looked at her.

"Don't mind if I do." He held out a casual bouquet with asters and wildflowers. "I couldn't resist these, though they can't rival your beauty."

Sarah bit her lip and turned away. How far did this man think flattery would get him? "They're pretty. Thanks." She stepped into the kitchen just off the foyer and pulled a vase from a cupboard. A moment later she had the flowers in water and arranged.

"Nice vase." He'd followed her into the kitchen.

"Thanks. It's from a local potter. I really like her work."

"I can see why."

She angled her head at him. Man, he was close. "They didn't make you sneeze?"

Corbin shook his head. "Most natural aromas don't affect me that way. Just artificial ones."

"Well, I left the perfume in its bottle tonight."

He grinned, a bit sideways. "Thanks. For the record, you don't need it. You smell terrific just the way you are."

Sarah stepped back. He'd been sniffing her?

"Ready to go? We have a six o'clock reservation."

She breathed. "Sure. Let me grab my purse. Where are we going?"

He escorted her down the steps to the parking lot and into a gleaming black pickup. "The Water Wheel."

Oh boy. Only the most expensive place in Riverbend. At least their premier chef, Lindsey, was on her honeymoon and wouldn't be peeking through the kitchen pass-through giving sly winks and thumbs-ups.

"Sounds nice," Sarah ventured when Corbin had started the truck.

He glanced across at her, and his hands flexed on the steering wheel. If she didn't know better, she'd suspect Mr. Flirt was nervous. Somehow that didn't dissipate the butterflies in her own stomach. Could it be he was actually interested in her, not just because she was female, not ugly, and twenty-something?

Question was, if she weren't a wee bit interested herself, why was she so nervous and tongue-tied? That line of internal thought could be an endless loop. "Tell me about your farm."

He shot her a smile. "My lifelong dream, but it couldn't have become reality so soon if I hadn't inherited it from my grandfather."

"I'm sorry for your loss."

"I miss him," Corbin said simply. "He was the one person who always seemed to understand me."

Sarah bit her lip so she wouldn't admit how hard he was to figure out. No need to go there yet, or ever. This was the only date they'd have.

They crossed the bridge into Riverbend and Corbin signaled a right turn at the first traffic light. A few minutes later he shut off the truck beside Riverside Park. A glow from the early-evening sun warmed the gazebo, flowerbeds, and manicured lawn. So peaceful, even with several children riding bicycles and tossing Frisbees. She let out a sigh she hadn't realized she was holding as she reached for the door handle.

Corbin touched her arm. "Allow me, please." In no time he'd come around the truck and opened the passenger door. She slid out, thankful for the running board to make the big step more manageable. He smiled at her as he took her hand.

Should she allow him that familiarity? What did it matter? It was only a few steps to the Water Wheel Restaurant at the end of the park. Besides, his hand was warm and his grip firm but not possessive. Somewhere this evening he seemed to have lost his gift of gab. This date might not be so bad after all.

Corbin seated Sarah in the fireplace nook he'd reserved. A row of candles in assorted shapes and sizes of holders flickered from the mantle, and a soft glow warmed the space from a hidden light source.

The waiter presented them with menus and took their drink order. No surprise that Sarah ordered pop the way she'd guzzled it at rehearsal. He settled for unsweetened tea.

Sarah turned a page and glanced up at him.

He'd been staring. Watching her. No thoughts of what food to order had yet crossed his mind. He quirked a smile at her.

"What are you having?" she asked.

Corbin opened the menu. This wasn't the sort of place a guy came with his buddies, so he had no idea what the options were. He glanced over the selections and pointed. "Steak, I think. Baked potato, vegetables in season, and a salad." Hard to go wrong with steak in an upscale place like this. "How about you?"

"Maybe the cordon bleu. That comes with a rice pilaf."

"Sounds good. Scallops for an appetizer?" Lindsey had once made those at Nick's apartment for a few friends. They'd been to die for.

"Oh, I cou—" She bit off the words. "Thank you. That sounds nice."

The waiter brought their drinks and Corbin ordered for both of them. Sarah seemed mesmerized by the flickering flames in the fireplace. For his part, he couldn't help watching the shifting glow on her face and hair.

"Thanks for coming tonight," he said at last.

She turned toward him, a question in her eyes.

"I'm glad you didn't turn me down. I'm surprised, actually. What made you say *yes*?" He held his breath. What was he hoping she'd say, that she found him as attractive as he found her?

Sarah folded the linen napkin in half and ran her thumb down the crease. "Lindsey made me promise to give you a chance."

Her words were so low he wasn't sure he'd heard correctly. "I have Lindsey to thank?"

"Don't sound so surprised. You know she chucked that bouquet directly at me. She has her own agenda, that girl."

"I guess I owe her one."

Sarah raised an eyebrow. "You two didn't plan it in advance?"

He grinned. "No, believe it or not." He leaned across the table. "So I'm thankful for her help. But I guess it's my job to make sure you have such a good time you'll be happy enough at the end of the evening to agree when I ask you out again."

His gaze held hers for a long moment. The firelight seemed to flicker in her brown eyes and add even more dimensions to the tones in her streaked hair. What was she thinking? That she'd like to smack her friend... or might she even be thankful already for the set-up? Whichever it was, Corbin was grateful for the reprieve.

She'd never have guessed he could be this gentlemanly and, well, nice. Though his quirky humor definitely peeked through a time or two, the dinner went well. Sarah was pretty sure the food had been good, too, but the memory that stayed with her would be more about the intensity in his blue eyes and the sexy grin that lifted one side of his mouth more than the other.

"Tell me about weddings," he said unexpectedly.

Sarah frowned. “What do you mean?”

He shrugged. “You said you’d never been on Team Bride before?”

Team Bride. Did he have to keep saying that? “Never as a bridesmaid.”

“That’s crazy. You must have lots of friends.”

She let her eyebrows go up. “Are you saying I’m an old maid? That all my friends must be married by now?”

He blinked. “Not at all what I meant.”

“I have plenty of single friends.”

“I, uh...”

“I’m just not very fond of weddings.”

Corbin leaned back in his chair. “I thought women were all over weddings. The ultimate party to plan. To be the star of the show.”

“Women are individuals. One size does not fit all.”

“I have a few sisters, and they’re definitely not clones of each other. But they agree on parties.”

“That’s nice.” A desperate need to change the focus shot through her. “You seem to like them, too. Not all guys do.”

“Sure do. Parties are great, and weddings are the best of them all.”

Sarah shook her head. He was for real?

He grinned at her. “I’ve been a ring bearer twice. Groomsman twice.” He checked them off on his fingers. “Now best man twice. Team Groom six times.”

Wasn’t this backwards? If there had been any doubt she shouldn’t date Corbin Morrissey — and there hadn’t been any — there wasn’t anymore. She needed to find a guy who wanted to elope.

“You said you’d been a flower girl? I bet you were the cutest one ever. I bet you drove the ring bearer crazy.”

“Not as crazy as he drove me.” She shuddered. Some memories were better left untouched. “I barely escaped with my life.” Her dignity certainly hadn’t been intact.

He laughed. “Sounds serious. Whose wedding was it?”

Sarah shook her head. “I don’t remember their names. They were my parents’ friends, I think. We moved quite a few times back then after my parents split up, and before Mom moved my brother and me to Riverbend.”

Genuine regret slid into his gaze. "I'm sorry. My folks went through some rough patches, but they grew together. They're a good example of a solid marriage now."

"It's kind of tough." Sarah toyed with her napkin. "So many marriages end in divorce. One of my friends is divorced already after only three years. Another is really struggling."

"Is that why you didn't want to stand up for Lindsey and Nick?"

She pulled her eyebrows together. "Who told you that?"

"Lindsey was ecstatic when you said you would. She was afraid you'd say no, but she wouldn't say why."

Good thing her best friend had showed a bit of restraint. "I really hope they make it."

"I know they will." Corbin spoke with deep conviction.

"You can't know that. You can't even know it for yourself, let alone for someone else. Things happen." She shrugged. "People change. Or maybe it's their true colors coming out. Nick was a real jerk in high school. I'd like to think he's changed, but what if he hasn't? What if, deep down, he's still the same guy? I don't want Lindsey hurt. She's already been through so much with her mom dying and all."

Corbin leaned across the table and wrapped both his hands around hers. "Nick changed, Sarah. He repented of his old ways and asked God to forgive him. He became a new creature in Jesus. Don't you believe that faith in Christ can change a person from the inside out?"

She opened her mouth and closed it again. Did she? Sure, she said she did, but she still guarded herself, just in case. What kind of faith was that? Faith. The evidence of things unseen. She pulled her hands away and laid them in her lap. "I do believe that. In theory. In reality, people are pretty messed up."

He regarded her steadily. "When I get married, it will be for life. My parents taught me love is a choice. It doesn't ultimately have a lot to do with fluttery feelings. Those can be fickle."

This was getting mighty personal for a first date. Even a wedding-inspired one. But she couldn't let his words go. "That's great, but marriage is two people. What if your wife decides she doesn't love you anymore? Leaves you? Has an affair?"

Corbin opened his mouth.

She held up a hand to forestall him. “You can’t deny it’s a possibility. People are human. Stuff happens.”

“I intend to love her so lavishly she’ll never be tempted to look elsewhere.”

Sarah laughed. She couldn’t help it. “I wish you all the best with that. Seriously. You’ll need it.”

She became aware of the waiter hovering just outside the alcove. “Can I interest you in dessert? We have a lovely turtle cheesecake this evening, or you might prefer a fall fruit compote with ice cream from Glacial Creamery.”

“No, thanks.” Sarah laid her napkin on the table. “I think we’re about done here.”

“Maybe next time,” Corbin told the waiter.

Right. Like they’d be back together. She bit her lip. But the thought of being that fervently loved was attracting. Could she be that woman? Did she have any desire to be?

A few minutes later they strolled the long way through the park back to the truck.

Corbin twined his fingers around hers, and she let him. “I have a question for you.”

“Isn’t it a bit too soon for that?” Oh, man, had she really said that out loud? He’d think she was flirting. Was she?

“Maybe.” He laughed. “So I’ll save the big one for a few weeks. We can build up to it. Where do you want to go with me next weekend?”

The quick answer would be nowhere, but it wasn’t strictly true. He’d been surprisingly good company and even had a serious streak. Intriguing. She caught herself nodding.

He bumped her shoulder. “That doesn’t answer my question, but I’ll take the affirmative. A movie? A picnic at the lake? A bike ride? Or we could catch the fall fair down at Arrowsmith.”

What happened to avoiding this clown at all cost? She couldn’t be so desperate for a date as to consider going out with him again. He’d probably take it as a sign they should be married or something. *Lavishly loved.* “Sure.”

Corbin laughed, swinging her hand. “Still not giving me much to go on, fair lady.”

"I'd like to see your farm."

"We can do that sometime, but the fall fair is only next weekend. I can pick you up at nine. Dress comfy with good walking shoes."

Had he actually just diverted her request? She hadn't been asking to see someone else's animals and produce, but a full day at the fair would be a real test. She'd know for sure by the end of it if he was as much a waste of her time as she'd thought at first.

Chapter Five

The clang of the Ferris wheel, the murmur and vibrant colors of the large crowd, and the aroma of hot buttered popcorn mingled with corn dogs welcomed Corbin as he slid out of the truck and rounded the front. He breathed in deeply. None of the odors twitched his nose. So far, so good.

Corbin opened the passenger door, and Sarah hopped down, her eyes wide. “Wow. I had no idea it was this big.”

“Didn’t you come here when you were a teen?” He would’ve been all over it.

She shrugged. “No, the midway came to Riverbend with the carnival rides. And the sharpshooter games. That’s all we cared about. My friends and I weren’t really into farm animals.”

And yet she wanted to see his farm, and he’d put her off. Why, on both counts? She probably expected something nicer than his place. He’d seen her apartment, at least from the doorway. Modern and airy, so unlike the tumbledown house Grandpa had left him. Also unlike the classic farmhouse as seen on television. Was he ashamed of his home? Not really... or he hadn’t been before. He’d have to think on that later.

Corbin wrapped his fingers around hers. “There’s more to do than the midway, and more to look at than animals. Come on! What do you want to do first?”

Sarah squeezed his hand. “Surprise me.”

She already had.

He paid their entrance fee and purchased a roll of tickets for the rides. He steered her toward the main pavilion. “Let’s see the winning entries.”

They wandered past the baked goods and preserves, past the gigantic pumpkins and towering corn stalks. The next long room housed the arts and crafts contests from photography to quilting. Sarah seemed more interested in the whole experience than he'd expected.

"Look at that pottery." Corbin pointed to the far end. "I wonder if your potter won an award."

"Let's go see." She dragged him forward.

He grinned and followed in her wake.

"No, it's by someone else, but kind of similar." Sarah's fingers caressed the handle of the blue-ribbon mug. "Maybe they don't let professionals in, but I wouldn't mind finding some pieces by this potter. I like the lines and colors a lot." She pulled out her phone and snapped a close-up.

Corbin memorized the artist's name. Sarah had good taste... or at least taste that matched his.

His nose warned him which pavilion was next. "Ready for the animals?"

"Sure! This is more fun than I thought."

Whew. Maybe his idea of a date wasn't as bad as he'd feared. The crowds thickened, adding to the noise and smell of the animals. Calves bleated, a rooster crowed, and somewhere ahead, a lamb bawled.

"Wow. So many animals. Do you raise this many kinds?"

They escaped into the bright sunshine of the fairgrounds.

"No, just chickens, pigs, and sheep for market, and a calf every year for family. I've thought of adding some llamas but there isn't an established market for the meat. Holiday's Hobby Farm has a few, and I hear people love seeing them."

Sarah nodded. "I've taken first graders out to Holiday's a few times. They do it up big with hay rides and everything."

"Right. I'm not in their market. I run a working farm, not a tourist trap."

She chuckled, bumping his arm. "Kids need to see your kind of farm, too. What do you say to a field trip sometime?"

Uh... no? But looking into her brown eyes, lit up expectantly, he couldn't quite get the word out. "Maybe sometime. Hey, are you hungry? I see the Yellow Bus." He pointed down the concession row. "Good food."

* * *

Sarah eyed the towering Ferris wheel and leaned closer to Corbin as they waited in line. "Probably eating before riding this was a bad idea."

He chuckled. "Maybe, but it'll be fun. I love these things. And then the zipper."

She shuddered. Figured he'd like the big thrill rides. "When should I tell you the spinning teacups are my favorite?"

Corbin laughed. "You crack me up." He handed a pair of tickets to the operator. "In you go, fair lady."

Well, she wasn't going to be a sissy in front of him, that was for sure. She slid into the seat, Corbin right behind her, and the operator latched the bar. The wheel shifted so the teens behind them could board their seat. Then again. In a few minutes she had a view of the entire fairground and all the pavilions. The seat rocked gently each time the wheel moved.

Then they were off. Sarah clenched the bar and closed her eyes. She was not going to scream, and she was not going to lose that sausage bun. Her gut rolled as the wheel turned and the wind whipped her hair. How could anyone think—

"I love the view!" yelled Corbin.

Why on earth had she agreed to come to the fair with him? This was crazy. She was going to die or, worse yet, embarrass herself. She snatched a glance at him. His hands were high in the air, and a gleeful grin stretched across his face.

She should not date Corbin Morrissey. She'd had a dozen reasons before today. Now she had at least one hundred.

The Ferris wheel slammed to a stop. The seat swung violently. Might it even flip around the bar? No. Whew.

A voice came through the sound system. "Sorry, ladies and gentlemen. We've got a bit of a problem here."

Somebody screamed.

This could not be happening. Sarah unpinched one eye to evaluate, but the ground was far below and she scrunched it shut again. Her fingers were so numb from clenching the bar it took her a few seconds to realize Corbin was rubbing her hand.

"Hey, you okay? They'll get us down."

No peeking. "C-can you see what's wrong?" Would they have to get fire ladders to get people back to solid ground? Why did this have to happen when she was on the ride?

"I can't tell." His voice sounded distant, like he was turned away from her. The seat rocked slightly. "There are a couple of people talking at the control booth, but no one is looking at the motor."

"Th-they should be. They should fix it."

A laugh came through the loudspeaker. "Okay, there's nothing wrong. I was just pulling your leg. But I'm not starting the wheel again until everyone takes their chance for a nice kiss."

He *what?*

Corbin laughed and lowered his voice. "I'll be happy to collect on that." He slid his arm across her shoulders.

Sarah found anger deep inside. "He staged this? I hope they fire him. That's just mean."

Corbin rested his cheek against her hair. "They won't. May I kiss you, Sarah?"

She pulled away. "Are you kidding me?" Her heart was still pounding overtime and it didn't have anything to do with the handsome guy beside her. "I want to get down now. Solid ground."

He kissed her cheek. "We'll be off in a couple of minutes."

"Not soon enough for me."

"I thought you liked the carnival. You said you and your friends used to come."

Yeah, she'd said that, but she'd forgotten about the rides she didn't like. She'd forgotten how many times she'd sat on a bench and watched her friends ride things she wouldn't go on. She'd forgotten how much cotton candy she'd eaten instead. "I think the rides are bigger now. Scarier."

The wheel turned to let riders disembark.

Corbin's arm tightened across her shoulders. "So I'm guessing the zipper is a no?"

There wasn't room to shrug him off. She took a deep breath and released it. "I'd rather not, but you may if you like. I'll wait."

"We're together." His fingers massaged her shoulder as the wheel lurched another notch. "Spinning teacups, then? I can live with that."

She was ruining all his fun. Why did he have to be a good sport about it? But hey, she'd tried. Somehow she'd survived the Ferris wheel, extra scare or not. "Teacups are good."

Finally it was their turn to get off. It was all she could do not to kiss the ground. They rode the teacups and got stems of cotton candy before wandering down the midway.

"Miss Jamieson! Miss Jamieson!" Two little girls barreled against Sarah, knocking her against Corbin.

She crouched and curved an arm around each child. "Elena! And Sophie. I've missed you in my class this fall. Now you're in second grade. Do you have Mrs. Christenson for a teacher?"

The brown-haired girl nestled against Sarah's shoulder as she nodded.

"She's nice, but not as nice as you," announced the blonde, dancing in front of them. "You are our bestest teacher ever."

Sarah smiled. Oh, how she loved teaching, and these two were something special. Chance words of her own had melded two little strangers who shared a birthday into best friends, a friendship that had turned them into true twins and sisters when their parents had fallen in love and married.

"Is this your boyfriend, Miss Jamieson?" Elena, the blonde, parked her hands on her hips and looked up at Corbin. "He's kind of good-looking, sort of like my new daddy. Did you know I have a new daddy, Miss Jamieson?"

"Elena, that's not a polite question," her mom said.

Sarah straightened and smiled at the girls' parents. "It's okay. I'm not sure if Mr. Morrissey is my boyfriend. I met him two weeks ago, and this is only the second time we've gone out."

Elena tipped her head. "Is he nice? He looks nice. I think you should marry him. Can I be your flower girl? Me and Sophie?"

"Elena!" The girl's mom clamped her hand on the child's shoulder.

"But we're all practiced up, Mommy. Didn't we do a good job for you and my new daddy? We sprinkled petals all down the walkway, just like you asked." She looked at Sarah. "They smelled pretty, too."

Sarah shoved the memories of her own stint as a flower girl into the dark recesses of her mind. Her experiences weren't relevant to the two cuties in front of her. “That’s very nice. As far as I know, Mr. Morrissey and I aren’t having a wedding, but I’ll keep the two of you in mind, just in case.” She held up her hand. “No promises, though, okay?”

“It will be beautiful.” Elena nodded as she tapped a finger to her mouth, deep in thought. “Sophie and me both look good in pink.”

“Okay, Elena, really. That’s enough out of you now.” Her mom reached out a hand. “Let’s go see which rides you and Sophie are tall enough to go on.”

“Yay! Rides!”

The dad grinned and winked at Sarah then reached for the girls’ hands and led them toward the carnival.

“Sorry about that,” Kelly said, leaning closer for a few seconds. “She’s going to keep us hopping for a long time.”

“Really, it’s okay. It’s a nice change from six-year-old boys asking to marry me. I’m used to nearly anything by now.”

Kelly stretched a hand toward Corbin. “I hope my daughter didn’t scare you off. I’m Kelly... Tomlinson, by the way. I still have to get used to saying that. Sarah’s a gem.”

“Corbin Morrissey.” He shook Kelly’s hand. “I’ve noticed she’s pretty special.”

Kelly grinned. “I’d better catch up with Ian and the girls. Nice running into you.” She turned and hurried away.

* * *

Corbin snagged Sarah’s hand. “Your students are lucky to have you.”

“Aw, thanks. Sorry they were so forward. Typical of Elena though. I’m not sure how many times she proposed to Sophie’s father.”

He chuckled. “Sounds cute.”

“For everyone but Kelly and Ian, I’m sure it was. Anyway, forget about them. Where were we headed?”

They’d already done the teacup, thankfully. For a sissy ride it was kind of fun, at least with her, but that didn’t mean he wanted to do it again.

Why on earth was he attracted to Sarah? Corbin couldn't figure it out. Sure, she was pretty, but so were a lot of other women, and Sarah didn't have the sense of adventure he did. Good thing? Bad thing?

Down the sharpshooter gallery, a stuffed purple dragon caught his eye, and he steered Sarah toward it. "Want one of those?" He leaned so close her hair brushed his cheek.

She angled her eyebrows as she glanced up at him. "You think you are a good enough shot?"

Better not brag too much. Besides, at a place like this it wasn't so much being a good shot as figuring out which way the gun veered. It might take a few rounds, but he'd get it. He waggled his eyebrows. "I guess we'll see."

He plunked down his money and picked up the toy gun. It was more likely to aim high or low than too far to the side, or it would be a menace. So... aim high then.

Poof.

He let off a shot and noted where it landed.

Poof.

Still too low.

Poof.

Getting closer.

Poof.

A little to the left.

Poof.

"Sorry about that, mister. Maybe another time."

"Like right now." Corbin dropped more cash on the counter. This time he dropped all five shots onto their targets. "I'll take the purple dragon."

The kid stared at him a moment before pulling down the three-foot-long stuffed animal and handing it across.

Corbin bowed. "For you, I will slay any dragons that come in your path." He presented the gift to Sarah.

She grinned and tucked the monstrosity under her arm. "What are you, my knight in shining armor?"

"I'm glad to hear you're finally realizing it."

Chapter Six

If I'd known you and Corbin were actually going to go on more than one date together, I'd have changed the time of our Thanksgiving dinner so he could come, too." Lindsey slouched into an easy chair in Sarah's living room a few days after she and Nick had returned from their honeymoon. "As it is, my step dad is taking Madison to his sister's for dinner on Monday."

"Sunday's great." Sarah stretched. "We're going for a bike ride Monday anyway. It's all good."

"Aren't you glad I made you promise to go out with him at least once?"

Sarah laughed. "Okay, yes. I think."

"Has he kissed you?"

If she were really falling in love — or at least like — shouldn't she want to talk about it? "Hey, want a cup of tea?"

"Evasion tactics, eh? No, I don't, but I think I asked a question. Has Corbin kissed you?"

"I don't think it's any of your business."

Lindsey burst out laughing. "That either means he has, and you don't want to talk about it, or he hasn't, and you wish he would. Which is it?"

Wishing? "No. No kissing." Though she'd wondered if he might when he dropped her off after the fair. She could still remember the intensity in his eyes as his hands caressed her face. Then his lips had brushed her forehead, and he'd been gone.

"What's holding him back, you think?"

It wasn't him. It was her. "Are you kidding me? We barely know each other, and besides, we're so different. I don't see how this can last."

"Sarah? I can't read your face. Do you like Corbin, or don't you?"

"I'm confused. I do like him, but he's so different from me. He's an *act now, think later* kind of guy."

"And you think everything. To. The. Death."

Sarah glared at Lindsey. "Whose side are you on, anyway?"

"Yours, girl. Definitely yours. I think Corbin is a great balance for you. And yes, you for him. It's okay to have different personalities. God made us all unique."

Corbin was about the most unique person she knew. "It's possible to be too different."

Lindsey tilted her head. "True, but sharing the same faith in Jesus provides a solid foundation."

"A good start, sure. But there are a lot more things. How you prioritize spending. How you raise kids—"

"Whoa! You guys have talked about kids? You're way more serious than I thought after only two weeks."

Warmth crept up Sarah's cheeks. "No, we haven't. I'm just thinking ahead."

Lindsey laughed. "That's your problem. It's like you're picking your retirement home before you turn thirty. Take things one step at a time?"

"Look, I'm trying, okay? You're my friend. Don't push me."

"Aw, Sarah. I'm not poking fun at you. I want you to be happy. I want you to see each new day as a possibility. To give Corbin a chance."

"I am." Sarah gritted her teeth. "We've gone out. We're going out again Monday. I don't know what more you expect from me."

"To relax and enjoy it?"

"I'm trying, but Corbin seems to think life is one big joke. Like that rock he got out of the river and duct-taped to a washer as the ring for your wedding rehearsal."

"You have to admit that was pretty funny."

"I suppose."

"Oh come on, Sarah. He knows when to be serious. He managed the real ring just fine during the wedding."

"True." Sarah rubbed the soft fur on the dragon. "He's the youngest of five kids, and the only boy. Everyone doted on him."

"He can't help that."

"No, I know. But I think it went to his head. I never know when he's joking or being serious."

Lindsey held up a hand. "And you like everything in its neat little compartments. You want comedy routines to be announced so you know it's okay to laugh."

"Is that so wrong? It's not that I don't like to have fun." Did she even know what fun meant, compared to Corbin? "It's just that he's almost never serious."

"So he keeps you off balance."

Sarah stared at Lindsey. "Yeah."

"Love does that. It messes with your equilibrium."

"Oh, good grief. I'm not in love with him. We've been on two dates, that's all." She wrapped her arms around the dragon, holding it close to her chest.

Lindsey reached across and grabbed the dragon's tail, but Sarah didn't let go. Lindsey laughed. "What did he say when he won this bad boy?"

Oh, man. Did she have to say?

Lindsey raised her eyebrows. "By the look on your face, it was pretty good. Spill, girl."

What did it matter? Years — maybe only months — from now Corbin would be long gone, and all she'd have was this plushy to remember him by. She thrust the toy at her friend. "Something about slaying all my dragons for me."

Lindsey pushed it back. "Sounds romantic."

It had been, in the dusk of the midway. Now, in the light of day, she wasn't sure. "After the fright I had on the Ferris wheel, he rode the teacups with me."

Lindsey burst out laughing. "Corbin in the teacups? Tell me it's not true."

"See, I don't even know why you and I are friends."

"Sarah, you're too much. Personally, I think Corbin is perfect for you. He stretches you out of your comfort zone—"

"A place I quite like, thank you very much."

"And it sounds like you stretch him out of his. That's good."

"Just because you've been Mrs. Nick for two weeks doesn't make you an expert in everyone else's relationships."

"Hey, girl, I'm on your side. You know how hard it was for me to believe Nick had changed since the jerk he was in high school? He needed a chance to prove to me that Jesus had made him a new man. It wasn't easy to accept, even while I was being swept away by all the anonymous gifts he sent."

Having a plush dragon gallantly presented to her was at least as romantic as all the secret admirer gifts Nick had showered on Lindsey.

"So I think you need to give Corbin a chance, too."

"What do you think I'm doing? We've gone out twice, and will again on Monday."

"But are you letting yourself see the good in him? Are you willing to see him as a potential life partner?"

Sarah opened her mouth, but closed it again when Lindsey put up her hand.

"He's a good guy, Sarah. He's a solid Christian man, and I think he's fallen for you. Open yourself up a bit and see where this takes you."

"You keep saying that as though I'm already singing the swan song."

Lindsey quirked an elegant eyebrow. "Aren't you? You're twenty-eight. It's okay to date with the future in mind. It's more than going to the fair like some teenagers."

"Hey! It was Corbin's idea." One she should've turned down, so he wouldn't see what a chicken she was.

"I didn't say it was *bad*. I just said there's more. A whole lot more."

"Yeah, well, you're married. I don't want to hear about the *more* part."

Lindsey chuckled. "We'll have that talk later, after Corbin's popped the question and you've said *yes*. Trust me."

Could she envision his proposal? Man, a guy like him would probably pull off something public and YouTube-worthy. Instead of being thrilled, she'd be mortified. She shuddered. "I don't think I can do this, Linds."

"What are you really afraid of?" Her friend's voice was soft with compassion.

Sarah clutched the dragon tight. "I don't know. It took a lot for me to stand up with you. That wedding I was in when I was a kid... I've managed to block most of the memories, but it was horrible."

"You've never told me what happened."

"I didn't really know the people. They were neighbors or something. All they cared about was that I was cute. The ring bearer was a couple of years older, and he was mean, and no one stood up for me."

"What kind of mean?"

"I took my job of dropping flower petals very seriously."

To give credit where credit was due, Lindsey did *not* roll her eyes. "I'm sure you did."

"At first he danced around me, picking them back up and returning them to my basket. When people began to snicker, he dumped out the whole basket, grabbed my hand and dragged me to the front."

"Uh oh. What did you do?"

"I burst into tears, yanked my hand out of his, and ran back to the pile of petals." Memory lane was so not a good place. Tears prickled her eyes along with the childhood humiliation.

"And then?"

"He ran after me and kicked the pile of petals, laughing as he scattered them."

"What a brat. No wonder you were scarred for life." Lindsey reached over and squeezed Sarah's hands.

"The junior bridesmaids came and dragged me to the front of the church. Someone dabbed my face with a tissue, and then I stood where I was told for the whole ceremony. It seemed really really long."

"No wonder you said you didn't want to be in my wedding party if there were preschoolers involved. I'm glad I didn't have my heart set on it."

"Me, too. Anyway, let's talk about something else. I've tried to forget that wedding ever since it happened."

"Corbin! Now there's a sight for sore eyes." Aunt Deb made a show of peering past him. "Didn't I tell you to bring a date for Thanksgiving dinner? I don't see her anywhere."

She'd been telling him to bring a date for years. Even on the rare occasions he'd been seeing someone, he hadn't dared inflict Aunt Deb on the unsuspecting girl. Wonder how Sarah would handle her? If she could manage thirty six-year-olds, surely his aunt could be dealt with.

"Corbin Jonathan. I worry about you." Deb dragged him into the house. "It was bad enough before, but now you live way out of town on that farm all by yourself. How are you even going to meet your intended if you never get out?"

He chuckled. "You make me sound like a hermit. It's not that bad."

Aunt Deb whirled and planted her hands on her ample hips. "Tell me three occasions in the past month where you could have met someone."

Corbin pretended to be deep in thought, scrounging for answers. "There was that wedding I was in a few weeks back. I headed up Team Groom, and there were some beautiful women on Team Bride." At least one.

His aunt zoomed in like a shark. "Oh? Tell me more."

"The wedding will have to count as two occasions. After all, there was a rehearsal and a wedding. Two different days."

"Same girls," Aunt Deb countered.

He'd pretend she hadn't said that. He couldn't very well count the dinner date with Sarah. "And I went to the Arrowsmith Fall Fair last weekend."

Her gaze narrowed. "By yourself?"

He held back the grin. "No, with a friend."

"A male friend or a female friend?"

"Female."

She slugged him in the arm. "Corbin Jonathan! You've been holding out on me. Tell me everything."

As if. "Not much to tell. We just met and have been out a couple of times."

"And you didn't invite her to Thanksgiving dinner so we could all meet her?"

"She had plans with friends. And besides, I'm not sure she's ready for you."

"Oh, what do you mean by that? All we have are your best interests at heart. What's her name?"

"Sarah." If he gave more information, Aunt Deb would look her up on Facebook, send her a friend request, and follow up with Corbin's baby pictures. No thanks.

"Well, listen up, Corbin Jonathan. Your uncle and I are celebrating our twenty-fifth wedding anniversary in two weeks, and we're having a big party here at the house. You will be here, and you will bring that girlfriend of yours, you hear? I'm not taking no for an answer."

He slung his arm across his aunt's shoulders. "We'll see."

Aunt Deb shrugged him away. "None of that nonsense. This is a very important family event, so it's the perfect time for her to meet everyone. After all, your parents and the twins will be here, too. We'll see if she's good enough for our boy."

"If you're going to come at her like a piranha, I'm not bringing her. You have to promise to be on your best behavior or I won't even extend an invitation."

She opened her mouth to speak but he held up his hand. "I mean it. She's not like this crazy family. She's quiet. Reserved. And if you scare her away, I won't come to your house for Christmas or Thanksgiving for five years."

"You wouldn't."

"Don't push, Aunt Deb. Sarah is too important to me to let that happen."

Aunt Deb smacked his arm, a wide grin crossing her face. "Well, now you've gone and done it. You're falling in love. I promise to be just the sweetest auntie you ever saw and welcome her in like one of our own."

Now why wasn't that a comforting thought?

Chapter Seven

"Do you do this route often?"

Sarah swerved her bike toward Corbin's. "Nearly every day when the weather is decent. This cycling trail is the main reason I chose an apartment on the east side of the river."

"A bit less handy to your job and the conveniences of downtown."

She shrugged. "It's worth it. And there's a Save-on-More Foods in the mall on this side and a banking kiosk. I don't go downtown often, unless I need a cupcake from Carmen's." She glanced his way. "Besides, you live further from the bright lights than I do."

His long legs, clad in ankle-length cycling pants, ate up the paved trail, but she didn't think she'd have any trouble keeping up. There might not be many good days left. Red-gold maple leaves crunched as their wheels rolled through, and a gentle breeze kept the day from being too warm. The blue sky had a hint of turquoise, perfect for October.

"I don't mind living out of town, but I sometimes miss having people around."

Of course he did. Not her, though. "I see enough people at work, so I'm happy to be a hermit evenings and weekends. Between all the other teachers, the parents, and the twenty-two kids in my class, that's enough interaction for me."

"Yeah, sometimes I miss having a real job." He pedaled harder, his bike pulling ahead.

"So why not have one?" She pushed to catch up.

"Because the farm takes too much time except in winter." He glanced at her. "I might work with Heath this winter if we get a lot of snow."

"Heath?" The name sounded familiar.

"He was on Team Groom, remember? He has a landscaping business, and in the winter he uses his Bobcats for snow removal."

"Cool. But that doesn't sound very people-oriented."

Corbin shrugged. "No, but it will get me into town, and there's always coffee time at Carmen's Cupcakes. Anyway, nothing's for sure. Depends how much snow we get, for starters."

He seemed kind of different today. Distracted. Maybe he'd decided he didn't want to go out with her after all, but hadn't known how to cancel their bike ride. She could be glad he hadn't just ghosted out of her life without warning. Yet, that is.

"So I was talking to Ms. LeRoy, the school principal, on Friday..."

Corbin glanced her way and grinned, crinkle lines showing around his eyes. "You're not in trouble, are you?"

That grin went a long way to dispel her fears. "No. So far I've managed to avoid trouble at work. But she said the field trip we'd scheduled for late October had to be canceled. I'd planned to take the kids out to Glacial Creamery so they could see how ice cream is made, but the owner was in an accident and they had to close the shop early this year."

"Oh, I'm sorry to hear that. The Desmonds, right? Everyone okay?"

See, Corbin was a nice guy who genuinely cared about people. She was safe with him. "Yes, I think so. Anyway, I was wondering about bringing my class out to your farm. I think it's important that kids know where their food comes from, don't you?"

"Uh, that's definitely true."

"Then may we come? Next week Friday?"

He scratched his neck as he glanced at her.

Classic evasive body language. "Or not, if you don't want us to. I can think of somewhere else." Not sure where, but this wasn't a good sign.

"I'm not sure kids will find my place all that interesting. It's just a farm. Nothing special."

"Corbin, I'm sorry for asking." She shot a look at him. Dare she say more? If they were ever to have a real relationship, yeah. "I asked to see your place before and you put me off. Is there something I should know?"

His smile looked forced. "I did, didn't I?"

She waited.

"It's just... kind of rundown. My grandfather left it in a mess and I'm working at fixing it up as I can, but it takes time. Time and money."

What was she supposed to make of that? "Everything takes time and money. Oh, and energy."

"Yeah." He shook his head. "I... I like you, Sarah. A lot. I didn't expect to want to spend so much time with you. More to the point, I didn't expect you to agree to go out with me more than once."

Whoa. Sarah's bike wobbled. She hit the brakes then dropped both feet to the paved path. The self-assured prankster didn't have all the confidence that seemed to ooze from his pores?

Corbin glanced over his shoulder then turned in a tight circle back to her. "Sarah?" He lowered his bike to the ground and straddled the front tire of hers, watching her. His hands covered hers on the handlebars as he took a deep breath, those blue eyes serious for once. "I think I'm falling in love."

"You-you are?" She hated that her voice came out in a squeak. He wouldn't joke about this, would he? He joked about everything else.

His thumbs rubbed the backs of her hands. "I know this sounds presumptuous, but you need to know I'm a farmer. My grandfather left me that piece of land because he knew I always identified with it." He cracked a grin. "And because I was his only grandson. It's not a fancy piece of land, and the house isn't that great, but it's mine, and I'm not leaving it."

This sounded like either a warning or a lead-in to a marriage proposal. She searched his face. More like a warning. This was his vulnerability.

Sarah extracted one hand and cupped his jaw. "I'd like to see your farm, Corbin." If he'd given her a warning, she needed to know what it entailed.

He leaned against her fingers slightly, and for a second she thought he might close the gap and kiss her. He didn't. "Want to finish this ride and then drive out? It's almost halfway to Castlebrook."

If she married this man, she'd be another thirty minutes from work, a long drive on icy rural roads. If she married this man. Now who was getting ahead of herself?

"I'd like that."

He brushed his lips across her forehead, and she nearly melted into a puddle. "Come on then. Race you back." He set his bike upright and mounted.

"No fair. Your legs are a meter longer than mine."

He grinned. "Excuses, excuses."

Corbin watched Sarah in his rearview mirror as her car followed his truck down the rutted driveway. He parked beside the house and waved her to the spot beside him.

What would it be like to have her drive in every afternoon after teaching her classes? She'd taken time to change into jeans and a peach sweater after their ride. Did she wear jeans to work? He opened her car door and she slid out, pushing sunglasses up onto her forehead and securing her long blond hair.

His breath hitched. There was nothing like seeing her on his turf — literally — to send his imagination wild. But before he could cut its tether, he needed to read her as she met his life. "Ready for the penny tour?"

Sarah nodded as she glanced around. Her eyes lingered on the house. Had she already catalogued the drooping roof over the veranda and the crooked steps? He always used the door around back. Safer, for one thing.

Her gaze met his. "Sure."

Corbin took her hand and steered her away from the house. First things first. "A lot of the farm is the way Grandpa left it. I've been making some improvements here and there as I've had time." Would she see the potential? Or only that it was rundown?

"What do you think my class will like to see?"

So she was making this trip a two-fer. Corbin exhaled. He'd play along.

They stopped in front of the chicken house. "These are always a favorite. Of course, there aren't any cute fluffy babies this time of year. You could bring them back in spring for that." If she'd ever want to return. "Baby chicks, piglets, lambs... enough cuteness to make your eyes bleed."

Sarah ran her free hand down the wire mesh. "That will turn all my students into vegetarians for sure."

"Not usually. Given a balanced worldview, kids usually figure things out. Besides, most of them are addicted to chicken strips and hamburgers. It doesn't hurt for them to know where those come from." She hadn't ordered vegetarian at the Water Wheel, had she? No. Chicken Cordon Bleu. Whew.

"So, those birds." Sarah pointed into the pen. "They're headed for nugget land?"

"Nope. The meat birds are already sold or in the freezer. Those are my layers."

"Layers?" She looked up at him.

"They lay eggs, which I sell to Loco-to-Go and a couple of stores."

Sarah nodded and turned away. "What else?"

He showed her the pasture where the pigs rooted, surrounded by an electric fence. Hmm. He'd have to make sure the kids understood not to touch that. Over the knoll, the sheep pasture. This year's lambs had already been sent to the abattoir, and the young pigs wouldn't be much longer. The horses followed them along the corral.

"No cows? And here I thought they were a farm staple."

"Grandpa kept an old milk cow. She's over in the far pasture with this year's calf."

"Interesting. I'm not seeing what will keep the children's attention for long, though they'll like the horses."

How about her own? He wished he could see what was going on behind those deep brown eyes.

"Kids like to run and play and experience nature. At least I sure did." Maybe they needed more structure. Corbin pointed to the area behind the house. "Let me show you the garden and orchard."

She fell into step beside him again, her fingers still tangled in his. "What kind of fruit trees?"

"Apples. Several heritage varieties and some newer ones, too. We're in the midst of picking." He reached up, plucked a Honeycrisp from a tree, rubbed it on his T-shirt, and handed it to her.

Sarah took a bite, removing a chunk of the red skin and white flesh. Her eyes widened. “Wow, that’s good.”

Corbin grinned. “They’re so much better fresh than when they’ve been packed in a controlled-atmosphere cooler for months.” At the side of the orchard, he pointed out the garden area. “Pretty much everything is off now. I’ve still got some tomatoes and greens in the hothouse to send fresh produce into town until the frosts are heavier.” Thankfully he’d run the tractor and rotovator through the garden last week, tilling in the hay he’d used as mulch as well as the weeds that had been left.

“How many people work for you out here? All this looks like it needs a full crew.”

Is this where he told her he didn’t really have a life? “Just me, most of the time. I have someone a couple of mornings a week through the summer to help with the weeding.”

She turned to face him. “Really?”

Better be honest. “That’s all I can afford at the moment. I’m trying to do some repairs, too. Grandpa let things slide the last few years.” Last few decades, really.

“It must keep you busy.” She crunched into the apple.

“It does.” He eyed her. Was she wondering how she might fit in? “But I love it. I can’t imagine living anywhere else with any other career.”

“You’re not kidding, are you?”

Corbin grinned. “Quite a shock, eh? Yep, I can be serious. And this is one of those times.” Should he take her in his arms and show her he could be serious about two things at once? Maybe better not.

Her gaze around the orchard seemed more speculative.

He held his breath.

“Okay. Any thoughts on what will keep my students’ attention here for a couple of hours?”

Corbin dared to breathe. “I was thinking... I have an old cider press. Think the kids might like to make apple juice? They could each take a liter bottle home.”

“Really?” Sarah turned to him with a smile. “That sounds like the ticket. Now we just need to pick a date.”

He’d picked one already. Her.

Chapter Eight

Sarah followed Corbin into his farmhouse, a classic style with dormer windows above the front porch. The kitchen floor was covered with ancient pitted linoleum and the cupboards looked to have been made with plywood, but renovators paid good money for salvaged sinks like the one under the six-paned window.

He stood in the middle of the space, hands fisted at his sides, staring past her. Nervous. Vulnerable.

"Wow, Corbin, you have so much potential here."

His eyes latched onto hers like a drowning man might grab a life ring. "You think?" A lilt of hope.

"So much character. Such good bones."

"I haven't had time to do much inside yet. I've been focused on getting the farm to pay for itself. I thought I might start on the house over the winter, but I'm not even sure where to begin."

Sarah had watched enough HGTV to have an answer for that. "Is the foundation solid?"

That cut off his words. He closed the few steps between them then reached for both her hands. "I don't know. Is it?"

Her breath hitched. He wasn't talking about the house anymore. She clutched his fingers. "What do you mean?"

"I'm not asking you to marry me. I know it's much too early for that."

No kidding. Sarah swallowed hard.

"But, well, this is what you're up against." He disengaged his hands and looped them loosely around her waist. "Do you want to keep moving forward and see where we end up? Or do you want to run while the running's good? Farm life isn't for everyone."

Someone must have hurt him. Who would have guessed his bravado masked such insecurity? She slid her hands up his chest and felt his muscles tighten before she cupped his face between both hands. "I haven't seen any reason to run yet," she whispered.

His eyes asked permission as he gathered her more tightly in his arms then tugged her against himself. "Sarah..."

She tipped her face to his and closed her eyes as his lips caressed hers, softly at first then with more intensity. How long had she been waiting for this? Possibly her entire life.

Corbin cradled Sarah against his chest and deepened the kiss. Thrill at her acceptance — no, her matching desire — shivered through him. This moment would change his life forever. He knew it clear down to his toenails.

Sarah. She's the one.

It would be easy, so unbelievably easy, to forget everything but her in this moment. He lived far from the road, far from town. There was zero chance in the world anyone would come in his driveway and discover them here.

But, no. That wasn't the next course to lay on the foundation they'd built thus far. He managed to remove his mouth from hers and buried his face in the crook of her shoulder with a groan. "Oh, Sarah."

She held him tightly as their breathing slowed in unison. "Corbin, I—"

He feathered his lips down her throat. "Yes, fair lady?"

"I want you to kiss me again."

"Gladly." But he'd keep better control this time. He tasted her mouth and sealed it possessively with a kiss then took a step back, catching her hands in his.

Sarah's eyes blinked open, looking a little dazed.

He probably looked the same. He trailed his fingers through her hair to smooth the muss he'd made, and she leaned into his touch. "Sarah, I love you." Had he ever spoken sweeter words?

She met his gaze, brown eyes filled with wonder. "I love you, too."

He'd certainly never heard anything sweeter.

"Want to stay for supper? I have burgers, and we can fire up the grill." She'd have to leave soon after, though. The temptation was going to kill him.

"I'd like that." She smiled tremulously. "Will you show me the rest of the house first?"

Corbin took a deep breath. Bathroom. Bedrooms. He couldn't do it. "You go on and have a look, and I'll get food started."

Her eyebrows furrowed slightly, and he smoothed his thumb over them.

"Go ahead. Snoop wherever you like. The stairs are just off the living room." He turned her and gave her a tiny nudge in the right direction.

"Okaaay." She glanced over her shoulder before ambling into the other room. Her hand slid across the antique oak table then she disappeared through the archway.

Corbin dared to breathe. Pretty sure he'd tossed his boxers in the laundry hamper and made his bed. She might find a layer of dust in some of the rooms, but not much out of place.

Her footsteps halted, and he forced himself to lean back against the counter rather than check what had caught her attention. *God? Is this for real? What have I done to deserve her?*

A woman's love wasn't deserved; he knew that. No more than God's love was. *Thank You, Jesus.*

The stairs creaked as she ascended, and Corbin turned to his fridge. He'd cooked up a big pot of potatoes yesterday, enough to make hash browns all week. He could make a big salad with lettuce from the greenhouse and some of the ripe tomatoes sitting on the counter. He'd picked up buns... yeah, he was good. No dessert, but then he hadn't expected to invite her out today. He'd planned to put that off for a really long time.

Corbin began preparations as he listened to Sarah move around upstairs. Seldom-used doors creaked, and so did the oak plank hallway. Three bedrooms. The bathroom. Her footsteps descended then moved into the laundry room that included the main floor bath.

He had the salad assembled before she reappeared in the kitchen.

"Oh, Corbin. I love your house."

He blinked. "Really? It's old. Rundown." Not what she was used to, from what he'd seen.

"But it has so much character." She came closer, stopping beside him. "So much history."

The hair on his arm strained the half-centimeter to hers. Okay, he couldn't resist. He set the blade on the cutting board and gathered her into his arms. "You're serious? You like it?"

"I've watched more HGTV than you'd believe. And if you followed me on Pinterest, you'd see my obsession with projects giving new life to antiques."

"I'm not that old. And I resent being called a project." Corbin kissed her forehead. "Also, what is Pinterest?"

"Silly." She grinned up at him then tilted her head. "Seriously?"

He chuckled. "No, I know what it is. Looked around the site once and ran out screaming."

"I have eighty-two pin boards."

He didn't even want to know. It sounded like an obsession. But maybe he could learn a lot about her by glancing over them. Hmm. Maybe later. "I'm ready to go out and grill the burgers. I'll do some hash browns on the side burner, if that's okay?"

"Sounds great. What can I do to help?"

"You can set the patio table if you like, and bring out the salad."

"You're on."

Sarah, wearing one of Corbin's over-sized hoodies, settled back into a lawn chair with a contented sigh. What a man of surprises. Between the farm-and-house tour, the spine-tingling kisses, and the delicious if simple meal, she felt like she'd entered a new dimension.

She glanced his way to catch his smoldering gaze on her. Gone immediately was the cool chill of an October evening. Who knew love was a heat source? Love. So unexpected.

"What are you thinking?" he asked, voice low and husky.

Good thing he didn't have a swing for two out here. She needed the distance as much as she hated it. But what a loaded question. "I'm thinking... I'm thinking today has been full of surprises."

Corbin nodded, his eyes fixed on her in the dusk. "It has, at that."

He seemed to expect more. But what could she say that didn't sound too presumptuous? "It will be interesting to see where God leads from here."

"It will." He reached across the span and caressed her hand. "Do you still want to bring your students out?"

"May I? On Friday. Next week. Is that okay for apple juice? I think they'll like it."

"Sounds good. I'll see if I can get Heath or Nick to give me a hand."

She opened her mouth to offer.

"You'll be busy with your class, and I can't expect the parents to know what to do on the technical side."

"Of course. That makes sense." Sarah turned her hand over so she could slide her fingers between his. "I'll double check with the principal and confirm with you in the next day or two. I don't see why it would be a problem, though. The day has already been set aside."

His cell rang shrilly in the evening air. He glanced at the phone and grimaced. "It's my aunt. I need to take this, if it's okay."

"Sure, go for it."

"Hi, Aunt Deb ... Right ... Yes, I remember ... No, you don't need to set me up with anyone, thanks anyway ... I know. You've mentioned it before ... Aunt Deb ... Let me get a word in edgewise here."

Corbin grinned at Sarah, shaking his head.

"Listen, I have someone to invite ... I told you about her, didn't I? I met a wonderful woman without your help. Hard to believe, I know ... I haven't asked her yet, but I'll let you know ... Uh, Aunt Deb? She's right here. I'm not answering that."

Sarah tipped her head, trying to catch his gaze. What did his aunt want to know?

"Saturday at four. Got it ... Aunt Deb, I need to go. I'll call you tomorrow ... Yes, everything's fine, but I gotta go ... Love you, too." He rolled his eyes and thumbed the phone off.

Sarah raised her eyebrows and grinned at him. "What was all that about?"

"My aunt is constantly trying to set me up with someone. She's sure I'm lonely and need a wife."

"Do you?"

The words hung between them then Corbin scratched the back of his neck. "Anyway, it's their twenty-fifth anniversary this weekend and they're having a party. She said if I wasn't bringing someone she'd find me a date."

Sarah chomped back the grin. "She sounds serious."

"Oh, yeah." He gave her a sidelong glance. "I was going to ask you on my own time, but she pushed my hand. Are you free Saturday? Would you be my date to their anniversary party in Castlebrook?"

This was scarily easy to answer. She'd be his date anywhere, anytime. "I don't have any other plans, so why not?"

"The *why not* might be Aunt Deb. No doubt she'll be looking for a diamond ring and a wedding date by the end of the evening."

"We don't have to let her push us."

"True." He snuck another look. "My parents will be there from Calgary. Two of my sisters. But none of them can hold a candle to my overbearing Aunt Deb."

So this would be the official meet-the-family date. Was she ready for that? Was Corbin? He didn't seem like it, but then he'd been reluctant to have her out to the farm, too, and look how that had turned out. She sucked in her lip, planning on another kiss or two before she drove back to Riverbend.

Wait. What if she were reading him wrong? What if he wasn't worried about what she'd think of his family? "Is it me?" Her heart thudded. "Am I not going to be good enough for them?"

He startled, his eyes finally holding hers. "No, Sarah. Never that. They will love you, I promise." He swallowed hard. "As I do. It's just you might not know how to take them. They tease a lot, and I know there'll be pressure. I'd just as soon wait a bit longer to send you into the lions' den, but..." He smiled at an angle. "I really don't want my aunt to go hunting down a date for me, either. I want you by my side."

"Then I'll be there."

“I hope you won’t regret it. Can I pick you up at two? Semi-formal is good. No bridesmaid dress.”

“So no tux for you?”

He chuckled. “Not this time. I’ll be in dress pants, a button-down shirt, and a sweater, if that helps.”

He’d be easy on the eyes. The man cleaned up nice.

Chapter Nine

"Corbin!" Aunt Deb swung the door open wide and crushed him against her, casting his memory back to the wedding reception line a few weeks back. "You made it." Then she seemed to notice Sarah. She looked from one to the other. "And who's this? I know I told you to bring a date — and I certainly meant it — but this is the first time you've actually obeyed me."

He reached for Sarah's hand and tugged her forward. "This is Sarah. Sarah, my aunt Deb."

Aunt Deb was an equal-opportunity hugger. Sarah disappeared into enfolded arms and came out a moment later looking dazed.

Corbin could sympathize.

"Aren't you lovely?" gushed Aunt Deb, holding Sarah at arm's length. "Where did you meet our Corbin?"

Sarah's eyes cast a plea in his direction. "We were both in the wedding party of mutual friends in September."

"Now there's a romantic way to be introduced! I'm thrilled he's finally met someone. I was about to take matters into my own hands, but I see I should have trusted him."

Corbin stepped between them, forcing his aunt to release Sarah. He slid his arm around her and grinned at Deb. "Yes, you should have. Now be nice to Sarah, or you'll scare her away. And trust me, I don't want to lose her."

"Oh, pshaw. I'm sure she doesn't scare that easily. She's put up with you for over a month already. Do come in."

Sarah trembled under his arm, so he tightened his grip on her waist as he guided her into the house. "I don't see my parents' car here yet."

"They'll be here any minute, and dinner will be on the table shortly. Then on to the celebrations!"

That sounded ominous, but he put on a brave smile. "What do you have planned?"

Deb leaned closer to Sarah. "If you think that boy is cute now, just wait until you see him as a five-year-old!"

Sarah glanced helplessly between Corbin and his aunt.

"Oh, no, Aunt Deb. You don't need to inflict your old wedding video on Sarah. Or on any of us, for that matter." It hadn't been his best day as a ring bearer.

She swatted at his arm. It would probably leave a mark. "Oh, you. It's Uncle Don's and my twenty-fifth anniversary party. Of course we'll be looking at old photos and such. So many happy memories."

There'd be no dissuading her. Corbin shrugged. "She's right about one thing, Sarah. I was a cute little kid. And wait until you see the flower girl I was paired with at the Double D wedding. You'll be jealous. She was all over me."

He'd been all over the flower girl, too. Why hadn't he remembered Aunt Deb would pull out all the stops? He only hoped his and Sarah's relationship could handle the next few hours... and his parents hadn't even arrived yet.

Sarah shook her head slightly as a little smile poked at her cheeks.

They followed Deb through to the kitchen at the back of the house.

"Corbin!" His sister flew at him, knocking him back a step. "Aunt Deb said you were bringing someone." She beamed at Sarah. "I'm Corbin's big sister, Amanda."

"This is Sarah," he managed to get into the half-second lull.

"I'm so excited to meet you!"

Sarah smiled. "Thank you."

By the way she hung back and clung to his hand, she was finding this as overwhelming as he'd feared. Might as well get it over with, though. "Is Michelle here?"

"Yes. She just ran down to the basement for another jar of pickles." Amanda turned back to Sarah. "Michelle's my twin."

"Th-that's nice."

Corbin leaned closer to Sarah. "I'm sure the only reason Aunt Deb invited them is because they were junior bridesmaids at the Double D wedding."

Amanda laughed. Was he super-sensitive because of Sarah, or was everyone being really loud today? “Oh, you know how Aunt Deb is. She was looking for an excuse to get the family together. We convoyed down from Calgary with Michelle and Mark.”

“Corbin!” shrieked Michelle as she ran across the room. “And you must be Sarah. Welcome to the family.”

“Um, hi.”

“Sarah is a first grade teacher.” He beamed at his sisters.

“Oh, that’s wonderful. You must love kids.” She pointed at herself and Amanda. “We both have boys that age. What a handful.”

By the glazed look in Sarah’s eyes, he needed to get her out of there. “We’re heading out to the back deck for some air. Let me know when the parents arrive, will you?”

“No hanky-panky now.” Amanda winked broadly.

As though he were sixteen. “Not to worry.” He put his hand on the small of Sarah’s back and nudged her ahead of him through the dining room and out the French doors. “Whew. Sorry about that.”

She let out a long breath. “You did warn me.”

“The good news is they live in Calgary and we only get together two or three times a year. Also, they will want to be your best friends. Not sure whether that’s good news or bad.” He wrapped both arms around her and pulled her close to his chest.

Sarah’s laugh sounded weak. “I’m not sure, either. I only have one aunt, and she’s unmarried and lives in London. I’ve met her half a dozen times in my life. My brother lives in Toronto and my mom in Vancouver. This kind of thing—” she tipped her thumb back over her shoulder “—just doesn’t happen in my world.”

“I can see advantages both ways.”

“I’m sure.” She looked into his eyes. “Please don’t leave me alone for even two minutes.”

“I might have to go to the bathroom sometime.”

She shuddered. “Can’t you hold it for six hours? Please?”

Corbin chuckled. “For you, I’ll try.”

A kiss or two later, Sarah decided she might be able to survive this family gathering after all. Maybe.

"Corbin! Deb said I'd find you out here. And your lovely girlfriend."

Time held still for one frozen second then Sarah turned in Corbin's arms.

"Hi, Mom. I'd like you to meet Sarah. Sarah, this is my mom, Lisa."

What a way for Corbin's mother to first see her, lip locked with her son. Sarah pulled up a smile as she met the middle-aged woman's gaze. "I'm so pleased to meet you."

"And I you." Lisa gave her son a significant look. "Interesting I had to learn about this development from my sister."

Corbin's arm around Sarah's waist didn't falter. "Oops, sorry about that."

He hadn't told his parents about their dates? Oh, man. But how could Sarah fault him? When was the last time she'd called her own mother? Besides, the relationship was still pretty new.

If it was that new, why had she started a secret Pinterest board for wedding ideas? Flipped through the bridal magazine another teacher had left in the staff room? Paused in front of the mall's lingerie shop?

None of it was anything to be ashamed of. She was twenty-eight and dating a handsome Christian man. Just because her parents had split up before they were her age didn't mean she was flawed, or that marriage was.

"We've been so worried about Corbin, living away out there in the country," Lisa was saying. "The life of the party turned into a monk."

Corbin's fingers twitched against Sarah's waist. "Not exactly a monk, Mom. Just waiting for the right woman to come along."

"Well, either way, welcome to the family, dear." Lisa kissed both Sarah's cheeks. "Deb says dinner is ready."

Bringing Sarah to this party had been a mistake. He should have invited his parents down one weekend or taken Sarah to Calgary, so she could meet them on her own terms. He'd known she didn't like crowds or a lot of attention.

There wasn't anything quiet about a Morrisseey-Shawnigan get together, and it seemed everyone peppered Sarah with questions. No one but him seemed to notice as she withdrew behind a curtain while right beside him at the dinner table.

Even Amanda's and Michelle's tales of their children's antics did nothing to restore the glint in Sarah's eyes.

Was the whole thing a mistake? Any woman who loved him was going to have to put up with his family. Yeah, they were rather boisterous, but he'd never seen that as a negative before he'd thought of bringing Sarah into their midst. Their older sisters had moved farther east, and the twins' husbands seemed to take it all in stride, though they disappeared to watch a hockey game often enough at family gatherings.

Corbin's wife would never have someone to disappear with like that. He was the only son, and the twins would always be a twosome.

He slid his arm across the back of Sarah's chair and leaned closer to her soft blond hair. "You okay?" he whispered.

She flashed him a quick smile. "I'll be fine."

Now why didn't she sound convincing? "Want to make a quick getaway right after dinner? We don't have to stay for the video or cake."

He felt her stiffen slightly. "I don't want to ruin everyone's evening."

"If you're sure."

Sarah nodded slightly.

She was right. The worst was likely over and, besides, he always got a chuckle out of the Double D wedding video.

He cupped his hand on her shoulder. "You'll see the first time I played on Team Groom. I was cute."

She sent him another small smile. "I can't imagine anything else."

"I can borrow it from Aunt Deb and show you some other time if you'd rather." The thought had merit. "We'll pop up a big bag of popcorn and watch it out at my place. Or yours."

"Corbin." She placed her hand on his leg. "Don't worry. It's all a bit overwhelming, but I'm an adult. It's okay."

He stared at her tanned tapered fingers against the black of his dress pants. That one right there — he ran his thumb down the length of it — would look terrific with a diamond on it.

The thought brought with it roiling emotions. Desire, protectiveness, and yes, a bit of fear.

He covered her hand and squeezed as he leaned into her hair. “I love you,” he whispered.

“Earth to Cory!” Laughter rang out around the table at Michelle’s jab.

“Still true,” he murmured against Sarah’s hair before facing his sister. “Yes? Someone called from outer space?”

“Nice one, Cory.” Amanda reached across the table for a high-five, but that would mean disconnecting from Sarah, and that wasn’t happening. He waggled his eyebrows at his sister instead.

Amanda rolled her eyes and sank back to her seat.

“Cory?” whispered Sarah.

He shrugged. “Childhood nickname that reappears occasionally.”

“Cute.”

He couldn’t tell if she meant it or not. Unlike a Morrissey, she didn’t hang every thought out on the clothesline for the world to hear and see. That had advantages and disadvantages.

Corbin rubbed that one special finger against his leg again. The Morrisseys and Shawnigans might be loud, but they were loyal, too. When they found love, they didn’t let go. He’d bet the Double D had their share of arguments. His own parents had certainly indulged in more than one shouting match behind closed doors. Yet here they were.

Amanda had left Mark once and landed back on their parents’ doorstep. Mom had marched them down to the church for counseling, and they’d worked things out.

Corbin was under no illusions. Marriage wouldn’t always be kisses and diamonds, sunshine and roses. But the rewards would be worth wading through the storms and thorns.

Would Sarah agree?

Chapter Ten

A wedding video would have to be easier to endure than that family dinner with everyone screeching like magpies. Corbin's sisters were probably very nice, but did they have to amp up the volume every time one told a story over top of the other?

The relative quiet of the basement family room soothed Sarah. Just a few more hours, and they could return to Riverbend. Corbin would have had his family outing, and she wouldn't have embarrassed him. Well, that was likely impossible, but at least she wouldn't have embarrassed herself. She wanted them to like her. Really, she did, but she'd never be able to fit in.

The room was packed with bodies. Sarah sat on the fuzzy carpet beside Corbin, leaning against a padded ottoman. He held her hand in both of his, the length of his body pressed against hers. With his rock-steady comfort, she could survive.

Don slid the disc into the player and fumbled around with the remote control until Amanda grabbed it from his hands and pressed a few buttons.

Deb leaned over to Sarah. "We had the old video formatted onto a DVD several years ago, along with our favorite photos of our big day."

Sarah smiled back over her shoulder. "What a great idea."

The first snapshots projected, bigger than life, on a 60" TV screen. Sarah frowned. Something about the bride and groom looked vaguely familiar. Had Sarah seen that lacy white gown with poufy sleeves before? Corbin's aunt hadn't been a tiny woman even twenty-five years ago, and she liked her hair just as big now as she had then. Maybe it was just that she still looked like the same woman.

A few photos later, shots of the entire wedding party came onscreen. Sarah caught her breath and stared. But when the beaming bride crouched beside the nervous flower girl, her gut clenched.

"That's me," she whispered.

Corbin leaned closer. "What did you say?"

"I said that flower girl is me." More photos flowed by. She'd never seen them before, but that didn't keep her from being certain.

He laughed. "No way."

"I'm serious."

Corbin leaned back. "Aunt Deb? Who was your flower girl?"

"A little neighbor girl named Sarah. Why?"

He stared at Sarah, questions in his eyes. "Did you keep in touch with her family?"

"No, sadly. They moved away right after the wedding, and we lost track of them. I heard the parents split up. Wasn't she sweet, though?"

"Very." Corbin slid his arm around Sarah's shoulders and tugged her closer. "Are you sure?" he whispered, clasping her fingers with his free hand.

The actual wedding ceremony came on the screen, now in video. Men in pink ruffled shirts, sparkling cumberbunds, and white tuxedos lined up at the front of the church.

The basement family room seemed devoid of air. Sarah's world narrowed to the déjà-vu on the screen.

"Positive," she whispered back as the first of three bridesmaids in pastel pink lace strolled down the aisle. Next, two junior bridesmaids pranced together.

A loud smack off to the side could only be Amanda and Michelle high-fiving each other for the umpteenth time today. "Weren't we the cutest ever?" asked Amanda.

Sarah's memories weren't anywhere near the adorable meter. She tightened her grip on Corbin's hand.

Then the flower girl appeared, her blond ringlets wreathed in pink flowers that matched her dress. She marched beside the ring bearer and clutched the basket with one hand while scattering pink petals on the orange carpet with the other. The ring bearer bent down and scooped petals back into the basket.

The wedding guests tittered, and he grinned at the attention. A few seconds later he grabbed the basket and swung around, flinging the flowers across the aisle and nearby guests, then waved at the videographer before dragging the flower girl toward the front.

The girl jerked free and stomped her foot.

Humiliation washed over Sarah along with the visual. She tried to pull her hand from Corbin's, but he didn't release it.

With her face puckered up in tears, the flower girl ran back to the petals and knelt, scooping them in the basket. The two junior bridesmaids followed her more sedately, took her by both arms, and hauled her to the front. Crying.

Everyone in Deb and Don's family room chuckled. Tears stung Sarah's eyes in pity for the little girl she'd been.

Everything flooded back to her. All the humiliation. "That was the worst day of my life." Her words seemed loud in the basement room. "I hated that Cory for years."

"I'm sorry. I shouldn't have done that." He even sounded sincere.

"Sarah, darling, was that really you? How could it be?" Deb patted her shoulder. "We all called him Cory back then. What a small world."

"I can't believe this." Emotion choked Sarah's throat. "That was such a horrible day. No wonder I've avoided weddings." She glared at Corbin.

"I'm sorry, Sarah. I was only five." He ducked his head.

The DVD paused.

"You've always been this way, haven't you? Aw, shucks, look at me. I'm cute."

Corbin spread his hands and looked at her with a pleading expression. "I'm sorry. It's who I am. I can't undo the past, or I would."

Sarah envisioned a lifetime of being the brunt of his jokes. He was still the life of the party, as his mom had said. Sarah had been traumatized enough as a child. She didn't need to keep going back for more.

"I'm sorry." From behind them, Deb sounded uncertain. "We don't have to keep watching it."

Sarah surged to her feet. "It's okay. It's your tradition. Your anniversary."

"But—"

"No, really. I'll be fine." Once she got over her shock, anyway. She stalked on wooden legs to the nearby powder room and splashed water on her face then stared at herself in the mirror. She wasn't that little girl anymore. The little girl who'd been alone among strangers who laughed at her, and when someone finally delivered her back home, she'd discovered...

Sarah burst into tears as memories poured over her.

Dad had been gone. Mom had the van packed, waiting, and her brother was having a screaming fit in his car seat. Mom unceremoniously strapped Sarah in beside him, still in her fluffy pink dress, and drove all night. They ended up in a distant town where they knew no one then moved several more times before ending up in Riverbend when Sarah was eight.

No one had mentioned Dad since Sarah had cried for him that night. Mom told her to shut up, that he was never coming back and good riddance.

Yes, that horrid day had sucked her into her shell and made it difficult for her to carry on. Was it even why she'd decided to be a teacher? She'd always felt an affinity for little kids who didn't quite fit in.

She hadn't fit in all through school. She still didn't. Her life was a sham. She'd always be alone, a scared child looking in through the window at someone else's Norman Rockwell life.

Corbin wasn't her ticket out of that situation. He was the reason she was there in the first place.

Corbin pressed his ear against the powder room door. All he could hear was the running faucet, and it had been going for five full minutes.

"Sarah?" He knocked again. "Are you okay?"

The door opened so quickly he nearly tumbled into the small space. Sarah stood forlorn, tears streaking her face and both arms wrapped around her middle.

"Sarah." He reached for her.

She pushed his hands away as she shoved past him. "Please take me home, Corbin. Or never mind. I'll just get a cab."

His heart ached. "Let's go."

Hurting eyes amid smudged mascara avoided his. "Thank you." She marched up the stairs to the main floor.

Corbin turned to the family room doorway, where all his relatives sat more subdued than he'd ever seen before. "Sorry to break up the evening. I'm taking Sarah home."

Aunt Deb surged to her feet. "I'll come say goodbye and apologize for the wedding. It never occurred to me, all these years, what that poor child must have felt like."

He hesitated, Sarah's blank stare still chilling his gut. "Might be best to save it for another time. Thanks, though. I'll tell her." Would there ever be another time? He nodded around at his family and followed Sarah up the stairs.

She stood at the front door with her coat on and her purse clutched to her chest. Hadn't taken her long.

"Sarah?" He touched her arm.

"Please."

Oh, Lord, the day had started with such promise. What was he supposed to do now? How could he fix something that had happened twenty-five years ago?

Sarah stared out the truck window. The vibrant autumn leaves dimmed in the gathering dusk. Like life. Headed into nighttime. Headed into winter.

Corbin had been all about the peppy praise music on the drive to Castlebrook. They'd talked over it, around it, and about it. Why couldn't he turn on the stereo now to cover the silence? Maybe he didn't have any dirges. That was about the only style that would fit.

Her gut, her heart, all of her being felt like one frozen, painful lump. She should've known better than to open up to someone, especially a guy like Corbin. Somehow she'd been attracted to fun. Laughter. Dreams of love.

Shuddering, she pulled her arms tighter around her middle, but it was too late to protect herself. The damage was done.

"I love you, Sarah. I'm sorry."

Sarah shifted slightly in her seat. He'd said that dozens of times in the past hour. She'd ignored him every time. She had to hold strong. Better to rip the adhesive bandage off in one quick move than linger and hope.

The lights of Riverbend gleamed ahead as they rounded the last curve on the mountain highway. Riverbend. It had always been a safe place for her. Now, all she could wish was that the school year was coming to an end and not just beginning, so she could apply for a position in a different district.

Mom had run from her problems, too. Blocked them out. Sarah was like her mother. Nothing new there.

She clenched her jaw as they drove past the car dealerships, then the mall, and finally pulled up in front of the apartment building beside the riverside bike path. One of her hands reached for the seat belt clasp while the other tugged the door handle.

Corbin's hand covered hers on the buckle. "Sarah."

She stared straight ahead. "I have nothing to say."

"Look, I understand why you're angry, but that happened a quarter of a century ago. I can't undo the past, no matter how much I'd like to. All I can do is apologize and prove my love for you now, today, is genuine."

Could she let the past go? His hand on hers warmed her. Terrified her. It wasn't enough to thaw her entire frozen interior, just enough to feel a little again.

Sarah pushed the button to release the seat belt and yanked her hand out from under his. "Apology accepted." She shoved the truck door open and slid from the warm interior into the chilly night air.

He bounded around the vehicle and grasped both her hands before she could take more than a few steps. "Thank you, Sarah."

She pushed him away. "It doesn't change anything."

"But—"

"There are no buts, Corbin. I can forgive the little boy." It would be a whole lot harder to forgive the ignorant behavior of the adults that long ago day. "But don't you see? You're still you. I'm still me. We're too different to make anything work long term."

Corbin shoved his hands into his jacket pockets. “I don’t agree. Differences are good. We complement each other. And besides, we have the Holy Spirit living inside us. He changes us and makes us more like Jesus. We’re not stuck being the same old people we always were.”

That stung. “So I’m a second-class Christian because I’m having trouble dealing with this?”

“What? No. I didn’t say that.”

A dozen thoughts ran through Sarah’s mind, but she managed to keep all of them from coming out her mouth while she took three deep breaths. “I’m sorry, Corbin. You’ll thank me later when you meet the right girl for you.”

“I’ve already met her. She’s you.”

Sarah backed up a couple of steps, shaking her head, as the ice solidified. “No. I can’t do this.” She turned and ran for the apartment steps.

Chapter Eleven

Corbin glanced around the dozens of people milling around the back of River of Life Church. He hadn't been here often, usually driving to the smaller church in Castlebrook he'd attended for years.

Nick had specifically invited him today, as it was his Sunday to preach. Being there for his buddy was his excuse should anyone ask. Not that he'd be believed. Everyone knew he and Sarah had been dating for the past six weeks and more.

Did they know it was off? His heart clenched. It couldn't be final. It was all a misunderstanding. She would put the past where it belonged and give him a chance to face the future together.

Wouldn't she?

"Hey, Corbin. Good to see you this morning." Lindsey peered around him as though looking for someone. "Where's Sarah?"

He kept his voice even. Mostly even. "She must be here somewhere. I haven't seen her."

Lindsey narrowed her eyes. "You didn't give her a ride?"

"Uh, no."

She chuckled. "Dating 101. Pick up the woman when you're going the same place anyway."

Corbin's jaw twitched. "Dating 101. Don't introduce your girlfriend to the relatives before your relationship is well established."

Lindsey was quick. He'd give her that. "Oh? She told me you were taking her to the anniversary thing. It didn't go well?"

"She told you about it before or after?"

"A few days ago, so before."

The music team began to play the call to worship. Lindsey grabbed Corbin's arm and steered him out into the foyer. "Tell me what happened," she said in a low voice.

The only thing he could think of worse than a fight with Sarah was driving a wedge between her and her closest friend. Corbin shook his head. "That should probably come from her."

"And she's not here." Lindsey bit her lip. "You're *sure* she's not here?"

"Her car's not in the parking lot, and I don't see her anywhere. And you haven't spotted her, either, I take it."

Lindsey shook her head, brows furrowed, as she pulled out her phone and tapped a message. She stared at it for a moment then put it away again. "She's not answering my text."

Did that mean Sarah was retreating from everyone, not just him? Not good. He breathed a prayer.

Inside the sanctuary, the worship leader welcomed the congregation into the service.

"I need to find my seat." Lindsey rested her hand on his arm. "Join me?"

Corbin nodded and followed her back into the sanctuary. She slid into the back row beside Heath.

The worship choruses washed over Corbin. He couldn't find the words. Couldn't find the tunes. He grasped the back of the seat in front of him and closed his eyes.

"Please open your Bibles to Philippians chapter three," Nick's voice intoned. "I'll read verses thirteen and fourteen from The Voice, and then we'll be shifting to the Old Testament."

Onionskin pages rustled around Corbin. He opened his Bible app and found the correct passage and translation.

"Brothers and sisters, I know I have not arrived; but there's one thing I am doing: I'm leaving my old life behind, putting everything on the line for this mission. I am sprinting toward the only goal that counts: to cross the line, to win the prize, and to hear God's call to resurrection life found exclusively in Jesus the Anointed."

Corbin stared at the words even as his heart reached out. Everything on the line. Even Sarah?

"In Isaiah forty-three, the prophet reminds his listeners of something similar: not to dwell in the past. The people of Israel clung to memories of the exodus from Egypt many generations before. Learning from the past is a good thing. Many times the people built cairns of rocks as reminders of God's goodness to them at specific times and places."

Corbin looked up at Nick, standing behind the pulpit. Who would have thought this day would come, when they were in Bible school together a few years back? That God would use Nick to put his own life in perspective?

"Hear the words of the Eternal One, beginning with verse eighteen. 'Don't revel only in the past, or spend all your time recounting the victories of days gone by. Watch closely: I am preparing something new; it's happening now, even as I speak, and you're about to see it. I am preparing a way through the desert; waters will flow where there had been none. Wild animals in the fields will honor Me; the wild dogs and surly birds will join in. There will be water enough for My chosen people, trickling springs and clear streams running through the desert. My people, the ones whom I chose and created for My own, will sing My praise. In truth, you never really called upon me, did you, Jacob, My people?'"

Nick paused and looked around the quiet sanctuary.

Corbin got the feeling he wasn't the only one to whom God's words spoke with piercing accuracy. Had he been so wrapped up in what had happened twenty-five years before — to say nothing of last night — that he wasn't trusting God for the future, whether or not Sarah was part of it? His love life — or lack of one — would have little impact on the fate of the universe.

He bowed his head. *Lord, I want Your best. I don't want to be one of those who never really called on You. I want to feel Your trickling springs and clear streams in my life. I want You more than anything. Even more than Sarah.*

Images of him letting go of Sarah, one reluctant finger lifting at a time, edged across his mind, followed by peace. Corbin settled into the pew to listen to his best friend expound God's word.

* * *

It was Monday morning. Sarah had gotten through Sunday by virtue of a long ride as far north as the bike trail went, then looping around to the highway and cycling home. She'd missed three texts from Lindsey and five more from Corbin. She deleted all of them without opening them.

She needed a plan to get her out of that looming field trip to Corbin's farm at the end of the week. She breathed a prayer — though why bother? When had God last listened to her? — and tapped on the principal's door before class. Then she got through her request as quickly as she could before Ms. LeRoy interrupted her.

The principal shook her head. "Sarah, we have all the permission forms back from the parents. The bus is reserved, and the chaperones are in place. I can't cancel the field trip with only a few days to spare."

Sarah shifted from one foot to the other, clammy hands clenched in front of her. "Please. I'll find somewhere else to take the classes. Let me try."

"The children are thrilled to see how apple juice is made. The other first grade teacher has units on apples scheduled all week." The principal glanced at the papers on her desk. "Looks like that is your lesson plan, as well."

"But—"

"Miss Jamieson, we are talking about the children's education. That is what field trips are for. If I'd known you had an emotional attachment to the man who owns this farm, I would have likely declined the plan to begin with, for just such a reason. But I did not know, and the arrangements are made. You will pull yourself together and act like a responsible, capable adult." Ms. LeRoy cracked a small smile. "Which you definitely are. You're a fine teacher, Sarah. I'm counting on you to hold it together and make this a memorable field trip for both classrooms."

Sarah took a deep breath. "Yes, ma'am. I'll do my best." She pivoted and strode out of the office as though she were in complete control. It wasn't over. She still had one card left to play. The trump.

* * *

On Monday, Corbin ordered a bouquet of flowers to be delivered to Sarah's apartment. On Tuesday, he sent a delivery from Carmen's Cupcakes and Confectionary. On Wednesday, he dropped a heartfelt poem into her mailbox. On Thursday, he tucked in a small box of chocolates. Hey, he could learn from the way Nick had wooed Lindsey.

His phone calls went directly to voice mail every time, and she continued to ignore his texts. He ought to be panicking by now, but he wasn't. Surely someone from Riverbend Elementary would let him know if the field trip had been canceled, and no one had. That meant Sarah and a whole lot of kids would invade his farm in the morning. He might not be able to speak with her privately, but he'd see how she was doing. God would show him what to do next. He had nothing else to cling to. Strangely, it was enough in this entire surreal week.

Sarah helped the last excited child into his sweater after the last bell. Outside the window, students streamed into the open doors of yellow school buses. More children abandoned lunch boxes and backpacks to climb on the playground.

She stood at the window, watching the colorful vision. These little ones meant everything to her. Teaching them numbers and letters, yes, but also to be fair and feel secure.

Now, what did she need to do to put her plan in motion for tomorrow? She turned toward her classroom, only then noticing Ms. LeRoy leaning against the doorway. Sarah's gut clenched. "Hi there. You startled me."

The principal strolled into the room and perched on a desk near Sarah's. "How has this week gone for you?"

"Um, not bad." Her mind scrambled to catch up. What was the purpose of this visit?

"You're looking well," Ms. LeRoy continued.

Better than she felt, no doubt. Her emotions careened into a pit. This conversation should not be happening.

"I'm glad to know things are fine. I'm sure there's no reason for me to worry that I might need to find a substitute teacher for your class tomorrow?" Ms. LeRoy's eyebrows angled upward.

Sarah opened her mouth and closed it again. Busted. "No, of course not." So much for that trump card. "My class is really looking forward to the outing." She gathered up her purse and paperwork as the principal smiled and nodded. She found herself walking down the corridor to the exit while Ms. LeRoy walked beside her, making small talk.

No sooner had Sarah escaped into the late October sunshine than the horn of a nearby vehicle honked. Lindsey.

Was it possible for the day to get worse?

Lindsey jumped out of her car and ran over to give Sarah a bone-crushing hug. "Girl! Is your phone broken? I've lost count of how many times I've tried to reach you this week."

"Um..."

Lindsey tipped her head and narrowed her eyes. "Unless you're avoiding me."

Sarah had never been that quick at a comeback. She stared into Lindsey's blue eyes a few seconds too long.

Lindsey looped her arm through Sarah's. "We're going to Carmen's. My treat. I'll drop you back for your car later."

"I'm busy." Sarah made a half-hearted attempt at breaking free. "I have grading to do tonight."

"You have the whole weekend for that. I'm not taking *no* for an answer. Consider yourself kidnapped."

Sarah would toss a prayer heavenward, but it seemed God and His angels conspired against her.

Chapter Twelve

Children poured out of the yellow school bus. Several adults whom Corbin did not recognize marshaled the youngsters into groups.

Heath elbowed him. "Your moment in the spotlight has arrived."

"Should've had you dress up as Santa Claus."

"Oh, come on. It's not even November yet. Besides, Santa doesn't do apple juice. It's all about the milk and cookies." Heath rubbed his flat belly. "I can hardly wait."

The stream of children slowed to a trickle. Where *was* Sarah? Worry attacked Corbin's gut. She wouldn't have sent a substitute, would she? Oh, man. He wouldn't put it past her.

"Come on, you're a natural onstage. Get with your program. Those chaperones are starting to wonder what to do with the kids."

His buddy was right, but Corbin's confidence had crashed with Sarah's absence. Where was the peace he'd found in his quiet times this week? He imagined reaching deep into that well and bringing up a bucketful. *Lord, You're in charge. As always.*

Corbin took a deep breath and rubbed his hands together as he stepped forward. "Welcome to Morrissey Farm! I'm happy you all have come today, and I hope you enjoy your visit."

He stuttered to a halt as Sarah stepped off the bus wearing dark jeans and a fitted navy jacket with pink ruffles from her blouse cascading over the front. Her hair had been gathered into a casual high ponytail with a pink tie.

She looked nothing short of amazing. A week ago he'd have expected to meet her gorgeous brown eyes, pull her into his arms, and kiss her. Maybe not in front of all these children.

Now she didn't glance his direction at all, but busied herself arranging students into a group around her. For protection?

"You were saying?" prompted Heath in a low voice.

Corbin blinked. "First we'll take a tour of the farm." He pointed toward the pair of Percheron horses harnessed to the wagon over by the barn. "If you'd like to meet the horses before the ride, please line up behind Miss Jamieson."

Her head jerked up and she stared at him, the bright dots high on her cheeks matching her accessories.

He smiled at her, trying to pour all the love he felt into his expression. Sure, he was putting her on the spot. Somehow he had to find a way to end this impasse. Today.

She turned stiffly. "Right here, class, if you want to meet the horses."

Corbin strode over to the wagon, Heath's low, "good job," ringing in his ears. He stroked Lucy's nose and slipped her an apple wedge.

"They're beautiful," a female voice said. "Are they a working team?"

Corbin met the woman's gaze. She was a pretty redhead nearly as tall as him, her eyes a warm green and flickering with interest. His nose twitched. A lot of perfume there. He tried to back up a step, but Lucy was in the way. "I use them when I can instead of the tractor. They're not suited to every task."

"I'm Steph Mabry. I heard you inherited this place from your grandfather, and I'm thrilled to have a chance to meet you."

"Uh, likewise. Corbin Morrissey."

Steph rested a manicured hand on his sleeve. "I know you're busy right now." She winked. "But I'd love to get together for coffee sometime. I sure do appreciate country living."

Words failed him.

"When my son brought the paper home about this field trip, I knew I had to take the day off from the bank and come along as a chaperone. It's hard being a single parent. Little boys need to be outdoors with lots of room to run around, and I just don't have access to that sort of thing in the apartment."

Corbin snapped his mouth shut and scratched the back of his neck. "I, uh. I'm sure." Was she seriously coming on to him? She'd practically proposed. What on Earth must Sarah think? He peered past Steph.

Sarah's brown eyes snapped dangerously from only a meter or two away, a row of restless children behind her.

"Excuse me," he said to Steph. "Duty calls."

She stepped aside and pointed out a curly redhead right behind Sarah. "That's my son, Reggie. Such a sweet boy."

"Great. Would you like to see the children settled on the wagon, Ms. Mabry? That would be a big help."

She smiled at him, head tipped to one side. "I'd love to. But do call me Steph." She waited a moment as though he would correct himself on the spot, but he made a show of looking past her. His nose stopped twitching from the scent overload as she moved out of his periphery.

"Right over here," he heard Heath say.

Good. Heath needed a woman in his life. Corbin already had one. He met Sarah's flashing eyes. Okay, he'd had one and lost her, but he wasn't giving up without a fight.

He fingered the halter. "This is Lucy, and that's Danny beside her. Lucy likes it if you touch her nose gently." Corbin beckoned to the redhead. "Reggie? Would you like to pet Lucy?"

The little guy nodded eagerly and stepped forward. "This is a big horse." Awe tinged his words as he reached up to pet Lucy. His eyes grew round. "It's soft."

Corbin grinned at the boy. "You're right." The kid couldn't be held accountable for his mother's actions. "Now go around to this side and climb up on the wagon, okay?"

He turned back to the line to see Sarah's clenched jaw. She motioned another child forward, and Corbin kept them moving around to the wagon after greeting the horses until only Sarah was left. "Want to pet the horse?"

She glared at him. "No, thank you." She followed the last student around to the crate Heath had set up for the children to climb onto the wagon.

Corbin shrugged, not that Sarah was looking, and met Heath's gaze. Heath's eyebrows twitched before Corbin swung himself onto the high seat at the front. He glanced back. "Everyone ready?"

A chorus of *yes* met his ears, and he flicked the reins over the horses' backs. "Move on, Lucy. Move on, Danny."

* * *

Reggie's mother leaned close to Sarah as the group watched the chickens scratching in their outdoor run. "I'm so glad I came today."

Sarah had never had this much trouble being gracious to one of her pupil's parents. "We needed the chaperones." Though Steph Mabry herself seemed to need one. Maybe Corbin did, too. He'd looked uncomfortable the first time, but seemed to have warmed up to Steph over the course of the last hour or so.

"A friend of mine from work who lives out this way has met Corbin a few times. She told me he was single, hot, and oh, so eligible." Steph sighed. "Wow. She was right. Isn't he a dream?"

Did Sarah seriously need to be part of this conversation? "Excuse me. I need to see to the students." She hurried around the chicken pen and crouched down between two children. As though they needed her at the moment.

Grr. That Steph Mabry, digging her claws into Corbin. The woman wasn't the least bit subtle. Was that how it was done these days? Maybe Corbin liked that sort of thing. He was rather forward himself. All that flirting he'd done at Lindsey and Nick's wedding.

Give him another chance, Sarah. That's what Lindsey had said to her just yesterday at Carmen's Cupcakes and Confectionary. *You can't hold what he did when he was five years old against him forever.*

Sure she could. Because he was still the same guy. Still playing to an audience. Still bringing up all those horrid memories of the day her parents split up. She could tell herself he wasn't responsible. Of course he wasn't. But deep inside, separating the two eluded her.

She all but snorted. Interest indeed. Ever since they'd climbed on the hayride, he'd completely ignored her. She wanted that, right? To close the door on what had been turning into a promising relationship and move on. Of course that's what she wanted. It's what she'd told him. It was the only way to stay safe. To be secure.

But did he have to start flirting with another woman so soon, right under her nose? Obviously Sarah meant little to him after all. If she were feeling charitable, she'd warn Reggie's mother, but hey, the woman was bringing it on herself, hovering beside Corbin every minute she could while Corbin turned smiles in her direction. Encouraging the hussy.

Sarah trailed behind the group as they made their way to the pole shed where several machines sat beside a huge bin of apples. At the front, Steph Mabry chatted away with Corbin, laughing gaily.

Corbin gathered the children around him. "Welcome to the apple orchard part of Morrissey Farm. We are going to make juice today, and everyone can taste some and then take a liter home. Have any of you ever made apple juice before?"

Several students' hands shot up, including some unlikely contenders.

"We picked the fruit a few days ago. This is an organic orchard, so we're not too worried about pesticides and stuff on the skins." He began to fill a wooden box with apples while he talked. "But still, there are birds and bugs around, so it's a good idea to wash the fruit." He picked up a hose and pointed the nozzle at the apples until water streamed out between the slats.

"Next, we have to turn all these apples into pulp. That's what this machine is for. It's pretty noisy when it's turned on. We'll put a few apples at a time into this metal part, and puree will come out the bottom. Any questions about it so far?"

Reggie's hand shot up. "What is puree?"

"It's like applesauce that hasn't been cooked. You'll see when we do it."

Reggie nodded, and his mom beamed at the child as though he were a prodigy.

Easy, Sarah. Reggie's a good boy. Don't vent on him.

"The pulp will be brought to this machine—" Corbin moved over a couple of meters "—and folded into cloth in layers. Then we use a small hydraulic jack to apply a lot of pressure to it. The juice is squeezed out and runs down into a bucket. We'll keep emptying the bucket into that stainless steel barrel. And that's all there is to it. It's pretty easy, but it takes some time."

"Does the apple juice taste good?" asked a little girl.

"It sure does," Corbin said seriously. "You'll find out in just a few minutes. Okay, I need some volunteers. I think your teacher told you to wear old clothes today, right? So if you want to help, you'll need to roll up your sleeves if they're long. I'm going to take care of this part with the noisy motor, and Mr. Collins there will take care of the press. Your teachers and parents will make sure everyone who wants to gets a turn, okay?"

"I can help you." Steph Mabry smiled at Corbin as though he were a famous movie star.

"Thanks. Miss Jamieson could use a hand organizing the children into groups."

Ha. No special treatment. Take that.

Students took turns putting apples into the wooden boxes and spraying water into them. They took turns dropping whole apples into the grinder and oohing over the puree it created. They took turns dragging buckets of pulp to the press, using dippers to lift the mash onto the cloths, smoothing them out, folding the cloths, and adding slatted boards between the layers. They took turns moving the handle of the small jack to increase pressure as juice bubbled out of the cloths and gushed into the bucket below.

Sarah carried a pail from the press to the barrel. Several wasps circled her head. She flinched away from them as she dumped the juice. There sure seemed to be a lot of the pests.

She glanced around. Several of the children flailed at the buzzing insects.

"I hope no one is allergic to stings." Corbin's voice sounded conversational. "Fresh, sweet juice attracts wasps. Swatting at them makes them angry and more likely to sting you, so it's best to stay calm and ignore them if you can. If you're allergic, go out of the work area, and they'll probably leave you alone."

Steph backed out of the shelter. "Reggie, come over here."

"But I didn't get a chance to help with the jack yet, Mama."

"I don't want you to get stung, baby."

Sarah managed not to roll her eyes. She didn't want anyone to get stung, either, but some parents didn't know how to keep their kids active in their peer group.

Reggie glared at his mom and turned back to his current job of ladling puree onto a cloth in the press. Steph's hands clenched, but she didn't argue.

“Do you know the difference between wasps and bees?” asked Corbin. “Bees pollinate plants and make honey, and they don’t sting people who aren’t bothering them. They’re fat and round and busy all the time. Wasps are skinny and mean. They’re happy to sting people for no reason at all.”

Reggie screamed and dropped the dipper, splattering apple puree across the cement. He bolted out of the work area. “Ow! Ow! Ow!”

Chapter Thirteen

Corbin flicked the switch to turn off the grinder. The sudden silence made Reggie's screams that much sharper. His gut plummeted. Getting stung was always a possibility, but plenty of juicing days went by without that complication.

Steph caught up to Reggie. "Baby, are you okay? Let Mama see."

Should he go over there, too? He stood, uncertain, as other children flinched and flapped at the air, backing out of the shelter. Another of the women went to Steph and her son.

Sarah stepped forward. "Over here, children. I'm sure Reggie will be fine. His mom is taking care of him, and Miss Thompson knows how to help his sting."

Right. The other teacher. Corbin dared to breathe as Sarah's composure settled him as well as the kids gathering around her.

"Who wants to keep helping Mr. Morrissey and Mr. Collins make juice?"

A few hands went up.

She nodded. "Okay, you may help. The rest of you, let's wash your hands from the hose to get the sticky off so the wasps won't be as interested in you. Then we'll sit down on the grass over there and talk about what we've learned today. Soon we'll get our picnic lunches from the bus and have fresh apple juice to drink while we eat."

Reggie's cries continued unabated while the other children lined up at the hose. Corbin couldn't take it any longer. Of course, it wasn't his fault the boy had gotten stung, but he was the host. He strode over to where Miss Thompson squatted in front of the boy, peering at his hand.

"Oh, Corbin!" Steph flung herself against him. "My baby."

Whoa. The twitch in his nose exploded into several sneezes as he tried to remove Steph's arms from around him and get away from her perfume. And from her. Easier said than done. He sneezed again. “Excuse me.”

“You poor thing. Are you allergic to wasps, too?”

He managed to get her at arms’ length. It took both hands to keep her there, so he could only turn aside for the next sneeze, not cover his nose. “Sorry. Not wasps.”

Her pretty face tilted to one side as her green eyes widened. “Then what? Miss Thompson, doesn’t that sound like he’s having an allergic reaction?”

“Perfume,” he managed to get out. “It’s your perfume.”

“Oh, I’m so sorry.” Steph’s hand covered her mouth.

As though that would help.

Miss Thompson glanced up. “Do you have any antihistamines for children, Mr. Morrissey? Reggie’s finger is quite swollen.”

“Uh, no. Just for adults.” How would it be possible for him to feel even worse than he did now? At least Steph’s hands had fallen to her sides and she no longer clung to him. She’d even turned back to her son.

“Oh, Reggie. Mama is so sorry. I should never have brought you out here to this farm where there are wild bees to hurt you.” She shot a glare at Corbin.

“It was a wasp, ma’am, not a bee.”

She fluttered her hand as though it made no difference. “I need to take my boy to the doctor. What if he d-dies? Where’s the bus driver?”

Miss Thompson patted Reggie’s shoulder. “He’ll be fine.”

“But how do you know? Look how red and puffy it is.” She tugged Reggie to her side. “Poor baby.”

Miss Thompson glanced at Corbin. “Reactions like he’s having are normal. The dangerous kind closes a person’s windpipe so they can’t breathe. We’d know by now if that’s what he had. He’s breathing just fine.”

“But you said... antihistamine...”

“That will help with the swelling and the itching, for sure, but there’s no panic to get to it. You might want to stop by the pharmacy and pick some up when you get back to town if you don’t have any at home.” She ruffled Reggie’s curls. “But he’s fine. Really.”

“If you’re sure...”

"Very sure."

The relief swept through Corbin even as Steph glanced between them, seemingly unconvinced. He nodded. "That's my understanding, as well. Someone whose allergies are life-threatening would already be in extreme distress." Or worse. It had been at least five minutes since the child had been stung.

Reggie peered past Miss Thompson to see the other children grouped on the grass around Sarah. "I'm okay, Mama. It's just my finger hurts. Can I go back to my class?"

"Sure you can." Miss Thompson took his other hand and led him away.

Steph looped her arm through Corbin's and smiled up at him. "I guess I'd better keep a bit of distance while I'm wearing perfume, hadn't I? So many kinds of allergies. I'm glad Reggie is okay."

Sarah glanced up as Reggie and the other teacher approached. For an instant her gaze met Corbin's then she looked away.

Corbin stepped out of Steph's grasp. "Excuse me."

"While I have you to myself for a minute..." She smiled, and her pencil-thin eyebrows jiggled. "I'm really interested in you. Would you like to go out sometime? I'll leave off the perfume."

Corbin took a deep breath. "I really don't know what I've done or said today to give you that impression. I'm in a relationship right now." He was, even if Sarah denied it. And yeah, he might've devoted a bit more attention to Steph than he should have today. Trying to make Sarah jealous, maybe? What a bad idea that had been.

"Oh." Steph looked at him uncertainly. "Well, if things change..."

"They won't." He didn't dare even smile at her lest she take it wrong. "Excuse me, please. I need to finish with the juice."

"May I talk to you for a minute?"

Sarah closed her eyes for a brief instant before turning at Corbin's warm voice. It sent shivers cascading through her. She swallowed hard. "Is Reggie okay?"

"He'll be fine."

Sarah tried to get some mental distance. “So I hear his mother is on the manhunt.”

Humor flickered in his brown eyes. “She probably will be for a long time to come.”

“Oh? When’s your first date?” Behind her, Donna Thompson arranged the children on the grass for their picnic lunch. Hopefully Steph Mabry was busy helping.

“Sarah, it is you that I love.” His eyes held hers. “I think I fell in love with you when I was five years old and never fell back out. There’s no other woman for me.”

He was declaring this with her entire class not a dozen meters away? What if someone overheard? At least he was keeping a bit of distance between them.

“I know you’re angry with me. I know my family overwhelmed you. I’m sorry, Sarah. I love you. Please don’t shut me out of your life.”

Tears threatened to flood her eyes. “I, uh...”

“Can I pick you up when you’re done at the school? I don’t want to say more now, when I know you’re at work. I wouldn’t have said anything at all, but you’ve blocked my calls and texts. I’ve been miserable all week. Please, can we talk through things?”

One more chance. Lindsey hadn’t managed to extract that promise from her, no matter how hard she’d tried. But the voice in her head wasn’t Lindsey’s. It was her own. Or maybe God’s.

Corbin waited, gaze fixed on her as he bit his lip. His hands twitched at his sides.

He deserved that chance. She nodded.

His face lit up. “Six o’clock? Maybe dinner and a bike ride?”

“Okay.” Sarah tried to compose her face before turning back to the children. Steph Mabry sent her a confused look. Not much she could do about that one, nor did she want to. If she turned Corbin away for good, would he wind up with Steph? That didn’t make sense. He’d just avowed his forever love to Sarah. She had no reason to believe he would be that kind of fickle.

And no matter how hard she’d tried to tell herself otherwise all week, she loved him, too.

But did she dare take the chance?

Chapter Fourteen

Sarah pulled into her apartment parking lot after work. Corbin would be here in a couple of hours, but was she truly ready to pick up where they'd left off?

An unfamiliar SUV was parked near the apartment door. The driver's door opened, and a large woman exited.

Sarah gasped. Oh, no. Corbin's Aunt Deb. How on earth had the woman found her?

"Sarah, darling. The Lord has put you heavy on my heart this past week, and I felt I needed to come talk to you in person."

"Um. Hi." Did she have to invite Deb in? It would be rude not to, but things with Corbin were fragile enough without the reminder his family would always be there, looking over their shoulders.

Deb enveloped Sarah in a suffocating hug. "I can't tell you how sorry I am about what happened at Don's and my wedding, and that you've felt the repercussions in your life ever since. I tried to find out where your family moved, as I wanted to send some photos and a thank you gift. No one in the neighborhood seemed to have a forwarding address."

Sarah managed to extricate herself from Deb's grasp then wrapped her arms tightly around her middle. "I'm sorry for making a scene at your party."

"Oh, honey. What a shock it must have been."

Truth.

"You and Corbin have been in my prayers all week. When I asked him, he told me he hadn't spoken to you since Saturday. That breaks my heart. He needs someone like you. Someone levelheaded and well grounded. He's a dear boy and like a son to Don and me. We were so thrilled to hear all about you and finally meet you in person."

"We spoke today."

Deb spread her arms and stepped forward, her face wreathed in glee.

Sarah backed against her car and tried not to wince.

"I'm so glad to hear that. You can't imagine how much time I've spent on my knees, asking the good Lord to love you both real good. To love you back to each other."

Had it been God's intervention? It had felt more like Lindsey's and Ms. LeRoy's. No. Deep inside, Sarah knew the Holy Spirit had been nudging her, too. Was nudging her now. She took a deep breath. "Deb? How can you learn to trust someone with your heart? Corbin's personality is so different from mine. I don't know how to let go." There was no way she could ask her own mother this question. Mom didn't know the answer.

Deb tilted her head and scratched her cheek.

Good. Sarah didn't want a snap reply. No clichés would do the trick. "Want to come in for a cup of tea?" It wasn't so hard to extend the invitation, after all.

"I'd love to." Deb fell in step beside Sarah as they headed toward the building. She remained silent and thoughtful while Sarah prepared a cup of tea for each of them. Then she cradled the cup between both hands and looked at Sarah. "It's not simple, I don't think. Here's one place to start, though. First John four verse eighteen says, 'Perfect love casts out fear.'"

Sarah shook her head. "That's no help. Corbin isn't perfect."

"I didn't say he was." Deb's face crinkled into a smile. "God's love is, though. It's His love that gives us courage. We won't find that kind of peace and faith in any human. If we try, we'll be let down, every single time."

"But then—"

Deb's hand covered Sarah's. "The first step is surrendering ourselves to God's love, and trusting Him to meet all our needs."

Sarah nodded slowly. "I've been a Christian since I was a teen, so I get what you're saying. But I think I keep grabbing control back. Not really trusting God."

“Especially when thinking of marriage?”

“Yeah. That.” Sarah sighed, staring into the steam lifting from her cup.

“Your parents’ breakup hurt you deeply, honey. Some men do prove to be untrustworthy. Sometimes it is the woman who strays. Sometimes a couple simply drifts apart. They don’t know how to bridge the gap and may decide it’s not worth trying. Some marriages end in divorce. But it doesn’t have to be that way.”

“But how can a person be sure?”

“You can’t know. Not one hundred percent. But you can do your part and trust God for the rest.”

Trusting God. There it was again. Trust God. Trust Corbin. She wanted to. *Perfect love casts out fear.*

“If your marriage is set on the foundation of God’s love and daily built with care for each other’s needs and prayer, you’ll make it through. The first while is full of passion and starry eyes. Those things fade, honey, but deeper joy and contentment take their place. When you find the right man, a man who loves the Lord with all his heart, it’s worth the journey a thousand times over.”

Was there any doubt Corbin had that kind of passion for Jesus? None.

Sarah took a tremulous breath. “Thanks. That helps.”

Corbin stood waiting for Sarah to open the door to her apartment. *Lord, please.* How many times had he murmured that prayer? It wasn’t even his real prayer. Not the one he really meant. *Lord, I put our relationship in Your hands. May Your will be done.*

The door swung open, and there she stood, her face wreathed in a genuine smile.

Hope leaped in his chest as he pulled a handful of fall flowers from behind his back. “For you.”

“Thanks. They’re beautiful.” She took them, and the brush of her fingers against his sent longing shivers through his body.

He followed her into the kitchen, where she pulled out her pottery vase and half-filled it with water before reaching for the asters and daisies. She arranged them, stepped back to look with her head tilted to one side, then fidgeted with them again.

"Sarah."

She glanced at him then away, her long hair falling to hide her face.

Corbin tucked a few strands behind her ear and cupped her chin in his hand. He couldn't do patience. "I love you, Sarah. I've missed you."

Her gaze caught on his. "I've missed you, too," she said softly.

He tugged her closer and wrapped both arms around her. After a few seconds, she relaxed against him. Her arms encircled his waist.

"Are you okay? I'm not trying to rush you." Yet if he could meet her in front of the justice of the peace and pledge his life to her this very minute, he'd do it without a second thought.

"I'm fine." She pulled back a little and looked up at him.

It was all he could do not to kiss her thoroughly. But he needed to know if they were really moving forward again. He slid his finger down the side of her face. "I'm so sorry about what happened."

"You've mentioned that." She swallowed hard. "And you're forgiven. Did you know I had a visitor after work today?"

A visitor? Corbin tipped his head. "No, who was it?"

"Your aunt."

Uh oh. That could be good or bad. By the evidence of Sarah in his arms, it had to be good. "Oh? What did she have to say?"

"Perfect love casts out fear."

Not what he'd expected to hear.

"I was afraid you'd hurt me again. Like when we were children. Like my parents did to each other. Like so many people do, ending up in divorce."

She was safe in his arms. Secure. "I'll never hurt you again."

"You can't make that kind of promise."

Hadn't she just said she'd overcome that line of thought? "I'll never do it on purpose, then. And if I ever do, tell me, and let me make things right."

"Your aunt reminded me God is the only one I can be sure of." Sarah's brown eyes glimmered with moisture. "But that's enough. He's enough for both of us."

Corbin kissed an escaped tear from below her eye. "God is enough." Then his lips brushed hers and pulled away even as his heart sang. "Come on. Let's go for that bike ride."

Chapter Fifteen

The glowing golden days of autumn had passed, and a gray chill permeated the air. Fallen leaves huddled against yellowed grass from yesterday's icy rain. They'd put their bikes into storage a few days ago, knowing snow would soon be coming.

Sarah barely noticed the chill, her gloved hand firmly tucked in Corbin's as they wandered the bike path toward her apartment. She glanced up at him and found him watching her from smoldering blue eyes as his grip on her hand tightened. The butterflies in her gut took to dizzying flight. Even amid the butterflies there was peace since the day Deb Shawnigan had stopped in to visit and helped her focus her gaze on the only One who deserved it.

Corbin leaned over and brushed her forehead with his lips. She could've used a much deeper kiss than that, even out here on the trail, but he seemed to have something on his mind. If he had bad news, he wouldn't be dragging it out like this, would he?

Perfect love casts out fear.

She could trust him, because he was trusting God. They both were.

They strolled into the parking lot just as a Panago delivery car drove in.

"That'll be for us." Corbin pulled her along as he sped up, digging in his pocket for his wallet.

The aroma of Mediterranean pizza made her stomach grumble as they climbed the stairs to her apartment.

Corbin quirked a grin. "Olives and extra feta, right?"

Aw, he'd remembered.

She unlocked the apartment door, and he set the pizza box on the counter before digging into the backpack he'd left in her coat closet before their walk. She tried to see what he had in his hand, but he blocked her view until the last minute.

She blinked. Pottery plates?

Corbin set a slice on the top one and handed it to her.

Sarah slid the pizza over a bit to see the plate more clearly. "Where is this from?" She looked up at him.

Corbin grinned. "From the potter who won the blue ribbon at the fair. I hope you like it. I bought two." He set another slice on a matching plate.

"I-I don't know what to say. I can't believe you went to so much trouble."

His eyes gazed deep into her soul. How had she ever thought he'd hurt her purposefully? He wouldn't. He couldn't. "It wasn't trouble. I wanted to. For you."

Emotion clogged her throat and oozed out her eyes. "Thanks." She set her plate on the table.

Corbin walked past her. "Want to watch a DVD while we eat?" He held up a disc.

A minute ago he'd seemed romantic. Now he wanted to watch TV? Men. Always so confusing, and today more so than most times.

They'd done a movie or two here in the past few weeks, so he knew his way around her system. She nudged the plush dragon out of the way and had a couple of bites of ooey gooey pizza while she waited. Soon Corbin slid one arm around her, his plate resting on the sofa beside him.

Sucking in her lip, Sarah stared at the TV as a rock formation came into view. The castle-shaped mountain behind Castlebrook? Not what she'd expected to see.

A digital Corbin stepped in front of it. "I'd offer you a castle if I could, fair lady, but all I have is a farm and a rundown house."

No way. She froze, not daring to glance at the flesh-and-blood man beside her.

The digital man smiled straight at her. "I have it on good authority that you've got eighty-two Pinterest boards and an HGTV addiction to help us with ideas for fixing it up."

Was this going where she thought it might be?

The camera zoomed in on a battle scene of toy knights and dragons on a rocky rampart. "I may not be able to offer you a castle, but here's what I can promise. I'll slay every dragon that dares to breathe his fire anywhere near you."

She swallowed hard as the camera swung back to his face.

"I'll love you lavishly every day for the rest of our lives. As best as I can, I'll model Jesus' love to you. Sarah Jamieson, will you do me the honor of becoming my wife? To have and to hold from this day forward? To be the head of our own Team Bride?" The man on the TV screen opened a small velvet box and held out a glistening diamond.

Sarah dabbed at tears dribbling down her cheeks as she became aware that Corbin — *her* Corbin, the man she loved — knelt in front of the sofa with that same box in his hands. Her shaking hands set the plate aside just before he spoke.

"Sarah? Will you marry me?"

Her lip trembled as she gazed into his expressive eyes. "I can't think of anything I'd rather do."

Corbin gripped both her hands in his as he fumbled with the ring.

She gazed in awe and disbelief as the beautiful promise slid up her finger like it had always belonged. Somehow she managed to get words past the lump in her throat. "Corbin. Thank you. I love you."

He picked her up as though she weighed nothing and twirled her around. "I love you, Sarah. Always have. Always will." His lips met hers and answered any questions she might've had as to his sincerity. "Do you know how much?" He set her feet back on the floor.

Like the sun, moon, and stars orbited her? She blinked. "How much?"

"For you, I would elope." He kissed her. "I know how you feel about weddings. About my relatives."

"No eloping." She shook her head. "Besides, I'm not afraid of your family anymore."

"Are you sure?" His eyes searched hers. "I want us to have the best possible start, and if that means just the two of us in front of God and a judge, I'm fine with that."

"I want a real wedding."

His eyes lit up. "Honestly?"

She'd made the right decision. Sarah nodded. "A small one."

"We don't need a big team of groomsmen and bridesmaids. No flower girl. No ring bearer."

"Just us and maybe Lindsey and Nick." She smiled at Corbin, suddenly shy. "After all, we can blame everything on them."

Corbin brushed his lips against hers, electrifying her senses. "I'm so thankful you agreed to be on Lindsey's Team Bride. That day changed my life."

"For the better, I hope."

"Absolutely, my fair lady." And he returned to the business of kissing her.

The End

A Riverbend Romance Novella
Merry Kisses
Valerie Comer

Chapter One

"Merry Christmas!" The young mom loaded big bags of toys into her buggy.

Sonya Simmons smiled back. "I hope your holidays are wonderful." *And that you can pay off your charge card soon.* She turned to the next customer in the long line waiting to check out of Toy Treehouse. "Good afternoon. I hope you found everything you were looking for?"

The elderly woman nodded. "I have a little something for each of my great grandchildren right here."

"That's terrific." Sonya slid the toys across the scanner and into a waiting bag. Why did everyone have to try to out-buy everyone else? Why was Christmas so commercial?

The woman paid and shifted the bag into the cart. "Thanks so much, dear. You have a merry Christmas, all right?"

"You, too."

"Look what I found for my granddaughters!" The next customer held up two fashion dolls with princess gowns.

"Oh, they'll love those sparkly dresses." Sonya smiled at Mrs. Bryant from River of Life Church. "These are from you, not from Santa, right?"

"Yes." The older woman sighed. "Santa has been curtailed in my grandchildren's lives."

Nice some families had the good sense to do that.

Mrs. Bryant tilted her head to one side. "I haven't seen you in church lately."

Of course she'd notice and comment. "I've been scheduled to work a lot of Sundays with Christmas coming on." Oh no, she'd said the word. A furtive glance over her shoulder revealed Deborah four tills over bagging for Annie. "You can see how busy we are, and we aren't even in full swing yet."

Mrs. Bryant leaned closer. "Surely your boss would let you have some Sundays off if you asked. The store can't be that busy of a Sunday morning."

Sonya shook her head. "I'm not asking for favors. Is this everything for you today, then?"

The customer's lips pursed as her eyes narrowed to a point beyond Sonya's shoulder. She slid her debit card through the machine.

"Please don't say anything to Deborah," Sonya whispered, leaning across the counter. "I need this job."

"As you wish. Merry Christmas, Sonya."

Sonya patted the bag of dolls. "Merry Princesses." Mrs. Bryant didn't seem to notice.

She began scanning the next customer's selections. "Did you find everything you were looking for?" Then she glanced up and caught her breath.

Tall, dark, and handsome was only a trite starter phrase. The man in front of her was all three, but so much more. Brown eyes twinkled above cheeks and a chin that had missed the razor for a few days. A jaunty Santa hat perched on his dark brown hair.

Why did he feel the need for a Santa hat? Why was Santa in *everything* to do with Christmas?

"For today."

Sonya blinked. "Pardon me?"

The man's grin widened. "You asked if I'd found everything." He indicated the packages heaped on the conveyor belt. "I've got today's list covered."

She took in the mound. No single toy was expensive, but they were going to add up. What was it with people and their need to buy so much junk? And why couldn't she have found a job less tied to the commercial aspect of Christmas? "Today's list?" Oh, good grief. She sounded like an idiot echoing him.

"I checked it twice."

"But..." *Never mind. Scan the toys, Sonya. He's just a cute guy. You've seen them before.*

Men his age — around thirty, she'd guess — weren't the most common customers in Toy Treehouse. The occasional few were usually accompanied by a young woman with a baby stroller.

Sonya scanned a talking doll followed by a 1500-piece puzzle followed by a baby rattle. Wait a minute. He was too young to have this many kids with such varied ages. She snuck him a furtive glance.

He grinned at her, eyes twinkling.

Conversation. She should make some. "Wow, you've got a big family." She should also think for a few seconds before opening her mouth.

"That's where the evidence seems to lead."

Maybe he was a doting uncle with plenty of cash, but his Carhartt work jacket didn't give that impression. She could head back into safe territory with a question like *Do you think we'll have snow before Christmas?* but that would mean saying the C-word. Also, what did it matter what he thought? There'd either be snow, or there wouldn't.

His jacket hung open, revealing a navy Henley-style shirt, untucked over faded jeans. He slid his card through the slot and glanced up, catching her watching him. A slow smile crossed his face, lighting up those eyes again, brown like hot cocoa. Except if her morning drink gleamed at her that way, she'd toss it in the sink. But his eyes? Different kind of sink. The kind where she might disappear and drown.

His grin widened.

Sonya ripped her gaze off him and handed over his receipt. "Thanks for shopping at Toy Treehouse."

"I'll be back."

"Me, too." Oh, Sonya. Dumb, dumb thing to say.

He chuckled. "Maybe I'll see you again then."

"Maybe."

Sonya watched him push the cart toward the exit. Why did it feel like he meant something beyond him buying more trinkets for his children? A guy with that big a family shouldn't be making the knees of toy store cashiers weak. He obviously already had as much on his plate as he could handle and, while she liked children as much as the next woman, she wasn't going to take on someone else's abandoned dozen. And then there was the Santa hat.

"Miss? I'm in a hurry here."

Sonya swung to the next customer in line as heat shot up her cheeks. "Sorry."

Heath Collins couldn't resist. He loitered in the wide corridor of Riverbend Mall outside Toy Treehouse, watching for a certain cashier. She hadn't been here yesterday or the day before, but now she was in sight, smiling at a customer. She turned away, her long brown braid swinging over her shoulder. His heart beat faster. She was so attractive even in that crazy green uniform with a giant giraffe design curving over her right shoulder.

He fingered the list for a party at one of the town daycares. The staff member who'd been in charge had called in sick, and they'd been happy to turn the list over to him. If he timed this right, he'd be at till #5 just before closing — his best chance at trying for some small talk and trying to get to know her a little.

Couldn't hurt to make an effort, right? He hadn't been able to get her off his mind since he'd been in a few days ago.

Sonya. That's what her badge said, smack on the horns of the giraffe. No trouble remembering her pretty name, or the fact she wore no rings.

Heath pushed a cart to the section of the store where action figures climbed both sides of the aisle. Left to his own devices, he'd have gone down to Chapters, the big bookstore just down the mall, and bought books for all the kids. But then he wouldn't have seen Sonya again, so maybe action figures were good, after all.

Consulting the list, he loaded the requested toys into the cart then angled toward his target. A large woman scooted a mounded buggy in front of him.

Heath groaned. Two other lines were open, each with only a few shoppers. It would look stupid to stand at Sonya's till, but she'd been the reason he'd come. Now what?

"Samantha can take you at number four." The manager rested her hand on Heath's arm and pointed out the obvious. "Almost closing time."

Sonya looked up from the toy she was scanning and her eyes widened slightly as they met Heath's. She glanced at his cart and her eyebrows pulled together.

Heath grinned. At least she'd remembered him. Making a scene wouldn't help, so he turned his cart into the shorter queue. A few minutes later his purchases were bagged. "Merry Christmas," he said to Samantha.

"Happy holidays," she replied.

He glanced at the manager, who hovered nearby, and read her nametag. "Merry Christmas to you, too. Deborah."

The woman's smile seemed frozen in place. "Season's greetings."

Okay, so... store policy? Whatever. Heath pocketed his wallet and pushed his cart toward the exit as Sonya bagged the last of the large order.

"I'm so glad I was able to find prisms! The kids will love seeing the colors dancing around on sunny days," the customer said. "Merry Christmas!"

Sonya smiled. "Merry Crystals." Then her gaze caught on Heath's and a little grin toyed with the corners of her mouth.

That did it. He was definitely following through. Heath edged his cart closer as the woman, waving, left the store. "Hi, I'm Heath Collins. I'm wondering if you'd like to catch a coffee when you're off work?"

His timing was perfect. One of the other cashiers rolled displays in from the mall corridor while Deborah tugged the security grille across the wide gap.

Sonya's eyes captured his for an instant then she looked down. "I, uh, don't go out with married men."

He held out both hands, tanned and rough from work, but no rings. "You're safe with me."

"Or single dads with a pile of kids."

Heath could be tempted to keep teasing. "Still safe."

Her brow furrowed. "But..."

"Shall we start this conversation again?" He was having way too much fun now. “Hi, my name is Santa Claus. Can I buy you a coffee?”

The smile slid off her face as she narrowed her gaze at him. “Santa?”

“That’s me.” He rested both hands on the counter between them. “Or you can call me Kris Kringle if you like. Or Saint Nick.”

“Seriously?”

Her reply wasn’t quite as warm as he’d hoped. “I’m not actually a saint, nor do I play one on TV.”

Her eyebrows rose. “Then where do you play one?”

Heath waved a hand. “Down the mall. At schools and daycares. At the old folks’ home. Nearly anywhere I’m asked.”

“You’re serious.”

“Sometimes.” Getting more so by the moment. “Now that we’ve established that I’m relatively safe, although not a saint, would you like to have a coffee?” He held his breath.

Sonya searched his face.

“Socialize on your own time, Sonya,” called the manager. “I don’t mean to rush you, sir, but it’s two minutes past closing, and we’re waiting on you. Unless there’s a problem with your receipt?”

Automatically Heath glanced at the long paper in his hand. “No, it’s all good.” He looked at Sonya, raising his eyebrows. “Tim Hortons has a street entrance. How long will closing up take?” Yeah, he knew he was pushing. Just a little.

“Fifteen minutes?”

His heart soared rather a lot, all things considered. He tried to hold back the exuberant smile. “See you there. Merry Christmas!”

She smiled back at him. “Merry kisses.” Then her eyes widened, and she clapped her hand over her mouth.

The manager whirled toward her. “What did you say?”

“Merry kisses,” Sonya mumbled, eyes downcast.

“Speak up. I can’t hear you.”

“Kisses!” Her chin thrust up as she narrowed her glittering eyes at Deborah. “I said *merry kisses*.”

The woman sniffed. “Yeah, right. To a man you don’t know? Haven’t we talked about how to respond to greetings? Please take your cash drawer to the office.” She turned to Heath, anger at Sonya obviously warring with her need to be polite to a customer.

“I was just leaving.” Heath pushed the buggy toward the small gap remaining in the security grille. Man, he hadn’t meant to get Sonya in trouble. Had she really said kisses instead of Christmas? That meant she was thinking of... well, he shouldn’t get too excited about her evasion tactic. It had backfired.

He paused, blocking the opening, and faced Deborah, who’d followed him to lock the store. “I’m sorry I distracted her. It was my fault, not hers.”

“She knows the rules.”

What could Heath say that wouldn’t get Sonya in even more hot water with her boss? Nothing he could be sure of. He nodded slowly and pushed the cart into the mall corridor. “She didn’t say Christmas, if that’s what you’re so upset about.”

“I heard what I heard.” The grille clanged shut behind him, and Deborah locked it.

“But I’ll say it. Merry Christmas.” It was the proper Santa Claus salutation at this time of year. He couldn’t help himself, but he could spare her the *ho, ho, ho.*

The woman on the other side of the grille raised one eyebrow then spun on her high heel and stalked away.

Good job, Saint Nick.

Chapter Two

Sonya bit her lip hard and stared at her boss. Her former boss. "You are seriously going to fire me because you think you heard me say the dreaded word Christmas?" She leaned closer. "Christmas is not a dirty word, no matter what you think." She was sealing her doom now, and she knew it, but she was past caring.

"I heard you say it, and then you lied. You expect me to believe you said *kisses* to a man you don't even know?"

She couldn't believe she had, either, but it was a fact. "You don't have to believe me, but it's true." Actually, Deborah did have to believe her, or she'd be out of a job. She already was. Her boss would never admit she'd made an error in judgment.

Sonya took a deep breath. "You may not celebrate Christmas, but most people in Riverbend do, and so do most people in Canada. I notice you're not against them buying Christmas presents for their kids in here. I bet Toy Treehouse is like nearly every other retail outlet in town. The sales in November and December float the store through the remainder of the year. If anything, you should be shouting *Merry Christmas* in the streets. Without it, you wouldn't even stay open." Which was a troubling statement about the job Sonya was leaving behind. All that commercialism paid her rent and bought her groceries.

Deborah crossed her arms and narrowed her gaze. "Are you quite done?"

"No, I'm not." Might as well go for it. "I get that there's more than one holiday in December. I get the whole inclusive thing. I even get not saying *Merry Christmas* to customers unless they say it first. After all, they might be in here for a birthday gift or, I don't know, a solstice gift. But it's just plain dumb not to allow us to say *Merry Christmas* back when a customer says it first."

Behind Deborah, Annie's jaw gaped. Samantha gave her a thumbs-up.

If she was going to lose this job — and she was now, even if Deborah might've had second thoughts earlier — she'd go out saying her piece. "Do you have any idea how strangely they look at us when we don't respond in kind? They think we are being downright rude. Some of them even say so."

"Anything else?" Deborah's toe tapped on the tile floor.

Sonya had blown it. She'd once entertained visions of gently explaining to Deborah how much the birth of Jesus meant to her. That opportunity was good and gone. *Oh, God, please forgive me for letting pettiness get in the way.*

She took a deep breath and met Deborah's gaze one more time. "I'm sorry for lashing out at you."

"Sorry isn't enough. I told you — all of you — that this was grounds for dismissal. Company policy. You can stop by Friday for your pink slip and final check. Please drop off your laundered uniforms at that time."

"I wasn't apologizing in hopes of making you change your mind. I'm sorry because I don't make a habit of losing my temper, and I regret doing so just now."

Deborah didn't even blink. "See you Friday."

Sonya raised her chin. "I might not make it in until next week sometime." She grabbed her coat and purse off the hook and left the office without a backward glance, tears stinging her eyes.

"You can't give me any more shifts, Deborah," came Annie's voice. "I've already got forty hours this week."

Sonya was halfway across the parking lot to her car when she remembered Heath Collins. She had a few things to say to a guy who played Santa, even if he was crazy attractive.

Fifteen minutes slowly ticked by into twenty, then twenty-five. Heath rotated his coffee cup against the table, round and round, while keeping an eye on both the mall entrance and the street door.

Had Sonya stood him up on purpose, or was she still hashing it out with Deborah?

Heath ran a hand across his stubble and grimaced. If he'd cost her her job... but surely she wouldn't get fired for a bit of flirting. Or for the word *Christmas*, which she hadn't even said.

No, she'd definitely said *merry kisses*. She'd been flirting, too.

Thirty minutes. The mall security guard dragged the grille across the entrance and latched it.

One door left, and Heath angled to focus on it. Was she coming, or wasn't she? How much longer would he wait? He didn't know her last name. Didn't have her cell number. If she didn't work at Toy Treehouse anymore, where would he find her again?

Of course, it shouldn't matter this much. He didn't even know her. There were plenty of other women in Riverbend, but no one had really caught his eye until yesterday. Until Sonya.

The street door opened, and a shaft of frigid air blasted in along with Sonya, wearing a knee-length black wool coat over black trousers.

Heath shot to his feet as relief washed over him. She was here. "Can I get you a coffee? Or maybe you prefer tea or hot chocolate. Would you like a doughnut? Or it's suppertime. I was thinking of getting a sandwich. Would you like one?"

She crossed the small coffee shop toward him, a tired smile creasing her face.

Man, he was blubbering. "Any of those sound good?" he finished lamely.

"I'd love a hot chocolate and a Canadian-maple-glazed doughnut. I have stew in the slow cooker at home, so I'll say *no* to a sandwich." She slipped out of her coat before he could round the table and help her. "But thank you."

"Okay. Here, have a seat." He pulled out a chair for her then headed to the counter.

A minute later he returned with a tray and set her hot chocolate and the treat in front of her. "I'm sorry I got you in trouble with your boss."

She tore her doughnut in half and shrugged. "It had been coming for a while."

"So is everything okay?" He dared to breathe.

"I guess it depends on your definition of okay. Know anyone who's hiring?"

"No way. She fired you?"

Sonya nodded and lifted the hot chocolate to her lips.

"I'm so sorry." Wow, that sounded totally inadequate.

"Like I said, it wasn't a big surprise, other than the timing. She was already short staffed. Now she's desperate, but she'll never back down. It's not her nature."

"What will you do? If there's anything I can do to help, I will. I feel so responsible."

"I'll pound the pavement for another job. It's a bad time to be looking because everyone already hired their Christmas staff, and then they often lay off workers come January. But I'll find something, I'm sure."

Heath heard the unspoken words. *Sooner or later.* "I'll keep an eye out and let you know if I hear of an opening. But, uh, I'll need your cell number."

A bit of life came back into her eyes when she met his gaze. "Now there's a unique pick-up line."

"I'm not the one who talked about kisses."

A flush rolled up her cheeks. "Deborah never did believe me. I can hardly believe it myself."

"Believe what?"

"I've become pretty adept at almost saying *merry Christmas* but not quite. But that was the first time I'd said something... ah, inappropriate while evading."

He reached across the table and covered her hand with his. "Inappropriate? Not prophetic?"

She pulled her hand away and lifted her cup. "Prophetic is an interesting choice of words."

Oh, how she dodged. He could enjoy this game. "Prophecy simply means foretelling the future. Maybe there are merry kisses in our future."

If he hadn't been watching closely, he'd have missed that quick snap of her eyes to his then away.

"I rather doubt it," she said instead. "I don't date casually. I have pretty high standards."

Heath took a sip of coffee and watched her face until she looked at him again. "And you've already decided I wouldn't meet them? Because you thought I had a dozen kids to buy gifts for?"

"No, sorry. You explained that." She hesitated. "I'm a Christian. I don't go out with guys who don't share my beliefs. I hope you understand it isn't anything personal."

"And if I said I was a Christian, too?"

Again with the quick sharp glance. "Then I'd ask you questions about your faith and about where you go to church."

"To make sure I wasn't just being agreeable so you'd date me."

"Right." She took a bite of her doughnut.

"But having coffee after work doesn't count as a date."

"I'm happy to pay for my own snack."

He shouldn't be having this much fun stringing her along. "No way. I invited you and, besides, I've already bought it."

"I can see that agreeing to meet you here makes it seem like I have a double standard. I was distraught and not thinking clearly." She pushed her chair back and stood. "I'm sorry, Heath. I should be going."

He leaned back in his seat. "But you haven't asked me the questions yet."

Her face clouded. "What questions?"

"The ones about my faith."

Sonya's fingers tightened on the back of the chair, and her brown eyes latched onto his, longer this time. "Pardon me?"

"I'm a believer, Sonya. I've lived in Riverbend not quite three years, and I attend River of Life Church. Even a small group on Tuesdays."

"Y-you do? But I've never seen you there."

"It's a big church."

"Yes, but..."

"That's where you attend? I've never seen you, either."

"Deborah refused to give me Sundays off. I've worked every single one since September and half the ones before that."

"Maybe it's a good thing you're rid of her."

"Maybe." She slid back into the chair. "Do you really go to the same church as I do? But that doesn't make sense. You play Santa."

It was his turn to be confused. "What's that got to do with anything?"

Sonya picked a bit of glaze off the top of her doughnut with a pink fingernail and popped it in her mouth. She eyed him and heaved a sigh. "I don't think it's right to lie to little kids. They have enough trouble keeping fantasy and reality separate."

His fingers began twirling his coffee cup again. "I see. So you think my job is right up there with the Easter bunny and the tooth fairy."

She raised her eyebrows. "Isn't it?"

"I don't see it that way."

"Of course you don't. Just another day at the office, right?"

Heath couldn't help his sardonic laugh. "Right. I work ten hours a week for one month a year as Santa, plus a party here and there. You can't seriously think I'm in this for the money."

Uncertainty crossed her face. "Okay. But why?"

"Why be Santa?"

"Why pretend to be."

Heath shook his head. Of course she'd distinguish. "I like making little kids happy. I like their hugs and their shy smiles. I like being a bright spot in their day."

"But it's a lie." She picked another fleck of maple off her doughnut.

"Sonya, *I* am real. I'm the guy who brightens their day."

"Only because you're in that red suit." She eyed him. "Must take a lot of padding."

He twitched a grin that she'd noticed. "I'm sure I'm not the only Santa who hits the gym on a regular basis."

She bit her lip and sipped her hot chocolate. "I'm sorry. I know millions of people can justify the whole Santa Claus thing. As a Christian, I think it takes away from the celebration of Jesus' birth. It's saying Jesus isn't enough, and we have to add a fat jolly man who bribes children into being good to make it worthwhile celebrating Christmas."

She… what? Heath opened his mouth and closed it. She kept right on going.

"What does that teach kids? The reward system. God doesn't give out little gold stars. We can't be good enough to deserve His gift. We lean on God's love and mercy for that."

"You have some good points."

Sonya blinked and met his gaze. "I do?"

"Sure." Heath leaned back in his chair. "I hadn't thought of it quite that way before. I still don't think being Santa is evil, mind you, but I've never believed in putting him before Jesus."

"Don't you think you're helping kids do that? And aiding their parents in telling lies to them? And then there's the whole commercial aspect of it. Don't even get me started."

And this was supposed to be a pleasant coffee with a woman he'd hoped to get to know better. He felt more like a dragonfly stuck to a piece of foam board. "I don't, actually. I have a job to do, and I do it to the best of my ability. I bring smiles and cheer to harried faces." More, too, but telling her now would make it seem like he was desperate for her approval. "Real people, Sonya. I brighten the day of real people. Yes, I'm acting a part. So do Hollywood actors."

"But everyone knows movies and TV shows are made-up."

"A lot of viewers think reality shows are actually real."

"You're trying to switch the subject."

Heath held up both hands. "Guilty as charged. I hope we can both agree that it is vital to keep Christ in Christmas and to bring hope and cheer to those who need it at any time of year."

Sonya nodded, but those brown eyes looked unconvinced.

Why was it so important she see things his way? "We may disagree on the best ways to accomplish those goals."

"Apparently so."

"Sonya, we've kind of gotten off on the wrong foot, but I'd still like to get to know you better." Why? He had no idea. "Can I take you out for dinner on Friday?"

She jolted to her feet, her chair scraping loudly on the tile floor. "I don't date Santa Claus."

Chapter Three

"No. I'm sorry, but we have all the staff we need."

"We might be hiring in May. Check back then."

"Do you have any experience managing an engineering office? We need someone who can hit the ground running."

That had been downtown Riverbend. Now Sonya sat in her car in the parking lot staring at the mall's log and stone entry. She did not want to go in. Not and run the risk of Deborah glancing out of Toy Treehouse at just the right moment to see her desperately searching for a job. Yes, she needed to get her record of employment, but Deborah usually disappeared later in the day, and that's when Sonya would go in. She'd already opened her file for benefits online, and the paperwork could wait another few days.

She also didn't want to go anywhere near the cordoned-off North Pole area between the food court and the big-box store at the end.

It'd been three days since she'd stalked out of Tim Hortons and left Heath Collins sitting there. How could she have been so rude to a pleasant, good-looking, Christian man who'd invited her on a date? But how could he defend Santa Claus? For seventy-two hours her brain had circulated those things like a blender. It wasn't like being Saint Nick was his full-time job. There couldn't possibly be enough money in it to see him through a year. So he was probably a seasonal worker or something. Desperate for cash, like she soon would be.

Sonya shoved the car door open and climbed out. The biting wind of early December howled down the Sandon River Valley hurling Arctic air towards the American border. It whipped her hair and knee-length skirt. She clutched her purse and the folder holding a stack of résumés against her wool coat and strode for the mall entrance as briskly as her high-heeled boots would allow.

Sonya shoved through the two sets of doors into the mall and headed straight for the bathroom to brush the mess the wind had made of her hair and to analyze her makeup one last time. She stared at herself in the mirror and pasted on a confident smile. At least as confident as it was going to get.

Eight more managers told her, "thanks, but no thanks," before she neared the North Pole display. Santa sat on his throne holding a little boy on his knee. A camera flashed. The little boy hugged Santa and whispered something to him, while Santa leaned close, nodding.

Sonya crossed her arms and leaned back against the window of one more clothing shop that didn't need another clerk.

Twenty or more kids stood in line, clinging to the hands of the adults beside them. The children wore their Sunday best... yeah, today's parents didn't call it that. Dress-up clothes? Party clothes?

Kelly Bryant from church — no, she was married now. What was her new name? It didn't matter. She stood in line with her two seven-year-olds.

Sonya's eyes narrowed. She'd thought better of Kelly. But wasn't that another young mom from River of Life Church beside her?

A sour taste burbled up Sonya's throat. Didn't anyone besides her stick up for Christ in Christmas anymore? Had everybody sold out to the whole Santa Claus thing?

Especially Heath.

He now held a toddler and a baby while the camera flashed in all three faces. The baby began to cry. Heath jiggled his arm and rubbed his fluffy white beard on the little one's face. The baby grabbed the beard, and it shifted dangerously.

It would serve him right if the kid yanked it clear off his face and all the waiting kids could see Heath was a fake.

She didn't want him to be a fake. In the short time she'd spent in his presence, he'd been sweet and funny. At least until she'd backed him into his corner of Santa's workshop.

Yep, she'd made a mess of it. Why, God? Why did the one and only man she'd wanted to take a second glance at — or a third, or maybe even a fourth — have to be someone who said he was a Christian but wasn't completely sold out?

She could hear Dad's voice already. He'd never accept a guy like Heath dating his baby girl.

Sonya pushed away from the window and glanced down the other side of the mall. How many more times could she take being turned away today? She took a deep breath. It wasn't going to be any easier if she came back tomorrow. She'd keep going until she ran out of résumés in her folder or the mall closed. Whichever came first.

Also, she'd stop thinking about Heath Collins.

Easy to say until she glanced back, one more time, and caught his gaze on her. A thrill ran down her spine when he lifted his white-gloved hand in greeting.

Never in a million years was she going to fall for a fat guy in a red suit.

It wasn't too late to keep that from happening. Was it?

Everything around him faded for a moment as Heath watched Sonya stride down the mall corridor, her black coat flapping over her black skirt that swished just above her tall black boots. He'd glimpsed a fuzzy peach sweater before she'd turned away, so it wasn't all doom and gloom.

Lord, please? Is there any hope for a relationship with her?

Why did he even want one, when she'd clearly enunciated her opinion of the favorite of his three seasonal jobs? Was it really wrong to dress up as Santa Claus and listen to the hopes and dreams of small children? Not when he could help them.

"Mr. Heath? Is that really you?" a young voice whispered.

Two little girls, a blonde and a brunette, stood before him in matching pink dresses, clasping hands. Behind them, Kelly from church winked at him.

"Ho, ho, ho." He opened both arms wide.

The little girls climbed onto his lap. "Are you really Mr. Heath or are you Santa Claus?" asked the blonde.

This would call for stroking his beard if he didn't have both hands occupied. "Maybe I'm both." He angled his lapful toward the photographer. "Smile for the camera?"

Both girls leaned in and kissed his cheeks as though they'd planned it in advance. The flash told him Destiny had nailed that one.

"How can you be both?" asked the blonde.

"I think you are many things, too. You're Elena, right?"

She nodded.

"You're a little girl, a daughter, a granddaughter." He squeezed the other child. "You're Sophie's sister."

"We're twins," announced Elena.

Heath grinned. The beard hid facial expressions well enough. He knew as well as anyone in Riverbend that the two girls shared a birthday but had only become sisters when Sophie's dad had married Elena's mom.

"So right now, I'm Santa Claus, and I'm here to find out what you want for Christmas."

"A baby sister," Elena whispered.

Sophie nodded.

Not the usual request. Heath shot a glance at Kelly, who stood a meter or so back. She grinned, lifted her shoulders, and shook her head. Looked like she had a good idea what the girls wanted.

"There are some things Santa can't promise, you know," he told them. "Baby sisters and brothers are presents only your mom and dad can give you."

Elena's eyes narrowed. "But our teacher told us Santa can give us anything."

Some teachers gave Santa a bad rap. "Requests like that are things to ask Jesus. He was a little baby once. He knows all about babies."

She pouted, parking her arms across her chest, but Sophie nodded. "Let's ask Santa for new princess dolls then."

Whew. Dodged a bullet. "That sounds like a good thing to ask Santa for."

"Come, girls." Kelly held out both hands. "We mustn't waste Santa's time. There are other children waiting to talk to him."

Sophie slid off immediately but Elena glared at him a second longer.

"I'll ask *Jesus* for a baby sister, then."

Kelly grinned and shook her head as she took both girls' hands. "Thanks, Santa."

A boy of about five climbed up next.

Heath turned his brain back to Saint Nick mode.

* * *

Sonya slid her tray along the counter at Tim Hortons. "A Canadian-maple-glazed doughnut, please. And a hot chocolate." She'd pretend that finding exactly one store in the entire mall with an opening made celebration worthwhile, even if they'd done no more than cheerfully accept her résumé.

"May I have a doughnut, Mommy?"

Sonya glanced behind her and met Kelly Tomlinson's eyes. "Hi there."

"Sonya! So good to see you. How are things going? Just a sec." Kelly leaned to the blond head in front of her. "You may share a doughnut, but you have to agree on what kind."

"The kind with sprinkles," announced Elena. Sophie nodded.

The girl behind the counter reached into the display case with a pair of tongs and set a confection on a plate. "Anything else?"

Kelly completed her order while the other staff member rang Sonya through. "Wait, Sonya! Want to sit with us? I could use some adult company."

"Sure." How long had it been since Sonya'd had time to hang out with friends? She didn't know Kelly all that well but, despite the age of the children, Sonya would bet she and Kelly weren't that far apart in age.

She waited then followed Kelly and the girls to a table by the window.

Sophie traced her fingers along the festive tobogganing scene an artist had rendered on the glass. "Will we have snow for Christmas, Mommy?"

Kelly flashed Sonya a grin. "I don't know, Sophie. I hope so. Here, Elena, do you want to cut the doughnut in half? Then Sophie gets to pick first."

Elena nodded and grasped the plastic knife. With upper teeth pressed firmly into her lower lip, she carved through the treat and pushed the plate across the table to her sister.

The halves were remarkably even. Sonya glanced at Kelly. “Now there’s a good trick.”

“You have to learn a few in this competitive business.” Kelly chuckled as she removed the mugs of hot chocolate from the tray and set them in front of the girls. Then she wrapped her own hands around a steeped tea. “So what have you been up to? I haven’t seen you at church for a while.”

Sonya hesitated. “I’ll be there this Sunday.”

Kelly’s eyebrows rose above the steam of her cup. “Great, but sounds like there’s a deeper meaning.”

“Oh, I was working every weekend at Toy Treehouse, but now I’m looking for a new job.” No need to explain the details.

“Mom said she saw you in there the other day.”

“Yeah. My boss and I didn’t see eye to eye on a few things.” Sonya shrugged, hoping she looked casual. “I’m sure something will show up. What have you been up to?”

“Keeping busy.” She poked her chin toward the girls, now devouring their treat while discussing the mural on the window and all the things they would do once it snowed. “I’m sure you heard I married Ian Tomlinson and acquired a second daughter.”

“I did hear. Congratulations.”

“We’ve had some adjustments as you can imagine, but we are doing well. I’m so thankful to the Lord for bringing us together.”

Sonya nodded. “That’s great. Wonderful.”

“And now my mission is to help all my friends be as happy as I am.” She leaned forward on her elbows, eyes sparkling. “Seeing anyone?”

Now why did a tall, dark, and handsome Santa slide through her mind? “Nope, not these days.”

Kelly waggled her eyebrows. “I just happen to know someone awesome who’s available.”

Why had Sonya thought it would be fun to join Kelly and the girls? She took a bite of her doughnut to keep from having to reply.

“He goes to River of Life, so you might have met him already. If I weren't happily married — and I am — I'd sure be looking twice. Do you know Heath Collins?"

Sonya inhaled a bite of doughnut, choking hard enough to get the attention of even the small girls. Kelly shoved a napkin into her hand, and Sonya coughed into it until her eyes swam. "Sorry," she gasped when she could.

"It hurts when you swallow wrong." Sophie patted Sonya's back.

"Mr. Heath is Santa Claus," announced Elena. "Mommy told me, and it's true."

"He's only *this* Santa Claus." Sophie pointed at Elena. "There are lots of Santas."

Elena rolled her eyes. "I know that."

"So tell me about Santa." Sonya slid her arm across the back of Sophie's chair. "What do you think of him?"

"He gives presents to kids at Christmas," said Elena. "If they've been good."

There. Didn't that prove that parents lied to their children and perpetuated the myths? Sonya's gut soured. Even Kelly and Ian.

"That's not what Daddy told us. Remember?" said Sophie. "He said it's play-acting to remember the real Saint Nicholas who gave presents to poor people."

"I *know* it's just pretend." Elena crossed her arms and jammed her elbows to the table. "But I like pretending to be a princess and I like pretending to have a horse and I like pretending about Santa Claus."

"It's Daddy who buys us Christmas gifts." Sophie wasn't letting up.

"And Mommy." Elena's face brightened. "Maybe we'll get twice as many presents this year now that we have both a mommy and a daddy."

"Enough out of you two." Kelly chuckled. "It's Jesus who gave Mommy and Daddy jobs so that we can give you everything you need... and a few things you want."

"That's what Santa said." Elena slurped some hot chocolate.

Sonya's eyes narrowed. "Santa told you about Jesus?"

Elena glanced at her mother. "I asked Santa for a baby sister for Christmas, and he said that was God's job, not his."

"That's because Santa is really Mr. Heath," put in Sophie. "He can't give away babies."

Kelly laughed. “That was a wise thing to say. He’s right. Babies are not Santa’s jurisdiction.”

“What’s ju... juris...?”

Elena stared at her sister. “It means it’s not his job.” She looked at her mom. “But me and Sophie want a sister.”

“Or maybe twins?” Sophie’s eyes grew round.

Kelly shook her head, still grinning. “Eat your doughnut and drink your hot chocolate. We need to get home to Daddy soon.”

Sonya joined the girls in having a bite then found Kelly’s gaze on her.

“I don’t think you got a chance to answer. Have you met Heath Collins?”

They were back to this? “We’ve met.”

Kelly leaned closer. “Isn’t he cute? And so nice.”

“Are you supposed to notice things like that? You’re married.”

“He’s not as cute as Ian, of course. I’m loyal, but I’m not blind.” Kelly watched her expectantly.

“He seems nice enough.”

Kelly spread her hands on the table. “I hear a *but* in your voice. But what? You must know something about him that I don’t.”

“But he’s Santa.” Sonya glanced at the two girls and lowered her voice. “Some hurdles are just too high to get over.” For Dad, at least, if not for her.

Chapter Four

Heath stood at the back of River of Life Church and scanned the people as they prepared for the Sunday morning worship service. Technically he was waiting for his buddy, Corbin, and Corbin's fiancée, Sarah, but, in reality, he was looking for Sonya.

He'd been attracted to this congregation when he'd first come to Riverbend. Its vibe was as close to a large city church as he'd found in a small town. The worshipers came in a healthy mix of ages, including a lot of teens, older singles, and young families. Today it seemed there were fewer gray heads than usual, and more women with long brown hair who might or might not be Sonya, at least from the back.

His heart jumped a beat. There she was on the far side, chatting with Kelly and Ian. The little girls bounced beside Reed Daniels, his guitar slung across his back, and gazed adoringly up at him as the three made their way to the children's wing.

Sonya tilted her head back and laughed, though Heath couldn't hear above the murmur of many conversations. Then her gaze slid past Kelly's and latched onto his. Her face sobered.

Kelly turned to see what had caused the change in Sonya's demeanor and beckoned to Heath with a big grin.

He could pretend he hadn't seen the invitation. He didn't want Sonya uncomfortable. But... why not? She made *him* uncomfortable — although he rather liked the sensation — so they might as well be even.

Just do it.

Heath's feet obeyed before his brain caught up. He hadn't seen her since Friday at the mall, and hadn't realized how empty his eyes had been. Now the vision of her filled his senses. The soft green sweater hugged her curves in a way the giraffe uniform never had. Her long brown hair flowed over her shoulders.

He nearly stumbled as unknown, but not entirely unwelcome, emotions slammed into him. He couldn't just walk up to her, gather her in his arms, and kiss her. Not in church. Not without permission.

Permission she was unlikely to give by the look on her face. Her brown eyes looked guarded, and those pink lips were definitely not lifted in invitation.

In one instant, Heath knew he could give up being Santa if that's what it took to win this woman. There were other ways to make children smile, and he'd find them.

"Good to see you, Heath." Ian's voice.

Heath blinked the dream away, and the world widened to include the Tomlinsons and the sanctuary of River of Life Church. "Hi. How are things going?" He smiled at Kelly. "Hi, Kelly. Hi, Sonya."

He pulled his gaze back to Ian as quickly as he could manage and caught the knowing grin on the other man's face.

The worship team began the musical prelude, reminding folks to find a seat.

"Why don't you join us?" Kelly linked an arm through his. "Unless you were waiting for someone else."

"I'd love to." This sounded like a better idea than Corbin and Sarah, whom he hadn't even seen. Heath turned to Sonya, but she stared past his head. "If you don't mind?"

Twin pink spots rode high on her cheeks when she looked at him. "Whatever you like."

If Kelly was matchmaking, she was efficient at it. She already followed Ian into a row near the back, leaving barely enough room for two more.

Heath bit back his grin. If Sonya had hoped the Tomlinsons would sit between them, the hope was dashed. "After you." He rested his hand on the small of Sonya's back as she passed him, then settled into the seat next to her.

He could get used to sitting pressed against her, hip to hip, shoulder to shoulder. He closed his eyes and breathed in the lilac essence she wore. *Lord? I don't remember ever feeling this way before. Is Sonya the one?*

* * *

Sonya tried to relax. She hadn't been in church for months and had been really looking forward to lifting her heart in worship, soaking in Pastor Davis's teaching, and joining in corporate prayer.

She hadn't counted on being wedged between Heath, of all people, and Kelly. Her friend hadn't taken Sonya's protests to heart the other day. The matchmaking was obviously in full swing, with Heath a willing participant like an adoring but overgrown puppy.

If only he weren't Santa.

If she'd met him in January, this might not have come up until she had a ring on her finger. Her heart jolted at the thought. Did she really like Heath enough to think things might've gone that far? That was silly. They'd just met.

A sideways glance showed Kelly's hand curved inside Ian's, her wedding band nestled against her engagement ring, which sported a diamond between two emeralds, representing the little girls. Had Kelly and Ian had deep discussions about whether or not Santa would play a part in family Christmases before they got married or even engaged?

Enough. She rose to join the congregation in *Joy to the World* as the opening song. Now that was what Christmas was all about: celebrating the Lord's coming.

"We've got one quick announcement before we resume worship. If you've got children ages four through eight, please sign them up for the Christmas party. It will be in the fireside room on the afternoon of Monday the twenty-first. Pastor Nick still needs two volunteers who are not parents. We are trying to offer a time when parents can finish up preparations or, better yet, take some quiet time to reflect on the birth of our Savior. Our own Santa Claus, Heath Collins, has a special time planned for the children. Check your bulletin for details."

Really, Pastor Davis? Even church isn't a safe zone? Sonya scrunched her eyes shut, but that didn't help get away from being pressed against Heath's side. She should've looked harder for a church like the one she'd grown up in after her move. Dad had had some suggestions, but she'd been attracted to the bigger congregation with so many young people.

Woodenly, she stood with the others as the next carol was announced. *I Heard the Bells on Christmas Day.* Why couldn't everything be about the birth of Jesus and the peace offered by His sacrifice?

Peace that was eluding her now. *Please, Lord. Help me stay focused on You.* She joined the carol on the second verse. Kelly's sweet soprano meshed with Ian's tenor on her right and, on the other side, Heath belted out a solid baritone.

The words to the carols familiar, Sonya kept her eyes closed and surrounded herself with the words and music.

After the closing prayer, Ian leaned forward to see past Kelly, looking from Sonya to Heath. "Kelly's got chili in the slow cooker. You want to join us for lunch, Sonya? Heath?"

Heath felt the tense vibration from Sonya's arm through both their sleeves. He shook his head as he glanced at his watch. "I'm due down at the mall in less than an hour. I'm Santa from two to four."

He felt more than heard Sonya's exhale. Irritation washed over him. Was he really that evil for bringing joy and hope to children? Why did he even bother trying to impress her in a positive way?

"Oh, too bad. We should have planned this for suppertime instead." Ian's hand slid around Kelly's shoulder, his shiny new wedding band gleaming.

"I'd change it, but I've already invited Sarah and Corbin and Carly and Reed." Kelly glanced at Heath then back at Sonya. "Can *you* come?"

Sonya hesitated. "Sounds fun, sure."

Would she have said that if he'd been going? Heath doubted it. "Maybe another time." He pulled to his feet. "I need to scoot so I have time to down the sandwich in my fridge before getting the red suit on. Try to have fun without me."

Kelly laughed. "Not sure if it is possible, but we'll try. Go make some little kids smile, you hear me? And don't promise baby siblings to any of them."

Ian, still rubbing his wife's shoulder, smirked.

"I don't make promises I can't keep, whether as Santa or just me." The words were more for Sonya than for Kelly, but she didn't look up. "See you all later."

He hated walking away with this unresolved between him and Sonya, but the jingle bells were tolling the time. He had to trust this one to God, at least for now. His conscience bit. What, he'd only leave it in God's hands until he had time and opportunity to do it himself? *Not the way trust works, Collins. Not at all.*

* * *

Kelly and Ian's basement suite smelled like chili and was packed with vintage Christmas decorations. A narrow tree stood in front of the wide window set high in the wall, but evergreen garlands spread the decor out like angel's wings on either side.

"Come on in, everyone. May I take your jackets?" Ian reached for Sonya's coat as she shrugged out of it. "Carly? Sarah?"

Sonya had missed out on friendships by being unable to attend church for so long. She didn't even know Carly, who sported a dainty diamond and had one hundred percent of shy Reed Daniels's attention. When had that happened? And when had Sarah met someone? Another diamond on that finger.

Well, Heath had foiled Kelly's matchmaking by having to work. And if he hadn't, Sonya would have come up with an excuse to head home herself. She tried to imagine Heath here, in this tiny apartment already packed with seven adults. Elena and Sophie had disappeared down the hall to their bedroom upon arrival.

Sonya turned to the open kitchen where Kelly mixed something in a Depression-era glass bowl. "Can I help with anything?"

Kelly grinned. "Sure. As soon as Ian adds the leaves to the table, you can give me a hand setting it." She scraped the yellow batter into a muffin pan and deposited it in the oven.

"Sounds good." Meanwhile, Sonya hardly knew where to stand and not be in the way. The other visitors drifted past her into the sitting area of the open plan. Looked like Sarah and Carly had plenty to talk about. Weddings to discuss, no doubt.

Sonya wanted one of her own someday. Heath's smiling face drifted across her mind.

"So." Kelly glanced into the living room then back at Sonya. "You never told me why you won't date Santa Claus."

Yeah, Sonya should have stayed home with her cat. "That reminds me. Is the church seriously having Santa at a kids' Christmas party? That really bothers me."

"Why?"

Sonya shook her head. "I just don't get it, I guess. I wasn't raised believing in Santa. It all seems so commercial. Don't you think the church should be a safe place from all that? It's like Christians saying *yes* to lies and greed."

"Whoa." Kelly studied her. "So that's what you have against Heath Collins?"

"Basically." Sonya couldn't get Dad out of her mind. Everything was so black and white in his world. It'd been easy when she lived at home, but she'd discovered a few other colors since moving out. Where to draw the line when it was up to her?

Kelly set the bowl in the sink and turned on the tap. "I don't see Santa as representing lies and greed. I see little faces lighting up with the magic of the season."

"But it's Jesus' birthday. What other magic do we need?"

"Saint Nicholas is like an object lesson. He shows us how to celebrate."

Sonya shook her head. "What do you mean?"

"I'm not saying it well, am I?" Kelly leaned back against the counter. "All I know is, I've always taught Elena that we give gifts to others to extend Jesus' love to them. And where there is giving, there's also receiving, so we have thankful hearts and appreciate the blessings we've been given."

Hmm.

"It's a bit more complicated this year with Ian and Sophie. Their traditions were different from ours, so we are all negotiating and blending. But the main idea hasn't changed. We use Santa and gifts to teach God's love." Kelly spread her hands. "I doubt we are doing it perfectly, but we have to work within the parameters of our Canadian culture. You should hear some of Sarah's stories. The things kids in first grade tell each other would curl your hair."

"I hear my name." Sarah appeared from nowhere. "Where are your linens, Kelly? I'll get started on the table."

"Me, too. How can I help?" asked Carly.

"You can help me convince Sonya that Heath Collins is one of the good guys. Even if he plays Santa." Kelly tossed a festive tablecloth at Sarah

Sonya felt a flush rise in her cheeks. "No fair ganging up on me."

"Ooh!" Sarah grinned at Sonya. "I've been wondering when someone would get Heath's attention. He's a friend of Corbin's and a really great guy."

Yeah, he seemed to be. And the protest of *but he's Santa* seemed like it would forever fall on deaf ears. Was everyone else right? Maybe it didn't matter as much as she thought. If only Dad would stay out of her head.

Chapter Five

Sonya paused in the doorway, bright smile in place. "Thanks for inviting me in for an interview."

The middle-aged woman glanced up from her paperwork with a slight frown. "Come on in and have a seat. Please give me a moment."

That didn't sound promising. Sonya sat on the edge of the orange plastic chair facing the desk. One minute slipped into two, maybe three. Keeping her smile in place was starting to become a challenge, no matter how badly she needed this job.

Finally the woman closed the file and dropped her glasses to the length of their beaded chain. She folded her hands and met Sonya's gaze. "I'm Ms. Zurich, the manager here at the Riverbend Shopper's Drug Mart."

"Pleased to meet you. I'm Sonya Simmons."

"Ms. Simmons. You're here about the opening behind our cosmetics counter, I believe."

"Yes, ma'am." Sonya nodded. "I've been a loyal customer for several years, purchasing all my makeup and personal supplies here. I'm familiar with the lines you carry."

"Do you have any experience working in this environment?"

"I have several years of retail experience."

The woman glanced at the paper on her desk. "Most recently at Toy Treehouse, I see. Which is not exactly cosmetics."

If there was a question in there, Sonya couldn't find it. She waited.

"I'll be honest, Ms. Simmons. The previous interviewee worked at the Shopper's location in Castlebrook for fifteen years, eight of those in cosmetics. She has exactly the credentials we're looking for and the references to back them up. Someone who can step in with no training and simply take over that department."

Sonya's head swam. "I see." The perfect applicant probably hadn't ever been fired, either.

"I would have called to cancel the interview, but she left only five minutes ago, and you were already here."

Like punctuality was a negative. Sonya rose. "Thank you for your time. Perhaps you'll have another opening soon for which you might consider me."

"Maybe." Ms. Zurich looked her up and down. "To be honest, most of our girls go to part-time hours over the winter until things pick up again in spring. If anyone leaves in the meanwhile, I'm sure the hours will be snapped up internally." She moved the paper off to the side. "I'll keep your résumé on file for six months."

Dismissed. Sonya managed to blurt out, "Thank you," one last time before turning and fleeing. She was halfway down the mall before she stopped for breath.

She blinked away tears and straightened her back. She'd known it was a long shot to find a full-time job with Christmas less than four weeks away. Somehow she'd allowed herself to build a ton of hope since the interview request this morning. Why should it surprise her that someone with perfect qualifications was ready to swoop in and nab the prize?

She'd put off finalizing things at Toy Treehouse. Somewhere in the back of her mind she'd hoped to be able to casually drop the news that she had a new job, a better job, when she handed over her uniforms and picked up her record of employment and final pay.

How much worse could today get? She looked through the toy store window. Only two tills were open, and lines of buggies snaked back into the display aisles. Would she go back if Deborah asked her? Just put on that stupid giraffe uniform and smile at customers and say *Merry Crystals* instead of *Merry Christmas*?

Sonya took a deep breath. She couldn't do it. Not even for a raise, which Deborah would never offer. Why ruin a different day dealing with Deborah? It wasn't like today could get any worse.

She strode down the aisle past trucks, cars, and construction toys. Past more couples looking at toys and a child who didn't seem accompanied. Not her problem. She pushed open the Employees Only door at the back.

The receiving area was stacked with boxes of toys leaning over the staff lunch table. The office door to the right stood ajar.

Sonya tapped on it. "Deborah? It's Sonya."

"Just a minute."

She heard a couple of drawers open and shut then the sound of a blowing nose. Uh oh. "If this is a bad time, I can come back later."

"No, come on in."

Deborah didn't look as confident as usual. In fact, she looked very small and worn down behind that mammoth desk.

Sonya set the bag containing her uniform tops on the corner of the desk. "Are you okay?" She didn't want to care, but even Deborah shouldn't look so depressed just before Christmas. Or any time of year, of course.

Deborah sniffed and picked up an envelope from a tray on her desk. "I'm fine. Here's your cheque and paperwork."

"Thanks." Sort of thanks. "So everything is all right? Did you find another cashier?"

The woman surged to her feet. "Everything is just dandy, okay? I hope you cleaned those uniforms."

Sonya backed up a step, clutching the envelope. "Of course I did."

"Good then. Have a nice day."

Another step backward, and Sonya's hand found the doorknob behind her. "I hope you have a Merry Christmas."

She was definitely not waiting for a response to that one. In seconds she was out of Toy Treehouse and down the mall corridor, where she stopped to stuff the envelope inside her purse.

Sonya glanced up and groaned. This stupid mall wasn't big enough. Now she was beside the North Pole exhibit with a side view of Santa's throne and the guy who sat on it. A line of expectant faces waited. A woman in a green velvet elf suit roved the line. See, someone like that would swoop in and gain Heath's love. They'd deserve each other, too.

The elf turned away from the children and coughed into the crook of her arm, a deep wracking cough that had Sonya's insides clenching in sympathy. Sounded like someone — especially someone who worked with children — should have called in sick.

* * *

Heath cast a worried glance at Destiny. He'd had his phone turned off while plowing last night's huge dump of snow from the mall's parking lot then half a dozen smaller lots downtown. When he got in the door at nine-thirty after six hours in the cab of his Bobcat, he'd set the alarm and collapsed for a three-hour nap.

If only she'd been able to reach him, he'd have told her to stay home. But who would have filled in as his elf? There wasn't really a backup Santa either, though he could probably bully Corbin into subbing if necessary. The farm was quiet this time of year. But Corbin would make a lousy elf.

Destiny coughed again, doubled over as the spasms wracked her body. Two moms took their youngsters by the hand and dragged them out of the line. He couldn't blame them, though the toddlers yelled and screamed.

Would anyone fault him for simply shutting down the North Pole today? But it was going to take more than twenty-four hours for Destiny to recover.

Something moved in his periphery. Someone. Sonya, peering inside her pink folder.

She hated Santa and everything he stood for. But... she needed a job, and managing the line didn't require significant training.

Heath whispered Santa-like responses — he hoped — to the little boy on his lap then set the kiddo down. He stood then jumped over the piles of silvery gifts that kept the line contained and strode toward Sonya before she could dash away.

Her eyes widened as she took in his quick strides. A glance darting down the corridor showed she would've bolted given a few seconds longer.

"Hi, Sonya."

"Um. Hi."

"How's the job hunt going?"

She straightened and looked him in the eye. "You broke rank to ask me that? You should get back to your adoring audience. They're waiting."

"I'd like to offer you a few hours of work." In the background, another coughing fit exploded. "Hear that? Destiny can't work. She needs to go home, but if I send her home, I have to close down the North Pole."

"I see that's a problem."

"It pays minimum wage and it's only ten hours a week through Christmas Eve. She'll need at least a few days off to recover, so this is temp. A cash job." He hesitated. Why even bother? She'd never do it. But still. "Please?"

"You must be kidding me."

"Not even a little bit." Heath scrambled for something more convincing and came up empty.

"You're desperate."

"Yes. But I wouldn't ask just anyone, even so. Give it a chance, Sonya? You'll help a lot of families get into the Christmas spirit."

She narrowed her eyes at him. "Do I get to tell all the little kids you're a fake Santa?"

He managed a lopsided smile. "I doubt it will come as a surprise to most of them."

That got her attention. After a few seconds she looked past him. "I sure wouldn't fit that uniform. She must be a size two."

Heath's heart leaped. She was actually considering it? "There's no need for the elf suit. It belongs to Destiny, and she loves wearing it. What you've got on right now is perfect."

More than perfect, really. She wore the same dark green slacks as she had at church last Sunday, but paired with a dark red sweater with bits of gold glitter on it. Very festive. But the best part was how attractive she was, no matter what she wore.

He quirked a grin. "So much better than a Toy Treehouse uniform with a giraffe looking over your shoulder."

That got a little smile from her. Behind him, he heard the kids' restless questions getting louder. He was out of time for this personal mission.

"Please, Sonya? Try it until five o'clock and let Destiny get some rest? Please give me a chance."

As the words came out, he recognized the double meaning. Yes, he needed someone to help at the North Pole, but he wanted her to give him a chance as well. To see if the attraction he knew she'd felt, too, could turn into something. Should he tell her Kelly would never forgive her for turning down this chance? No, better not push his luck that far. Still...

He leaned a little closer, filling his senses with her presence. "You can say Merry Christmas all you want."

Chapter Six

If she hadn't met the poor elf's gaze through yet another coughing fit, Sonya would be at home right now, curled up under a quilt with a purring cat, a mug of homemade cocoa, and a good book.

Instead, she hoped the camera really did auto-focus and that the little kids wouldn't ask her if Santa was real. Heath Collins was real enough in his padded red suit, shiny black boots, and preposterous fake facial hair. Real enough to make her heart speed up every time she glanced his way and met his gaze, which was often as children clambered up into his lap and then back down to be replaced by the next one. She hadn't realized there were this many kids in Riverbend.

The first break in the line didn't come until nearly the end of the posted time. Heath rose and stretched to one side then the other.

He had no right to look so attractive in that ridiculous suit. "Hard work sitting on your gilded throne for hours?" Sonya wouldn't know if he flashed her a grin from behind that white beard.

"It's my other throne that's the problem."

Surely she hadn't heard right. "Your *other* throne?"

Heath came down the steps and reached for his toes. "Yep. The one in my Bobcat has even less padding than this one."

"In your Bobcat?" Man, she needed to stop mimicking him.

This time she caught the twinkle in his eye. Not exactly the kind of twinkle she'd always associated with Santa. "Did you notice the neatly cleared parking lot out there? Must've been six inches of snow overnight."

"It hasn't stopped."

"I think you're telling me the lot needs to be plowed again." His shoulders drooped.

"Probably." She shook her head. "That's really your other job?"

"One of them." Heath stepped out of the North Pole and glanced up and down the mall. He stuffed the white gloves into a pocket. "Not a lot of shoppers left."

Sonya remembered the cozy scenario waiting for her at home. "Do you close up early then?"

"Not with this gig." He beckoned. "Come on. You've been on your feet for over an hour, and at least we can sit down while we wait for more children."

The grouping of leather benches did look inviting, so she strolled over and sat down. Not that an hour on her feet was enough to topple her.

Heath lowered himself to the bench kitty-corner to her, knees all but touching hers. "So... how did it go, being an elf?"

She hesitated. "Not too bad, I guess." So long as she didn't have to tell her parents about her new job. But not being able to see Heath's face was driving her crazy. How was she supposed to read his facial expressions? Trusting just his eyes was terrifying, because he never stopped looking at her.

He reached over and captured one hand in his. "Define not too bad?"

Sonya stared down at his long fingers. At his callused thumb stroking the back of her hand. Not bad at all.

But... he was Santa. She made a half-hearted effort to disengage, but he didn't seem to catch the hint. Truth to tell, the warmth, the contact, felt kind of nice. How long since anyone had really cared about her?

He wasn't *just* Santa. "You said plowing snow was another of your jobs. How many do you have?"

Heath's fingers twined around hers. Had she really turned her palm up to accept his? "Three, if you count this one."

Did he need to remind her? Not that she was about to forget. The red sleeve with its white trim rested on her knee. "What do you mean, if you count it?"

He shrugged. "Jobs are a means to pay for life's needs. Being Santa is different. Yeah, there's compensation, but not enough, if you know what I mean. I do it for the kids. To help me remember that people are the most important thing. Everyone needs hope."

Her mind reeled. "Hope from Santa? How?"

"I'm not sure I can explain it." Heath met her gaze for a moment then looked down.

Did he find their clasped hands as fascinating as she did? "Try?"

"I hate the commercialism of Christmas. It seems everybody is just focused on gifts. On getting more stuff."

Whoa. "Isn't Santa an enabler of that attitude?" More like the driver.

"Sure, some children ask me for the newest video game and other toys. But lots of them have completely different requests. Some of them want their parents to stop fighting. Or they want the bully at school to stop picking on them." He sighed. "Some of them want a warm jacket that fits. And a few ask me for food."

"I had no idea." The words escaped before she could censor them, but she wouldn't take them back if she could. "That must be heartbreaking. To see real needs and not be able to..." Wait. She stared at him. "But the parents give names and addresses so we can mail the photos."

He nodded, his eyebrows peaked. Like he was waiting for something. For her to connect the dots, maybe.

"So if there was a way to link them with the children's requests..."

Heath reached into his chest pocket and removed a small spiral-bound notebook.

"You..." Sonya's mind raced with the possibilities. "You're already doing that."

He flipped it open and handed it to her.

Jordan: girl about 4. Baby sister. Dance class & tutu.

Sonya turned the pages, scanning several more notes. "Do you write them all down?"

"Most of them. It's fascinating, really. Every child has hopes and dreams, even when they're only two or three years old." He grinned. "The babies are there just so Mom can put a Santa photo in their baby book but, once they can talk, they have endlessly entertaining things to say."

"So Jordan wants dance lessons. I think I remember her. Corkscrew curls? Lessons can't cost that much."

"You'd be surprised." Heath laughed. "They add up."

Sonya narrowed her gaze at him. "You've checked?"

"I might've." He scratched the back of his neck.

Was he saying he actually fulfilled Santa's gift-giving role? There was more to this — to him — than she'd ever dreamed.

"Not that I, uh, have a secret wish to wear a tutu and dance in front of anyone."

Sonya squeezed the fingers that still clasped hers. "Why not? You're obviously into dressing up."

He gave her a rueful grin. "That's a little much, even for me."

"Oh, hey, I figured it out."

"Hmm?"

"You said you had three jobs. So the other one is teaching dance class?"

He rose, pulling her up with him. "Not so much. I wouldn't mind learning though. One on one. With the right teacher." He raised their clasped hands, set his other on her waist, and pulled her two steps to the right. "And the right partner." Then left.

"I don't really dance." Okay, not at all, but for the first time it seemed rather appealing. The movements Heath led her through to the canned music in the mall's sound system could give way to so much more. She blinked. "But I could learn. Maybe."

Heath's hand on her waist sent a ripple effect up and down her body. Or maybe it was the mint on his breath or the intensity of his brown eyes, looking into her so deeply she couldn't help wondering if he could see straight to her skitterish heart. Her senses swam.

"I don't think I can sign us up until January, but would you like to go for dinner?"

"I'd like that." She would. She really would.

"Tonight?" he said softly.

Sonya lifted her eyes to his and nearly lost herself in their brown depths. She nodded. Whoever would have guessed she'd fervently wish to be kissed by Santa Claus?

She peered into the mirror and swept mascara over her long lashes. Then she stepped back, right on the cat, who yowled.

"Sorry, Tangle." Sonya scooped the calico up and gave her a quick rub as she eyed herself critically. This was as good as it was going to get. If Heath could give her a second glance when she wore that ridiculous giraffe uniform, he obviously wasn't too picky.

Sonya turned one way, then the other. Dark gray slacks, a white cami, and a subdued purple-and-gray striped sweater. Her black boots added a couple of inches of height.

She set the cat down and gathered her hair in both hands. Maybe she should wear it up. No. She'd already decided on down. Loose. This wasn't a formal event.

When was the last time she'd been out? Six months? Eight? She heard the buzzer from the apartment building foyer, and she pressed the button. "Hello."

"It's Heath. May I come up? I have something for you."

Sonya'd planned to meet him downstairs. She shot a quick glance around her apartment. "Sure." What would it look like to him? How much of her personality showed in her space? Would he notice the lack of Christmas? Well, she was who she was. "Behave yourself," she whispered to Tangle.

A light tap sounded on her door and she swung it open. Heath stood in the hallway holding a giant poinsettia. "For you." He grinned and leaned closer, his lips sweeping her cheek. "Merry kisses."

Her face tingled. It was all she could do not to touch the spot. As it was, his cologne lingered between them. Belatedly, she reached for the beautiful plant, its base wrapped in red foil. "Thank you. It will look perfect on my table."

Sonya set the poinsettia on the runner her grandmother had quilted for her a few years back. "It's stunning." She stepped back... right into Heath.

His hands clasped her elbows, steadying her for a second before letting go. "Sorry, I didn't mean to startle you."

His nearness was intoxicating. She shifted to one side, needing a bit of space to keep her head. Just because the guy was cute, funny, and a Christian didn't mean she could let her guard down quite this quickly.

Heath tipped his head to one side, examining her with his warm brown eyes. "You look terrific."

"So do you." What was that about thinking before she spoke? But it was true. He'd ditched his Santa suit for a navy jacket, partially unzipped so a dark red turtleneck peeked out, and he wore black jeans. He looked more than terrific. Amazing.

"Wow, you have a lot of plants." He glanced around the living room with appreciation. "You must have a green thumb."

"I hadn't picked up a poinsettia yet, though." She wouldn't have, either. Wasn't that just buying into the Christmas hype?

Tangle hopped up onto the runner and sniffed the new addition. The cat never seemed to learn to stay off the table. Sonya scooped her away and deposited her on the floor.

"Oh, I didn't realize you had a cat. Poinsettias are poisonous. That's probably why you didn't get one."

He could think what he liked. "This is Tangle. She'll be fine now that she knows what it is. She's not a plant eater."

Heath lifted Tangle and rubbed her ears. The cat nearly melted in his hands. He chuckled and set her back down then turned to Sonya. "May I help you with your coat?"

Any guy that liked her cat was a winner. Okay, Heath was a winner half a dozen ways. If it weren't for Santa, he'd be perfect. "Thank you. It's hanging in the closet behind you."

She held her breath as Heath settled her coat over her shoulders then slid his fingers behind her hair to untuck it. His touch lingered a few seconds, warm on her neck. "Ready?"

Sonya turned and found herself in his arms. She took a half step back. Not quite ready, no, but getting closer by the minute.

Chapter Seven

Heath captured Sonya's hand as they stepped out of the Water Wheel restaurant some time later. The wonderland of Riverside Park, decorated for the Christmas season, spread out in front of them. If he were in a fairy tale, he'd like if it lasted a bit longer. "Want to walk for a bit?"

She nodded. "It's beautiful."

"The wind's died down." Now the fresh snow drifted by more like a whisper, caught in the glow of millions of tiny white lights winding around trees and lining the path. A path that — thankfully — was somebody else's responsibility to keep cleared, though at least a centimeter had fallen since it had last seen a shovel.

They paused at an intersection. Sonya lifted her face to the night sky and closed her eyes. Her long lashes brushed her cheeks as she took in a deep breath and let it out slowly. A falling snowflake caught on her lashes and another kissed her nose.

Heath stood, mesmerized, still clasping her gloved hand in his. She was so beautiful, and she didn't even seem to notice it. This wasn't a pose begging for a kiss. She was lost in her own moment, and he a mere observer. One that was being tugged in, though. Closer.

Did they really have a chance of a future together? The question wafted Caribbean breezes across him, alternating with Arctic blasts. Was he ready for a forever relationship? There had been plenty of first dates over the years. Even a few seconds and thirds. But no girl — woman — had rocked him to the core of his being.

Kiss? Too soon? He tightened his grip on her hand more from reflex than thought.

Sonya's eyelashes blinked open, the tiny snowflake melting away. "I love winter," she said simply. "I love all the seasons, but winter the most." She took a step toward the river, pulling him into step beside her.

Heath barely trusted himself to speak. "What do you like best?"

She swooped her free arm around the park. "Snow. It makes everything fresh and clean. It clears the air and energizes me. I feel so alive."

He tried to agree, but could barely get out more than a murmur. At the moment, it was Sonya herself who made him feel alive. Aware of every red blood cell racing through his veins. Aware of this moment in time with perfect focus and clarity.

She swung their clasped hands and picked up the pace when all he wanted to do was linger. "How about you? What's your favorite season?"

The fingers of her white glove twined around the gray of his. They came into his line of vision then swept backward. And again. "Whichever one it is, I think," he said at last.

"Pardon?" She glanced at him.

He stilled the hands that joined them. "Every season has its own beauty." *And I want to see* your *beauty in every one.* But no, that was way too forward for their first date. First of many. First of a lifetime?

"So... you like snow?"

Heath gazed into those eyes, gleaming with the reflection from nearby lights. The whole park glowed with sparkling lights, soft shadows, and lazy flakes wandering earthward. "I love snow."

Too late he realized her intent as she bent, scooped a handful from beside the path, and threw it in his face.

"Hey!"

She giggled, a sound that fit the park's magic, then took off at a run. He ran after her, slipping a bit on the path before abandoning it to take a shortcut across the knee-deep drifts. When he closed in, she flung another handful at him then ducked, still giggling.

Heath wiped the snow off his face and grabbed her around the waist, dragging her against him as he tumbled backward into the snow bank. Mistake. She sat on his belly and rubbed more into his face.

Three times was definitely not an accident. None of them had been.

He twisted and dumped her into the snow beside him. Her laughing eyes shone up at him above cheeks rosy from chill. Above lips curving in invitation.

Heath scooped a handful of snow and pressed it into a tight ball with both hands.

"You wouldn't dare!"

"You don't think so? I'm just accepting the challenge you've set before me." He pinned her against the snow with one arm and a knee, showing her the snowball. Then he carefully slid it across her forehead, across her cheeks, and across her mouth in a slow zigzag.

She stared at him, eyes wide.

Heath tossed the snowball over his shoulder and heard it skitter down the path. "I just want you to know I could have smeared your face with that. I could have scrubbed it into your hair." The brown hair that lay splayed across the white snow with a sparkle of its own. "I could have pushed it down your neck." He leaned even closer. Mere centimeters separated their faces. "But I didn't."

"I would've deserved it." Her words were only a breath, as soft as the gently falling snow.

"We don't always get what we deserve," he whispered back. He bent the remaining distance and brushed his lips across hers just once, never breaking contact with her eyes as they widened.

"Heath?"

Did she have any idea what that brief connection had done to his insides? Fireworks ricocheted from side to side throughout his entire body. Heath rolled over and clambered to his feet before offering her his hand. A moment later she stood on the path facing him.

Heath stuffed his gloves in his pocket and fingered the clumps of snow out of her long brown hair. It was a mess — a gorgeous mess — tumbling past her shoulders and down her back, where it curled against his fingers as though laying claim.

Time stood still. His hands abandoned her hair for her waist and tugged her closer, which was barely possible.

Her arms wrapped around him as she nestled against his chest.

Heath inhaled. Exhaled. Felt her matching breath. *Lord? I hope this is Your answer, because I'm going for it.*

He brushed his cheek across her damp hair then dropped a petal-soft kiss on each eyelid in turn, feeling the flutter of her lashes in response. Her face tipped to welcome his. This time, when his lips met hers, it was a seal, not a request.

Sonya's knees all but dissolved under the sensations coursing through her body. Only the contact with Heath's lips kept her upright, as though they provided a magnet that held her in place. She clung to him with all the strength she could muster and felt the muscles in his arms around her ribcage ripple in response. His hands splayed across her back. Even through her coat she could feel the warmth of his touch.

Heath deepened the kiss, claiming her, and she responded in kind. She was his. He was hers. For all the flirting she'd done in the past five minutes — daring him to catch her and conquer her — she hadn't expected the depth or the tumultuousness of her emotions. She didn't give way lightly, though Heath had seen little evidence of reluctance.

Never had she felt more alive. She'd waited twenty-seven years for a connection this deep. Could this really be love? The true, forever kind of love that Kelly, Sarah, and Carly claimed found them over the past few months?

Was Heath the one?

He pulled away, just far enough to rest his forehead against hers. "Sonya." He sounded out of breath. Like his, her lungs were starved for air. It was all she could do not to gulp in deep mouthfuls, but every other cell of her being was starving for this man. To repeat the soul-changing experience she'd just had.

Sonya stretched the tiny space between them and caught his mouth again, tasting him, a bit more controlled this time. He responded with tantalizing kisses, lightly exploring her mouth, her cheeks, her throat.

A few minutes later he slowed then stopped, his face pressed against hers. Only the movement of his hands against her back and hips proved the restraint he exercised.

"Heath..."

He turned his face to hers, gaze holding her as securely as his hands. As his lips just had. “Sonya.” His voice was husky. Unsure. “Are you okay?”

Define okay. “Yes.” Her voice cracked. “Are you?” Was he sorry? He couldn’t be. He’d come back for more as surely as she had.

“Not even a little bit.” Questions in his eyes, he lowered his mouth to hers one more time.

Sealed with a kiss. If she’d never known what that meant before, she did now.

Chapter Eight

Everything had changed.

Heath found it difficult to concentrate on what the kids said to him on Friday at the North Pole. Hopefully his notes would make sense later. Maybe his distraction was so extreme he spoke gibberish to the children. Maybe he'd be called on having an off day. But didn't everyone have one occasionally?

He sure didn't feel off. If anything, he felt more *on* than ever. More alive. But yes, distracted as he watched Sonya run the other half of the system. She chatted with parents, got their info and payment if they wanted a photo — and most of them did — clicked the camera, and handed out candy canes with a glow she hadn't had yesterday.

Maybe he was glowing, too. Would it show to the North Pole's visitors? Would it show in a mirror? Or did one have to be a participant of last night's amazing kisses to feel like the red carpet leading to the Santa throne was merely something to float above?

Sonya bent to talk to a little girl of about eight in jeans and a long-sleeved T-shirt. Her hair had definitely not seen the bristle side of a brush yet today. Weird. Most parents went all out dressing their kids up for their annual Santa photo. But this girl also didn't seem to be accompanied by an adult. Sonya glanced at him and, for a second, he forgot what he was supposed to be doing.

Right. The little girl. She stalked toward him, arms across her chest, glowering.

Uh oh.

Heath held out his hands, but she was having none of that sitting-on-Santa's-lap nonsense. She stayed just beyond reach, staring at him.

Maybe someone had just found out that Santa wasn't real? If so, he could explain. "Hi there. What's your name?"

"Bailey."

"That's a really nice name. What would you like for Christmas?"

"Why do you care?"

Whoa. It was all Heath could do not to rear back. At least his gaping mouth didn't show behind all the white whiskers. He hoped. "Because I'm Santa. It's Santa's job to make wishes come true." Probably not the best answer, but she'd caught him flat-footed.

"Only little kids believe that. Stupid kids."

Heath's mind raced. *Help me here, God. What do I say to this jaded child?*

"You're just mean, anyway. Last year I asked you for stuff and you didn't even come at all. Some of my friends say you don't always bring what they ask for, but at least you go to their house and give them *some*thing. What did I do wrong? I tried to be good."

Bailey set her little chin, but Heath could see tears shimmering in her eyelashes.

He stared at her, helpless. "Did your mom mail your letter to the North Pole? The address is Santa Claus, North Pole, Canada, H0H 0H0." Like ho ho ho, but she was in no frame of mind to hear the joke.

"No, I came here. My friends told me you were real. Nobody said I had to send a letter. That's dumb. I can hardly read."

"But you got presents from your parents, right?"

She blinked back tears. "Maybe my mom sent a letter saying I hadn't been good. Telling you not to come to our house. Did she?"

Heath shook his head. "I didn't get a letter like that." What mother would...?

"She thinks Christmas is dumb. Now I know why. You're not really real. You just look real."

"Do you know the story of Saint Nicholas?"

Bailey narrowed her gaze. "Who's that? What's he got to do with anything?"

Heath glanced at Sonya and the lineup. Eight moms and their children waited. A woman checked her watch. Kids whined and fidgeted. He didn't really have time to take this child aside right now.

“Listen, Bailey. I’ve got about an hour before I close down for today. Can you come back? I want to tell you that story.” And the story of Jesus, too, but he’d get to that in good time.

She angled her head and looked at him. “Maybe.”

“I hope you do. I’ll be watching for you. And ask that nice lady for one of those papers, okay? We usually tuck them in with the photos, but you don’t want a Santa photo, do you?”

By the twitch of her chin, he’d guess not.

“See you in an hour?”

“I said maybe.” She stalked back toward Sonya, the only easy way out of the North Pole setup.

Sonya glanced at him with a question in her eyes then bent to Bailey, offering her an invitation to the church children’s party in a couple of weeks. The little girl looked at it and shoved it in her pocket without folding it.

Heath breathed a prayer for the child who hurt in ways Santa could never fix. Only Jesus could. He’d get the girl’s last name and address from Sonya — at least if Bailey didn’t come back — and hand that in to the ministerial association early. One of the pastors would make a home visit.

He held his hands out in welcome to the toddler who came next, deposited in his lap by an eager young mom. “Hi there. I’m Santa. What’s your name?”

* * *

Sonya packed the camera away at the end of the hour then turned to the laptop where she’d recorded all the addresses for sending Santa photos.

Heath slid his arm around her and she leaned into him for a moment, though the sight of the red velour arm and white glove still caught her off guard. “Just closing up. Do you think that little girl will come back?”

“I don’t see her anywhere.” He sounded worried. “I want to wait around for her, though. Do you mind?”

She looked up into his brown eyes, itching to remove the white whiskers so she could see his whole face. And maybe steal a kiss, though that might be quite inappropriate in public. With Santa, anyway. Her face flushed at the thought of her father seeing that.

Heath didn't seem to notice. He scanned the shoppers scurrying past, some heading toward the food court and others away.

Sonya looked, too, but no child in jeans, blue shirt, and scraggly hair appeared. She reached to shut off the laptop.

"Just a sec." Heath put his hand on hers. "Can I get her last name and street address first? In case she doesn't show?"

"What was her name again?" Sonya scrolled through the list.

"Bailey." Heath watched over her shoulder, his warmth on her back making her want to lean into him.

Something niggled at Sonya's mind. "She didn't want a photo with you..."

"I know. I'll get over it." She heard the grin in his words.

"No, you don't understand. I only get that information to mail the pictures. Otherwise there's no need."

Heath's hands rested on her arms and turned her around. "We have no way to find her. That's what you're saying."

Sonya nodded, staring at the big black button on his chest. "Sorry. I didn't know."

"You had no way to. And making her give it anyway would have been wrong under the circumstances." Heath released her abruptly and strode away, out of the North Pole and into the stream of shoppers. He turned this way and that, obviously looking for the child.

It had been a full hour since she left, though. If Bailey didn't know how to tell time or her mom had taken her home, there wasn't much they could do about it.

God, I know Heath feels really bad about Bailey. I pray that you will take care of her and give him a chance to talk to her.

Huh. Who would have known she'd ever pray for Santa Claus? A little grin poked at her cheeks as she finished packing up. She didn't have a lot of choice whether to wait for Heath or not. He'd picked her up and given her a ride this afternoon, and home was clear across the bridge and too far to walk. She did have his number recorded in her cell. If he disappeared for too long, she'd send him a text.

With all the equipment packed up, Sonya settled down with a novel on her phone to wait.

Heath dropped onto the leather sofa in the middle of the mall corridor beside Sonya.

She set her cell aside and pulled her knees up to her chest. "Find her?"

"No." He rested his elbows on his knees and stared down at the tile floor. He'd motored through every store, glancing up aisles. Odds were good that she wasn't even in the building. That she'd gone home long before.

Sonya's hand rubbed his back. "Why does it matter so much? You must have met other kids who didn't believe in Santa." She let out a sardonic laugh. "I was one of them."

"Why didn't you believe?" He angled his head to see her, but didn't shift enough to make her stop that soothing circular motion.

"My dad told us other people lied to their kids. That Santa was a big game made up by adults to fool kids."

"Sounds like there's more to the story." Heath held his breath. Would she confide in him? A visual of Sonya and him cradling a baby between them slipped into his mind and settled in with a near desperate longing. But it would be vital they agreed on Santa's place in Christmas.

Could he give up the magic of Santa Claus himself to make Sonya happy? How important was it to him?

Not more important than her. He'd walk on hot coals if it would keep those kisses and back rubs coming. If he could marry her and grow old by her side until he looked like Santa with real whiskers instead of fake.

Heath's back chilled when she removed her hand. "There's always more to the story," she said flatly. "Are you ready to go?"

He caught her hand in his and turned toward her. "I'll just take a minute to change." He searched her face, but her eyes only connected with his for an instant. He lifted his duffel bag from the pile of equipment beside Sonya. "I'll be right back."

Chapter Nine

She was dating Santa Claus. Falling for his easy charm, the twinkle in his deep brown eyes and the ever-present grin on his face. Letting him kiss her. Okay, fine. She'd kissed him back. Maybe even instigated a few of them.

Sonya surged to her feet in her small apartment and paced to the patio door that led out to the balcony. She'd hardly slept for trying to figure out if her life had gone off its rails or only just found them.

Santa. Who'd ever have thought it? She could just imagine bringing Heath home to meet her parents. "Mom, Dad, I'd like you to meet my boyfriend, Santa Claus."

Her insides sank in ice.

She'd let two phone calls from her parents go to voice mail. She could handle their *told you so* about the toy store job. But she just couldn't tell them about Heath. Not yet. She couldn't go there with them until she knew it would last.

A gray sky hung over Riverbend, shrouding the nearby mountains. A darker ribbon of gray — the Sandon River — wound past the monochromatic town. Snow, the great equalizer, covered roofs, yards, and streets alike. Two plows worked the streets in the downtown core, their engines barely audible in the distance over the deep hush. Somewhere down there Heath and his little Bobcat cleared parking lots. He said he started at three o'clock in the morning if there was much snow. It took him six hours to clear his contracts.

Sonya rubbed her arms and turned from the glass, a flimsy barrier from the chill outside. On her table, the bright red poinsettia, the only hint of Christmas in her apartment, beckoned her closer until she reached for its velvety leaves.

It shouldn't have to be this way. Just because her parents never had a tree or made a big deal of the season didn't mean she couldn't. Everything had been laser-focused on Jesus' birth in her childhood. They'd exchanged small gifts, sure, but on Christmas Eve, probably so neither she nor her brother could pretend some red-suited guy accompanied by a herd of reindeer had brought them. Christmas Day had been for church and turkey dinner.

Which was the right way to celebrate? Her upbringing battled with Heath's vision as though both had sharp swords. One thing she knew for sure. The birth of Jesus was worth everything and deserved to be recognized. Without that momentous occasion, there would have been no sermons on hillsides. No parables. No miracles. No death and resurrection that provided salvation to all who believed.

Sonya crossed to her television and found the Christmas music channel with the hokey crackling fireplace. Strains of *Silent Night* filled the apartment. She fixed a mug of hot cocoa, picked up her Bible from the coffee table, and curled up to read the age-old story one more time.

Whether Heath was right or her parents, she could count on the gospel of Luke to keep her foundation solid and sure.

The rich aroma of potato chowder teased Heath awake. A cat sprawled across his chest, reminding him he wasn't at home. Not that anything he cooked smelled as amazing as that soup. He dragged his fingers down the cat's back, all that was required to start her motor.

"Did you have a good nap?"

Heath angled his head until he could see Sonya, silhouetted in the light from her kitchen. "I'm sorry. I didn't mean to."

She sauntered toward him, sat on the coffee table, and reached for his hand. "No problem. You looked awfully tired when you stopped by."

Right. He'd had a question for her. "What time is it?"

"Two."

Heath shot upright on the sofa, the quilt that had been covering him spilling to the floor. “Seriously? I must’ve slept four hours. You should’ve woke me up. I can’t believe I did this to you.”

She smiled. “You needed it. How long can you go, burning the candle at both ends?”

He scrubbed his hands through his hair. “Another three weeks? Until Christmas is over.”

“You’re going to get sick like Destiny did. And then who will be Santa?”

“Destiny. That’s what I stopped by to tell you. She’s feeling better, but still coughing a lot. She’s wondering if you can do today and tomorrow, too. Then there are no North Pole hours Monday and Tuesday, and she thinks she can be back for Wednesday. What do you say?”

Sonya looked at him thoughtfully. “I think I can do that. It’s not like I’m gainfully employed anywhere yet.”

“Something will show up. Hey, if you know how to drive a Bobcat…?”

She smiled. “Not in my skill set, but it does look fun. Do those things really do a zero-turn radius?”

“Pretty much.” A woman of continual surprises. “Now where did you learn that term?”

“Heard it somewhere.” She shrugged. “I made some soup. Are you hungry?”

“It smells awesome, and I’m starving.”

She rested her hand on his knee. “When is the last time you ate? You sound like you need someone to take care of you.”

Heath captured her hand and leaned closer. “Are you volunteering?” When she didn’t shift away, he stretched a smidge further and brushed his lips against hers. Whoa, that tingle was as good as food. “Because the position might be open.”

Sonya inhaled sharply and met his gaze before surging upright. “Come on over to the table.”

He stood and wrapped an arm around her. “Thank you, Sonya. And to answer your question, I had a couple of sandwiches in the cab this morning.” His stomach rumbled. “That was a while ago.”

She dragged him over to the table and pushed him into a chair before going into the kitchen. A moment later she returned carrying two bowls of chowder.

Heath caught her hand as she sat down. He bowed his head. “Thank You, Jesus, for coming to Earth as a tiny baby so that we could have forgiveness and eternal life. Thank You for Sonya and for this awesome food she’s prepared. In Your name, amen.” He caressed her fingers. “This smells amazing.”

Sonya smiled. “Dig in.”

Now he had one more reason to keep this woman in his life. How long had it been since he’d tasted homemade soup? His mom rarely did more than open a can. The velvety texture and subtle flavor tantalized his mouth and satisfied his stomach. A few minutes later he’d polished off a second bowl.

“You really plowed snow for seven hours, mostly before dawn?”

“All in a day’s work.” He reached for a warm biscuit and slathered butter on it. Then he paused with it halfway to his mouth. “Oh, man. I crashed on your sofa without an invitation and now I’m eating you out of house and home. I’m sorry.” And her without a job. Could he be any more of a heel?

“Heath.”

He set the biscuit down. “Yes?”

A little smile toyed with the edges of her mouth. “It’s okay. Really. I don’t get to cook for anyone other than myself very often. It was fun to wonder what you might enjoy that I had the ingredients for.”

“I can’t remember when I enjoyed a meal this much.”

Sonya’s eyes slipped downward. “It’s not anything special.”

He reached across the corner of the table and lifted her chin. “Everything you touch is special. Because you are.”

She sucked in her lips, not meeting his gaze.

“Don’t you believe me?” he asked softly. “You’re amazing, Sonya. Absolutely amazing.”

Sonya glanced at him then away.

If it was a ploy to make him keep talking, she was pretty good at it. But he didn’t think so. What had happened in her life to make her so unsure of herself?

Heath slipped from his chair and knelt beside hers, sliding an arm around the back of it and reaching for the fingers clenched in her lap with his other hand. "Sonya."

She didn't respond, but that might have been a tear at the corner of her eye.

"Sonya, look at me. You are a beautiful woman with a love for kids and a generous heart. You're an amazing cook. You've created a real home in this apartment, unlike the bachelor pad I live in."

Tangle twined around his ankles, little motor headed from zero to sixty. Heath grinned. "Your cat adores you, and she should. I'm well over halfway in love with you myself."

She snuck him a glance, and his stomach clenched. Too much, too soon? He hadn't intended to say those words yet, not because he hadn't been thinking them morning, noon, and night for several days, but because he didn't want to rush her. Scare her. But maybe they were better out in the open.

He tightened his fingers around hers and held her close as he buried his face against the crook of her neck amidst her luscious hair. "Thank you for letting me into your life. I won't hurt you, ever. I promise."

Sonya trembled then turned slightly to wrap her arms around his shoulders.

Heath gathered her up, lifting her off the chair and over to the sofa where he sat with her in his arms. He brushed his fingers through her soft, thick hair and cupped the back of her head as his lips searched for hers. They were easy to find.

Her mouth moved against his with as much passion as he felt building up in him, teasing him yet making promises at the same time.

Heath's hands roved her back as he reveled in the sensations coursing through him. He'd kissed a woman or two before in his day, but never before had it threatened to topple him. He pulled back with a groan, desiring anything but.

Sonya wasn't ready to stop. She held his face between both her hands and nuzzled his forehead, his eyes, his cheeks — unshaven — before settling back against his mouth.

He drowned again, and when he came up for air, he knew he had to stop. Now, while he could.

* * *

Heath was good with the kids. He held even the smallest babies up to his white whiskers and smiled for the camera. Sure, there was always a toddler or two that took one look at him and freaked out, but he even managed to soothe many of them into cooperating.

The battle continued in Sonya's mind as she managed the moms and tots in the lineup. She was falling for this guy in a big way. There was no pretending otherwise for the passionate and very merry kisses they'd shared. When he wore anything but the Santa suit, the reservations were easy to push aside. Even seeing him in action wasn't a real deterrent. It was only when she forced herself to take a long look into the future that the doubts welled up again.

She turned to the laptop to enter the information for the next Santa photo, and caught movement beyond the piles of glittery gifts. Shoppers hurried by in both directions, so how could one motion catch her eye? No, it was the stillness of one small body amid the flurry.

Bailey.

The child watched from a distance, hands stuffed in her jeans pockets.

Sonya took an involuntary step closer as Bailey's gaze latched onto hers. Then the girl was gone.

Someone desperately needed hope this Christmas season.

Chapter Ten

"It's the least I can do." Heath guided Sonya into the Save-On-More supermarket not far from River of Life Church. In the foyer, he plugged a dollar coin into a buggy's handle and disengaged it from the row.

"But—"

He dropped a quick kiss onto her sweet lips. "Okay, you do have a choice. You let me buy groceries to cook with, or I'll go back to eating ramen noodles and day-old sandwiches from the Petro-Canada." He waggled his eyebrows at her. "You don't want gas station food on your conscience, do you?"

Sonya sighed. "You drive a hard bargain."

Whew. He pushed the cart into the produce section of the store. "Have at it. We're not leaving until this thing is rounded on top, okay? Whatever you need."

"Then we shouldn't start with produce. It will get crushed."

"See? I know nothing about this process. I shop at the Petro-Can because there are only four kinds of soup to choose from, and their fruit choices are bananas, oranges, and apples. When they have any."

"I can't believe you shop there. Besides fuel, I mean."

"Fresh coffee. Pop." He grinned at her as she tugged the cart into the baking supplies aisle. "I can even get a hot dog or a slice of pizza there."

Sonya shuddered. "You want pizza? That can be arranged."

He nudged her. "I knew you'd see it my way."

A smile peeked from both her mouth and her eyes. "You're impossible."

"I'd like to think that anything is possible." Now that he had her attention, he leaned for another kiss.

She stepped back, shaking her head, but smiling. "We'll never get done in here if we keep that up."

Heath pulled an imaginary zipper across his mouth. "I'll dream of merry kisses with every step we take through this store. What do we need here? Flour? Sugar?"

Sonya nodded and reached for a bag of sugar, but Heath snagged it first and set it in the buggy. "I hope this means there are cookies in my future."

"What's your favorite kind?"

"Hmm. Christmas cookies? Gingerbread men with icing and coconut and those little sprinkles."

She turned and stared at him as he licked his lips.

"What, you've never had those?"

"My mom didn't make special cookies."

Heath slid his hand over hers on the shopping cart handle. "Your parents didn't really do Christmas." Would she confide in him soon?

"Not the trappings everyone associates with it, no. Just Baby Jesus." She grimaced. "I'm sorry. That came out wrong. The Savior's birth is the only part that matters, anyway."

Her apartment, cozy and full of character, but not full of Christmas. No tree. No decorations. No visual reminders of the holiday season. "You don't have to do things the way your folks did," he said softly, scooting the cart to one side to allow another shopper to pass. "You can choose a different way, unless their way makes you happy?"

She stared down at their entwined hands. "I always thought it did."

His heart surged out of proportion to the five whispered words. "Not anymore?" Because could he really give his heart and his entire future to a woman who spurned so many of his favorite things about one entire month of the year? And kids... man, he wanted babies with Sonya. But they'd have to agree on how to raise them. Santa might not be the only thing.

"It's just... it's just all so commercial, you know? It's all about what we can get."

"Not for everyone. Most people find a balance. For every gift that's received, someone is the giver. Usually that someone has spent time considering what kind of gift will make the person he loves happy." Like him. Wondering if it was too soon to give Sonya the Christmas gift he wanted to offer more than anything else.

He was nuts. He'd only known her three weeks. Yet somehow, it seemed enough. He'd made a snap decision to move to Riverbend three years before and never regretted it a minute. Same with starting his own landscaping business when he hadn't been able to find work. When he jumped, he was all in.

Maybe when he fell, too. He hadn't been looking for love, but Sonya had found him anyway. He asked God every day to guide his footsteps, but he hadn't been praying for a wife. He hadn't even wanted one. Sure, in the vague future, but it hadn't been an immediate need. That had changed in a hurry.

The shopping cart shuddered as Sonya dropped a bag of flour into it.

Heath started. He'd been so lost in his own thoughts he hadn't even noticed. "I'm sorry. You should have let me get that."

"Five kilograms, Heath. Not that heavy." She smiled. "If you've got a recipe for ginger cookies, I'll give them a try. What else do we need?"

"Really?" Heath put his hands on her waist and gave Sonya a little twirl, nearly running into an elderly woman. Thankfully she looked more amused than annoyed.

"Molasses, right?" Sonya clutched the shelf beside her.

The old lady moved on.

"Molasses. I think so. I've never had this much trouble concentrating in my life."

"Being Santa messes up your brains?"

"Being with you does. My brains, my heart, everything." He reached for her again.

"Heath."

He stopped. "What?"

"We need to finish in here. You have to be at the mall in two hours."

Right. "It will seem strange having Destiny there and not you. I'll miss you."

"Heath."

He loved the way she said his name. "Say that again?"

"Say what again?"

Heath leaned closer. "My name."

She jabbed him lightly with an elbow. "Which kind of molasses should I buy?"

"Molasses?"

"For the cookies."

Did it really matter? He selected a small carton. "Can I help you decorate them?"

"You'd better. I've never done it before."

He put on his best puppy dog look. "Tonight? When I'm done at the mall?"

Sonya chuckled. "Maybe tomorrow. I might call Kelly for instructions. But don't you have to get some sleep before plowing at three in the morning?"

"I can sleep next year." That's how he felt, too. Like he wanted nothing more than to spend every minute savoring Sonya's tentative steps toward celebrating.

"Says the guy who keeps falling asleep on my sofa."

"Uh." She had a point. "It's for Tangle's sake. She needs a cat nap, so I feel obligated to provide a place for that to happen."

She grinned, shaking her head. "You're crazy, you know that?"

"I try." Anything to make her smile.

"Sonya?" A short, thin woman with curly red hair stopped beside them. "It's Sonya Simmons, right?"

Sonya turned toward the woman and reached out a hand. "Yes. And you're Carmen. How's the cupcake bakery doing?"

"Crazy busy this time of year." The woman smiled as she shook Sonya's hand. "Well, always, to be honest. Listen, I really wished I could offer you a job the other day when you came in, but my staffing is full."

"I understand."

"But I looked over your résumé later and noticed you've taken the bookkeeping course at College of the Rockies over in Castlebrook."

"Yes, I did. I received my diploma two years ago."

"I need to hire someone trustworthy to do the bakery's books. I just can't keep up with it anymore as well as everything else. It's not a full-time job by any means, so I hesitate to even ask if you might be interested. I'd hate to switch to a new bookkeeper when you find something more permanent."

A myriad of emotions rolled across Sonya's face. "Really?"

Wait. Sonya did books? What had she been doing working retail?

"Really. You have no idea what a mess my paperwork is in, or you might run for the hills. All I know is I make a deposit every day and there's enough in the bank to pay for supplies and staff. I work my magic in the kitchen, but numbers…?" She shuddered.

"I'd love to."

Way to go, Sonya. Heath leaned back against the shelving in the aisle, unable to help the grin that spread on his face.

"Can we get together one evening between Christmas and New Years so you can get an idea what you're up against?" Carmen fished out a business card. "You pick the day. What works for you?"

Sonya looked a little dazed. "Um, the Monday sounds good."

"The back door of the bakery at about seven, then? And, of course, bookkeeping is worth more to me than another server up front. It's considerably fewer hours, but it pays twice as well."

"Wow. Thank you. I'll be there."

"Whew. That's one thing I can cross off my list. I look forward to handing everything in that department over to you." Carmen waggled her fingers in Heath's direction and gave her cart a nudge. "Merry Christmas."

Sonya stared after her. "Merry Christmas."

"Congrats," Heath said softly. How amazing that he'd been privileged to be present. "I didn't know you were a bookkeeper."

"I-I'm not, really. I mean, I took the course, but I don't have any experience."

"Looks like you'll be getting some."

She turned a worried frown toward him. "What if I can't do it?"

"I bet you can. In fact..." He searched her face. "I kind of need a bookkeeper, too."

Sonya stepped back as her brows furrowed. "Santa has such a list of income and expenses?"

"Not Santa, Sonya. My landscaping and snow removal business."

"You do landscaping?"

"I sure can't plow snow for twelve months. Even if I lived in Tuktoyaktuk that wouldn't be possible."

"But I never knew."

He reached for her hands and tugged her closer. "I never knew you were a bookkeeper. I guess neither of us have told all our secrets yet." Heath brushed his lips against hers.

She gave him a tremulous smile. "I thought we'd agreed the supermarket was a no-kissing zone."

"Then we'd better hurry up in here, or I can't be held responsible. I feel a kiss attack coming on."

Chapter Eleven

"Thanks for letting me join you." Sonya rolled cinnamon-and-ginger infused dough over Kelly's kitchen table. "I've never done this before and needed some expert help."

"And here I thought Heath might be willing to give you a hand."

Sonya glanced sideways at her friend. "I said expert."

Kelly burst out laughing. "Hard to believe there's anything that man isn't good at. He sure knows how to project confidence."

Now there was an understatement. Sonya plucked a loose bit of dough from the table and popped it in her mouth. Molasses and spices exploded against her tongue. Wow. "Is this thin enough?"

Kelly patted the dough. "It's a little thick in the middle, still. So tell me more about you and Heath. Sounds like you two have been spending a lot of time together."

Sonya nodded. "He's amazing."

"What did I tell you?"

"Pretty much exactly that."

Kelly raised her hands in the air and danced a little jig. "I can't believe how excited I am for you guys."

"It's too early yet for that kind of celebration." Didn't seem like it, though. Every minute she spent with Heath felt more right than anything in her life ever had.

"Why say that? You two aren't eighteen. What's the point in taking it slow, once you know?"

"That's the thing. I *don't* know."

"Hmm." Kelly set several festive cookie cutters on the table then began pressing out snowflake shapes. "Is it still the Santa thing?"

"Yeah. Still that."

"Well, you two have one advantage Ian and I didn't have."

"You mean not having kids already?" Oh, man, had she really said that to Kelly? They didn't know each other that well. It was none of Sonya's business that Kelly had spent seven years as a single mom.

"Kind of." Kelly shrugged. "We met in March, had a whirlwind courtship, and married at the end of August. Santa — and how each family celebrated Christmas — never came up before we'd tied the knot."

"Oh. I see how that could be a problem."

"We both conceded a lot. My mom has always been really into Santa. I know some kids feel crushed when they figure out Santa has not, in fact, slid down their chimney in person every Christmas Eve for their entire life. Accompanied by Rudolph. That was never a big deal for me. Mom played Santa up to the hilt, and I went along with it, loving the magic of it all."

Sonya had to know. "Were you guys Christians at the time?"

Kelly nodded. "Yep. I understood that the Baby in the manger was more important. That He was the reason we gave gifts and did all the fun stuff for Christmas. It was like His birthday party."

Huh. "So how did you find out?"

"I was eight when I confronted Mom. I'd suspected before, because there are always kids who feel it is their job to straighten out the believers."

Sonya winced.

"So I asked her if Santa Claus really came down our chimney or if she'd bought the gifts and pretended."

"And she said?"

"She asked if it wasn't a fun game of make-believe, and I had to agree. She told me it was now my job to help make Christmas magic for other people. That it creates a stage for talking about Jesus."

Life without that stage sure hadn't offered Sonya many opportunities to share her gratitude at her Savior's birth. Would being less antagonistic make a difference? Her mind drifted to young Bailey. *Lord, I pray You'll send someone to her and her family to demonstrate Your love to them in a complete way.*

Sonya fitted the cut-out shapes together on the baking sheet. "So you did the same thing with Elena?"

Kelly put the first tray of cookies into the oven and set the timer. "More or less. I did mention the pretend aspect a bit more than my mom did. But Ian and Sophie... they did things differently." She glanced sidelong at Sonya. "No talk of Santa bringing gifts. Face it. If you don't have to buy a gift from Santa and a gift from the parents, you save money, so it's easier to explain how to live within your means."

As a bookkeeper — now that Sonya was allowing herself that title — that made sense.

"Mom had trouble explaining to me how Santa could give me a plastic pony with a mane and tail I could comb while other kids from rich families got real horses like I'd asked for. I figured Santa could right the injustices of the world and treat all kids equally. It really bugged me that he didn't."

Sonya nodded. "See, that's one of the things that bothers me about the whole Santa scenario."

"Anyway, Ian and I realized in September that we had to come up with a united front for both girls. Their expectations were so different. You know Elena. She started talking about what Santa might bring her before the new school year started. She wasn't happy when Sophie kept correcting her."

"I guess not."

Kelly set aside another tray of cookies and began rolling out more dough. "They're good girls, and they truly love each other. They have their moments — don't we all? — but we've found many compromises. One of those is with Santa. Ian agreed a little more magic in Sophie's life might be a good thing, and we agreed on adjusting Elena to more reality. We sat both girls down together and had a good family talk." Kelly rolled her eyes. "One of many, I assure you."

"I bet." At least she and Heath didn't have two seven-year-olds to make their adjustment to each other that much harder. They had time to find the compromises that would work for them. If any were possible when her family entered the equation. Kelly's mom had accepted Ian, even though it changed her way of doing Christmas. Could her dad ever accept Heath?

"It sure frustrated my mom," Kelly went on. "Elena is her only grandchild. Well, besides Sophie, now. She wanted to keep the game going for longer, but we told her it was over."

Sonya couldn't resist. "I hear the girls want a baby for Christmas."

Kelly spread her hands across her flat belly. "Does it look like they'll get their wish?"

Sonya started to giggle then more and more laughter erupted until Kelly joined her. The timer broke into their hilarity a moment later, and Kelly rescued the first pan of perfectly browned cookies.

Heath followed Ian and the two little girls into the Tomlinsons' basement suite. Warmth and laughter enveloped him along with the aromas of molasses and roasting beef. The girls kicked off their snow-covered boots, and Ian reminded them to set them on the rack and hang their coats before running into the kitchen. The men followed more slowly.

Sonya looked terrific with her hair tied back, her cheeks flushed, and her eyes dancing. A bright red apron with ruffled edges covered most of her jeans and navy T-shirt.

He rounded the table without conscious thought and slid one arm around her then kissed her lightly.

"Mr. Heath is kissing Miss Sonya," Elena stage-whispered.

The conscious kicked in.

"Are they going to get married?" Sophie whispered back. "Maybe they'll have babies. Twins, like us!"

Heath dropped another quick kiss on Sonya's mouth. He wouldn't let those girls sabotage anything. "How may I be of service?" He turned to Kelly, but she was no help, wrapped in Ian's arms and getting a smooch that made Heath look like an amateur. Well, maybe he was.

"I think supper is ready. The slow cooker has been smelling awesome for the past few hours." Sonya stepped out of Heath's grasp, crossed to the counter, and lifted the lid.

"I'm starving!" Elena wilted dramatically to the floor.

"Daddy is going to carve the roast. Can you two help Miss Sonya put all the cookie cutters in the sink? After we've eaten, all of us can decorate the cookies."

"Is Mr. Heath going to help?" Sophie glanced at him from under her eyelashes.

Heath knelt beside her. "Do you mind? I really like decorating cookies. I especially like adding lots of coconut."

She nodded. "I like coconut, too."

"It's a deal, then."

Later, after the meal was cleaned up, Heath took his place back at the table between Sonya and Sophie. He helped the little girl spread butter icing on an angel-shaped cookie then watched as she carefully arranged tiny silver ball candies. At the other end of the table, Elena doused an entire cookie with multi-colored sprinkles in two seconds flat.

Heath caught Sonya's gaze as she grinned at him. The two children were so different, yet somehow this blended family seemed to work. "What can I pass you?" he asked Sonya.

She reached up and touched his nose. "Oops. You have some icing there." Her eyes glinted.

This was the Sonya he loved best. The flirty, playful one, like the evening of their first date. Without breaking their gaze, he found the icing bowl with his fingertip then touched her cheek. "Oh, no. You do, too." He kissed it off, and it tasted deliciously like peppermint and Sonya.

"Hey, you two." Kelly's laughing voice held warning.

Heath glanced at the little girls, both of whom were watching him and Sonya with wide eyes. "I'll get even with you for that later," he whispered in Sonya's ear. "Now be a good example for the children."

Her eyes danced. "I didn't do anything. You really did have icing on your nose. You still do."

"Uh huh."

"You do, Mr. Heath," Elena said decisively. "Miss Sonya, can you help me with an angel? I want one like Sophie's."

"Sure." Sonya turned to spread icing on another cookie while Kelly moved several completed confections to the counter.

"This is the Mount Everest of cookies." Heath added a chocolate chip belt to a gingerbread man. "Who is going to eat them all? I'll do my best, because I wouldn't want Sophie or Elena to get sore tummies."

"Mommy said we are making them for the Christmas party at

church." Elena glanced up from the profusion of red glitter on her angel.

"That's right," Kelly agreed. "We'll keep a few out so the girls can have one each day, but the rest are going in the freezer for the party. How many kids do you think are coming, Heath?"

"I really don't know. I'm not in charge of anything but my part of the program. If all the church kids come, we'll have forty at least, and if they bring friends..." He spread his hands wide.

"I invited my friends," said Sophie. "Gracie is coming, and maybe some of the others."

"That's awesome." Heath glanced at Sonya as she continued icing cookies.

"Still not sure how this fits as a church event," she mumbled.

"I can't wait to see!" Kelly passed a snowman shape to Sophie. "I think you and Nick and Lindsey have some great ideas, and I'm glad Pastor Davis and the board got behind it."

Sonya sucked in her lip and added a sliver of black licorice to a sheep's leg. Hopefully she'd dunk the rest of the cookie in coconut, officially making it Heath's favorite combination.

He leaned closer to her. "Will you come and help out with the program on Monday? I'd love to have you there."

"They wouldn't let me," said Kelly. "I tried to sign up, but Lindsey said parents weren't allowed. She wouldn't let Sarah either, because she's a teacher."

"Reed and Carly are doing music with the kids, aren't they?" put in Ian.

Heath nodded. "They have something special planned." He glanced at the girls and grinned at their rapt attention. "But I can't say what it is. I'm not allowed."

Elena rolled her eyes. "No one tells me anything."

"I like surprises," said Sophie.

"Sonya?" asked Heath softly.

She glanced at him sideways. "I think I have to."

He caught his breath. "Have to?"

"I need to figure out your angle. Before it's too late."

Too late for what? He had a guess or two. A lot rode on next week's presentation, but God would work it out.

Chapter Twelve

Well over fifty children crowded into the fireside room at River of Life Church, with more voices from the corridor beyond. Across the space, Sonya and Lindsey helped a group of children with a Christmas craft, while at a second table, other volunteers led another craft.

Heath let out a long breath. A lot rode on this program. He'd been the one to approach the pastoral team with this idea. He could be glad his buddy Nick, the church's youth and family pastor, had seen potential, and developed it together with his wife, Lindsey.

But not only had this become a big deal to the church families, over the past week, it had become a big thing between him and Sonya. She still hung back, just a bit, as though waiting for the other shiny black boot to fall.

Please, Lord.

This month had done wonders for Heath's prayer life. Not just for his relationship with Sonya, though that had been a lot of it, but for the needy families the ministerial association had been able to pinpoint. And for the little girl, Bailey. He'd seen her a couple of times, but she always disappeared before he could get anywhere near. He'd met so many kids in the past few weeks. Why this one refused to leave his mind, he didn't know.

"Look, Mr. Heath. See what Miss Carly helped us make?" Elena held up a half-walnut shell containing a bead with a face painted on it and a scrap of Christmas fabric tucked to its chin. "It's Baby Jesus in the manger. See? There's fishing line, so we can hang it on the tree."

"That will help you remember Jesus' birthday." He crouched down beside her.

She nodded soberly. “Not everybody knows about Jesus. Some kids only know about Santa Claus.” Elena leaned closer. “But did you know some kids don’t even know about Santa?”

“That’s hard to believe in Canada. Don’t they ever come to the mall?”

Elena grinned. “I know. But Santa doesn’t come to their house.” She pressed her hand to her forehead. “I get so mixed up about it. I know Santa is pretend and Jesus is real.”

“It’s tough to remember everything all the time. Even for grownups.”

She tipped her head at him and sighed. “Really? Sophie always remembers.”

Heath forced the grin to stay off his face as he glanced around. “Where is your twin, anyway? She’s usually right beside you.”

“She invited her friend to come, and she’s not giving up waiting at the door.”

“Wow, good for Sophie.” Heath pointed at the other craft table. “Are you going to do that one, too?”

“I sure am, Mr. Heath!” And off she bounded.

Heath made his way through the busy room and out into the corridor as several children entered. Sophie wasn’t among them. He headed for the church foyer, rounding the final corner just as a little girl came in the big doors. “Bailey!” called Sophie. “You came. I knew you would.”

Bailey? Heath’s heart nearly stopped as he melted back into the shadows. He’d only caught a glimpse, but it couldn’t be another child with the same name. Had she kept the invitation she’d crumpled into her jeans’ pocket two weeks back?

Heath shook his head. Could she even read it? Let alone figure out the place and time by herself? Maybe the unknown mean mother had dropped her off after all. That would be an answer to prayer right there.

The two little voices came toward him, and Heath beat a hasty retreat to the fireside room. Would Bailey recognize him? Unlikely. At least not until he donned his Santa suit later, but she’d recognize Sonya.

Heath worked his way through the group of children as Carly passed out jingle bells, castanets, and tambourines. “Sonya!”

She turned at his voice, a smile on her pretty face. “Hey, handsome.” She lifted her hand to his cheek.

For some reason, she seemed to like his face with a day-or-two-old beard. Definitely worth leaving it. He resisted the impulse to lean in for a quick kiss. Best keep focused with sixty-some kids in the room. "Don't look now," he whispered, "but see who just came in with Sophie?"

She leaned around his shoulder and her eyes widened. "Bailey," she breathed.

"Yeah, God worked some kind of miracle to get her here. She'll recognize you, I'm sure."

Sonya nodded. "Should I go over to her, do you think? Or avoid being seen?"

"I'm not sure." He closed his eyes for a second. "Ask God. That's all I've got."

"Wait. I gave her the invitation, so she'd expect me to be here, right?"

Heath gave his head a little shake. "Of course. I should've thought of that."

Reed strummed his guitar and asked the children to match the rhythm with their instruments. Heath glanced back as Sophie and Bailey shook two sets of bells, adding to the cacophony in the room. They were seated on the carpet in the midst of the group, which was reason enough to stay back and let events play out.

"When do you need to go get ready for your talk?" Sonya asked.

"Not for a few minutes." Heath leaned on the wall and pulled Sonya against him so they could both watch and sing along. "I can keep you company for now."

She leaned back, her head resting against his shoulder and both her hands covering his around her waist.

This. This was as close to heaven as Heath could get on Earth. At least for now.

Sonya watched the children's delighted faces as Heath, dressed in his Santa outfit, came onstage. Several of the church teens acted out the story of the first Christmas as Heath told the tale. Then he talked about how the story of Jesus' birth had spread around the world and how different cultures celebrated it with gift-giving. Pastor Nick, dressed up as Saint Nicholas in long robes and elaborate head-piece, invited Elena to the front. He then demonstrated how in some parts of Europe, the village priest visited each household on December fifth, taking the children on his knee to bless them for the coming year.

Soon Corbin entered dressed as Sinterklaas, lamenting that his white horse was not welcome inside the church. He handed out candy to the kids as he and Heath recounted the Dutch traditions.

By the time Reed appeared as the British Father Christmas, Sonya had settled into a chair at the back of the room, amazed by the thousands of little details that had gone into this presentation. Young Bailey sat between Sophie and Elena, as enthralled as any child in the room.

Why hadn't Sonya ever stepped way back and looked at the whole Santa Claus legend like this before? She still didn't think parents should lie to their kids, but Elena and Sophie seemed well-adjusted. Turfing Santa completely was like throwing the baby out with the bathwater. Look what it had done to Bailey.

Look what it had done to her.

A woman's voice came from the corridor, rapidly growing louder. Lindsey surged to her feet and headed to the door, Sonya at her heels. Lindsey opened the door just as the woman pushed on the other side of it.

Sonya's mouth dropped. Deborah? What on Earth was her anti-Christmas ex-boss doing in a church — at a children's Christmas party, no less?

"You?" Deborah's eyes blazed. "I should have known it was you. I saw you acting out at the *Santa* display at the mall."

Sonya jerked back a step. "Should have known what was me?"

"Where is she?"

Lindsey took Deborah's arm and shifted her back half a step, shutting the three of them out into the hallway. "I'm sorry. My name is Lindsey Harrison, and my husband, Nick, is the youth pastor here at River of Life. Would you mind telling me what all this is about?"

"My daughter. Someone gave her an invitation to this thing, and I told her no way. But then she got it into her head to come anyway, against my wishes. She's in there. I know she is."

"Y-your daughter?" Sonya's brain buzzed. "I didn't even know you had a child." *Bailey*. That would explain so much. Deborah was exactly the kind of person who would produce a jaded child like Bailey.

Sonya should know.

"I had to bring her to the mall a few times this month when her after-school care fell through. I know she went down there and gave Santa Claus a piece of her mind." Deborah's voice vacillated between anger and satisfaction. "But the worst thing?"

There was more? Sonya stared in fascination, peripherally aware that a few meters down the corridor, the other door to the fireside room opened and Santa Claus — Heath — strode toward them.

"Hello, Deborah. What seems to be the problem here?"

Sonya cringed. Was he being too forceful? Deborah would stomp all over him if she thought so.

The toy-store owner pivoted on a sharp heel. "You."

Heath spread his white-gloved hands wide. "Me. Yes. What can I help you with?" He glanced from Deborah to Sonya and back again.

"Heath. I think Bailey is Deborah's daughter."

Deborah spun again, her finger jabbing toward Sonya's chest. "Aha. You admit you knew. And you tried to turn my child against me. Well, I've come for her now." She turned a narrow glare at Lindsey, who leaned against the door. "Please move. You have no right to keep my daughter here without my permission. Do I need to call the RCMP?"

Sonya stepped closer to Lindsey. "I'll go in and get her." There really wasn't anything else she could say, was there? Deborah was right. It wasn't their place to interfere with how she raised her child.

Lindsey didn't move out of the way. "Just a sec, Sonya. I have a question first."

Deborah sputtered.

Lindsey raised her hand. "One question. You said there was something else. A worse thing. Care to elaborate, so we have all the facts?"

Deborah glared at each in turn, but must've come to the conclusion she couldn't overpower all three of them to get in the fireside room. Reed's guitar and the not-so-melodic sound of dozens of children singing *Away in a Manger* drifted through the door.

The woman turned on Heath. “It must be your fault. I don’t know whose else it could be.”

He held up both hands. “What happened?”

“Some man who said he was the pastor of a church showed up at my house last night. He said someone had given our name as a family in need of Christmas cheer.” No cheer was evident in her tone.

Memories crashed over Sonya. The neighbors who’d meddled, who’d made Dad as crazy as Deborah was right now. Sonya and her brother had cowered in the corner as Dad raved. It hadn’t been any of that neighbor’s business whether she and Brian had gifts under their non-existent tree or not. Was that what Heath had been doing, thinking he was making it better for Bailey? Because that wouldn’t be the result.

She turned to look at him, to read the reassurance on his face, but the blank expression didn’t give the reassurance she craved. “Heath? Do you know anything about it?”

“I-uh...”

The clamor in her head grew to a deafening pitch.

He took a step closer, glancing between her and Deborah. “I can explain.”

Sonya didn’t see how.

Chapter Thirteen

He didn't have time to explain. Sixty kids poured out of the fireside room. Deborah grabbed Bailey's arm and towed her down the corridor ahead of the tide without a backward glance. Little ones gathered around Heath, wanting to whisper secrets in Santa's ear.

Somewhere in the midst of the melee, Sonya disappeared.

Heath's heart — his entire being — ripped in two. He and Nick had planned this event for months, working over the details of presenting Santa as a bridge to celebrating Jesus' birthday. He couldn't toss aside all these children and race down the church corridor to find the woman he loved above all others.

Sonya would have to wait, but what had caused the blank sheet of white on her face? What was going on in her mind? Surely she would give him the chance to clarify. *Please, Lord. Let it not be too late.*

He could explain. He really could. But she needed to be willing to hear his words, and the panic in his chest told him that might not happen.

Lindsey cast him a worried frown. Parents arrived to pick up their offspring and were greeted with walnut mangers and gingerbread cookies. Heath recognized one Sonya had labored over, a bell meticulously lined with silver balls. She'd used tweezers to make it perfect.

Heath wasn't perfect. He was just an ordinary guy who loved Jesus. When he blew it, he made amends and carried on. His stomach roiled. If only. If only.

* * *

She should've stayed to help clean up. After all, she'd promised Lindsey. But that meant facing Heath in front of their friends. Facing Heath at all, really.

Sonya mumbled an apology to Lindsey and ran to her car. What possible explanation could he have, and for what? Had he known Bailey was Deborah's daughter? He couldn't have. Sonya had worked for the woman for months and hadn't known she had a child at all.

But somehow he'd figured it out and sent someone over. Somehow he became one with that neighbor from Sonya's childhood. Somehow Bailey cowered because of Heath, and Sonya cowered with her.

He'd convinced Sonya that maybe Santa Claus wasn't the most evil representation of Christmas. Thank God she'd come to her senses before things had gotten any deeper. Being that child again pushed his words aside. Even his kisses.

Tears froze on Sonya's cheeks as she started her car. The church parking lot was plowed. Probably Heath's doing. Pitoni Street wasn't in quite as good of shape, but she wasn't more than fifteen blocks from home. A good cry, a hot shower, and a snuggle with Tangle might give her strength to survive.

Thanks to Heath, she had enough food in the apartment to stay put until after Christmas. She would shut off her phone, ignore the door, and skip the party of all Heath's friends out at Corbin's farm. She winced. They'd become her friends, too. Kelly. Carly. Sarah. Lindsey.

It was hard to see through her tears and the fogged windshield, but she made it to her apartment without causing an accident. So far, so good. She jerked her car door open and dashed for the main doors.

"Sonya! There you are!"

Not Heath. Not his voice. He couldn't have gotten here ahead of her, anyway. She stopped dead, just like when she'd played frozen tag as a child, then turned slowly around. "Dad?"

"Where were you? Didn't you get my message?"

"M-message?"

He strode toward her. "It's freezing out here. Let's go inside."

Her insides felt icier than the wind chill. Dad had sent a message? When? How could she have missed it?

Sonya unlocked the door to the apartment foyer then started up the stairs, her father on her heels. She opened the door to her own living space, and a meow from Tangle welcomed her.

"You should really give me a key to your place in case this ever happens again. I do come through Riverbend on business sometimes, you know."

Mechanically, Sonya removed her coat and boots. "Can I offer you a coffee or tea?"

"Tea would be good." Dad moved past her into the living room. "What have we here?"

Sonya leaned against her kitchen counter and pressed her eyes shut. "What's that, Dad?" But she had a pretty good idea. Kelly had offered her a garland and a few ornaments and, like a fool, she'd accepted them. She'd have to see Kelly long enough to return them. Sonya squeezed the bridge of her nose then filled her kettle. The sooner she got through this visit, the sooner she could go back to crying.

"Sonya, Sonya." Dad's chiding voice came from further away.

In the kitchen, Sonya got out two mugs and a teabag. The honey jar. A teaspoon. She lined them up carefully three centimeters from the edge of the counter and waited for the kettle to boil while timing her inhales and exhales. When the tea was ready, she took both cups to the table, but that was a mistake. How many times had she and Heath shared a meal here in the past few weeks? Too many.

"Sonya, it seems you have forgotten the true meaning of Christmas." Dad strode over to the table and gripped both her shoulders.

She stepped back until he dropped his hands. "Your tea is ready."

"We need to talk."

About the tea, the decorations, or something else? All she wanted was peace and quiet to cry over Heath. To try to regain some of the peace Jesus came to bring. She had no clue where it had gone.

No clue.

"Your mother says you've been too busy to talk lately." Dad waved his hand toward the living room. "Now I see why you've been pushing her away."

"What on Earth are you talking about?"

"Christmas is a holy day, Sonya. Don't you remember that's where the word holiday comes from?"

She gripped the back of her chair.

"You're in danger, daughter. I see signs that the world has found its way into your heart."

He hadn't changed. His way was still the only right way. Sonya stared at him, trying to see him through fresh, compassionate eyes. She went the long way around the table and came back carrying the items she'd borrowed from Kelly. They were so few it only took one trip.

"This, Dad? This is a felt wall hanging that says Love, Joy, and Peace on it. This is leading me astray how, exactly?"

"The holly symbols around the words are of pagan origin."

Sonya shook her head. "Dad, give it up. God made the holly plant, same as any other. These words remind me of why Jesus came to Earth. Seeing this in my home brings perspective." She squared her shoulders.

Dad sputtered.

"As for this plush kitten with its paws wrapped around a gift? I don't know if you noticed, but I have a cat. I happen to think Tangle is cute, and I like this decoration. Unless you've changed your mind, gifts in themselves are not evil."

He glowered at her. "The cat is wearing a Santa hat."

Sonya took a deep breath. "So it is."

"You should..."

No. It wasn't right. *He* wasn't right.

She held up her hand. "Dad, let me make something clear. I'm twenty-seven years old and moved out of your house five years ago." Fear had kept her bound, though. Fear and legalism. "This is my home. I make my own decisions, and I pay my own rent." With Carmen and Reed both hiring her for bookkeeping — and hopefully Heath — she stood a chance of continuing to pay for it.

Dad's face deepened to an alarming shade of red.

Please, Lord, no heart attack. I can't handle that on top of everything else.

"Look, Dad. I love you. I really do. But you don't control my life anymore. Sit down, please, and drink your tea before it gets cold."

He slumped into the nearest chair. “We tried so hard to teach you right from wrong. First your brother. Now you.”

“Oh? What’s Brian been up to?”

Dad stirred his tea. “He refuses to have anything to do with us. He left his wife. He left the church. I don’t know where we went wrong.”

Whoa. She should have tried harder to keep in touch with her brother. Maybe it wasn’t too late. Sonya stroked the words on the hanging again. Love. Joy. Peace. Those hadn’t been exemplified in her household growing up. No wonder she was having such a hard time trusting Heath. How much different his upbringing must’ve been.

“I’ve made a choice, Dad. I’ve chosen joy over fear. I’ve chosen love over legalism. And I’ve chosen peace over strife.” As she said the words, she felt them soothe a little of the pain in her heart. She could choose to listen, too. She could choose to allow Heath to have different motivation than that neighbor long ago.

The foyer door buzzed. Sonya surged to her feet and pushed the intercom button. “Who is it?”

“Heath. Can I come up? Please?”

“Yes.” She pressed the door release and waited. One. Two. Thr—

“Who’s that?”

Dad was slower than she’d expected. “My boyfriend, Dad.” At least, she hoped so after what happened. It was a good sign Heath was on her doorstep.

“Your b—? But you never said anything to your mother.”

For a dozen reasons.

A light tap sounded before her door swung wide open. Heath. In his Santa Claus costume.

All the words he’d rehearsed fled straight out of Heath’s mind when he saw the scowling gray-haired man standing behind Sonya.

“Dad, I’d like you to meet my boyfriend. Heath, this is my dad. Mr. Simmons.”

The wild joy at being introduced as her boyfriend got shackled and caged the instant he met the chilled eyes of her father. What had Sonya said about her parents and Santa? This was definitely not the best first impression he could make.

"Pleased to meet you, Mr. Simmons. Your daughter is a wonderful woman." Heath stuffed his white gloves in his pockets and reached for the other man's hand.

The gesture was not returned.

Uh oh. Heath pulled off the Santa hat and whiskers then ran his hand through tousled hair. He hadn't shaved, either. The fake whiskers stayed on better with that bit of traction. Besides, Sonya seemed to like that bit of growth.

Mr. Simmons crossed his arms and widened his stance.

Heath unbuttoned the Santa jacket, shrugged out of it, and hung it. Padded red pants: on or off? He had sweats on underneath. They were at least as decent as the Santa pants. He took off the shiny black boots and stepped out of the red pants.

No one said a thing the whole time. Heath glanced from Mr. Simmons to Sonya. Her face was still pale beneath smudged makeup. Had she been crying?

For better or for worse, Heath was here. He'd been introduced as Sonya's boyfriend, so he'd act like it, regardless of the way they'd left each other less than half an hour before.

He closed the gap and took Sonya in his arms. He kissed her. Once, though everything in him demanded more. Her dark eyes never left his as he turned them both toward her father, arms around each other.

Heath had never experienced such a wall of silence in his life. "So, Mr. Simmons. It's good to meet you." Wait, he'd already said that part. "I hope you had a pleasant trip. Were the roads clear?"

Her dad's eyes focused on Sonya. "May I speak with you alone for a moment?"

Sonya's chin came up. "No. Anything you want to say, you can say in front of Heath."

The man jerked his head toward Heath. "When did he move in?"

Sonya inhaled sharply.

Heath slid his hand up and down her back. "This is Sonya's apartment, not mine. I live across town. But I have visited here before."

Had a nap or two on that sofa. Not that her father would want to know that.

"He came in and practically undressed. No wonder you have pushed your mother and I out of your life."

"I am fully dressed. See? Shirt, pants, even socks."

Mr. Simmons didn't look at him. "But worst of all, he pretends to be Santa Claus. Sonya, come home with me for a few days. Let your mother and I pray over you, that God will forgive you."

Beneath Heath's hand, Sonya tensed. *Please, Lord. Help her to choose wisely.*

"Dad, I am not coming home with you. I'm an adult, and this is where I live. I cannot tell you how angry I am that you accused Heath and me of living together. You had no cause to say that." She breathed in deeply then let the air out in a slow, shuddering breath. "You think the worst of me right away. It's like you want to."

Mr. Simmons shot Heath a narrowed look. Now that Sonya had proven she had a spine against him.

"You have my word, sir, that I have never taken advantage of Sonya nor treated her lightly. I love your daughter with everything in me. She is a treasure." This was so not how he'd meant to tell Sonya. "I'd like to have a good relationship with you and Mrs. Simmons. For many, many years."

Mr. Simmons glared at him. "I have no words to say to a boy who leads children astray with lies." He held out his hand to Sonya. "Come."

"No, Dad. I am not coming with you."

"You have made your decision. Don't come crying to your mother and me." Mr. Simmons grabbed his coat from the closet and yanked it on. He plunged his feet into his boots and bolted out the door.

Sonya sagged against Heath. He scooped her into his arms and headed for the sofa. "I love you, Sonya," he murmured into her hair as she released her tears. "I love you. I'm here for you. Always."

Chapter Fourteen

I'm sorry, Heath. I'm so sorry I didn't trust you." If she begged him a thousand times, would he forgive her?

"Sonya. It's okay. Really."

It couldn't be that easy. "But I—"

He kissed her. "You don't have to earn my love. You have it. All of it."

"But—"

He put his finger across her mouth. "I'm not a boy who plays make-believe and tells lies, Sonya."

Those words of Dad's had to have stung. "I'm sor—"

"Listen, sweetheart. Okay?" Heath tightened his arms around her, holding her securely. Safe. She was safe in his arms.

"Jesus died for your sins. You know that, right? Once for all. You accept His gift and then you have a new relationship with Him. He doesn't withhold it on bad days. It's steady, like the Earth turning on its axis."

She burrowed her face into the crook of his neck and nodded.

"I'm not God, and I can't claim to love as perfectly as He does. But I'm also not Peter Pan, who refused to grow up. I don't have my head in Neverland... or even the North Pole. It's here in Riverbend. With you."

Those silly tears just kept flowing. She'd practically soaked Heath's shirt by now. But the words soothed. She did know that about God's love. She did. Dad might try to manipulate her by giving or holding back favor, but God didn't. Heath was human, though. Given a few years, would he be like Dad?

"Sweetheart, God is my lifeline. I want His love to flow through me every single day. It's why I am Santa. Why I did the program today. I want to help point kids — families — to the best gift of all, salvation through Jesus. I don't do it perfectly. I know it. But it's what I want more than anything."

Sonya tried to imagine Dad saying anything like that. It wasn't possible. Dad might say God was love, but a harsh love. A behave-yourself-or-you'll-get-punished love. Not this peace and assurance Heath spoke of that dribbled into every crack in her dry, aching soul.

"Sonya? Speak to me."

"Heath." She tightened her arms around his neck. "I love you, too. I don't think I knew what love was. Even God's love." She pressed her lips to his.

He pulled away after the briefest kiss. "Are you ready to hear about Deborah?"

She took a deep breath and nodded.

"A neighbor of hers reported her to Child Services for neglect on Friday."

Sonya stiffened and sat up straighter. It hadn't been Heath?

"Just listen. Child Services sent Deborah and Bailey's names to the Riverbend ministerial association's list to receive Christmas hampers. Nick and Ian took a basket of food and a few gifts over yesterday evening." He held up his hand. "I didn't know anything about it until today. I didn't have a chance to tell you. And honestly I wasn't completely certain it was the same Bailey until I saw Deborah. I'd never heard their surname."

Sonya felt very, very small. She'd done a lot of jumping to conclusions, none of them with any grounding. "Oh."

"One more thing, in the interest of full disclosure." Heath's dark eyes looked deeply into hers.

Uh oh.

"The Santa thing at the mall. All of it. I let you believe that the mall administration sponsored everything. They didn't. They gave permission and space, of course. But they contracted it out."

Sonya bit her lip. "Then who? You? On your own?" That couldn't be right. It took more than one guy to set up that whole array. Somebody who wasn't half exhausted from plowing parking lots every night.

"The ministerial association. They wanted a way to reach into the community and help meet families' needs. The ones who seemed to need help went on the hamper list."

"And they knew exactly what each child wanted for Christmas

because of your notebook and the address lists for the photos."

Heath nodded and swallowed hard. "Are you angry?"

Sonya pulled back. Should she be?

"I didn't tell you everything."

Yesterday, she'd have been furious. This morning, too. Now? After Dad's display and seeing — feeling — the contrast between Dad's version of love and Heath's? She knew without a doubt which one was closer to God's. All she felt for Dad was pity. And for Mom, too, living in a marriage where everything she did wrong was held up for inspection. Sonya couldn't imagine Heath ever doing that.

"I'm not angry," she said slowly. "I would have liked to have known, but I'm not sure I was ready for it."

Heath's lips brushed hers, and her senses reeled.

"Thank you for being so patient with me," she whispered against his lips.

"Loving you is always my pleasure." And he kissed her thoroughly.

"Jingle bells, Santa smells, a million miles away..." Elena belted out the lyrics at the top of her lungs then dissolved into giggles.

Heath reached across the hay-covered wagon and tickled the little girl.

Sophie sniffed his jacket. "Mr. Heath doesn't smell. Except like peppermint. And maybe like Miss Sonya's perfume." She nestled against him.

No matter. Heath made room for her as well as Sonya. A more perfect Christmas Eve would be hard to imagine with their friends around them. Corbin and Sarah perched on the front of the wagon as Corbin drove his team of horses, festooned with jingling harnesses. Nick and Lindsey and Reed and Carly sat along one side, winter boots dangling above the snow-covered fields, glistening under the full moon. Ian and Kelly snuggled against a pile of bales in the middle of the wagon while the little girls — or at least Elena — ricocheted all over.

Heath nuzzled into Sonya's hair. "Have I told you today that I love you?" he whispered.

"Once or twice, but you may tell me again."

He would, too. Over and over. "It's a beautiful night. Almost as beautiful as you." The air was crisp, but not fierce. At least it wasn't snowing, or he'd have to be out on the Bobcat in just a few hours. But no, this was a night off. A special night. One, he hoped, he'd remember forever with the intense clarity he felt at the moment.

"It came upon a midnight clear," Reed sang out. By the next line, everyone was singing along. From that carol, they moved into another. Then another, all capturing the birth of the Christ Child, the embodiment of love. Heath closed his eyes, breathed in the essence of Sonya, and held her as close as winter parkas and prickly hay would allow.

After a while the carols faded away. Soon after, Corbin's gentle, "Whoa," brought the horses to a halt.

Heath had no desire to move. He felt the bump as the horses were unhitched and Corbin and Sarah led them away. Rustles in the hay told him some of the others had climbed off the wagon. Crackles and a flare of heat on his face told him someone had tossed a few logs on the bonfire Corbin had started before the hayride. Still he reclined, holding Sonya close against his chest.

"What is it, Mommy?" Elena whispered.

"Shh. It's mistletoe. Go hold it over Miss Sonya's head."

Heath opened an eye as Sonya stirred. Elena blocked the moon with her sprig.

"What happens next, Mommy?"

"You say, merry kisses, everyone."

"Merry kisses!" yelled Elena.

Even knowing it was coming, Heath jumped at the volume in Elena's voice. He grabbed her around the middle and tumbled her into his lap. "You want a kiss, little girl?" he growled.

She wiggled and screeched. "No, not me. You're supposed to kiss Miss Sonya!"

Heath blew a raspberry against her cheek.

"No! Not me. Yuck." She pulled out of his grasp and jumped off the side of the wagon.

Kelly collapsed on the hay, howling with laughter. "Now you see what Ian and I have to put up with? All. The. Time. Times two."

Heath threw an armful of hay in her direction.

Kelly rolled away. "Oh, that was just too funny for words."

Sonya sat up, still in the crook of Heath's left arm. "Things have gotten rather noisy around here in the last few minutes."

"They have, haven't they?" Heath said conversationally as he gathered more hay and tossed it at Kelly. "What's a guy got to do to get some privacy?"

"Stay five kilometers away from seven-year-olds?" Kelly jumped off the side of the wagon.

"And their mothers," added Heath.

"Ha, probably," Kelly tossed over her shoulder as she joined Ian beside the fire.

"Where are they all now?" whispered Sonya, looking around.

Heath counted the silhouettes around the fire. Everyone was accounted for. He groped around in the hay.

"What are you looking for?"

"This." He held the sprig of greenery — it felt oddly like plastic — over Sonya's head. "You heard the orders. It's time for merry kisses."

"I think that can be arranged." She closed her eyes and leaned closer.

He held the mistletoe between their faces. "Wait a minute. Do you still think it is inappropriate?"

She looked at him and reared back a bit at the sight of the greenery. "What?"

Heath swung it back and forth like a slow pendulum. "Or perhaps... prophetic?"

Sonya grabbed the mistletoe and threw it over her shoulder. "Want to fulfill some prophecy?"

"Would I ever." He tasted her lips, once, twice, then gathered her in both arms and deepened the kiss.

"They're kissing," announced Elena.

Heath pulled back and grinned at Sonya.

"Caught," she whispered, a twinkle in her eyes.

"Are they going to get married and have babies?" asked Sophie. "Why can't we have babies at our house?"

"What do you think?" whispered Heath, his hands cradling Sonya's face. "Want to?"

"Want to what?"

"Get married and have babies?"

"Is that a proposal?"

"It might be, if you were going to say yes."

"I might, if you asked."

He kissed her again. "I might have to give that some thought."

Sonya rubbed her nose against his. "You might want to get on that."

Heath swooped her up as he stood then deposited her feet back on the planks of the wagon.

She gasped and clutched him around the neck.

He could get used to that, but he disengaged her hands and held them between them. "So, I've been thinking."

"Oh?"

From behind him, over at the fire, Reed began plucking out the melody to *I Saw Mommy Kissing Santa Claus* on his guitar.

Heath dropped to one knee and tugged a small box out of his jacket pocket. "Sonya Simmons, I love you. Will you marry me? Will you share merry kisses with me every day for the rest of our lives?" He opened the velvet box and held it out to her.

Sonya gasped and her eyes widened as the diamond shimmered in the full moon. Both hands flew to cover her mouth. She stomped a little jig in place, her gaze never leaving the diamond. "Yes, yes, yes!"

"She said yes," called Elena.

A few chuckles sounded from the fire, and a bit of clapping. One wolf whistle.

"Does that mean they're having a wedding?" asked Sophie. "I love weddings. Maybe we could be flower girls again."

Heath pulled the ring out of its nest and reached for Sonya's left hand. "May I?"

She nodded as he slipped the ring on that precious finger. "Oh, Heath. It's beautiful."

He stood and gathered her back in his arms. "I love you, Sonya. With all my heart."

"I love you, too." Her lips caressed his, sending shivers through his body. "Always and forever."

The End

Author Biography

Valerie Comer lives where food meets faith in her real life, her fiction, and on her blog and website. She and her husband of over 35 years farm, garden, and keep bees on a small farm in Western Canada, where they grow and preserve much of their own food.

Valerie has always been interested in real food from scratch, but her conviction has increased dramatically since God blessed her with three delightful granddaughters. In this world of rampant disease and pollution, she is compelled to do what she can to make these little girls' lives the best she can. She helps supply healthy food — local food, organic food, seasonal food — to grow strong bodies and minds.

Her experience has planted seeds for many stories rooted in the local-food movement, such as the six-book Farm Fresh Romance series, the Riverbend romance novellas, and the Garden Grown Romance series to debut in 2016.

To keep up with what's happening next, visit her website at www.valeriecomer.com or scan the QR code. You'll find her blog, many links, and all her books. You can also sign up for her email newsletter there and get a bonus short story set in the Farm Fresh Romance world. She looks forward to your visit!

Made in the USA
Monee, IL
29 September 2021